Praise for
Celeste Ascending

"Kaylie Jones' novels are a pure joy to read, and *Celeste Ascending* is splendid!"

—WINSTON GROOM,
author of *Forrest Gump*

"*Celeste Ascending* is a luminous portrait of a young woman confronted by contradictions: the chasm between longing and contentment, the material sickness of American culture versus the ascetic life of the artist, and the hard fought scramble towards grace that necessitates facing the biggest contradiction of all, who we are and were versus who we are becoming and want to be."

—ROBIN HEMLEY,
author of *The Last Studebaker*

"Celeste's journey is irresistible and involving from the first page. She is both familiar and exceptionally brave—and the grandmother is magnifique!"

—ALICE ELLIOTT DARK,
author of *In the Gloaming*

"*Celeste Ascending* teaches us all the importance of telling ourselves the truth if we're ever to find our souls. In Celeste's journey to come to terms with her family, her men, her drinking, and her life, she shows us the perils of self-deception and the rewards of bravery that start her on the road to herself. I was cheering for her all the way."

—BARBARA ESSTMAN,
author of *Night Ride Home*

"I'm falling over myself trying to say why I think *Celeste Ascending* is Kaylie Jones' finest work. Such energy! Few writers achieve this level of vigor, vibrancy, passion, feeling. Fewer still can match the feeling with an equal measure of descriptive skill—of places, scenes, bedrooms, bars, rainy streets. Kaylie Jones imperceptibly drew me along until I was helplessly hooked."

—SHANA ALEXANDER,
author of *Very Much a Lady* and *The Astonishing Elephant*

"Friendship, love, and despair are knitted together with such skill and without sentimentality. I love fighters like Celeste."

—JENNIFER JOHNSTON,
author of *How Many Miles to Babylon?*

Celeste Ascending

A NOVEL

Kaylie Jones

Perennial

An Imprint of HarperCollinsPublishers

**OTHER BOOKS
BY KAYLIE JONES**

As Soon As It Rains

Quite the Other Way

A Soldier's Daughter Never Cries

HarperCollins books may be purchased for educational, business, or sales promotional use. For information please write: Special Markets Department, HarperCollins Publishers Inc., 10 East 53rd Street, New York, NY 10022.

First Perennial edition published 2001.

Designed by Nancy Field

The Library of Congress has catalogued the hardcover edition as follows:

Jones, Kaylie.

    Celeste ascending : a novel / Kaylie Jones. — 1st ed.
      p.   cm.
   ISBN 0–06–019325–5
   I. Title
   PS3560.O497C45 2000
   813'.54—dc21   99-35290

ISBN 0–06–093134–5 (pbk.)

01 02 03 04 05 ❖/RRD 10 9 8 7 6 5 4 3 2

Acknowledgments

I wish to thank Trena Keating, my editor, for her keen and rich observations; my dear friend Shaye Areheart for her fine critical eye; Peter Matthiessen for his kindness and guidance; James Ivory, Ruth Prawer Jhabvala, and Ismail Merchant for their inspiration; David Weild IV for explaining mergers and acquisitions; and Kevin Heisler, whose faith never wavered.

Also Cecile and Buddy Bazelon, Carolyn Blakemore, Gabrielle Danchick, Henry Flesh, Joy Harris, Nan Horowitz, Beth Jones, Gloria Jones, Ellie Weiler Krach, Tim McLoughlin, Kimberly Miller, Haig Nalbantian, Dayle Patrick, Lucy Rosenthal, Ina Shoenberg, Kate Sotiridy, Liz Szabla, Janine Veto, Kathleen Warnock, and Renette Zimmerly for their readership and kind encouragement.

The generous support of the Virginia Center for the Creative Arts, where I spent two extraordinary summers working on the novel.

And my student at MS 54, Derby Clarke, for permitting me, on page 134, to print his poem.

Before Nathan, there had never been this overwhelming feeling of wanting someone so much. Only one other time in my life had I felt so completely alive—the trip my mother and I took around Italy. Both were colored by a certain recklessness. We seemed to be attempting to stop time; but what we feared from the future, I had no idea.

—CELESTE M.

One

I HAD A FRIEND in high school named Sally Newlyn who explained what had gone wrong with God's plan for the world. During one of her schizophrenic episodes, she told me that God had given mankind a finite number of souls. He set them free in the sky where they orbited silently until they were needed for the newly conceived. He intended for the souls to be reincarnated so that humanity would grow more generous and wise with each generation. But God had underestimated man's propensity to go forth and multiply, and so, on our planet today, millions of bodies were roaming the earth searching in vain for a soul.

We were sitting cross-legged in an abandoned shed we'd discovered in the woods, passing back and forth a thermos of rum and Coke. I listened to her with rapt attention, because she often spoke important truths when she stopped taking her medication. Sally's eyes were on fire, and I reached out and felt her pale forehead, but it was cool to the touch.

"That's what's wrong with me, Celeste," she said close to my ear in her small, urgent voice as tears fell from her eyes. "I didn't get a soul."

"Oh, Sally," I said, pulling her into my arms and holding her tightly, as if that could keep her demons away.

* * *

WHEN I WAS a sophomore in college, she killed herself.

I learned of Sally's suicide on a December morning when an old friend called me on the hall phone in the dormitory. Afterwards, I sat alone for a long time in the communal kitchen, listening to the midweek silence. I tried to get on with the day but I couldn't move. I remembered what Sally had told me several years before about God's plan, and I could not shake the thought from my mind.

I began to look into people's faces, searching their eyes for a glimmer of their souls. It became a compulsion; I pictured the inside of their heads as a room—something like the set in Beckett's *Endgame*—with no doors, only two windows looking out onto the world. If I could furnish the room, or at least see the view from the windows, a little corner of their soul was revealed.

I remembered Sally's eyes, and in them I could still see a warm and sunny greenhouse crowded with rare and rich-smelling plants, fragile and in constant need of care. But as she grew ill, the light in her eyes slowly dimmed, and in the greenhouse of my memory the plants shriveled up and died.

I lost my mother when I was ten, and although I remembered her well, I could not recall the event with any certainty. Trying to spare me pain, my father had filled my child's mind with reassuring stories that tenaciously lodged themselves in my imagination, leaving little room for the truth. In my mother's eyes I imagined an exotic French boudoir, with a mauve chaise longue, silk tapestries of naked demoiselles covering the windows, risqué lingerie peeking out from a closet, old clothbound books strewn everywhere, and in a corner, a bar for the many guests she might have had in real life, but never did.

* * *

AT TWENTY-EIGHT, I found myself in a small, dark apartment in New York City, quite alone. Having lost almost every person who had ever meant anything to me, I confronted my own soul-room for the first time. In mirrors, my blank eyes stared back at me. The walls and floor were bare. The windows looked out onto a dirty airshaft, a brick wall.

And then I met Alex, at a Fourth of July party on a chartered yacht, the way people meet in movies.

During the past six months, I had managed to get to my teaching job at Columbia University; to the public school in Harlem where I taught creative writing to eighth graders; and to the Korean deli: familiar places and preplanned destinations.

When summer finally came and I was relieved of my teaching obligations, I locked myself in my apartment, and began putting together my first collection of short stories.

Sometimes, in the evening, I went down the hall to visit my neighbor

Lucia. She was in the throes of a love affair with a rock and roll roadie called Soarin' Sammy. Lucia had met him on the set of one of her music videos.

They had never been outside of her apartment together. It had been going on—off and on, but mostly on—for over three years. I always knew when he was visiting because she would stop answering her phone, and the music would start pounding so that her door would hum with the vibration.

For long stretches there would be no mention of him, then she would begin to expect him again. "Soarin' Sammy should be coming by," she'd say in her heavy voice.

That summer we holed up, waiting for a storm to pass, like two commuters who'd forgotten their umbrellas. We watched old movies on her VCR and drank wine or brandy into the late hours. Around the corner there was a bar I liked, a small, dark place. Sitting in there one night, after we'd both had a number of cognacs, she made me promise I'd accompany her to this upcoming Fourth of July party. The Slimbrand company had rented a private yacht that sailed around lower Manhattan. Lucia, who had produced several commercials for them, had received a gilded invitation in the mail. It was a black tie affair. Last year, she told me, there had been music and film stars, a Top Forty band, and rivers of champagne.

I promised, and forgot about it. But on July third, she called to remind me. I told her I had other plans.

"Yeah, like what," she said. "Like lying around reading Emily Dickinson poems?" She sighed heavily into the phone.

"I like Emily Dickinson," I said.

There was a long pause. Then she said in her lumbering voice, without anger, a mere statement of fact, "Maybe you should go see a shrink, Celeste."

I would never consider it; in my family, we were stubborn and resilient and took our "hard knocks" in silence, with fortitude.

So I put on my best summer dress, low-cut, drop-waisted, emerald-green silk, which I had bought for a cousin's wedding, my high-heeled Evan Picone pumps, which I saved for special occasions, and my mother's long strand of pearls that blushed pink in the light. I braced myself with several shots of frozen Stoli and waited for Lucia to ring the bell. She arrived promptly; dark and sensual with her large mouth painted crimson, she wore a black Spandex dress that accentuated her full breasts and wide hips, fishnet stockings, and big, shiny black pumps like Minnie Mouse wears.

As we boarded the yacht, I wanted to spin around and run back across the walkway. The upper deck was all windows and resembled an aviary crowded with rare birds. The yacht cast off; Lucia and I headed for the bar. On the way, she ran into her Slimbrand executive in black tie and I found a waiter with a full tray of glistening champagne glasses. The band started to play Motown hits. Unable to hear a thing Lucia and the executive were saying to each other, I went outdoors. Manhattan's lighted windows formed a glorious halo in the indigo sky. A tall, wide-shouldered man appeared beside me, elbows leaning comfortably on the railing. His dark blond hair was brushed back from his broad forehead. Little glasses glinted on the bridge of his nose, and below that was a substantial, firm mouth and square jaw. In his pin-striped suit, he seemed poised, content with who he was in the world.

"It's spectacular, isn't it?" he said. I looked over my shoulder to see whom he was addressing, and realized it was me.

"It's overwhelming," I said. "I've never seen it from this perspective before."

"I was born and raised in Manhattan," he said, "and I still think it has the best skyline in the world."

"Better than Singapore?" I said. "I've never been there, but it looks pretty impressive on the Discovery Channel."

"Better than Singapore. I go there quite often on business. I'm Alex Laughton."

He extended his hand and smiled. He had a firm grip and his eyes were steady. Alex's teeth were perfect, not one of them out of line, and very white.

Inside, the band was playing "Respect."

I didn't meet men like him. In fact, I hadn't met any men in a long time. I used to go out on surrogate dates with my best friend Branko, who had been as familiar and dependable as Christmas.

"I'm Celeste Miller," I told him, shaking his hand. I brought my champagne glass to my lips, but it was empty.

A waiter passed by carrying a tray of bubbling flutes, and Alex briskly exchanged my empty glass for two fresh ones. A little nervous, I began to babble. I told him I didn't often go to such parties. He asked me what I did.

"I teach English lit and creative writing at Columbia. I got my Ph.D. there a couple of years ago. Now I'm an adjunct professor. Once a week, I go up to Harlem and teach kids creative writing in a public school. But really I'm a writer."

"What do you write?" His glasses picked up the city lights and glinted as he gazed at me.

Lucia came by, apologized for abandoning me, and explained that the Slimbrand fellow wouldn't stop talking. He was considering her for another job.

"Can you believe this line?" She merrily quoted in a high-pitched singsong, " 'Plastic, it's fantastic!'

"They're competing with Playtex," she explained. "Plastic applicators."

"That slogan is obnoxious," Alex said.

He introduced himself to her. Lucia looked him up and down, and finding me in good company, she went back to discuss more business with the Slimbrand fellow.

I asked him what he did for a living.

"Investment banking. I'm a managing director in the M&A group at Griffin Silverstein."

"MNA?"

"Mergers and acquisitions," he said vaguely. Not that a more detailed explanation would have helped clarify this. He might as well have said the Enema Group. There was an uncomfortable silence. Then he said, "My mother is a doctor with Feed the Children. She works primarily in Central Africa. Her job is a little like yours, I guess."

"Just like it," I said with an ironic laugh. "You Wall Street guys think it's a real jungle up in Harlem."

He looked down, blushing, and shook his head. He murmured, "Good one, Alex, you moron."

"I'm sorry," I said quickly. "It's just that I've never had any problems up there at all."

After a pause, Alex asked again, "So, what do you write?"

"Short stories. I've published several stories in magazines. Literary magazines." I felt uncomfortable saying all this, as if it weren't enough, as if I were apologizing.

"I don't know anybody who writes fiction. You must be really good to teach at Columbia."

I didn't tell him that writing well was not a prerequisite for teaching at Columbia, that the university treated adjuncts like slave labor, and we were still grateful to the administration for the job. I liked that he was impressed.

Alex told me he was an only child, that since he and his mother were often traveling, their paths rarely crossed these days. She'd been married and divorced twice. When she was home she descended on the nation's capital like a plague, he said, shouting about the awful living conditions of America's underprivileged masses. Alex admired her. He said he admired women who were ambitious and independent—although politically he and his mother were in different camps.

"I haven't voted since Carter," I said. This fact really seemed to worry him.

"It's our right, our democratic right," he said, looking intently into my eyes. "It's what makes this country great."

"Where's your father now?" I asked, changing the subject.

"He's in Jersey. But he may as well be in Alaska. I've been on my own a long time," he said serenely.

"So have I."

The yacht circled the Statue of Liberty, gleaming like an emerald tower in the sleek black water. Fireworks tumbled from the sky as though angels were emptying their treasure chests, and in the distance, Manhattan twinkled like the palaces in the fairy-tale books my mother used to read to me at night.

I gasped as just above our heads a firework exploded and then whistled dangerously as it careened toward the river. Alex pressed me to his wide chest. He smelled of one of those manly leather-and-spice colognes. I felt small against him. "I saw you as soon as you came in," he said close to my ear. "I thought you were European, French or something."

"I'm half-French," I said, surprised.

A waiter passed close by and Alex grabbed two more champagne flutes. We toasted Independence Day, I held my glass tight in my hand, and with my head all in a whirl, tears threatening to rise, I buried my face in his hard pectoral muscles and breathed deeply.

"I'm sorry. My best friend Branko . . ." my voice trailed off, the right words out of reach. Alex stroked my hair and held me as the city lights flashed by. I felt safe there, as I had when my mother and I rode the Ferris wheel, pressed against each other, screaming out at the night.

The waiter came by and my hand shot out for another glass of champagne.

We must have talked and talked, but what we said escapes me, lost in a swirl of champagne. It seemed no time had passed at all and then the yacht docked and guests began to stumble off. Alex led me through the crowd, across the walkway to the glistening black pavement. Lucia was standing there, looking at us with amusement.

Alex hurried us away from the dock. He said it would be impossible to find a cab there. Indeed, the guests were rushing into the street with their arms up. I wondered if he would ask me to have a drink; go back to his place. I would not refuse. He walked us uptown a few blocks, then stepped out into the empty street and whistled loudly. As if on command, a taxi came careening around the corner and screeched to a halt before us. Alex held the door for Lucia, then me. I hesitated, not knowing what to do or say to him. I was certain I'd never see him again.

"Would you give me your number?" he asked tentatively.

"Got a pen?"

"I have a photographic memory for numbers," he said with a confident smile. I told him my number. He stooped and kissed me with open lips, not at all inhibited by Lucia's watchful gaze. A passionate kiss that lasted many seconds. He stepped away.

"Watch your dress." He shut the door and pressed his hand to the glass for a moment. I watched him through the rear window as he receded, then disappeared into the darkness.

Lucia was telling me that I was silly to have been so scared to go. I was thinking that I would surely never hear from him again.

* * *

THE NEXT MORNING a dozen red roses arrived with a note that said only, "From Alex Laughton."

He must have looked up my last name and initial in the phone book, and searched for the number that matched the one I'd given him. With a last name as common as Miller, this was no small feat in New York City.

I went back to sleep for three hours, unplugging the phone as I always did. When I awakened there were three hang-ups on the answering machine.

"I guess I should tell you I've been married before," Alex said the following evening, a Wednesday, at dinner. He had chosen a California grill on the Upper East Side. The space was enormous and brightly lit by track lighting. I strained to hear him over the din of cutlery and echoing voices.

"Any children?" I asked; the obvious question. He shook his head. I was relieved and hoped my face didn't betray me.

It had taken me a long time to get ready. Alex had no idea how many times I'd called Lucia long-distance. She was away on a job. She'd grown irritated and told me to pull myself together. I missed my old roommate Candace sorely. In the old days, Candace would have picked a dress for me. She might even have come along on the date if I couldn't face it alone. In the stark bedroom Candace and I had once shared, I glanced quickly at myself in the mirror, half expecting her to appear behind me and rearrange my hair. "Where the hell are you?" I muttered. A draft from the air-conditioning passed over me like a flutter of wings, and I began to shiver.

I had asked Alex to come pick me up. I had been afraid to go into the restaurant alone, but I would never have told him this. I realized that he had no idea what he was getting himself into. He thought we were two normal people sharing a nice dinner. I reached for my vodka gibson; the delicate faceted stem of the glass reflected the light like a diamond as I twirled it. The liquor crackled nicely against the back of my throat, warming my chest and stomach. I wanted to down the whole thing, but nursed it instead. Who knew how much Alex drank, or if he'd even order a second cocktail, or wine, or would he drink plain water? It would be impossible for me to sit through dinner on plain water. I decided to order wine by the glass.

He was telling me that his wife had been a part-time model who was trying to finish law school at Fordham. Her name was Mimi.

"What happened?" I asked.

"I don't know. Didn't work out." Since then, he'd been what he called a serial monogamist.

"Better that than a serial polygamist, I guess." A laugh escaped from me. He seemed disconcerted. I composed myself.

"I want to settle down," he said, dead serious. "I want children."

I glanced uneasily at my reflection in the floor-to-ceiling window. I looked poised and sensible, perhaps even beautiful to him, in my pale green cotton sweater and long skirt. A tall, dark-haired woman ambled by behind me in the smoky glass of the window. She wore a skintight, sleeveless emerald green dress. Her arms and legs were thin and taut, and she wore emerald earrings and a matching choker. She was probably a model. I had always wanted to be taller, and bone-thin, straight-haired; in fact, all the things I was not. I turned back to Alex, and felt myself disappear under his gaze.

I took a last sip of my martini and speared the pearl onion, popping it into my mouth. I wanted another drink. Alex had finished his rum and tonic. He called the waiter over and ordered a bottle of California Chardonnay. Thank God. My relief was so extreme that for a moment I couldn't remember what we'd been talking about.

The topaz-colored wine arrived. The waiter poured. I reached for my glass, but the gesture seemed greedy, so I set it back down without taking a sip.

I blurted out, my mouth dry, that I had only been in love once, and that the feeling had lasted for years and years, and that with this fellow, I'd lost a piece of myself that I'd never been able to recover.

"What was his name?" Alex asked, the tips of his ears reddening.

What a lot of heavy baggage I had. I didn't know if I had the energy or the enthusiasm to go through it all again. I didn't want to talk about it, and shook my head.

"I'm going to take care of you," he said. He reached across the table and took my hand. He invited me to have dinner at his apartment on Saturday night. He said he would call me when he was ready to leave work.

"You work on Saturdays?" I asked.

"Well, not always," he said.

* * *

I WAITED BY THE PHONE until he called at nine P.M. He said his secretary had ordered dinner for us and it would be waiting with the doorman when we got there. I imagined that I would be spending the night.

His Upper East Side penthouse apartment was on the thirty-eighth floor and had a large, gleaming white kitchen with an open counter on one side that faced a dining/living room area so long and wide you could have put a bowling alley in there. The tall windows faced southwest, offering a magnificent view of the Manhattan skyline and Central Park. A wide balcony ran the entire length of the apartment. Alex opened a sliding glass door and stepped out. I couldn't, it was too high up for me and I had a terrible fear of heights. I stayed inside and walked around inspecting his things. There were a few large art books on the Chinese coffee table, and a picture book on the history of tennis, but no others.

He had installed track lighting on the ceiling, which carefully high-lighted the Oriental rugs over the mossy green carpeting, the Chinese tapestries and scrolls on the walls, the dark cherrywood furniture embossed with gold bamboo leaves and charging dragons. The large, plush couches were a darker, mossier green than the carpeting.

"Nice stuff," I called out to him, thinking that he must have had a designer help him.

"I got most of it in Hong Kong," he said. When I didn't join him outside, he came back in and shut the door. "But it's real, old colonial stuff from the mainland."

A sleek black cabinet ran the length of the far living room wall and in it stood a shiny black TV, VCR, tape deck, compact disk player, an electric guitar and huge amplifier, and all the accompanying paraphernalia. The remote controls were lined up like little coffins on top of the TV. At my place, I had a small black and white with no cable and not even a single coffin.

"You play the electric guitar?" I asked, surprised.

"Not so much anymore," he said.

His secretary, Lorraine, had ordered a crabmeat salad with all kinds of vegetables and greens. Unsure of whether he had wine in the house, or if his secretary would have the good sense to order a couple of bottles, I had brought an expensive white Bordeaux from my grandmother's vineyard. Americans usually dismissed white Bordeaux, but my grandmother had long ago taught me that this was one of the finest wines of France. I was hoping Alex would ask me about my choice, but he just poured liberally, never glancing at the label.

In his hand-carved four-poster king-sized bed, in the dark, my lips reached hungrily for his wide mouth. A rapacious mouth, a predator's mouth. His body was strong and smooth, and he was graceful and sure of himself. An athlete. In fact, I'd learned tonight that he'd been a tennis champion at Yale and at Choate, and a soccer standout before that, in junior prep school.

He liked to kiss, to lick, to suck as much as I did. We were very good together. Excellent, in fact. All-conference, at least. He didn't talk or make a sound. Not a sound. I liked to make a lot of noise, especially in an apartment as big and safe as his, with walls so thick there were no noticeable neighbors in any direction. Several hours passed, and still not a word, not a sound from him, only a hissing exhale of breath, a shudder of his wide back.

* * *

THE NEXT SATURDAY, we had brunch and then walked down Columbus Avenue. I stopped in front of an Italian shoe store to admire the summer pumps.

"You'd look hot in those red ones," Alex said in a murmur that sent a shiver from my throat to my crotch.

"I've never worn red shoes," I said.

He took me by the arm. "Why don't you try them on?"

"I can't afford them, Alex!"

In the store I noticed that women looked at him. He sat back comfortably in an armchair and asked me to walk back and forth in front of him in the red shoes.

"I have nothing to wear with these, Alex!" I protested.

He took a platinum Visa card out of his wallet. "We'll get you something to wear with them."

"God, you landed yourself a jewel," the salesgirl murmured, looking up with big eyes from her crouched position as she slipped the shoes from my feet.

Two

FOR MY BIRTHDAY, he took Friday and Monday off and we flew to Bermuda for a long weekend. Alex had not taken a single sick day or vacation day in two years and had recently been ordered to take some of the time that was due him.

In our spacious room at the White Bone Beach Hotel, we were greeted by the big red blinking message button on the telephone.

"Shit," Alex said, dropped his sports coat on the bed, and punched in his work number.

"Yes, George," Alex said. "The letter went out to the board of directors, what, on Wednesday? What's the stock trading at today? Still twenty, and we offered to purchase at twenty-five . . . "

I went to the window and opened it. A few hundred feet straight down was a large terrace and a bean-shaped electric blue pool; a few hundred feet farther down some steep stone steps lay the aquamarine ocean and bone-white beach. The sun was hot despite the wind and there were still umbrellas and beach chairs and people swimming in the churning surf. A thatch-roofed bar catered to the guests who were tanning themselves on the chaise longues.

Alex said, "Put a call in to company counsel, ask if they received our letter. Ask if there's a response."

I waited for a while, but Alex had kicked off his loafers and stretched out on the bed. He did not appear to be getting off the phone anytime soon. I opened my bag, took out a bathing suit and the second volume of Marcel Proust's *A la recherche du temps perdu*—nice light beach reading, I now thought. I'd secretly hoped to impress Alex not just with my intellectual acumen but also with my linguistic talents. I changed right there, hoping to distract him. He barely glanced my way.

"You tell them that we're prepared to put out a press release. That we'll contest it in the press. We'll take out a fucking ad in the *Wall Street Journal* and force the issue! We'll squeeze their balls!"

When I was done changing, my wrap snug over my hips and the suntan lotion and other necessities in my new beach bag, I waved to him to indicate that I was leaving. He held up an index finger. Was he indicating that I should wait? I waited.

"Well, you call them, George, and find out what they have to say. I'll wait right here. You call me back and we'll figure it out from there. What else?"

Fifteen minutes later he was still on the phone, so I walked out, shutting the door a little harder than necessary.

* * *

THERE WAS A very nice waiter on the beach who wore a blue sports coat over a white shirt and bow tie, white and blue striped Bermuda shorts, and knee-high black socks and dress shoes. He looked like he'd walked out of his house that morning and forgotten to put on his pants. Every time he appeared with his tray and a fresh piña colada for me, I felt like laughing. After a little while I didn't feel angry at all.

The sun was low in the sky by the time Alex showed up wearing long black swim trunks. He had a few inches of fat around the waist, but he was a splendid sight. Still lightly tanned from summer, with large biceps and chest muscles, a tight, round ass and muscular legs, he turned women's heads on the beach. When he sat down at the edge of my chaise longue, I slipped my hand up one of the swim trunks' legs. He grabbed my hand and threw it aside.

"Don't do that, people can see."

"Are you going to apologize to me for ruining this whole day or what?"

"How many of those have you had?" he nodded toward the empty glass.

"Just two."

Ha! Proust lay unopened at my side. Many years of practice had taught me to avoid slurring and to control my muscles so that most people would never even know.

"Good book?"

"Great book!" I said with conviction. When my friend the waiter came back, Alex ordered two piña coladas.

"So did George work out whatever it was he needed to work out?"

Alex shifted around. "Not really. They can't do anything without me, I swear." After a pause he said, "I'm going to play some golf tomorrow. I wanted to go scuba diving but they say it's all fished out around here."

"Whatever," I said gloomily. "I'll just hang here with our nice waiter who forgot to put his pants on this morning."

Alex didn't laugh. Our piña coladas arrived.

"What's the matter, Alex?"

"Nothing," he said. "I'm just not used to being on vacation, that's all."

We drank the piña coladas and then two more.

Later, when we dressed for dinner, I realized why Alex hadn't laughed. He had Bermuda shorts as well, and looked, as the waiter had, as if he'd forgotten to put on his pants.

"Where did you get those?" I said, trying to hold back a giggle.

"Last time I was here," he said, annoyed. He had a habit of stamping his feet and sliding them back slightly, like a bull about to charge.

"And when was that?"

He hesitated. "My honeymoon."

"Well, goddamnit, Alex, couldn't we have gone someplace else?"

"It wasn't the same hotel," he said, straightening his collar. "And stop using that language, Celeste."

"Oh, excuse me. You can swear all you want on the phone with George but I can't use the word *goddamnit* in my own hotel room?"

"That's different," Alex said, "that's work."

It was the beginning of a long night.

After dinner, he gave me a little black box and inside was a pair of ruby studs.

"Wow, they're beautiful. What good taste you have, Alex!"

"I sent Lorraine to Tiffany's during her lunch hour. She loves doing that kind of stuff."

It occurred to me that his secretary had probably been the one who looked up my phone number in the phone book in order to find my address and send me a dozen long-stem roses. Somehow none of this sat well with me but I thought it prudent to keep my mouth shut. Instead I had another after-dinner drink.

Many hours later, we found ourselves in the outdoor disco, set up under a long thatched roof on the beach. A glittering disco ball hung from the center roof beam and showered the empty dance floor with little circles of light. It must have been two or three in the morning; we were the last customers, and the blond Australian bartender, who was also drunk, was telling us Sheila jokes. The music suddenly died, and the lights were turned up, so that in their glare the cigarette-strewn dance floor and bar area, the overflowing ashtrays and empty glasses and sticky spills were a dismal sight. Alex fled, pulling me behind him along the path and up the steep, narrow steps to the terrace and the now dark, bean-shaped pool.

"Oh, Alex, let's go skinny-dipping! There's no one here."

Alex looked around. "No," he said.

"What a square," I said, and jerked free. I dove into the deep end in my black evening dress, sandals and all. The world seemed so quiet and peaceful down there that I considered staying. I wondered if Alex would jump in to save me. When my lungs began to ache for air, panic forced me to push for the surface. I grabbed the edge of the pool and looked around, gasping for breath. Alex had gone.

I have a hazy recollection of standing under a tepid shower with my arms pressed up against the tiles to steady myself, and Alex appearing behind me, naked and hard. He lifted me up and turned me around, thrust himself into me as my back and head slammed into the tiles. Next we were on the floor, wet, then I'm pressed, facedown, over the edge of the bed with him standing behind me.

The next morning I was so sore I felt like I'd been in a rodeo.

"I think we have a fascinating method of communicating," I said to him as I inspected my swollen face in the mirror. He lay prostrate on the bed with a pillow over his head.

* * *

A FEW WEEKS LATER, in the beginning of November, we were watching a late-night movie, *A Kiss Before Dying,* in bed; Robert Wagner was about to push his pregnant girlfriend off the roof of the municipal building.

Alex said, "Isn't it incredible? She has absolutely no idea who she's in love with!"

"I know!" I said. Naked, we'd pulled a sheet up from the floor and twined it around ourselves. His whole apartment smelled of him, of that leather-and-spice cologne. Pillows, sheets, towels, and now, even I.

Chinese take-out containers stood on a tray on the bedside table, and our clothes were strewn everywhere. Alex had just gotten home from work, and I'd come over straight from the bar where Lucia and I had been sitting for several hours.

"How come you never talk or make any sounds when you're fucking?"

"Don't say *fucking*. It bothers me."

"All right," I said, "screwing, then. How come you never make any sounds or talk when we're screwing?"

He was mad now, his face became flushed and a frown crossed his brow. I punched him in the arm, "Come on, lighten up!" Perhaps Lucia and I had had too many cognacs. I was pushing my luck.

"It started at Choate, I guess," he said, and shifted his weight around uncomfortably. "You learn to be quiet."

I laughed, thinking of young Alex Laughton inchoate at Choate. "So you were doing those naughty homosexual things then—"

"Listen, Celeste, I don't like it when you talk like that."

"I'm sorry."

Alex said suddenly, "Why don't you move in? Then you'd be here when I got home. You wouldn't have to travel across town late at night."

I swallowed, and caught my breath. "So soon?"

"Why not? My place is so much nicer," he said simply. Alex wouldn't stay at my apartment. It was cramped and too "bohemian."

"I can make this apartment perfect for you," he said. "And why pay two rents? I'll get someone to build you bookshelves for all your hundreds of books, wall to wall. With an alcove in the middle for your desk. We'll turn the guest room into a really nice library/study. Your cinderblock-and-boards shelves are college stuff, Celeste."

I was mad now. So what if I couldn't afford custom-made shelves? I was doing what I wanted with my life.

"This is a little fast for me, Alex. I can't do things this fast."

A formal shroud of politeness fell over his eyes. He moved away and kept a foot of space between us for the rest of the film. I became frightened.

"I just need a little more time."

As the film credits began to roll, I said, "Maybe I'd better go home."

"If you like," he said in an indifferent voice that I didn't recognize.

I took my time getting my jacket, to give him an opportunity to stop me, to put his arms around me, but he did not.

Even in my own apartment I still smelled of him. That cologne had rubbed off on my hand towels in the bathroom, on my own pillowcases.

I couldn't stand it and ran down the hall and knocked on Lucia's door. She was in her nightgown. The light at her back illuminated the cotton fabric, exposing the dark forms of her wide thighs and large, round breasts.

"Hey," she said in a gloomy voice, "what's up?"

"Let's go have another drink," I said.

"All right; let me get dressed."

Sitting at the bar in the spot we had vacated only a few hours before, I felt much better. I warmed a Martell brandy, twirling the snifter around in my palm, and watched the light glowing amber inside the glass. I took a sip, felt the familiar splash-and-burn make its way from my throat to my esophagus, hit my stomach, and then a feeling of grace wafted over me. *Fuck him,* I thought. *I don't belong there anyway.*

"Let's stay until the place closes!" I said to Lucia.

"What's the matter, Celeste?" she asked. "What the hell happened?"

"Nothing. I'm sick of him," I said. "He's such a tight-ass."

"Yeah, well, Soarin' Sammy he's not," she said, dead earnest.

* * *

BETWEEN MIDNIGHT, when I left Alex's, and ten-thirty A.M., when I came to, there were ten hang-ups on my answering machine. At eleven, Alex finally left a message. I lay in bed and listened as he talked to the machine. An image pierced through the pain and fog: I was dancing to the jukebox, crotch to crotch with a gorgeous Puerto Rican bodybuilder, the lights spinning round and round. Having run his hands up under my shirt, he was just about to unsnap my bra when Lucia grabbed my arm and dragged me away.

I swiftly turned my back on the thought and pulled the pillow over my head.

"Celeste?" Alex's voice rang through. "Call me as soon as you can, okay? . . . Listen . . . I love you, Celeste. I hope you know that. Don't forget, we have that fund-raiser tonight. They're honoring the CEO of Chemical Bank."

My brain was pounding on the walls of my head, trying to get out.

By four o'clock I was able to construct a coherent thought and this was it: this was no way to behave at my age. I called him back.

Ten minutes later, the phone rang again and I didn't pick it up. "Hallo, this is Esteban, we met last night," said a deep, gravelly voice.

My heart started to pound in my throat. How had he gotten my number? Had I given it to him?

I erased the message as soon as he hung up.

* * *

FOR THE OCCASION, Alex had bought me a tight-fitting black velvet dress with a low-cut tulip-shaped neckline, a matching velvet evening bag and pumps. I wore my mother's pink-hued pearls and antique pearl earrings. We sat at a round table with eight other couples I had never met but whom Alex knew through his business dealings.

I kept my mouth shut and smiled till my ears ached, feeling sure that this way no one would identify me as the impostor I was. The waiters were fortunately quite liberal with the wine.

The man to my left wanted to know how Alex and I had met. I told the romantic story of the Fourth of July cruise. He nodded approvingly. His wife leaned across him and told me conspiratorially that Alex was one of the most "eligible bachelors" in New York City. That she and her husband had been trying to fix him up for years, to calm him down. Her husband nodded. "He works seven days a week," he said with a rueful smile, "sixty, eighty hours, no problem. Married guys with kids, like me, we hate him."

After the steak au poivre, during the champagne and profiteroles, we were shown a video on the life and achievements of Mr. John Fairfax Jr., CEO of Chemical Bank. He was big on giving to museums, and had donated many millions to the Metropolitan Museum of Art.

"The Metropolitan Museum!" I grumbled in Alex's ear. "Jesus Christ, I can think of a few places that could really *use* that money. Like the program I work for in Harlem, The Writer's Way, they could sure use it! Or how about just setting up a fund to send some of those kids to college? Jesus, Alex, the Metropolitan Museum!"

"Shhh," Alex hissed. His glasses twinkled in the candlelight. I couldn't see his eyes. "Museums need money, too."

"Keep the poor in the ghettos, right?"

"Stop it, Celeste. Don't get mad at me, I give tons of money to Feed the Children every year." His jaw was tensing. I could see he was getting angry. "You sound like a socialist."

"I am a socialist!" I said with conviction. I had never given politics much thought, but at the moment, I felt very much like a socialist. The couple I had been talking to looked down, embarrassed. Alex began to laugh, a low, rumbling chuckle I found very appealing. He squeezed my knee under the table and I let out a little cry that made the other couples turn in our direction.

I began to stay at Alex's in the mornings, reading for my classes, trying to get used to the place. There was a closet in the living room, right next to the garbage chute, and every bag that dropped down sounded like a body falling through the floor above.

One night, after I'd awakened in a sweat over a bad dream, I sat in the dark living room and counted the blinking red lights to calm myself: the microwave, VCR, the cable box, the little round lights of the electric mixer mounted on the kitchen wall, the rectangular light on the answering machine, and the digital clock on the coffeemaker. I opened the fridge. A bottle of Moët champagne, a bottle of Evian, and some ancient barbecued chicken wings in a plastic delivery container. It was as if no one lived here.

I came upon the remnants of his former wife, Mimi, in remote corners of the apartment. There were lipstick cases and a little makeup mirror with a flowery pattern on the back in a drawer of an antique vanity that had belonged to Alex's grandmother. I found an eye-pencil sharpener and some perfume samplers—Poison, appropriately—in the back of the medicine cabinet.

Once, while Alex was at work, my shoulder knocked a large, rectangular plastic picture frame off the bathroom wall. The frame fell apart, and a small stack of photos slid out from behind the one of Alex and his mother playing tennis at some club. They were naked photos of Mimi. In one she posed arched and growling, leonine, her blond hair teased out and the eyeliner black and curving to points at the corners of her light blue eyes. Her skin was pale and her body reedlike, her breasts just the right size, a handful. How could Alex have been in love with someone as different from me as this? And why had he saved the pictures?

* * *

NOT LONG AFTER THAT, we went to a dance club on a Saturday night with a friend of Alex's from his college tennis team. The fellow was still in awe of Alex ten years later, sidling up to him like some kind of large dog. He had some Ecstasy and offered Alex and me each a hit. I waited to see what Alex would do. He swallowed the white pill dry, without giving it a thought. Mine went down easily with a shot of tequila.

Alex danced beautifully, lithe and graceful and perfectly in rhythm. He barely moved, but his movements were rolling, coordinated. Even on the dance floor people cleared the way for him.

When we got home I was so high I couldn't sleep after we'd made love twice so I put on the Discovery Channel and watched a show on sperm whales. I felt that the world was a grand and wonderful place.

I said, "All right, Alex, I'll move in. But would it be all right if I put some real food in the fridge?"

"You know I work late almost every night," he said evenly. "And sometimes things come up. Like my boss wants me to take someone out to play golf or to dinner . . . "

"If I cook my boeuf Maringo you'd goddamn well better be home for it, or else!" I said, and laughed. He didn't laugh, so I punched him in the arm.

"I'm serious, Celeste."

"Alex, lighten up, will you? Why the fuck did you ask me to move in if you didn't really want me to?"

"Don't swear like that, it bothers me. I do want you to move in. I just want you to know how things are."

"I know how things are, goddamnit."

"God, you're so crude sometimes," he said.

"Crude?" I cried. "Crude? Well, screw you, Alex. I just told you I'd move in. Isn't that what you want? Make up your fucking mind!" I grabbed my clothes from the floor and dressed to go.

His doorman smirked at me as I marched unsteadily out of the lobby and into the street. A taxi blared its horn.

* * *

ALEX USUALLY CALLED every hour, and if the answering machine picked up, he hung up. But this day, there were no calls from him at all. I raised the receiver once to make sure the phone was working. By nightfall, my anxiety had risen to a crescendo and I was pacing the floor.

Someone knocked; I thought it was Lucia and opened the door. It was Ethel, the deaf old lady who lived next door.

On the day seven years earlier that Candace and I had moved in,

Ethel opened her door, peeked out, and said, "I'm dying of cancer so I can't help you." Candace and I stood there, loaded down with boxes, and just stared at the shriveled old woman. Candace's face got blotchy, which always happened when she was trying to control her emotions. "Oh, I'm sorry—excuse me, please," Candace said, and rushed into our apartment with me on her heels.

As soon as the door was closed, she covered her mouth and held her nose to stifle her nervous giggles and slid down the wall to the floor. "What an awful thing to say—I don't mean to laugh, but really."

Now Ethel's clawlike hand gripped the door frame as her knobby foot slipped across the threshold. The scent of stale vodka and cockroach spray clung to her. She glared at me, her face scrunched up in a wince of outrage.

"It's so bad today, Celine," she said, her voice warbling. "My son hasn't called me in three weeks."

Her trouble was always cataclysmic, and never her fault. Often she had the DT's. "There's a crater in my ceiling and water's leaking all over the floor! Rats are crawling down! They let you live like niggers in this building!"

Once she called the firemen in the middle of the night and in their zeal they tore her door off its hinges. Occasionally she ran out of vodka, which was the issue this afternoon.

"Celine," she said, "they disconnected my phone again. I'm entertaining tonight. Call the liquor store for me, will you? Order me a pint of vodka. Smirnoff's. That kind."

As I was making the call to the liquor store, I considered ordering a new bottle of Stoli for me and Lucia, but then I remembered with a shudder the smell of vodka on Ethel's breath, and didn't.

The young German couple upstairs began to fight.

I looked around my crowded living room, at the fold-out futon couch, the dust balls in the corners, the dingy windows, my unpaid bills. No messages blinked on my answering machine, because lately I had neglected friends and family. Against the far wall stood my cinderblock-and-boards bookshelves, so crowded with books that I'd started piles on the floor. I'd kept every book I'd ever read, although a few were missing that people had borrowed and never returned. Long ago when I had thought about the future, I'd dreamed of myself as successful, and married, and safe. Looking at my reflection now in the cheap mirror that hung on the door, I wondered what on earth had happened. Where had the time gone?

Alex had promised to build me wall-to-wall shelves for my books. *Lucia will be home soon,* I said to myself. *Don't panic.*

The room grew dark, the radiator hissed and thumped. There was a grille on the fire escape window, and the light across the street projected diamond shapes onto the floor. Ethel was watching *Live at Five,* and the overenthusiastic voices of news anchors seeped through the wall. I remembered that I still had a bottle of Stoli in the freezer. I went into the kitchen and poured a shot into a thin glass and took a long, icy, syrupy sip.

Better.

What now? I thought.

When I was completing my Ph.D. in Comparative Lit at Columbia, I found temp work as a word processor at various law firms at night. My father, an attorney, once said, chuckling at the irony of it all, "You tried to get as far away from lawyers as you could and here you are, working as a lawyer's secretary."

I gazed at him calmly while my heart pumped blood behind my eyes.

"Gee, sometimes you look so much like your mother, you scare me," he said, turning his eyes away guiltily. "You know I'll pay for law school, Celeste. Anytime, anyplace." He said the last magnanimously, and for a moment my system seemed to completely shut down with the realization that I truly did not like this man whose genes I shared. Then he shook his head, as if the whole thing were simply beyond his control. Rage burned in my esophagus like hot soup swallowed too fast.

Thank God *for the money your mother left you,* I told myself again as the old, unnameable fear tightened its grip. She had made me the sole beneficiary of a large life insurance policy that had been supporting me for over a decade, but the money was running out.

You can always sell her emerald ring, I told myself. *You can always sell her pearls.*

But then what? In less than a year, I would turn thirty.

For many years, I had taught at Columbia while compiling my notes for my dissertation on the works of two concentration camp survivors— Primo Levi, who refused to perish at Auschwitz, and Varlam Shalamov, who survived Stalin's Siberian Kolyma camps. I had often considered quitting, getting a full-time job, but Levi and Shalamov kept me from doing so. If two such great writers had managed to survive the worst conditions the world had to offer, their souls intact—*and write such beauty*—who was I to quit? I was nothing but a spoiled, rich girl; I'd never had to fight for anything in my life. What right did I have to quit?

They had described brutality and death, but also the random gifts of life—a scruffy shrub laden with wrinkled, frozen berries that Varlam collected with trembling fingers in a wasteland of snow; a pipe leaking droplets of clean water that Primo discovered when everywhere around him people were dying of thirst. Sometimes the gifts came from the reckless acts of generosity of other inmates, gestures that cost them their lives. In such a wasteland, on some days the tiniest flicker of human dignity had kept them alive, and they had, for me, best depicted the darkness when describing the flickers of light.

I had started many letters in my rudimentary Italian to Primo Levi, but they seemed trite and unconvincing and I never mailed one off. I could not write to Varlam Shalamov because he would never receive my letters. He was imprisoned in a Moscow insane asylum, until his death in 1982. Five years later, in April, Levi died.

The television news had been making me cringe for years: ghetto babies burned to death in firetrap buildings; children raped by their own fathers, burned by their mothers' cigarettes. When Levi died, I stopped watching the news and began to look for a volunteer position teaching in the public schools. For eight months I fought the New York City school system's bureaucracy, and then an opportunity to teach in Harlem just fell into my lap. I had been there for three semesters now, and I was prouder of this than I was of anything else I'd ever done. But today, none of it, not even the kids with their wide-open faces and fresh and gorgeous poetry, could bring me peace, because fear once again had its clawed hands around my throat.

I thought of Alex's warm, bright, sunny apartment, where nothing ever leaked and the floors were straight. He lived in a world where wastelands did not exist, where pain and fear were just obstacles to overcome, like correcting nearsightedness with a handsome pair of glasses.

His life would surely go on without me, barely disrupted; the city was filled with women who would gladly take my place. Rage and jealousy churned in my stomach, my mouth was dry, my knees numb.

It was dark, and Lucia still wasn't home.

I remembered what Lucia had said last winter when in a particularly blue mood. "Oh my God, I'm thirty-three already. I've been living in this dump for ten years! I don't want to be here at forty, fighting with that drunken lout of a super over the fucking heat!"

I went back to the kitchen and poured myself another stout shot. The hours passed. At ten o'clock, I heard the news come on at Ethel's. I could no longer face the black hours before daylight. No amount of Stoli would calm my fears. With a shaking hand, I reached for the phone.

"Hello?" Alex said, and I heard an edge of anxiety in the one word, and I knew everything was going to be all right. I felt drugged, overcome by relief. Suddenly there was no fear, no black hole, and I could no longer remember what had caused me to argue with him the night before. I saw nothing ahead but easy sailing and blue skies.

* * *

I MET ALEX'S MOTHER, Aurelia, on New Year's Eve. She was in town for a few days. We went to a party at the Fifth Avenue apartment of their rich cousin by marriage who had recently sold his business magazine to a midtown conglomerate for an inconceivable sum. His wife had decorated the vast living room with an array of oeuvres by famous artists—Magritte, Calder, Duchamp. Behind the paintings the walls were deep red. The robust couches and armchairs were upholstered in a lush green and red floral pattern. Long, dark green velvet drapes, embossed with gold fleurs-de-lys, hung in folds beside large windows that revealed a beautiful view of the Met and the park beyond. There wasn't a single book in the entire apartment, but there was a surfeit of Dom Perignon champagne. Aurelia and I stood by one of the windows discussing the view while I tried to keep my balance in my high heels by surreptitiously holding on to the thick drapes. Aurelia wore a green and blue sequined jacket over a black turtleneck and slim black slacks. The track lighting ricocheted off the sequins and made little blue and green spots of light dance on her face and neck.

Suddenly she said, "Alex is crazy about you. He's been so lonely. He doesn't socialize much with his schedule. I guess you could say he's a workaholic, like his mother." She smiled. "Be prepared, he's going to surprise you."

Just then Alex emerged from the crowd and strode toward us with a determined expression on his face. He took me by the arm and pulled me toward the window, behind the curtains. He'd timed his arrival so that there were less than three minutes left to the countdown. He kissed me hard as he slid his hand into his jacket pocket and produced a little velvet box. The box remained in my hand, a corner digging into my palm as he held me tightly. When he released me, I opened it and found a large round diamond solitaire, which threw off sparks of color against the black velvet background. *Oh, to have such things,* my mind whispered.

"Marry me," Alex said in a murmur close to my ear. "I've been looking for you for a long time."

"Did your secretary pick this out as well?" I asked him, smiling to show I was kidding. I couldn't resist.

"Actually, she came with me. Just say yes, Celeste," Alex said.

"How old is this Lorraine anyway?"

"She's a grandmother," Alex said, finally cracking a smile.

I could feel his mother's presence behind the curtain; she seemed to be holding her breath.

"Yes," I said, completely overwhelmed. My mind was saying, *Why me? Why me?* As the crowd began to shout the countdown, he kissed me again, not waiting for midnight. We emerged from behind the curtain engaged. Alex was beaming.

"He wanted to surprise you but I told him not to put you on the spot," Aurelia said with a bright smile. Her dark blue eyes were unfathomable.

* * *

IN EARLY FEBRUARY, a few days after the announcement of our engagement appeared in the *Times,* the phone rang at eight-fifteen in the morning. Alex had left for work hours earlier. I was sound asleep.

"This is Mimi. Who's this?" she said.

Later, after hanging up, I came up with cutting responses like, "This is Alex. I forgot to tell you, I had a sex change." But at the time, I was so taken aback I simply said, "Celeste."

"Oh. Well . . ." She proceeded to tell me in a high-pitched breathless voice that she wanted to come by and fetch her Christmas tree lights.

"Isn't Christmas over already?" I asked, befuddled.

"Well, honey, they're for a party. But see, I can't come up to the apartment because I have an order of protection against Alex."

An order of protection? What the hell was she talking about?

I mumbled that I'd leave the lights with the concierge in the lobby.

I put her Christmas lights into a plastic bag along with every little feminine by-product I'd found in the apartment since I'd moved in two months earlier.

Once I'd regained my composure, I called Alex at work.

"Alex, what's this shit about an order of protection against you?"

"It really bothers me when you swear, Celeste, you know that."

"Just tell me what the fuck is going on, Alex."

He sighed deeply. "It's nothing. It was nothing. When we were breaking up I got kind of pissed off at her and punched a hole in the wall. Nothing, really. She overreacted."

"All right," I said, unconvinced. "But you could've told me. I didn't need to hear it from her."

"She's high-strung," Alex said, as if that explained everything.

Three

THE SECOND WEEK of April was so warm, it broke records. Mostly I stayed in the cool, quiet apartment, watching the world steaming away outside the thick, soundproof windows. Across the avenue, in the canyon between two tall buildings, there was a little public park with benches where business people came to eat their lunches in their shirtsleeves. I wondered what they all did for a living and if they were happy.

* * *

ON FRIDAY NIGHT, Alex and I drove his shiny black, tank-like BMW to my father and Anna's house in southern Connecticut. It was a grown-up's car, and sitting back against the soft, chestnut-colored leather seats, I felt like a little girl. I can't say that I didn't appreciate how impressed Anna looked standing at the front door, waving to us as we drove up in a sputter of gravel.

Anna was thrilled by my "catch." She had always been certain that I couldn't take care of myself. She'd been calling for days now, insisting that it was time to have my wedding dress fitted, even though the wedding wasn't for another two and a half months. Anna seemed to think that if the invitations were mailed, and the dress bought, and the wine ordered, the chances that the event would take place were greatly improved.

Their large shingled house stood on a hill overlooking Long Island Sound. We had cocktails and a late snack on the wide porch, facing the luminous water. The lights of Long Island's north shore blinked across the Sound. A nice breeze had stirred itself up after the sultry day, and everyone was cool and relaxed.

"I swear, I've never seen an April like this, have you, dear?" Anna asked my father. He seemed to ponder the question as if it were of the utmost importance to give her a precise and definite answer. Such was his habit in all conversations, one I assumed he'd picked up from being a corporate lawyer for over thirty years. Finally he shook his head and asserted that he had not.

"I wonder what this presages for early July?" Anna asked worriedly. She was already imagining rain on my wedding day. The ceremony was to take place in the garden, then we would all gather at the yacht club for the reception.

*   *   *

SATURDAY MORNING, Anna drove me to her seamstress's shop. The dress was an antique eggshell-colored lace gown that clung to my body over a silk slip. Anna had spotted it in a local antiques boutique, and called me immediately. Alex was not thrilled with the idea of an antique, but Anna had been right about the dress. She had insisted that I leave it in Connecticut so that the minor alterations could be done there, figuring that I probably would not have taken care of it in New York until the last minute, if at all.

Anna stood behind me and watched in the mirror as the seamstress stuck pins here and there. Perched on the little stool in front of my reflection, I watched the lovely bride in the large mirror. She seemed perfectly poised and sensible, and I felt I was watching a film of someone else's life. Inside, a strange, hot sensation of embarrassment assailed me.

"Your mother's pearls will look divine with the dress," Anna said. "And what you need to do now, dear, is take a little piece of fabric to one of those shoe stores that specializes in dyeing satin pumps, and you'll be all set. Now, what about a veil?"

"I don't want a veil," I said.

"But you must have a veil!" Anna cried. She had embraced the wedding plans with a passion she had previously shown only for birth control, the pro-choice movement, and golf. She had no children of her own.

"You *are* stubborn!" Anna laughed, crossing her arms and throwing her head back. "When you were, oh, ten, I believe, I took you to Central Park, to the carousel. You got on and I waited for you at the gate. I waited and waited. You wouldn't come off! Do you remember? How you screamed and yelled when I made you leave. I could never get you to listen to me, even back then. All right, you don't want a veil, so you won't have a veil. How about a little tiara of flowers?"

I looked at Anna in the mirror, puzzled. I had no memory of a day at the carousel with her. I remembered vaguely my mother's presence and the carousel, but not Anna. For some reason, this sent a chill through me.

"I never went to the carousel with you," I said in a formal voice that came from the pretty, poised bride in the mirror and did not sound familiar. Anna frowned in midsmile.

"What are you talking about, Celeste? Of course we did."

* * *

I AWAKENED with a start the next morning, in the bedroom that I had slept in for half my life, to the squawking seagulls and the clatter of lawn mowers. Still thinking about the carousel in Central Park, I could not remember the day Anna was talking about. I recalled many other days from that time, but there was a certain haziness to the images.

Who had I been, then? What had been my hopes and fears?

The shelves and walls of my old bedroom offered no clue, for I had come home after my sophomore year of college, and in a moment of resolve, emptied my shelves and closets of all my old belongings. Once and for all I wanted to bury the childish and needy Celeste whom I had never liked much. I unceremoniously packed everything into boxes and shoved them in a dark corner of the attic. Now, as I tried to form a picture of myself as a ten- or twelve-year-old girl, I could not remember the books I had read, the toys I had played with, or the clothes I had worn.

Alex turned over and reached out for me as he opened his eyes. I kissed his shoulder, sat up, threw off the sheet, and got out of bed.

"Where are you going?" Alex asked, sitting up and running a hand through his lovely dark blond hair.

"Up to the attic," I said.

"What for?" he asked sleepily.

"I don't know. I'm not sure. I'll be back in a little while."

The air in the attic was close and still. The early sun shone through the windows in slanting beams that seemed opaque and tangible. Specks of dust danced in the light. The boxes were not hard to find. They were exactly where I had left them ten years before.

I opened the first one and came upon my large, clothbound fairy-tale picture books: the Brothers Grimm, Hans Christian Andersen, Mother Goose. Beneath them were *Les fables de la Fontaine,* and every single French-language version of *Tintin* and *Asterix le Gaulois*, special-ordered by my French mother who had feared that I would grow up "too American"; and below them, my *Bobbsey Twins* and *Nancy Drew* mysteries. I could not remember the plot of a single *Nancy Drew*, only vague images of haunted houses. In the next box were my bears and dolls. They seemed sad, all jammed together and suffocating in the dark. I took them out and made a halfhearted attempt to smooth their fur, hair, and clothes.

In the next box I found my posters: characters from *The Lord of the Rings*; a barefooted Cat Stevens; a miniskirted Carly Simon, and a frizzy-haired Carole King. Folded neatly were my hip-hugger bell-bottom jeans, tie-dyed T-shirts, and Indian beads. I held up the old khaki army satchel I'd used as a book bag, embroidered with butterflies, flowers, and a huge peace sign. At the bottom of the box I found my senior prom dress, a pale blue gown of tulle, wrapped in plastic, along with the corsage of white roses and baby's breath, given to me by my date, Sebastian MacKenna. Beside the dress was a large jewelry box my mother had given me that played a little tune when you opened it while a tiny ballerina twirled around in front of a mirror. The little lock had long ago lost its key. I lifted the lid, but the ballerina wouldn't twirl anymore. The box was filled with Sebastian's letters in their envelopes, held together with a ribbon. Underneath, I found letters from his brother, Nathan.

"You've been up here for ages." I looked up to find Alex standing in a beam of light. I closed the box quietly, putting it aside.

"Hi," I said, and smiled. "I'm sorry, I just started thinking about all this stuff up here. I haven't looked at it in years."

"Getting married makes people nostalgic," he said. Alex crouched down beside me and put a hand on my shoulder. He gazed at the tie-dyed T-shirts strewn by my crossed legs. "Oh God, remember those clothes?" He laughed. "My mother wanted me to have Beatle boots, you know. But I wanted penny loafers, so I could look like my dad. Square at twelve."

His eyes landed on the box filled with picture books. "You should keep these," he said, serious. "One day you could read them to our children and say, 'These were my books once.'"

Children! What a thought. I smiled, nodding foolishly.

Alex reached his hand into the box, and like a cardsharp, drew out a volume that had not been there a moment before: the 1977 *Sand-*

piper, my high school yearbook. How could I have overlooked it? I wrenched the solid navy-blue clothbound book from his hands.

"Oh, come on, let me see your picture!" Alex said, reaching for it. I gripped the book to my chest and sighed as he tried to pry it from my hands. As we struggled over the volume, a cardboard picture frame with a gold lining slipped out. In the cloud of dust our fuss had raised, I watched Alex lean over and pick it up, and unfold the prom photo of Sally Newlyn and Sebastian MacKenna and me.

Sebastian stands in the middle, looking businesslike and in control of matters in a gray fedora and gray suit. On his right arm is Sally, her skin milky white against the crimson velvet of her long dress that fits her perfectly. It was her mother's prom dress, kept in storage for over twenty years. Above her ear, pinned to a barrette, the corsage of red roses Sebastian gave her pokes out. Fine, straight black hair falls to her shoulders. Her oval face, sporting tiny dark freckles at the nose and cheeks, is wide open, her smile immense, verging on an explosion of hysterical laughter. I am on Sebastian's other arm, smiling coyly for the camera in my pale blue dress, overwhelming in its puffs and folds, my white roses pinned above my breast. My Farrah Fawcett hairdo looks like a palm tree, with dark blond fronds falling in layers around my face.

"The three of you went together?" Alex asked.

"Yes. Sally was in the hospital up until a week before the prom. By then everyone was paired up already." Images of that evening came flooding back, the crowded dance floor, the bottle of vodka in Sally's handbag, the lights twirling around us as we danced, the three of us together, except for the slow songs, when Sally and I would take turns with Sebastian. Quickly, I added, "We had the best time. Until the football players pulled the urinals off the wall of the men's room and we all got thrown out of the country club."

"Who's the mortician?" Alex asked with a smile.

"Sebastian MacKenna. Last I heard he was a Navy pilot. He joined up after college. His dad worked for Exxon. His family moved away. They moved a lot."

We sat in silence as the dust settled around us. A frightful pang of anxiety gripped my heart. The yearbook lay in my lap. I opened it to the first page.

SALLY NEWLYN, JUNE 1977, was written there in bold letters.

"This isn't yours," Alex said thoughtfully, pointing to the inscription.

"It must be," I said, but then realized with a shudder that Sebastian and I had bought one yearbook for the two of us, as an act of faith and eternal devotion. After graduation, he had kept it. It was inconceivable to me that I had packed up Sally's by mistake.

* * *

WHEN I HAD come home for Christmas my freshman year, Mrs. Newlyn called to inform me that her daughter was back in the hospital. Sally had to be put in a straitjacket because she was tearing out her hair, punching the walls, screaming that she had left her yearbook at my house and absolutely had to get it back. Her doctor was adamant that Mrs. Newlyn try to find it.

Mrs. Newlyn said that she'd turned her house upside down, and asked me to look for it at mine. There was a certain iciness in her tone that had been there since Sally's first bout with mental illness. I felt that Mrs. Newlyn somehow blamed me, or at the very least wished that I had been the one afflicted, instead of her own, very good little girl. I had searched everywhere for the yearbook, but never found it.

* * *

"THIS JUST CAN'T BE," I said to Alex, my voice rising insistently. "It wasn't here. I know it."

He looked at me strangely and said, "You probably just packed it without seeing it, what's the big deal?"

"No!" I said. I sat there, stunned, while Alex took the book from me and silently began to flip through the pages. He came across a large photo of Sebastian, tall and tow-blond, in his baseball uniform, poised at the plate with the bat over his shoulder. Across his slightly bent legs in the white uniform, he had written in his left-hander's tilting script: "Dear Sally—I know this year has been hard for you, but don't forget we love you 4-ever."

All the inscriptions were similar: "Dear Sally, you're the nicest, sweetest person I know, and I know everything will be great in your life from now on." "Dear Sally, remember when you ran the mile in 5:12? You were the greatest." Further on, there was a page-sized picture of our local beach, gray in the winter light, with the Sound almost black beyond it. High above, seagulls hovered, white V's in the dark sky. The yearbook staff had printed a poem I had written earlier that year for the *Sandpiper Press* on the photo. It was about a girl walking alone on a winter beach, looking out at the stormy ocean and trying to picture it on a summer day.

"This is a nice poem," Alex said.

Below it I'd written: "My dearest friend—I know that everything is going to turn out the way you want it to, so don't worry. I'll always be there for you. Remember, 'Winter, spring, summer or fall/all you got to do is call/and I'll be there/yes I will/you got a friend.' —Carole King." It seemed so silly now, attributing the verses to Carole King, as if anybody on the planet wouldn't know, or would accuse me of plagiarism.

Alex turned the pages back to the senior portraits. He was looking through the N's. There was a blank, pale square where Sally's picture should have been. She'd penciled in a self-portrait, with her hair sticking straight out around her head, and her eyes huge, bulging and crossed, and a zero with a bar through it at the center of her forehead. She used to sign her notes and letters with this symbol. I had found this wise and deep on her part. Below the blank frame, the caption read: "Sally Newlyn, Best Girl Athlete, Everyone's Friend. Unavailable for photograph."

"She wasn't there when they took the pictures," I said to Alex. "Something was wrong with her brain chemically. She was in and out of the hospital for most of the second half of our senior year."

"You mean she was crazy?"

I looked at him, his handsome face, so clear in its understanding of things, as though he'd rolled over all of life's sticks and stones like a mountain stream. Our upbringing had not been that dissimilar—he had a stepmother, I had a stepmother. We had never wanted for anything in the material sense. At seventeen, we each were given a car, all that. But he'd never *lost* anyone, and that, I thought, made a big difference in how we perceived the world.

I thought about his question for a moment. Doctors had attached names to Sally's illness, and the names changed, along with her medication. "An imbalance," they said at first, and put her on lithium. When that didn't work, they called it "clinical depression" and put her on some mood elevator. Finally, when nothing seemed to help, they said she was "schizophrenic," and put her on new drugs that made her lethargic and fat. We did not live in a community that liked to delve into disaster. She was ill—this was an accepted fact, but her parents, our teachers, and our friends behaved as if she had a rare but curable infection. We were all afraid of the word *crazy*.

It was, I remembered with a shudder, what my father used to shout at my mother in fits of rage: *You goddamn crazy bitch! You're crazy, Nathalie, you know that?*

Calling somebody crazy was like calling them junkie, faggot, or whore.

"I guess she was crazy," I said, feeling guilty, for I remembered that in the midst of her bouts with despair and madness, she'd said the most brilliant, intuitive, unexpected things. She'd predicted my future with an accuracy that now seemed staggering.

"What happened to her?" Alex asked.

I'd never spoken to him of Sally, or of that period in my life. As I thought about what to say to him, all sorts of images came rushing back, and crowded out my breath.

"She killed herself," I said, attempting to sound neutral. "She jumped off an overpass in New Haven and landed on the highway."

"Jesus, what a horrible thing to do," he said.

"No." I felt I had to defend her. "She did what she felt she had to do. I think it took a lot of guts."

"I know those overpasses," he said. "Jesus."

I'd never belonged to any church. I'd never been baptized. But after I heard about Sally I went to the Catholic church in town and lit candles for her, praying on my knees to God, "Please, if You exist, please let her into heaven." It seemed such an outrage, such a terrible injustice, that she should have to suffer in purgatory for eternity after having suffered so much in life.

"I don't know. Maybe she wasn't planning it," I said. "Maybe she was just out walking over a bridge, and then . . . I don't know."

"No one just goes out for a walk on an overpass," he said quietly.

"What does *that* mean, Alex?" I said in a menacing tone I knew scared him. He looked at me as if he thought I was about to throw one of my "fits." Whenever I felt tears threatening, I would run and lock myself in the bathroom until it passed. He'd sit on the couch and read a newspaper and act as if it never happened. I couldn't stand to have him see me like that. I wanted to change. I wanted, in fact, to become more like him—calm, rational, objective. He'd never seen me cry.

"I'm really sorry," he said. His eyes were dark and luminous and I thought that perhaps he understood, perhaps great pain had not escaped him entirely. We sat in silence a long time.

* * *

FOR THE REST of the day, images of Sally, of my mother, of Sebastian and his brother Nathan, came to me unexpectedly, like impromptu visits from old friends you really don't want to see and so you hide, pretend that you're not home. But they kept returning, especially that night back in our apartment, as I lay in bed waiting for sleep. Not another word on the subject was uttered, yet Alex and I had made love almost violently, throwing sheets and blankets to the floor. Now he was sleeping soundly beside me. After a while I got up quietly and went to the kitchen, remembering that there was half a bottle of white wine in the door of the fridge. I poured myself a glassful, then took the glass to a chair by a living room window and sat in the darkness, trying to make peace with those I thought I'd left behind a long time ago.

Four

MY FRENCH MOTHER'S railing against America had started off as a joke between us, "to break the silence," she said, of our large house. By the time I was eight, an edge of anger and frustration had infiltrated her lightheartedness; and my father, who worked long hours in the city, who was silent and distracted when he was home, moved farther and farther away from us. One day he took a studio apartment in New York and started coming home only on weekends. Then, he'd lock himself up in his study and appear only at meals, safe and formal affairs in which Mathilde, the French cook, would serve us from fancy trays and my mother would never yell because she thought it not *comme il faut* to involve the servants in family disputes.

* * *

I WAS TEN at the time; my brother Jack, thirteen. He was not interested in us, and didn't come home except to change and sleep. My mother had lost control of him, given up hope. She talked incessantly of taking me away to Europe and leaving my brother and father behind.

"What is this sports, sports all the time?" she'd say in her heavy French accent. "They watch the football like it is the great truth of life. I tell you, that is the only way men can talk to one another in this country. They watch the football, sitting in a row so they don't have to look in each other's eyes, and they say 'Ah, nice pass,' and slap each other on the back.

"Your brother is formed already, just like your father, girls and cars and games, games! I met your father on the ski slope in Grenoble. Ah, I was so young and beautiful then. America was everybody's dream. I was so stupid! And he was so handsome with his white American teeth!

Look how strong are his Wasp genes. Out of two, only you look a little bit like me, not much."

I went back to the kitchen for a second glass of wine. The bottle was nearly empty, so I finished it off. I hid it at the bottom of the trash can under some plastic bags, wondering if Alex would notice. On my way back to the armchair, I caught sight of my reflection in the dark window. In a pale nightgown, hair tousled, carrying the wine glass, I looked so much like my mother that for a moment I stood frozen before this apparition.

I sat down and squeezed my eyes shut, fighting back tears.

* * *

MY MOTHER IS PACING the kitchen in her stained, pale blue bathrobe with safety pins of all sizes pinned to the lapels. Her hair is a mess of thick curls, the color of a freshly plowed field. Fingers of sunlight reach through the jungle of plants that grow in front of the large window and refract off the ice in her amber drink. I watch her from my tall stool at the butcher block in the middle of the room. Beside me, her ashtray is overflowing.

Her voice whispers to me, "You are not too old yet to have your mind opened up. I tell you something, you don't feel like being an athlete, I tell them to go to hell. I write you an excuse to gym class. This world is too small. Nothing exists for these people outside of these walls!"

I understood even then that my mother was terribly unhappy, that my father did not love her the way she wanted, that she had no friends to speak of in our community. She was unhappy, and no one else seemed to be, or if they were, they didn't advertise it. I began to feel uncomfortable at school around the wholesome, happy kids who fit in so easily and seemed to have no time for doubts. And Sally Newlyn, jockette and running champion, who wore the school colors and went to Halloween parties as the Statue of Liberty, was the child I hated and envied most.

I followed my mother around the house in the afternoons. She padded from room to room, the drink always in her hand, inspecting things, paintings, vases, ashtrays, up close, and then squinting at them from a distance.

"All this—" she'd make a sweeping gesture, a cigarette smoldering between her stained fingers, its ashes falling on the pale carpet. "All this means nothing. Don't forget what I am telling you, Celeste. Ah, let's go back to France. Let's *go!*"

But we never did. She raged mercilessly about her own mother, who sat "like the rock of Gibraltar" in an ancient chateau near Bordeaux. "That old woman will die before she sees me again."

She had incurred the wrath of "the rock" by marrying my father, a "low-class American." It didn't matter to my grandmother that his family had been here since the Revolution; all Americans were by nature low-class. My mother and I had tested the waters with a two-week visit to Bordeaux the previous summer, but it had ended in disaster. For my mother, the thought of going home to *her* mother represented failure, and therefore disgusted her. She had never worked, could not conceive of it, so her talk of moving with me to Italy, to Florence, to Venice, to Rome, was just that.

* * *

SPRING. I like the walk home in the rain from the school bus stop, just beyond our gate, the sound of rain pattering on the cool green leaves in the garden. I open the kitchen door. No lights are on in the house. I call out for my mother and hear my small voice echoing through the large rooms. Something has happened. I'm afraid to go upstairs. I walk around switching on all the lamps until the whole ground floor is ablaze with light.

My father came home from New York, unchanged, apparently unmoved, except now he seemed tired. He could not look me in the eyes; I wondered if I brought to mind things he'd rather forget.

"Where is my mommy?" I asked this stranger, glaring up at him.

"Your mommy had a weak heart," he told me. "She had a heart attack. But don't worry, she didn't suffer. She simply went to heaven to visit God."

* * *

THERE WAS A FUNERAL, of course. Our neighbors and friends were amazed by our courage, our will as a family to go on. A few days later, in school, I was standing by my locker, laughing coyly at something a cute boy had said, when Sally marched up to me in her perfect pleated skirt (she wore shorts underneath as a precaution against exactly such randy boys) and said to me in a shocked little voice, "You shouldn't laugh like that, what's the matter with you? Your mother's funeral wasn't even a week ago."

"Go to hell," I said to her, and watched her coldly as her face turned purple and she spun on her heels and stormed off in a pout.

My father must have given up his studio, because now he was home every evening. I began to water my mother's jungle of plants, and to watch him in silence.

Incapable of showing us affection, he decided to offer us a sense of organization. He told my brother and me that he expected certain changes. Dinner at seven sharp.

This was the new routine:

"How was your day today, Celeste?" he'd ask at dinner, gazing at the plate our new housekeeper Paloma had set before him. Mathilde had quit, just after my mother died.

He'd had his martini or a scotch on the rocks and there was a bottle of French wine on the table. My mother had collected red wine, and it seemed my father was determined to finish off her vast cellar as soon as possible. We were allowed a few drops in our water. I tried always to get more, mostly because it was not allowed, and because I loved the color and the secret magic of the ruby elixir that made my father feel warm and tender toward the world.

"So, Celeste?"

"I'm fine, Daddy," I'd say. "Everything is fine."

"And what about you, young fellow?" he'd ask Jack.

"Oh, I'm fine, too." And to make our father happy, Jack would add something about football practice, or a new organism he'd inspected under the microscope in science class.

"Well, that's terrific," our father would say, nodding with relief, and he would begin to eat. After a while he'd start to relax, the lines in his face becoming softer, less angry. As if by magic, the vague, cold look would disappear from his eyes. He'd talk about the law firm in words that sounded to me like mathematics, which I had already started to fail.

One by one, my mother's plants shriveled up. Nothing I did seemed to help.

A month passed; I had an accident on my bicycle and broke my leg. One day a tall, thin, blond lady appeared in my bedroom and sat down to read me a Nancy Drew mystery.

"Who are you?"

"I'm Mrs. Smith. But you can call me Anna."

"Do you know anything about plants, Mrs. Smith?"

"Anna. A little, why?" She smiled down at me, her eyes curious and alert.

"All my mother's plants in the kitchen are dying."

"I'll take a look." She patted my cast, stood up, straightened her skirt, and was gone. Moments later she was back, this time with a tall, thin frosted glass that smelled bitter and lemony. "You've been overwatering them," she said. "Now, would you like me to read to you? I certainly hope you and I will become friends."

She read me an entire Nancy Drew mystery. It took all day. Every once in a while she'd cry out gaily, "Break time!" and go downstairs to refill her glass.

*   *   *

SOON THE PLANTS were thriving again. She even replaced the ones that had died. But the kitchen lost its jungle look; now it seemed more like an English garden, with carefully arranged flowering plants, all variations of the same hue.

Within a year my father married her.

Once, my mother had told me when I was having a problem with a particularly bossy math teacher, that it was better to kiss the asses of persons of authority if they had the power to control your life. When Anna moved into our house, I did everything possible to gain her confidence. I grew quickly to depend on her for advice concerning minor, everyday obstacles, like needing new shoes, losing a schoolbook, or needing help with homework. But we never became friends.

Apparently my mother had not given Jack the same advice, and from the moment Anna stepped through the door in her white bridal suit and little hat with a sprig of white flowers, the two were at war.

*   *   *

I CAME TO THINK of her as a dainty queen from a fairy-tale book, living behind magical fortress walls. She seemed to peer out at the world through the narrow balistrarias, from where she shot poisoned arrows at her enemies. She believed she had a panoramic view of the world from her castle, and no one could tell her that it wasn't so.

* * *

Jack rushed into the kitchen around supper time like a black tornado, filthy from football, and headed right for the fridge. I was sitting at the butcher block, reading one of my Tintin comic books for the thousandth time. I looked up and watched Jack drink from the milk carton. His fingers left black streaks on the white surface. I gasped, for dirt upset Anna more than anything. But he was taking his time, probably hoping that Anna would walk in and catch him. Since she hadn't come in, he put the empty carton back in the fridge and set about making a sandwich, tearing the plastic wrappers off the cold cuts and leaving them on the counter with the open mayonnaise and mustard jars. Just then Anna pushed through the swinging door, making a swish of wind, a tall glass tinkling in her hand.

"Oooh, macho man! It excites me, *Jacques,* to observe such grace and charm!" she cried.

And Jack, who hated nothing—nothing—more than being called by the French name that adorned his birth certificate, burped, smiled, and walked out carrying his sandwich, leaving dirt and grease stains on the swinging door, and a trail of ham and mustard and mayonnaise on the floor.

I watched her reach into the freezer and take out the gin bottle with a dramatic flourish. She poured a generous shot into her glass. Several ice cubes from the ice cube maker followed with a loud clinking splash.

"God knows I try," she muttered, pushing her hair back with the flat of her trembling hand and taking a large swig of the drink with the other.

A year later, Jack took to drinking from a tequila bottle at the living room bar, his eyes glaring at her. He left empty condom wrappers in the ashtray of the car. Anna complained to my father, but he would just laugh and tell her that boys will be boys. As Jack's rebelliousness grew—he quit the football team, started failing classes—Anna's tone became more and more saccharine, even ebullient. Watching, I wondered if he might consider it a victory if she ever wept or tried to hit him. But she continued to pretend that the war did not exist, all the while firing her sugar-coated arrows at him.

I was quiet, reserved, and had few friends. In school I hung out with the exchange students from France, and the precocious "radicals" who at twelve were singing inflammatory songs about Vietnam. I excelled only in language and literature. When Sally—everyone's little darling—saw me coming down the hall, she made a wide circle to avoid me, and walked by with her nose in the air. Her parents had an American flag on the antenna of their station wagon. I'd heard from other kids that her brother was over in Vietnam, a captain in the Marines. Her family went to the Episcopal church on Sundays. Her mother, a little, dark-haired pixie of a woman, was a member of the DAR, the school board, the PTA, and volunteered in all the charities. Sally was the best girl athlete in the junior high and could outrun almost all the boys.

I hated her, foremost because I wished I could run like that.

In phys ed I had always been a failure. It was not so much that I was physically uncoordinated, but rather that I was terrified of failing, of looking stupid, of being laughed at. We were judged by how we performed, and my distinct lack of practice in the gym was an unfortunate handicap that I couldn't surmount. I was picked last for the teams, while Sally was always a captain, usually of the winning team.

Several years passed in this attitude of general avoidance, until, at the beginning of tenth grade, our class was moved to the new high school, an enormous one-story red-brick edifice that spread out across the town's highest hill. It had been built, at great expense to the taxpayers, in a Romanesque style around courtyards, so that from every class we had a garden view. Sally and I were horrified to find that we'd been placed next to each other in homeroom. For the whole year we would share all our classes, except for the electives.

The first day, I said good morning to her in a cool and formal manner. She responded in kind, and soon we were saying hello to each other in the halls. We were like two species of monkeys glaring at each other through the bars of adjoining cages. Sitting next to her day after day, I realized that she was not a phony. She hated gossip. When other girls talked about a "slut" or a "cock tease," which pretty much covered the range of possibilities, Sally would look away uncomfortably and say, "Oh, gad, hang it up, will ya?"

* * *

ONE MORNING in homeroom, she reached over and ran a finger across a butterfly I'd embroidered on my jeans.

"How pretty!" she said. "Did you do that yourself?"

"Yes." And then, for some incomprehensible reason, I added, "I'll do one for you if you like."

"I wish I could wear stuff like that! My mom would have a cow. But thanks anyway."

We gazed at each other and there were smiles on our faces. We no longer feared each other, and in that moment I felt redeemed, as if I had passed across some threshold, into a world of happiness and light.

* * *

LATER THAT DAY, in phys ed, we lined up in the chill October air for a soccer game. I stood at the perimeter of the group, shivering, with my arms crossed over my chest. Sally, captain as always, didn't appear cold at all in just a T-shirt and shorts. She stacked her team with the best athletes, frightening Amazons with muscular legs and arms—and then, she called out my name.

"What, are you totally nuts?" an ox of a girl cried out.

"Yeah, Sal, what's up?" another teammate said in a deep voice.

I tiptoed over to their side, head hanging guiltily as the jockettes peered at me with scorn.

"Look," Sally whispered to me, "you're probably just scared, see. It's easy! Just kick the heck out of the ball. It's fun! It's no big deal if you miss."

Sally flew through the air, yelling orders and flipping her dark hair away from her eyes. Her legs and feet seemed as coordinated as arms and hands; she could do a jig around the ball and keep it moving, kick it anywhere she wanted, even flick it behind her into the goal. She kept sending the ball in my direction, but I invariably froze.

"Come on, kick! Kick it, Celeste!" she cried.

I attempted one good kick. As my leg flew out, I saw my foot dangling there at the end of it, limp and useless. I sent the ball skidding into the legs of the captain of the opposing team.

"It's all right! At least you kicked it! That was good!" Sally cried.

We did not speak much outside of gym class, but there, she had made me her pet project. For our midterm, we were to perform in one of the four gymnastics disciplines—parallel bars, mat, horse, or balance beam. Sally spent entire gym periods helping me with exercises on the balance beam. She was under the impression that I had good balance.

On the day of the exam, the teacher, a tall black woman with a morose face, stood on the sidelines with her arms crossed while Sally directed my efforts on the beam. I managed a fairly steady pirouette, a few good skips, and a meager, shaky somersault without falling off. I received my first B-plus in gym.

Afterwards, I watched Sally tumble across the mat, performing front and back flips, cartwheels, and splits in every direction. She had brought a little cassette recorder from home, and the song "Tiny Dancer" by Elton John bounded off the gymnasium walls. What she lacked in grace she made up for in the sheer strength of her arms and legs. She could jump higher than anyone, and was not afraid to try a somersault in the air. She landed on both feet with a loud thump and an expression of angry concentration on her face. I stood there watching, dumbfounded by my own admiration.

"Why aren't you taking a shower?" she asked me after class while we were both getting dressed.

"I took one this morning," I responded, feeling shameful.

"God, you really *are* French aren't you?" she said with a strange smile.

"You didn't take one either," I remarked.

"I have my period," she said. With that, she took an extremely large Tampax out of her book bag, slammed her locker shut, and headed for the bathroom. A moment later she came back, pinching her fingers together and sniffing at them, making a disgusted face. "I *hate* that smell," she said. "Deodorant tampons don't make it go away at all. I washed my hands about a million times! Being a girl is so gross."

* * *

"*VOOLAY . . . VOOLAY VOO* oon glassay? Damn, I'll never get this," Sally muttered. We were in homeroom a few days later, and she was poring over her French textbook, pulling on her hair.

I turned to her. "When's your test?"

"Tomorrow. Damn. I hate this foreign language stuff. My dad might get posted to Paris, can you believe this crap? Now they're making me learn frog-talk!"

"I speak French. I can help you."

"Really? That would be so cool."

She invited me to go home with her after school and stay for dinner.

We ambled along the quiet, winding roads. She told me she wanted to be an Olympic long-distance runner. She was on the cross-country team, she said, running five, sometimes six miles a day after school. She ran barefoot like the American Indians. Today, though, she was taking off so that I could help her with her frog-talk. She told me the coach wouldn't let her run more than five miles a day because her bones were still growing, and he wanted her to be the number one runner for the mile in the spring.

"Have you ever smoked cigarettes?" she asked me.

"Yeah, a couple times, with my brother Jack."

"Gee, is he the *cutest*! . . . I really would like to try smoking," she said, "just once, though. Just to try. They say it gets you high the first time."

She told me that besides her older brother the Marine captain, she had an older sister who was married and had a baby. Once we got to her home, a nice, two-story stone house set back in the woods, she got some milk and cookies from the kitchen and took me up to her bedroom under the roof. She played a Carly Simon tape on her little cassette player and showed me an album full of pictures of her five-month-old niece Suzy, who'd been born three months premature.

Sally gave me a face massage, reading the directions over her shoulder in a book and using a cucumber cream she'd bought at the health food store downtown.

"What about your French test?"

"We'll get to it . . . My mom says all this pressure point stuff is hocus-pocus, but I believe in it."

My first face massage was exhilarating. My family never touched one another. This intimacy, which seemed so natural to Sally, made me long for a sister. I felt quite exposed as I lay on her bed with my eyes shut, while she twisted my face into all kinds of odd expressions.

Then she did my nails with a little kit, buffing and filing each one, clipping off the excess skin around the moons.

"You always want the moons to show," she said.

"Why?"

"Because it's chic. That's what my mom says."

Carly Simon was singing, "We have no secrets/We tell each other most everything/About the lovers in the past/And why they didn't last . . . "

"She's so in love," Sally mused. "I feel like I'm in love, but not with anybody in particular, you know. Just in love. Next week I'm going to get my ears pierced. I've wanted to for years but my mom says it's sleazy if you're too young. You look like a foreigner or something." She gasped, then looked to see if mine were pierced. "I used to hate you, you know," she said, not looking up. Her cheeks were shiny and red, like apples.

"Yes, I know," I said.

"I thought you were a snob. Plus, you didn't act sad when your mom—well, you know. It was like you didn't care what anybody thought. Now I think you're the most interesting person I know. Your clothes are so cool and you walk so straight, like you don't have time for silliness. Boys like that, you know, they like girls who don't pay them any attention.

"I found my mother's diaphragm," she whispered suddenly. "I was looking through her underwear drawer, for fun. Did you ever see a diaphragm? It's as big as a salad dish, I swear! How does she get it in there?" She laughed, embarrassed, her face scrunched up into crinkles. Then she winced. "I don't know, the thought of them doing it kind of makes me feel sick. I *hate* it." She looked at me as if she expected a response.

I tried to imagine my father and Anna "doing it," and the thought was definitely unappetizing. I nodded in agreement.

She told me about her brother the Marine. She said her parents were getting very strange letters from him and were worried. "This is a secret," she warned me, a finger over her lips. I nodded solemnly.

"The troops are starting to pull out, but he's got some big job in Saigon so he has to stay. My dad was in World War II, he landed on Omaha Beach five days after D day. My brother's letters are getting so *weird*! In his last one, he said the war was a *mistake*! Can you imagine? He asked my dad to take the American flag off the antenna of the station wagon!

"What do you think we should do?" she asked me, looking very serious.

"I have no idea."

"I told them to take it off. He could *die* over there. But you know what my mom said? She said, 'Everyone will notice!' It's true, isn't it? Everybody notices *everything* in this town."

I just shrugged my shoulders and flipped over the tape.

Five

THE FIRST DAY of school after the Christmas holidays, there was a new boy in our homeroom. The teacher introduced him as Sebastian MacKenna and said he had just arrived from England. His eyes were velvety-brown, soft-looking, and his hair was a straight and silky blond. He looked a little like Robert Redford in *The Way We Were*. He was on the round side, but this only added to his charm. He was simply adorable.

"Sebastian is a pretty unusual name," Sally said, leaning toward his desk.

"My mother read *Brideshead Revisited* and she fell in love with a character whose name was Sebastian," he explained. He pronounced all his consonants, his vowels were sharp. He seemed self-possessed, well-mannered, and slightly shy.

"What were you doing in England?"

"My dad works for Exxon. We move around. In London, my brother and I went to an all-boys school for three years. This is a big change." He laughed and blushed. "My mom was very happy over there, being that she's an Anglophile from way back."

Sally looked at me, I looked at her. Anglophile, that was a new one on us.

During recess, I saw my brother and another boy sneaking off toward the woods to have a smoke.

"That's my brother, Jack," I told Sebastian, nodding in their direction.

"How funny, he's with my brother."

Sally, Sebastian, and I were still standing around when they came out of the woods a while later.

"Hey, Bass, how's your first day?" his brother said. He was a little taller than Sebastian, dark-haired, with similarly shaped eyes, but his were a strange hazel-green with gold specks, and in them there was something mischievous and sharp, something smoldering. He had a rosy mouth, soft-looking lips, and a nose that was not small but turned up slightly at the end. He was wearing a pair of faded blue jeans with holes at the knees and a bald patch right where the bulge was. I had to force my eyes away.

Looking Sally and me over, he added knowingly, "I see you're already making new friends."

I saw from my brother's eyes that they had smoked more than just cigarettes. A strange, acrid odor, subtle and elusive, rose from them. I was about to go into a pout, because I believed that marijuana led people to more serious drugs, as we'd been informed in health class. My brother noted my sour expression and became more considerate than usual.

"Nathan, this is Celeste and this is Sally."

"Ladies," Nathan said, bowing slightly, but never taking his eyes off us. After a moment, he added, rubbing his hands together briskly, "This is going to be a riot. No fucking rules like in London. No fucking A levels! Clear sailing all the way to graduation!"

* * *

A RUMOR BEGAN drifting around school that Nathan had received a genius score on his IQ test, but we suspected he may have been the source. Nevertheless, his British education had put him so far ahead that, according to Jack, Nathan could outtalk his teachers in every subject.

This was certainly true in Advanced French, the only class he and I shared. He had read every book on the curriculum, and would sit back comfortably at his desk, legs spread wide, tapping a pencil on the desktop, and ask Mlle Spiegel questions in French that she was unable to answer.

Nathan and Sebastian were both left-handed, but Nathan wrote in block capitals, even in French. This annoyed Mlle Spiegel, who said there was a *type* of handwriting specific to France. She had forced the rest of us to learn it. My French handwriting was exactly like my mother's, which frightened and appalled me.

One day she handed Nathan back a paper on Sartre and existentialism with a B-plus scribbled on it in red. She'd taken points off for his handwriting. We heard a loud sound of crumpling paper and turned to look. Nathan had made the paper into a ball between his solid hands. Holding it reverently, he threw it in a graceful arc that landed in the wastepaper basket by Mlle Spiegel's desk. There was no expression at all on his face.

I couldn't imagine doing such a thing—what if he'd missed?

* * *

SEBASTIAN WAS THE KIND of boy parents *wanted* you to go out with. Teachers, mothers, traffic cops—everyone seemed to like him. He had a sweet, honest face, calm and focused, that made you want to just turn everything over to him. Sally and I talked him into buying us Eve cigarettes—they seemed so chic with a ring of pale flowers around the filter—and of course the saleslady in the drugstore believed him when he said they were for his mother. The three of us rode our bikes to a field at the end of a dirt path in the woods, and smoked until our heads were spinning and our feet could no longer feel the frozen ground. Then Sally and I took turns kissing him with our mouths open, like in the movies.

I could tell that Sebastian kissed me longer, and that his back and arm muscles relaxed with Sally in a way they didn't with me. But it was easy to pretend that his affection was equally apportioned between us.

Sally and I went over to Sebastian's one afternoon. Mrs. MacKenna made us iced tea and put some Oreos on a plate. She was petite, fine-boned, pretty like a porcelain doll. Her voice was low and steady, her movements precise and refined. Sebastian looked very much like her, he had her coloring and her dark brown eyes. He called her "Mother."

Mr. MacKenna, we'd found out just that day from Sebastian, was still in England, "wrapping up loose ends." When we'd asked him why they'd come ahead, Sebastian said it was because of school.

The pale blue living room was crowded with stiff-backed antique furniture. On the baby grand a few school portraits showed the boys as children, along with one family photograph. I was dying to inspect them, believing that some great secret would be revealed to me. Nathan's and Sebastian's youthful faces smiled at me blankly; there were spaces between their front teeth. The photograph of the four MacKennas was a recent formal portrait, probably taken at the photographer's studio. The three men, the father in the middle, stood stiffly around Mrs. MacKenna sitting in a chair; she was the only one smiling. Mr. MacKenna was suntanned and youthful-looking. Nathan had inherited his mischievous eyes.

Nathan's nose, however, came from his mother. It then occurred to me that Sebastian had his father's nose, a fairly substantial, masculine one that was not remotely delicate.

* * *

SALLY TOOK A QUART of rum from her sister's house one Friday night and we drank it with orange juice, the three of us, in an abandoned shed we'd found in the woods. When it began to pour, Sally stood up, tore off her clothes, and ran out into the teeming rain. Sebastian and I sat there, stunned, as her voice cried out some invented Indian rain chant, which drifted in to us on the wind.

"Oh, come on Bass, let's go!" I said, pulling off my clothes.

"If we get pneumonia, don't blame me," he said, and stood, tugging at a sneaker as he fell backwards into a wall.

I couldn't feel the cold, only the rain splattering against me as the whole world lit up to day in a flash of lightning. There was no fear, no notion of danger. I screamed out Sally's Indian chant and danced in circles, arms spread wide.

"I am here, goddamnit!" Sally yelled up at the lightning sky.

"I am here!" I shouted. The treetops swayed black and phantasmagoric against the flash of light. "I am here!"

Soon afterwards, Sally retreated to the cabin and Sebastian followed. I remained outside in the rain. My blood seemed to pulsate with a feeling of power I had never known.

When I finally went in, they were both dressed, and I quickly grabbed for my discarded clothes. Sally, unsteady on her feet, moaned, "I'll never drink alcohol again."

"God, I will," I cried. "That was great!"

* * *

ONCE, WHEN JACK and Nathan were hanging out in Jack's room, the door was ajar so I stood outside, attempting to eavesdrop.

"Hey, Celeste! Come on in!" Nathan yelled. I could hear my brother grumbling.

I knew it was only a reprieve that would be rescinded at any moment, so I sat primly, quietly, on Jack's desk chair and did not wrinkle my nose at the stink of dirty socks and rancid beer emanating from the piles of clothes on the floor. They were smoking cigarettes and drinking beer. That acrid-sweet smoke filled the air, and I knew they had been smoking pot and that

I'd hear about it from Anna later on. Nathan began waxing philosophical on Olivia of the huge jugs, a senior who wore so much makeup she looked twenty-five. He was saying that she gave excellent head. "It's because she's Catholic." He was lying back on my brother's bed with his hands crossed behind his head. "As long as it's not fucking, it's not a mortal sin. I swear to God, though, Catholic girls, if you can get them to do it, are the best."

"What does that mean, she gives excellent head?" I asked.

Nathan turned to look at me and Jack began to laugh. "It means she gives great blow jobs," Nathan said without blinking.

"You're lying," I said.

"I kid you not. Don't you know that song by Lou Reed? 'But she never lost her head/even when she was giving head/she said, Hey babe, take a walk on the wild side . . .'" Then he said with a sharp laugh, "Celeste, we're destined for each other. Do you know we have the same birthday?"

"You're such a liar."

He sat up and took his passport out of his back pocket. I presumed he carried it for identification, since he didn't have a driver's license yet. It was wrinkled and rounded to the shape of his behind. He reached his arm out to me, and as I took the passport our fingers touched. I felt a stab in the heart, not unlike the electric shock I'd gotten when I stuck a knife in the toaster at the age of five, but this one was pleasant.

I flipped to his picture, attempting to calm my shaking hands. And there on the page, grinning up at me, was a younger Nathan in a funereal black sports jacket and tie. His birth date was October fifteenth. He was exactly two years older than I. Expecting him at any second to ask for the passport back, I flipped through it quickly, attempting to gain some sense, some knowledge of him. There were pages upon pages of colorful visa stamps—Paris, Rome, Istanbul, Marrakech, London . . .

* * *

A NUMBER OF WEEKS LATER, I came across him sitting on a rock in a field behind the school. It had just begun to snow and, with a few minutes to spare between classes, I'd stolen out for a moment to look. Nathan was sitting there alone, in a large black knitted sweater and his old jeans, smoking a cigarette. The white flakes fluttered about and landed on his dark hair and sweater. He seemed preoccupied, maybe even sad. I hadn't seen him like this before.

"Hi, Nathan."

He looked up, smiled faintly. I stood a few paces from his rock, hands clasped before me. It was a cold and windless day and neither of us had our coats. "Is everything all right?" I asked after a while.

"I think my parents are breaking up," he said neutrally. "Sebastian doesn't know. Suspects it, I'm sure." He took a deep drag off his Marlboro and then tamped it out against the rock. Then he took what was left of the cigarette apart and scattered the tobacco at his feet. He took the filter apart, too, and scattered that.

After this meticulous operation, he looked at me quite seriously and said, "They don't really talk to us. I mean, my father's supposed to be coming in a couple of weeks, but this morning my mother made it sound like he wasn't going to stay."

"I won't say anything, I swear." It was hard to breathe. I wanted him to trust me.

"I've been watching you a long time and do you know that you're by far, by quantum leaps, the prettiest girl in any room you're in?" he said matter-of-factly. "It's interesting because I don't think you know. Most girls who are as pretty as you are a real pain in the ass. Boys are terrified of you."

Breathless, I said, "Sebastian isn't scared of me."

Nathan just gazed at me with that serious expression, his lips curving into a smile. His eyes appeared particularly green against the backdrop of white.

With my heart in my throat, I told him something I'd never told anyone: that it didn't really matter to me what I looked like from the outside, because inside I didn't exist. "It's like I can't feel my outline in space!" I said.

"I feel that way most of the time," he said. "Some days I feel like a ghost in my house, like my own family doesn't recognize me."

He stood and stretched his legs. "It's damn cold," he said.

I followed him back toward the school. When we approached one of the countless side doors, he stopped, took my arm, and walked me around the corner of the building. There was a dusting of snow on the pebbles that crunched beneath our feet. He pressed me into a corner where the ground was littered with cigarette butts. His tongue, gentle and forceful at once, explored the inside of my mouth, and it seemed to me that I could feel him all the way down to my feet. After a while he looked at me.

He appeared about to say something, but changed his mind. Shaking his head, he walked away, back into the school, and did not look back.

That particular corner of the school became a magical spot, and even the dirty old cigarette butts took a place in my heart, for they and the falling snow were the only witnesses to my moment of utter bliss.

* * *

A LONG, LONG TIME passed and, although he did look at me with a different sparkle in his eye, he never acknowledged what had happened.

"Want to come over?"
Sebastian and I were standing by the school buses.
"Sally's got track practice."
"I know. Want to come over anyway? No one's home. Nathan's got his Harvard interview."
"Good!" I huffed, as my heart sank.

Walking down the dark, wood-paneled hallway of the MacKennas' house, I paused in front of Nathan's closed door. Sebastian put a tentative hand on my shoulder and spun me around so that my back was pressed up against Nathan's door. Sebastian's tongue found mine, circled, waited for my reaction.

I kissed him for a while. Then I turned my face away and placed my head on his shoulder.

"Can I see Nathan's room?"
He pulled back and gazed at me. "What for?"
"I'm just curious."
Sebastian, resigned, pushed the door open and stood aside like a bored old museum guard. I felt sorry, but not enough to stop.

Nathan's room was oddly spare except for one wall, which was lined with books arranged by author. I had never seen so many books in one room. I went and perused the titles, my eyes landed on the S's— *Last Exit to Brooklyn* by Hubert Selby Jr., Shakespeare's sonnets and plays, *The Gulag Archipelago* by Aleksandr Solzhenitsyn, *The Confessions of Nat Turner* by William Styron, Jonathan Swift's *Gulliver's Travels*. My eyes drifted, landing here and there. I saw *Pale Horse, Pale Rider* by Katherine Anne Porter, Plato's *Republic,* poems by Sylvia Plath. There did not seem to be any logic to his taste. I hadn't read any of these books, except for a few of the Shakespeare plays that had been forced upon me in English class, but I had heard of most of these writers, except for Hubert Selby Jr. and Sylvia Plath. Later, during my college years, I made it a point to read every single one of the authors I remembered from Nathan's shelves.

His single bed was covered by a dark blue blanket and light blue sheets. On his bedside table lay *The Happy Hooker*. I'd heard this title whispered among the older girls in the school's bathrooms.

"Oh my God!" I said, remembering Sebastian. "Doesn't he *care* what your parents think?"

"I guess not," said Sebastian glumly.

I perused Nathan's albums, which took up almost the whole length of one shelf. He had records by Lou Reed, David Bowie, Herbie Hancock, Jefferson Airplane, whose hits I'd heard on the radio, and then he had totally unexpected ones by bands like the Beach Boys, and the Supremes, who at that time were uncool even by my incredibly limited standards.

Nathan seemed more enigmatic than ever.

I wanted desperately to search his dresser, look at his underwear and socks and find a secret diary, but I knew this was not possible, and that Sebastian would be irreparably upset.

"Let's go to your room," I said, feeling restless, dissatisfied.

I let Sebastian touch my breasts. I unbuttoned my blouse and lay back, shutting my eyes. His hands were uncertain, shy. I felt he deserved this gift. I liked him a great deal and had no desire to hurt his feelings. Yet it was Nathan I thought of whenever Sebastian's lips touched mine.

I couldn't wait to get into bed at night so that I could replay the fantasy that I had created for Nathan and me. It was exactly like watching a film: It is a warm day in spring, the clearing where the shed stands is speckled with flowers. I ride up on my bicycle, looking for a quiet place to read. Nathan is walking across the field toward me. He smiles, waves. I drop my bike and go to him. Very much as he had that day outside the school, he takes my arm and leads me toward the shed. Once inside, he presses me into the wall and kisses me hard. He lifts my legs and wraps them around his waist, I can feel his cock getting hard against my crotch; he unbuttons my shirt, kisses my neck with his soft wet mouth, my neck, then my breasts; and since I don't know exactly where to go from here, the picture fades to black.

Wanting more, so much more, I'd start it over again at the beginning, adding dialogue—Nathan tells me he loves me more than anything in the world and will never stop loving me. I tell him I feel the same way. When we get to the sex, my imagination overloads and the picture once again fades.

* * *

LATE IN THE SPRING, Jack drove a carload of us to a neighboring town to watch Sally run the mile in the state championships. Once we were seated, I never took my eyes off of her, as if I could make her win by the sheer force of my will. As the runners prepared at the starting line, Sally's expression was so concentrated that she appeared naked, as if she had shed every ounce of propriety and decorum and couldn't have cared less. Her eyes stared at some point in the distance, while her nose wrinkled and her upper lip twisted into an eight. When the gun went off, she sprang ahead, running with her torso slightly forward, her legs and arms pumping so hard she seemed like a film of herself on fast-forward. She tore away from the other front-runners after the first lap.

People were screaming and jumping up and down on the bleachers as she crossed the finish line. The announcer stated her time—5:12. Sally had broken the high school state record. People were saying that in a few years she'd surely be a candidate for the Olympics. I ran down to the field and hugged her. I kissed her sweat-drenched cheek. Her bright red face showed nothing but surprise and elation. I was so proud of her that I forgot I was envious of her for having such talent and determination.

In July Sally's father learned that he was being transferred to Paris for a year. Sally was told that she had to go, because it was a once-in-a-lifetime opportunity, and her parents couldn't bear for her to pass it up. Although her parents promised to find her a place to train, she was disconsolate.

She burst into my house sobbing like someone had died. Naturally, I turned to stone. I couldn't bear tears or shouting. She threw herself facedown on my bed and I sat with my back against the headboard.

"Fuck Paris. Fuck the 'experience of a lifetime,'" she sobbed.

"I'm sure it'll be great," I said. "Don't cry, Sally, please."

She looked up at me, her face contorted and tearstained.

"You're the best f-friend I ever had." Her head dropped, jerked back in a convulsion of sobs, and I forced myself to pat her shoulder, mumbling inanities.

* * *

WITH SALLY IN PARIS and our brothers in college,
Sebastian and I ended up spending all our time together. One day, in
the hall, he put his arm around my shoulders as he was telling me some
small secret, and I didn't move away. So he left his arm there, and we
began to walk around in this manner. Our new status wasn't news to
anyone but us. I often told him I loved him, adding quickly, but not *that*
way.

* * *

AROUND THIS TIME, his father moved back from London.
I sometimes was invited over for dinner on a weekend. To me, Mr. and
Mrs. MacKenna seemed like the happiest, most stable couple in the
world, always smiling at each other across the dinner table, and calling
each other "dear." Nathan was away at Harvard, and my exchange with
him outside the school seemed to have left the realm of reality and
become only a fantasy.

* * *

I MADE SEBASTIAN steal Nathan's copy of *The Happy
Hooker*. I had him read parts aloud to me when we were alone. There
was a section on Xaviera's favorite masturbation techniques that completely flipped me out.

"It's entirely normal to masturbate," Sebastian said reasonably.

"Do *you* do that? I don't!"

"You should," he said.

When Xaviera described female orgasms, I was certain she was
making it up and told Sebastian so. But he said it was true, "Women
can have orgasms, too."

"Would you know what to do to make that happen?" I asked.

"Probably. But you should experiment by yourself."

I looked at his kind, smooth face and solid, nice thighs in their pale
corduroy Levi's. I liked what I saw and I knew now that I had him all to
myself, that I could do anything I wanted, cruel or kind, and he'd take
it in silence and never walk away from me.

"Are you in love with me?" I asked Sebastian.

"I've been in love with you since the first time I saw you," he said
flatly.

"So let's do it."

He sat there, stunned, thinking, then he said, "All right, but we have to plan. We don't want to do anything foolish. Maybe I should call Nathan and ask him about condoms—of course, I'd never say it was you," he added quickly.

"No, don't do that." His mention of Nathan made the air catch in my throat.

"Well, I'll have to buy them, but I really don't know what kind to get," he said thoughtfully. "It's legal, isn't it, if both partners are underage?"

He pulled a bunch of colorful foil packets out of his down jacket pocket and sat on my bed. The entire house was dark except for the bedside lamp. My father and Anna had gone to Bermuda for a long weekend, leaving their thoroughly dependable and studious teenage daughter alone.

"These are lubricated," he said in the soothing tone of a doctor about to administer an injection, "and these are not."

I was in my best Lanz of Salzburg nightie with yellow daisies and lace at the neck. I felt more like I was about to have surgery than sex, and Sebastian's tone was not helping things.

He slowly removed his clothes as he sat on the edge of my bed with his back to me. "Nathan used to say," he mused, "that one should always take off one's socks."

"Bass—" I said quickly. "I need to tell you something about Nathan—"

He looked at me sideways. "No you don't," he said. "You must think I'm completely blind, or stupid."

A dark room, his dark body so close, his head pressed into the crook of my neck. His smell, sweet like shampoo. The silence is frightening, and there's no sound at all coming from us. His movements are gentle, tender; I feel no pain. I feel no elation, no sadness either. Tomorrow I will remember every detail with utter detachment. I don't bleed, but afterwards, in the bathroom, I notice those other lips have changed shape, are no longer flat and smooth but protrude outward as if to give a subtle kiss.

* * *

SOME TIME IN APRIL, I was pushing my bike up the MacKennas' driveway when I saw an unfamiliar, dented Volkswagen

Rabbit parked in front of the garage. The front door was open, a pair of blue jean–clad legs and a behind were sticking out. It was Nathan.

"Hi," I said.

Swiftly, he sat up. "Hey, Celeste. Lost my damn hash pipe. How's life?"

His face was sunburned to a baked-clay color; the area around his eyes formed two white circles where his sunglasses always sat. There were clothes, towels, an empty tequila bottle, and beer cans all over the back seat.

"Just drove up from Fort Lauderdale yesterday," he said.

"How's school?"

"Cool in every department except work. I can't seem to get it together." He looked at me for a long moment with his probing eyes.

"You and Bass are fucking, aren't you?"

I opened my mouth to speak but no words came out.

"Thought so. I can see it in his face. Saw it right away. You probably initiated it. Am I right? You've been reasonably careful, I hope?"

I nodded.

"Good." He went back to looking for his lost pipe. From under the dashboard, he said, "I thought it would be me. I guess I have no right to be jealous."

Incomprehensibly, I began to cry. As if he could feel this happening, he immediately got out of the car and came toward me and my bicycle.

"It—it—doesn't feel like anything," I sputtered. When he was within touching distance, I held up my hand, palm flat to his chest. "Stay away from me." I was blinded by tears, incapacitated. I had never cried in front of another person.

"All right," he said. His face had collapsed, as if he'd dropped a mask he'd been wearing, along with his hash pipe. After a moment, he went back to his car, got in, shut the door, and just sat there. I went up to the window and leaned in.

"You're a bastard, Nathan." I did not wait for his reaction, but turned and rode fast down the driveway.

Six

THE DAY SALLY returned from Paris, she ran six miles barefooted with the cross-country team.

On her first Friday back, the three of us went out in Sebastian's parents' Volvo. We squeezed into the front seat and to celebrate, drank a bottle of gin mixed with Kool-Aid. This was our usual entertainment on a Friday night, the quality and quantity of liquor depending greatly on what we could steal from our parents without getting caught. I did not like gin, but it was the only bottle Sebastian had been able to steal from his mother's bar that particular night.

Sally was telling us about the American ambassador's son, Jeffrey Davis, whom she had met at school in Paris and had dated for the entire school year.

"He had a whole floor to himself that was bigger than our entire apartment! Oh God, I can't believe it—but I've got to tell you guys this!" she said, and burst into a high-pitched giggle.

"Come on, out with it," coaxed Sebastian.

"Well . . . I smoked *pot* with him!!"

"Oh *no!*" we cried in unison, "Sally, you bad girl!"

Bass and I had smoked our first joint together some time ago. It was a rare gem given to him by Nathan—Panama Red with a few drops of hash oil. Sebastian hallucinated, while I merely shrank into a corner of the old shed and wept.

"And I let him feel me up!" Sally said with disgust.

I downed my fourth drink, and suddenly angry for no reason, said, "Well, that's nothing. Bass and I slept together."

Sally stopped laughing, her face freezing in an expression of hilarity, and then collapsing as if she'd been slapped.

"You're kidding me, right?"

We were silent. Sebastian looked away. She opened the passenger door, leaned out, and threw up.

"That's disgusting," she wailed. "Gross me out totally! Well, better you than me, that's all *I* have to say."

Sebastian had many friends on the baseball team who would have been thrilled to take Sally out, but she wasn't interested. She kept up a correspondence with Jeffrey Davis, who was back in Washington. His father the ambassador had been forced to resign due to a scandal involving alcohol, a transatlantic flight, and two TWA flight attendants.

I was sitting on my bed on a school-day afternoon in the late fall, looking through college catalogs and applications, when the door flew open and Sally came in, barefoot in her sweat-drenched gym shorts and T-shirt. Her face was pale and drawn.

"What's the matter?" I asked, worried.

"I don't know. I didn't feel like running today."

She had run about five miles with the team, through a wooded area behind the school, and decided to leave the group and run to my house.

"What's wrong?" I asked. "Are you sick?"

She sat down on the rug and crossed her mud-flecked, muscular legs.

"I'm upset, and it doesn't really make sense."

I was afraid this was going to be about Sebastian and me, and I felt myself shutting down, my mind floating off.

"Remember years ago I told you my niece Suzy was born three months premature? Well, I just found out last night that it's not *true*! Marianne was pregnant when she got married." She stood up and burst into tears, clenching her fists. "Sex is disgusting! Those gross positions! All that huffing and snorting and screaming with some guy's fat ass going up and down on top of you! How could you *do* that?" With that, she began to emit the most terrifying high-pitched wails, and dropped to the rug with all her force. Anna came running up the stairs.

"What's the matter?" Anna said. "What on earth is going on?"

I looked at her and grimaced. Sally's face had contorted and she was frantically rocking back and forth, screaming like a person being tortured.

"My mother just let it slip!" she shouted. *"By accident!"*

I sat frozen on my bed. Anna wrapped her arms around Sally's shoulders and tried to hold her still.

"There, there," Anna crooned.

"*Lies! It's just a bunch of lies!* They lie to you your whole fucking life they tell you to be a good little girl and do what I say and then one day they just let their lies slip like they're nothing, nothing! My sister is disgusting. She's a hypocrite! She's been *fucking* Brad since high school!"

She threw Anna's arms off and rose. "Oh, *fuck* this," she said, and stormed out, slamming the door.

Anna and I looked at each other.

"Do you think I should call Mrs. Newlyn?" Anna finally asked. "I hate to get involved."

"I don't know. What do you think?"

"Have you ever seen her like this before?"

I shook my head.

"I think I'd better call Mrs. Newlyn." Anna plucked at her plaid skirt, tucked a curl behind her ear, squared her shoulders, and headed for the door.

Sally became lethargic, moody, disinterested. But she continued to run.

The next Friday night, she drank twice as much as we did. Once in a while she'd laugh ghoulishly to herself. I realized as I sat next to her in Sebastian's parents' car that she was not thinking about her sister Marianne, but about other things, so disturbing that I could not begin to understand, and did not want to ask.

* * *

THE FOLLOWING WEEKEND, she got falling-down drunk on eggnog at an early Christmas party. She dragged Sebastian and me outside to look at the stars.

"I'm going to predict your future," she said in a childish voice. "Bass," she punched him hard in the arm, "you'll grow up to marry a nice Wasp girl and have three, maybe four kids. You'll have a nice job with the government—something very boring but solid. You'll never marry Celeste because Celeste is just beginning her journey. You'd be happy enough with her, she'd be bored to death with you.

"Celeste, you're lucky the first one was Bass and not Nathan. If it'd been Nathan, he'd have dumped you by now and you'd be vicious and pissed off and twisted into ugly knots. Nathan is either going to become famous or kill himself with alcohol or drugs. What you want,

Celeste, is danger. You don't want the truth *now*, but someday you will. Do you know what people say about your mother?"

"Stop! Stop it!" I shouted. For a moment, I couldn't breathe, and I knew that if she'd said one more word I would have jumped on her and stopped her with my hands.

"Okay. Okay," she said. "But I have to tell you this—you're going to get swallowed by a sperm whale, just like Pinnochio."

With that, she fell to her knees and threw up on the frozen grass.

"Good," she said, getting up. "Now that's all out of me." And she walked unsteadily away.

She was admitted to the Clearwater Institute for Mental Health on Christmas Day. Her friends were not allowed to visit.

"She talks about you and Sebastian constantly," Mrs. Newlyn told me cryptically over the phone. I wondered if Sally had told her mother or her doctors that Sebastian and I had sex. After a pause, Mrs. Newlyn went on.

"She's very upset about something but we can't seem to find out what. The doctor thinks she needs time away from her friends and family and daily routine." The coldness in Mrs. Newlyn's voice made a large fish start flopping around in my stomach.

A few weeks later, Mrs. Newlyn called to say that Sally had a salt deficiency in her brain and that soon, with lithium, her condition would be under control. Everyone was acting like she had pneumonia or something.

Sally came back to school in February and quit the track team.

"I never ran for me," she said, shrugging. "I did it for everybody but me."

* * *

SALLY HAD BEEN back a week when she turned to me in the crowded hall, her eyes filled with outrage, and screamed, "I bet you didn't tell Bass how you fucked *Nathan* in the shed, did you? I *saw* you!" She was leaning toward me, her hands in fists, like a furious child.

Faces turned and stared. I was paralyzed, and in that instant I began to calculate—how could she have witnessed my fantasy if she was in Paris? Flushed, I watched Bass's face. Doubt scurried across his eyes; I saw its dark presence and gasped. I felt as guilty as if what she'd said was true.

"That never happened!" I protested. "Sally! Did you forget to take your pills?" She banged her head into her locker and remained there, immobile, for a long time. The school bell rang. Sebastian was still looking at me, but his eyes had cleared now. Sally turned to me, pale again and composed, and said, "We're going to be late for class."

For a few days, I held my breath, praying for her pills to work, for whatever it was to go away and leave her alone.

In English class, in the middle of a discussion on *Robinson Crusoe*, Sally turned to me and screamed, *"You bitch! You stole my fucking money!"*

Miss Wilson and the students turned their eyes to me with questioning expressions, as if maybe for a split second reality were standing on its head and they believed me capable of such a thing.

"You're out of your mind!" I protested, "I don't need your money!"

Miss Wilson came toward us with her paperback of *Robinson Crusoe* pressed protectively to her chest.

"I swear I didn't take her money," I told Miss Wilson.

But Miss Wilson was not concerned with that. "Are you all right, Sally dear? Would you like to go to the infirmary?"

"What do you think I am, crazy or something?" Sally shouted.

After the echo of her voice died, there wasn't a sound in the room.

I realized then that none of us were prepared for this. We didn't understand.

* * *

SHE RETURNED FROM Clearwater the second time, in April, and we went to a disco party with Sebastian. Without warning she disappeared and I found her in the ladies' room, leaning close to the mirror, apparently applying lipstick.

"You want to go home, Sally?" I asked, concerned. When she turned around I gasped. She had pierced her bottom lip with a safety pin. Blood trickled from the closed pin, down her chin.

"Celeste! Celeste, I'm so glad to see you." She grabbed me by the shoulders and brought her tearstained face close to mine. "I fucked a guy in the nuthouse. We waited till all the nurses and other nuts were asleep, then we'd sneak into each other's beds. Oink, oink, like little pigs. But not as good—never as good—as with this huge cucumber I stole from the kitchen when I was on serving duty 'cause see, they gave *me* responsibilities, 'cause I was *way* normal compared to the others."

Panic-stricken, I ran out to find Sebastian, who was standing just outside the door.

"Help her, Bass," I said, choking back tears. "She's totally flipped."

He went in. A flock of tittering girls came flapping out.

Minutes later, he emerged, grasping Sally firmly by the arm. She looked reasonably calm now, the grotesque safety pin had been removed. The blood and streaks of mascara had been washed from her face. She held a square of toilet paper to her lip.

"We're going home," he said calmly. "This evening is over."

But of course, nothing was over. There were new diagnoses, new pills, new doctors.

She came back to school again late in the spring. It was a glorious day, the three of us were together again. Sally's new medication made her lethargic and heavy. As we sat on the cafeteria steps, taking in the noonday sun, her face wore a contented, relaxed expression.

"Can you believe," she said evenly, "that I'm adopted?"

She explained in neutral tones that she had been the bastard child of an incestuous affair and that just this morning her mother had put drops of arsenic in her orange juice.

"She's so *stupid* to use arsenic, it smells like almonds. Anybody knows *that*." She turned to Sebastian and me with an exasperated smirk. "You don't believe me," she said, searching my eyes. "I know Bass believes me."

Sebastian looked heartbroken in his silence. He stood and walked to the principal's office to call Mrs. Newlyn.

Sally had stopped taking her pills because they made her feel tired and fat, but Mrs. Newlyn convinced her to start again and she came to school the following week.

"Everything is going to be fine, now," she told us. "It really is. We'll be like we were before."

* * *

SALLY HAD NO DATE for the prom, and we could not let her sit at home, so going as a threesome seemed the only solution. Sebastian invited her formally, in a little card with roses on the front.

Her mother got the crimson dress out of storage. Sally was happier and calmer that night than I'd seen her in a long time. Until the football players got rowdy and pulled the urinals off the wall of the men's room. Uniformed guards rushed into the banquet hall and rounded us up like cattle.

Sally's face twisted into a knot of hopeless rage. She went up to the first football player she could find and slapped him hard across the face.

"How dare you act like this?" she hissed between clenched teeth. "Don't you know you'll have to pay for this in your next life?"

* * *

THE DAY BEFORE I left for my Little Ivy League college in Massachusetts, Sally called and asked me if she could stop by. She had taken a turn for the worse again in July and had spent most of the summer at home with her mother, watching television. Mrs. Newlyn said it had a marvelously calming effect on her.

It was raining that day and water flowed from the eaves in a comforting murmur.

She sat on my bed with her yearbook open on her lap.

"Look at all the nice things people wrote for me," she said.

"I know. Everyone has always loved you."

"I think I'll go to the community college for a year, bring up my grades, see what happens. You'll be nearby. And Bass'll be at Columbia—not too far away. We'll get together and it'll be like old times."

I nodded, looking away.

"I see things nobody else sees," she said.

"Yes," I said, "but don't tell me, Sally. I don't want to know what you see."

"I need to tell you one thing—I used to be in love with Bass. I was so in love with him, I thought I was going to die. But I saw how he kissed you, how he looked at you, and I knew I didn't have a chance. I was so jealous!"

"Don't say things like that now, Sally. What's the point?"

"Do you still love Nathan?" she asked me, searching my eyes.

Abruptly she changed the subject. "My mother is a thwarted woman. She never had a life of her own. This whole town is filled with women like her who are afraid. I used to be afraid but I'm not anymore.

"My mother has hidden talents, she can talk to animals, did you know that?"

My heart sank. "Oh, God, Sally."

"It's the truth. But I'm not going to live my life like she did. I'm going to join the Peace Corps."

"That's great!" I said.

She grabbed my arm and brought her face close to mine. "Don't settle, Celeste. Go get what you want. For me, okay? Don't forget what I told you. You have an *ancient* soul. You have to protect it."

"Okay, Sally."

* * *

DURING THE CHRISTMAS holidays Mrs. Newlyn called me to tell me that Sally had returned to Clearwater. Months away from home had freed me, and now I didn't want to return to the nightmarish responsibility of being Sally's best friend.

She told me that Sally was in a state of obsession over her lost yearbook, which she was certain she had left in my room the last time I'd seen her. I was equally certain I'd watched Sally put the book in her knapsack, and told Mrs. Newlyn this. But I promised to search for it, which I did. I never found it.

Mrs. Newlyn never forgave me for not finding it, for not going to Clearwater to visit Sally, for not writing.

* * *

IT WAS SEBASTIAN who called me on my dormitory hall pay phone the following December, in the middle of finals week, and told me that Sally was dead. Her parents did not know what had propelled her suicide.

I hoped that she did not think ill of me before she died.

Sebastian had been a better friend to her than I. He had kept in touch. His voice was slightly distant on the phone. I did not blame him.

After I hung up, the phone rang again, and thinking it was Bass calling back, I picked up.

"Celeste, this is Nathan. I heard about Sally. I just thought I'd call."

It did not even seem strange that he knew my voice immediately.

"How are you?"

"Flunking out of Harvard."

"Why?"

"I don't know, I took some time off to figure it out, but it didn't help. So now we're both sophomores, how's that for fate?"

There was a moment of silence in which I could hear his even breathing, and my mind saw his lips pressed against the phone. I felt that jolt of electricity again as my mouth went dry.

"Nathan, I think I'm flipping out over Sally. I can't *feel* anything."

"I need to see you, Celeste," he said in a quiet voice.

"Why?" I asked, confused.

"Because I've never stopped thinking about you and it's time," he said.

"I'm in the middle of exams," I said desperately, trying to anchor myself.

"Drive up after you finish. Please."

"All right," I said. "Tomorrow."

The next day, a light snow was falling as I drove southeast toward Boston. I felt lighthearted, free, filled with trepidation and desire. I did not feel guilty over Sebastian or Sally; I'd left them behind in my dorm room, the way one would an old moth-eaten coat at the first sign of spring.

Seven

ALEX AND I were on our way to southern New Jersey to spend the night with Chester and Babs, his father and stepmother, who were throwing us an engagement party. Outside the BMW's tinted windows a desert of factories and empty lots rushed past. It was a beautiful spring day, but you never would've known from the dismal landscape. I was sick with a serious cold. I'd awakened that morning with a scratchy throat and pressure in my sinuses; by noon, the virus had launched an all-out offensive.

I pressed my forehead to the glass. Alex was telling me that he loved me in the beige linen suit he'd bought me for the occasion. I felt as though my head were encased in a jug of tepid water.

The suit was expensive, attractive; something you might see on a Wall Street executive—the skirt just above the knees, the jacket with a cinched waist and padded shoulders. It felt like a disguise, but that was all right by me. Mostly I wore long skirts, loose tops, or drop-waisted dresses.

Alex drummed his fingers on the steering wheel, sighed. His new cellular phone rang. It made a bulge like a small handgun in his jacket pocket.

"What is it, George?"

George talked for a while and then Alex said patiently, "That doesn't change anything. If you want to get the bride to the altar, you have to get her wet first. You can't take her by force. Court her."

What on earth was he talking about? Alex listened for a while and then said, "The controlling party is worried about getting senior management positions for his kids, that's all. You know those Latin types. Big families."

Apparently some huge deal was about to go through in Argentina, and George, whom he'd sent down there, couldn't seem to handle things without calling every thirty minutes. I was becoming annoyed.

"What would happen if you just turned that thing off? Would George have a heart attack or what?"

"This is very serious, Celeste," Alex said, containing a sigh of impatience. "The timing couldn't be worse." To George he said, "Well, carve out something that's going to be attractive to them, goddamnit! You know how to do this, George."

"The timing couldn't be worse for me, either. I'm sick as a dog," I said to the window.

* * *

I THOUGHT THAT perhaps he was nervous about seeing his father's relatives and friends all gathered in one place. This hadn't happened since his father's wedding to Babs some ten years before. Maybe it was easier to plan a huge takeover deal over the phone than to think about his family. I didn't mention my thoughts to him, and put my hand on his thigh instead.

I hadn't seen any of my relatives in years either, but I couldn't have cared less what they thought. The only time they had gathered in one room—the Wasp paternal side and my mother's French clan from Bordeaux and Paris—was at my mother's funeral. My French grandmother had not come. She wrote a tight little note explaining that her husband (her third) was ill with gout and couldn't be left alone, but I was certain it was because she was still angry at my mother over the fight they'd had the previous summer. Nevertheless, whatever my grandmother's reasons, I decided on the day of the funeral, at the age of ten, never to see her again.

Alex maintained that all the divorces and remarriages in his family hadn't affected him in the least.

* * *

CHESTER HAD WORKED in the city for thirty years, for a large commercial bank, but had recently been prodded into early retirement. In the ten months I had been with Alex, I had met his mother twice, "between flights"; but I had met his father and stepmother only once, when they drove into the city the day after Christmas and took us to lunch.

It had been my responsibility to find a suitable restaurant, and I chose a nouvelle cuisine French restaurant that was hip, but not too hip for Chester and Babs, whom Alex had described as "a bit square" and not particularly fond of "foreign foods," especially ones that used garlic.

Unfortunately, on the fateful day, I forgot the restaurant's address.

"I'm so sorry," I said from the back of their Buick. "It's around here somewhere."

Babs's gleeful voice jumped in, "But this is *fine*! We're having a little tour!" She had long dark hair twisted up in a chignon that was held together by large silver combs.

"I remember now," I said. "It's not on Third Avenue, it's on Second."

"It's such a beautiful day," Babs mused. "Must be at least fifty degrees. Whatever happened to white Christmases, I wonder?"

"It's sixty-two," Alex pointed out. "Must be the hole in the ozone."

"Is it really sixty-two?" said Babs. "I could have sworn the radio said low fifties."

"Sixty-two," Alex repeated.

"Well, I'll be. What do *you* think, dear? Does this feel like a sixties kind of day to you?" She turned to Chester and with her long red fingernails flirtatiously tickled the hair at the base of his head, which was shaped exactly like Alex's.

"Yes, love, it does seem that look is back," Chester said. "I see girls everywhere in bell-bottoms."

As we perused our menus, Alex said, "The fish here is good. Not too garlicky."

"What will you have, love?" Chester asked Babs.

"Just a small salad." She smiled wanly at the waiter who stood nearby, and absently rubbed her temples.

"Oh no," said Chester, "a migraine coming on?"

"Just sinuses, I think. I'm fine, really." She winced.

Chester ordered a hamburger; Alex and I, the sole meuniere.

We exchanged presents. Alex gave his father, "from both of us," some kind of state-of-the-art tool, incomprehensible to me, for the carpentry workshop he kept in his basement. Chester had a passion for making Quaker-style furniture in his spare time. Alex handed Babs a gift-wrapped Bloomingdale's box that held an imitation Hermès scarf he had bought from a Senegalese street merchant.

They oohed and ahhed for a moment, then fell silent.

Chester gave Alex a complicated, bright yellow scuba diving watch, and Babs handed me a very large hardcover book wrapped in green paper with a big red bow. It was the latest Danielle Steel novel.

"Thank you so much," I said.

"Alex has told us how much you like to read! I *love* her, don't you?" Babs said with a pleased smile. I smiled back and asked about her sinuses.

Alex told Chester about his latest promotion at the investment firm (he was the youngest managing director in the history of the company) and he asked his father about a Mexican television company called Grupo Telemedia that was attempting to buy L.A. television stations from one of America's oldest and most longstanding companies, Chadwick Broadcasting. They talked about this for a while and I stared at them, dumbfounded. Babs, I noted, was covering her mouth and pressing her fingers up under her nose, attempting to stifle a yawn.

Chester had a benevolent, elastic face that seemed utterly unperturbed.

Babs wrapped an ice cube in her napkin and applied it to her forehead, right between the eyebrows. She shut her eyes tightly and winced again.

After a moment, Alex looked at Babs, then said in a honey-coated voice, "If those headaches are as bad as you say they are, Babs, you really ought to see a doctor."

"I've been to *twenty* doctors if I've been to one, Alex dear," she said, sighing.

Alex frowned, looking extremely concerned. "Well, maybe they just weren't the right *kinds* of doctor, Babs. Maybe it's psychosomatic, did you ever consider that possibility?"

Babs laughed through her nose and said, "Alex, you're so amusing!"

"Hey, Dad," said Alex, "I just read the greatest book. You might like it. By Primo Levi; it's called *Other People's Trades*. Celeste gave it to me—"

"*You* read a real book, Alex? It must have been under duress!" Babs laughed. She turned to me. "When Alex was engaged to Mimi—you know, of course, she was a veritable clothes horse (no, I wanted to say, the only photos I ever saw of her were bare-assed naked)—well, she had him reading *GQ* and shopping at Saks! All those little Italian-cut suits with shoulders out to here! Now it's back to Brooks Brothers, thank God. And *books*! This *is* an improvement!" The smile on her face was so sincere and sweet, you'd have thought she was talking about a brand-new litter of kittens.

Alex was frowning at his stepmother, but Babs pressed on with her earnest smile. I looked to Chester for a clue, but he was also smiling, a big, elastic, happy grin that spanned his entire face.

Now as we sat in the car, Alex's cell phone rang again. The thought of being on display with a cold of this magnitude made me disconsolate. "Just do what you have to do, George," Alex said after a while, and closed the phone, a fat, gray rectangular contraption with a long antenna. He turned to me.

"I wonder if Edgar Marx'll come. He's kind of artistic. He's a big producer. He likes young women, if you know what I mean, so watch out. His wife is an alcoholic."

I took out my Neo-Synephrine and squeezed two large shots into each nostril.

"Celeste, you're only supposed to use that stuff every four hours. That's the third time you've used it and we've only been on the road an hour."

"I can't breathe, Alex," I said, irritated.

I tried to sleep. After a while I attained a pain-filled half slumber; I could still hear the rhythmic ticking of the engine, and my sinuses squeaking and gurgling inside my head as if they had indigestion. Then I slipped into blackness, oblivion. I awakened with a start, with no sense of time having elapsed, not remembering where I was. I looked around quickly. There was Alex, sitting beside me, talking to George in Argentina. Relieved, I closed my eyes again.

We drove up to the three-story white colonial with a manicured lawn on a quiet, winding street. Alex was a guest here as much as I. We were offered our choice of room and he chose the renovated attic, since it was the farthest away from Chester and Babs's bedroom. While Alex went off to the country club to play tennis with his father, I collapsed on the bed and slept fitfully for several hours.

Alex finally shook me from sleep thirty minutes before the guests were to arrive.

"Poor girl," he said. "Maybe a hot shower would help." Not just my head felt ensconced in a jug, my whole body seemed to be moving as if through water. I went to Babs for help. Behind her closed bedroom door I could hear her moving around. I knocked, feeling like an intruder. She was still in her bathrobe.

"Babs, I really feel terrible. I'm sorry, I don't know what to do."

"Oh my dear," she said soothingly. "I know what spring colds can be. Here . . ." She led me into her large, white tiled bathroom that glinted in the light, and opened the medicine cabinet. On the marble vanity table were little glass bottles and vials lined up like an Amazon army conscripted in the war against age.

"Here we are. Liquid Sudafed!" she cried. "A miracle drug." She filled the little plastic cup to the brim with the evil-looking red liquid. "Drink up!"

I tossed it back and it hit bottom like molten lead and then spread warmth and comfort upward toward my chest and extremities.

"In twenty minutes you'll be good as new. Now, you must get dressed, my dear. All these people are dying to meet you! What a pity your father and stepmother couldn't come. We would have loved to have gotten acquainted with Charles and—Anna, isn't it?—before the Big Day."

"They were really touched you invited them," I lied. "It's hard for them to get all the way down here from Connecticut." As I said this, my father's irate voice rang in my head: "Oh God, how're we going to get out of this one?"

Babs gave me the bottle of Sudafed "for later" and I took it upstairs to our attic room. The ache began to disperse, and my nose cleared somewhat. I dressed languidly, had trouble with the small details—my mother's pearls, the diamond earrings Alex had given me, my high-heeled pumps. I went into the bathroom to apply mascara, something I did only on rare occasions. My face looked pale and bloated, oily from sickness.

Alex appeared in the mirror behind me, all ready in his gray pin-striped suit and floral tie.

"The suit looks great! Feeling better?" he asked hopefully.

"Yes, actually." I tried a small smile. We heard the doorbell sound. Cocktail party voices greeted each other on the landing downstairs.

"Uh-oh. You're a real sport," he added solemnly. "I love you. I'll go down." He gave me a hug from behind. "Take your time."

Once he was gone, I filled the little plastic cup and drank another shot of Sudafed. It was only as I descended the stairs that I realized I was already quite tipsy, and the reasonable part of my mind was telling me to cool it, that it was going to be one of those unquenchable thirsts, the ones I had been so conscientiously avoiding lately, which ended up with me waking up the next morning with no idea of where I had been. As the reasonable voice said take it easy, the other, stronger voice laughed derisively, because what I wanted now, more than anything, was a drink.

I floated toward the bar, where Babs was playing bartender.

"Thank you so much for the medicine," I intoned. Babs was quite beautiful, with her tall frame and angular face, her perfect chignon, large onyx and gold earrings, matching necklace, and charcoal gray suit.

"Oh, but you're so very welcome, my dear!" Her voice rang in my ears, as if coming from a great distance, down a long tunnel.

"You're beautiful, Babs," I said.

She gasped, not used to candid talk, I suspected, then laughed gaily, blushing. "Compliments will get you everywhere with me! May I fix you a drink?"

"What goes with Sudafed?"

"Let's see, maybe white wine?"

"Sounds great."

She filled a long-stemmed glass to the rim and handed it to me with a little napkin. The wine sparkled like a jewel as it caught the light. "Now relax, dear Celeste. This is a celebration!"

* * *

MY WINE WAS too soon gone. I felt bereft. A tall, gray-haired man in a kelly green sports coat was talking to me about golf. It seemed not enough time had elapsed to go back to Babs for more wine, so I waited patiently for him to ask me if I needed a refill.

"Are you a golfer, young lady? Alex is quite a golfer, I'm told. An all-around athlete. When I was younger I thought golf was for old people," he was saying in an incredibly loud voice, the voice of Wasps at the dinner table that reminded me of my departed paternal grandfather. "Now I'm old and I see all these youngsters out there at the club every day. Why did I wait so long, I ask myself?"

"Precisely," I said, smiling.

"So you *are* a golfer!" he shouted.

"No, but my stepmother plays. She's pretty good, too." This was not a lie, but I would not have been above lying, if it meant pleasing him and getting another drink.

"Say, would you like a refill there?"

Congratulating myself, I handed him my glass.

Only a moment later, it seemed to be empty again. This time I went to the bar myself, only to find Chester had relieved Babs.

"Celeste! This is my dear friend and employer, Mr. Hendrake. Please meet Celeste Miller."

Mr. Hendrake's face looked like an enormous pink nipple, everything puckered and scrunched toward his pursed lips that greedily sucked at his glass. I smiled politely at Mr. Hendrake as a dangerous laugh began to rumble in my chest.

Mr. Hendrake told me about computer software. I listened intently until my glass was empty. Chester was generous with the wine; as soon as he refilled my glass, I excused myself with a big smile, and swiftly floated off.

"Ain't that just too cute," I heard Mr. Hendrake say behind me. "She misses him already."

Time stopped. I found myself speaking to the infamous Edgar Marx, producer of Broadway shows.

"I'm the only Jew here," he was telling me as he looked over the crowded room. He was also tall, with silver hair, in a square-cut sports coat. "But I don't take it personally, ha, ha!" I perceived a wink and continued to smile. His face swam before my eyes. I stood, quiet, demure, smiling, leaning up against the grand piano for support.

"I make more money than all of them put together . . . but, you win some, lose some. Name of the game . . . say, did you see *The Secret Sharer* yet?"

"No, but I love the book." Were there actually words emanating from my mouth? It was hard to tell.

"Never read the book. But it's a hell of a play. I'll send you a pair of tickets next week . . . "

I was grateful to hear him responding; I realized that I had indeed spoken and that I was still in control.

"Say, sweetie, can I refresh your drink?" I felt his hand cupping my hipbone.

"Sure," I said, "why not?"

Shortly he was back.

"Have you ever read John Cheever, Mr. Marx?" I was proud of the effort I was making to speak sanely and crisply. I perceived that he had heard me, for he was nodding.

"Call me Ed, please. In the *New Yorker*, sure."

"Doesn't this party seem Cheeveresque?"

"Hahaha!" He paused and looked at me, then said, "In what way do you mean? Oh, here's my wife, Elizabeth."

She descended like an enormous black bird with a jowly red throat and filled up the entire frame of my vision. Her poor face was ravaged by bloat and wrinkles. It was clear she believed her husband was trying to make me.

"This is Alex's fiancée," he told her quickly, an edge in his voice.

"It's so nice to meet you," I said; my words sounded too slow, too enthusiastic.

"Right," she said. "Marx, get me a drink."

While he was gone she said, "I'm not Jewish, you know."

I smiled, speechless.

"Yes," she continued, "and I've learned the hard way that it's a mistake to crossbreed."

I felt my face turn to stone in some kind of gargoyle smile. And here was Alex, to the rescue, hugging me tightly to his side. It was like leaning up against a refrigerator. I looked up at his beautiful face, his perfect features, his expression always so controlled.

"How are you, Mrs. Marx?"

"No better, no worse than the last time you saw me," she muttered. I wanted to run away from this woman as fast as possible, but I feared that if Alex let go too suddenly, I would totter and fall on the floor.

He turned his attention to me. "Are you feeling better, Celeste?"

"*Much* better!" I cried.

"I'm glad!" He smiled. "You're a real sport. Maybe you should slow down on the wine, Celeste. Better get something to eat. Buffet's ready."

Eating was out of the question. What I wanted was another shot of Sudafed, the miracle drug. The room was now spinning like a carousel, tinkling music, laughter, bright clothes, I felt a dizziness close to vertigo, reminding me of somewhere else, a long time ago . . . I smiled reassuringly at Alex. "I'm off to powder my nose," I said, ever so careful to enunciate, because Alex had seen me like this before, and I turned to climb the stairs. Movements ever so precise. Extremely proud. Handling myself like the real sport Alex said.

Carousel. Carousel. Good or bad? Very important, when dealing with memories, to figure that out. I was feeling a terrible knot of anxiety in my chest. I sat on the edge of the bed and it began to rise and fall like the shiny black stallion with the gold saddle and leather reins.

* * *

IT'S MY TENTH birthday, October fifteenth. I am on the carousel in Central Park with my mother, who has been laughing and whooping like a cowboy through the whole ride. She is in a short royal blue dress and matching jacket, and tight black leather boots up to her knees. As our horses begin to slow in their rhythmic rise and fall, the merry, tinny music seems sad, filled with a false lightheartedness.

"No! No! Again!" I am starting to panic, because I know that in a moment it will end and my mommy and I will once again be thrown out into the real world, where she is so desperately unhappy.

As our horses come to a halt, the carousel's guardian, a short, round, elderly man with a beret and a ruddy complexion, is standing below us, on the ground, smiling.

"*Vous êtes françaises?*" he asks my mother.

"*Oui, bien sûr.*"

"I heard you earlier. From where?"

"*De Bordeaux!*" she cries. "But we live here now. My husband is an American." I fear she might just start to cry, as she does sometimes for no apparent reason. Her pretty, tight dress is hiked up on her thighs as she straddles her gray horse with a silver harness.

"I'm from Marseilles," the old man says. "I am here for fifteen years but still I miss home."

"Ah, yes. I do know," my mother says, laughing sadly.

"You look like Brigitte Bardot," he tells her. "But you are even more beautiful." We've heard this before, and my mother usually cringes, but she takes it as a compliment and offers him her charming, doleful smile. "My little one doesn't want to get off," she tells him.

"Well then, have another spin on me!" he says, tapping the nose of my mother's horse. "Stay as long as you like."

Much later, for we have been spinning for hours, it seems, he waves us off, standing beneath one of the carousel's high archways. Our heads are giddy, our feet unsteady on the ground.

"Come back soon!" he yells after us. "I'm here every day, for fifteen years!"

"We don't get into the city much," my mother calls over her shoulder.

"Just the same," he says, "come back. I'll remember you."

"God bless you," my mother says, and blows him a kiss.

* * *

NOT EVEN A YEAR has passed, it is summer, and Anna, my father's new friend, has taken me to the Central Park Zoo. She has been coming around lately, taking on little chores. Anna is hoping this trip will lift my spirits, but the animals appear so sad in their ugly cement cages that I begin to cry. Desperate, Anna suggests the carousel. I assent, suddenly enthusiastic.

We can hear the tinny music from way down the path. I begin to run, run! as if a minute will make a difference in whether or not I'll find the old French guardian there. All at once, it seems of paramount importance, even though I haven't thought of him since that day.

Anna buys me a ticket and sits on a bench with her feet primly crossed in her sensible shoes and I wait, crazed with worry, for the gate to open. But I see him, standing in a far corner of the grand hall, watching serenely as the horses and carriages spin round and round. The music is the same—gigantic, hopeful, filled with loneliness. The platform stops rotating and the chain is unlatched. I run to him.

"*Monsieur! Monsieur!* Do you remember me?"

He looks down at me for a long moment and then his face breaks into a smile. He asks after my mother, "*Ou est ta belle maman qui resemble à Brigitte Bardot?*"

"*Elle est morte, monsieur,*" I say, and can't look at him. The words are new, never spoken by me before. "She is dead. *Elle avait le coeur faible.*" I translate for him what my father has explained to me. "She had a weak heart."

"*Pauvre petite,*" the man says, placing a hand on my shoulder. He murmurs, "I am certain she is happy in heaven with the good Lord. Let me put you on my best horse. He's the fastest of my black stallions and he'll carry you away!"

He lifts me in his arms and I wrap mine tight around his neck. I am so grateful, I can't even tell him that I don't want to ride, I want to stay with him on the ground, watching the others. I bury my nose in his denim shirt and let out a tiny sob for her, the first. It is also the last for many years.

I'd been weeping with my face in a pillow. Raising my head a few inches, I saw through a blur that the pillow was streaked with mascara. I stumbled into the bathroom and vigorously washed my face. Looking at myself in the mirror, I saw that I was basculating as if on a ship. Clearly there was no hope of reapplying mascara. I congratulated myself on my astuteness, and settled for an eye pencil, some rouge and lipstick. I brushed my hair, my teeth. My eyes were bloodshot, but thank God there was Visine in my *toilette* kit. I considered taking another swig of Sudafed but decided that this might not be wise, and instead planned to have another glass of wine.

Light on my feet, fortified by the release, I descended the stairs. I was reminded for some reason of the costume ball scene in *Rebecca,* when the second Mrs. DeWinter descends the stairs in the absolutely wrong, wrong dress.

Fade to black.

*   *   *

I **WOKE UP PARALYZED,** bewildered, and uncertain of where I was. I stretched out my arm and felt along the sheet to see if someone was next to me—thank God, I was alone. Then I remembered that I was engaged. Alex was not there.

What on earth could have happened?

He was standing beside the bed. "How are you feeling, Celeste?"

I detected a note of sarcasm in his voice. "I'm sick."

"You certainly didn't act sick last night," he said. My head began to pound as I attempted to formulate a retort, but he threw himself down next to me and kissed me.

Afraid he might smell my breath, I turned away.

"Everyone *loved* you! I'm so proud of you. What a sport."

I decided that the only thing you needed to succeed with this crowd was the ability to smile and shut up. After a moment, he asked, "What were you and Babs talking about in the kitchen?"

What were Babs and I talking about in the kitchen? Was I in the kitchen? I decided to hedge. "Which time was that?"

"Later, when you were helping her clean up."

I tried very hard to form a picture of the scene. Nothing came to mind.

"Nothing special," I said. "I can't remember, really."

"You two were laughing like hyenas. I guess you'd both had a lot to drink by then," he added.

I realized that Alex felt threatened by this budding friendship, but I couldn't appease his anxiety, as my mind was utterly blank.

"Not me," I said quickly. "It was the Sudafed."

Miraculously, my cold was better, or perhaps my hangover was so bad I could no longer feel the pain of my cold. Alex went to the bathroom and came back with two Advils, a glass of water, and the bottle of Sudafed.

"Get that stuff away from me!" I said. Just the sight of it made me want to vomit.

"It's raining," Alex said. "I thought we could take a drive to the mall. I'll buy you a present for being so charming to the old folks."

"I can't, Alex. I'm really sick. What time is it?"

"Nearly noon."

*　*　*

I SHOWERED, dressed, and made my way gingerly down to the kitchen. Even my fingertips ached as they touched the banister. I felt seasick, heartsick, and ashamed.

Everything was in order. You'd never have known there had been a party here. Babs was sitting in the breakfast nook in her robe and slippers, reading the *New York Times* Arts and Leisure section. Her long dark hair was down around her pale face. She seemed vulnerable without her chignon, and slightly melancholy. When she looked up at me I saw her bloodshot, swollen eyes and imagined she felt pretty much the way I did.

"Good morning, Celeste, dear—or shall I say good afternoon? How's that cold?" She patted the chair beside her. "Come sit next to me. Would you like some coffee?" Babs's smile was generous and intimate. *Good God,* I thought, *what on earth did we tell each other last night?*

A wave of nausea coursed through me as something came to me in a flash: Babs at the sink, washing glasses, while I sit at the counter nearby, incapable of anything but keeping my head propped up on my hands. "Mimi was so stupid," Babs says, "she didn't know the difference between World War I and World War II! How she managed law school is beyond me." She throws her head back and guffaws, a gold molar glinting in the light. Turning back to her sudsy glasses, she adds, "Alex wasn't 'sophisticated' enough for her, however—she had an affair with an Italian count, and Alex was *very* angry *indeed*."

Jittery-kneed, I took the seat beside her in the breakfast nook. I wanted to ask her about the order of protection. But what if she didn't know about it? What if she was Alex's enemy? She might use it against him in some underhanded way.

Alex was down in the basement with his father; the murmur of their voices and the whizzing of power tools seeped up through the floorboards.

Babs and I sat in silence; she continued to read while I watched the rain dribble down the window pane.

"My dear Celeste," she finally said in a low, quiet voice, "I hope Alex will give you what you need . . . I know I'm much too deep for Chester, but then, when I met him I was forty-five, my husband had just left me for his secretary, and I had four teenage children. Sometimes I want to take Chester by the collar—" She lifted the newspaper and shook it. She stopped, stared at it, then crumpled it and threw it aside. "But then, I suppose, denial can be a blessing. It's so much easier to live that way. It's just that—well—Alex is so violent-tempered. And you are truly a dear, sweet young woman." After a pause she added, "I'm sorry about that Danielle Steel novel. Sometimes I'm such a bitch, I just can't stop myself!"

I smiled weakly with what I hoped was an understanding look. What did she mean by "violent-tempered"? I was afraid to ask.

"I lost my mother too at a very young age," Babs went on. "I'm still avoiding that pain."

I gazed at her, bewildered, as tears rose to my eyes. Had I told her about the carousel? I could not bring myself to ask her about this either, and not remembering seemed a calamity. I swore to myself I would never drink liquor with Sudafed again. I would not drink any alcohol for a month. Say, three weeks. Well, perhaps two. Now, at least, I knew I would never wake up in a stranger's bed. There would always be Alex to lean up against, pillar of stability that he was.

"Oh, God, Babs." I covered my face and breathed to calm the panic and bile that kept rising in waves to my throat. "I don't know what I'm doing."

She took one of my hands and held it in her lap.

I laughed mirthlessly. "I'm a coward," I told her. "I'm afraid of being alone."

"Then that must make me one, too."

We sat in silence for a long while and watched the rain pelt the window as the coffee cups grew cold in our hands.

Eight

A TERRIBLE LETHARGY overcame me after Chester and Babs's party. My cold had set up camp for a long siege inside my head, but I didn't mind. For five days I stayed in bed, relishing the fact that I had an excuse. I read, and watched the Discovery Channel, where I learned about life in far-off places and scientific facts about the behavior of sharks, dinosaurs, ants, crocodiles, wild dogs, and apes. I felt soothed and mentally nourished.

By the following Saturday I was ready for an outing, and Alex suggested we go back to Bloomingdale's to continue our registering extravaganza. Already the gifts had started to arrive. I never opened the boxes, but waited for him to get home from work. It was amusing to watch him rip open the wrappings with a child's voracious enthusiasm. Sometimes I'd tease him, and he'd call me a Trappist monk and grin sheepishly.

For years I'd lived sleeping on a futon and watching a black and white TV. I had lived with just enough money to survive with the basic comforts, and the riches that populated Alex's life were still foreign to me. While his concerns had been to fill his life with such riches, mine had been simply to survive long enough to complete my work, and become a writer.

Yet that Saturday, as we walked slowly through the Bloomingdale's living room and bedroom displays, the back of my throat began to ache with an incomprehensible longing. On a waxed wood dining table spotless crystal glasses and silverware gleamed near deep red plates, spotlighted like jewels from some ancient and revered culture. I felt like an intruder in an opulent world of order and satiety.

I went and sat on the couch and crossed my legs. Alex sat in the armchair beside me. We smiled at each other in silence. I caught a glimpse of us in a large gilded smoky mirror that hung on a nearby wall and for a moment was overwhelmed with happiness for the nice, serene young couple I saw there. I smiled at our reflection; Alex reached for my hand, squeezed it tightly.

As we continued to explore, the Positano display caught my eye and I stopped. We had registered for these dishes. I had liked the simple, childlike, indigo blue fish hand-painted along the borders of the plates and mugs. I picked up one of the large plates and admired it, trying to imagine what I would cook to serve on it.

"I like these, Jane," a young man standing next to me said to his companion.

"They're *Italian*," Jane responded dismissively. "We're going to *France* on our honeymoon, Howard. Daddy said we could go to *Limoges* and pick out our dishes there."

"Will they be that much cheaper in Limoges, though?"

"Who cares! We'll be able to *say* we got them in *Limoges*."

I put the dish down and looked at the couple from the corner of my eye. Howard was a dark-haired man in his late twenties, probably a businessman attempting to look relaxed in his weekend Gap bermudas and cotton oxford shirt. Jane was in khakis and a pink Lacoste shirt with the collar turned up, her very blond hair pulled back tightly in a ponytail. She wore a gold Cartier watch, and her diamond solitaire was what Alex would call a skating rink. Like mine, in fact. On most days I looked at it with surprise and awe, as if I still could not believe that it belonged to me. I looked down at my dress, one of my favorites, a faded Putumayo floral print that was five years old, and Portuguese espadrilles whose rope soles had started to unravel.

What the hell am I doing here? I thought, and hurried away.

I found Alex in the cookware section, examining an enormous Le Creuset orange pot that cost $300. "Wouldn't you like to have this? You could make dinner for tons of people. We could have big dinner parties . . ."

We went upstairs to the restaurant for lunch. We stood in line for twenty minutes while the two ladies in front of us discussed how it was nearly impossible to get a good manicure anymore since the Koreans had taken over the nail salons. By the time we sat down, I'd lost my appetite.

Alex paused in midbite of his big chicken salad sandwich on a baguette. "What's the matter?" he said worriedly.

"I—I don't know." My face felt cold, I probably looked pale. "I feel like I don't belong here, Alex."

"You belong wherever you are," he said. "I've worked like a dog to be able to afford whatever I want in life. Just enjoy it, Celeste. Don't think so much."

* * *

ALEX LEFT FOR MEXICO on Monday. He would be gone four days. Restless, I went over to visit my old neighbor Lucia that afternoon and we sat on her couch and smoked a joint. I rarely smoked pot. Soon, troubling thoughts began to invade my mind. *You don't miss him. You should be missing him more.* I remembered too late how the last time I'd smoked pot with Lucia I'd sworn I would never smoke again; and now, here I was, stoned and unable to undo it. I felt like my skin was transparent and she could see everything that was going on inside me. The sharp tang of his cologne suddenly wafted over me. I sniffed at the ends of my hair, my hands. Where was it coming from? Had it permeated my pores? Lucia was staring at me with a concerned look.

"Let's go get some food. I'm freaking out over here," I said.

We went around the corner to the Yellow Rose cafe for an order of deep-fried morels. We sat at the bar. Lucia ordered a frozen margarita. Patrick, our handsome, fortyish bartender-actor friend, waited for my order. Lucia waited too. Everything was happening in slow motion, the pause so pregnant with innuendo it was like a badly directed Pinter play. I was sure they were thinking that everything in my future hinged on my decision of whether or not to have a drink. I had not had one since Chester and Babs's party and it seemed a good idea to continue on this track; yet this endless silence was unbearable and I decided that a margarita would surely help me get unstoned. And there was that leather-and-spice smell again, driving me crazy.

"Lucia, do I smell like him? Like that aftershave or whatever it is he wears?"

She came forward and sniffed me like a big dog. "I can't smell anything," she said. "But then my nose is always stuffed up."

A while later, halfway through the drink, I began a litany of unhappy complaints. I noted foggily that my tolerance to alcohol must definitely be waning. I couldn't believe I was telling Lucia in detail about Alex's ex-wife Mimi and her order of protection.

"I fucking hate that he didn't tell me!" I cried in conclusion.

"I'd be a little more concerned about what he did to her," Lucia intoned.

"He said he didn't do anything to her."

Lucia just stared at me. "Right. One word of advice . . ." She popped another mushroom in her mouth and chewed it with great relish. "Forget it."

"That's two words!"

Patrick, who had been eavesdropping on the twists and turns of our lives for the past several years, came over with two fresh, frozen drinks and set them in front of us on little white napkins.

"Congratulations," he said to me. "These are on the house."

How could I say no? It was unthinkable. So we sat there and discussed marriage in general, and mine in particular, with Patrick, who from time to time would empty the bottom of his margarita blender into our glasses after he'd filled an order, until it occurred to me, sometime after the dinner crowd had dispersed, that I was drunk. Alex would be trying to call from Mexico. How many hours ago had I left home? Perhaps four . . . There would be at least five hang-ups on the answering machine by the time I got home. He would think I was having an affair. I felt guilty for no reason.

I put a quarter in the phone and called his voice mail at work.

"Hi, Alex," I enunciated very clearly. "Listen, I'm with Lucia on the West Side. She is on the verge of a mental collapse—I may end up staying on her couch tonight. Well. Good-night. I love you."

With that, I hung up and breathed a sigh of relief. I went back to the bar and bought a pack of cigarettes from Patrick, who reminded me that I had quit smoking over a year ago. Alex had once said that it was a good thing I didn't smoke because the taste of tobacco in a woman's mouth made him feel sick.

"What the hell," I said. "It's just one night."

"Gimme one," Lucia said, reaching for the pack. "You know what's wrong, Celeste?" she said in her saturnine way. "You're getting cold feet."

On Wednesday a Federal Express package arrived from Lucia— twenty individually gift-wrapped pairs of socks; gold socks, silver socks, neon socks, gym socks, socks with stars and stripes, in fact, every kind of sock imaginable. Her note read: "Celeste, for your cold feet."

I was laughing with a certain amount of uneasiness when the phone rang. It was Alex in Mexico.

"Hey listen, I want you to come meet me down here."

"Down here where?"

"Well, in Mexico. This deal just went through between Grupo Telemedia and Chadwick Broadcasting and these Mexican guys are really happy. They offered me airline tickets and a great place to stay for a week. It's a resort they own somewhere near Matlan. Best diving in the Western Hemisphere. I'll fly to Matlan from Mexico City. Meet you at the airport."

A free trip to Mexico. I'd never traveled on the spur of the moment in my life. "But what about my kids up in Harlem? I have class with them next Tuesday."

"Your *kids*?" he said with a chuckle. "They won't even notice. It's *spring,* the term's almost over. They don't want to be writing poetry in this weather."

It was true that they were getting harder and harder to control and their attention span was shrinking. On days like that they ran my battery down so low, I came home wondering what the good of it was anyway.

"Come on, Celeste, let your hair down," Alex said. "It's beautiful down here."

I decided to call Ellie Horowitz, their teacher, and find out if I could reschedule my class for Thursday or Friday of next week. When that turned out to be fine, I had no more excuses.

*   *   *

THE AERO ZAPATA plane descended toward Matlan in a torrential thunder and lightning storm. A crack of lightning split open the charcoal-colored sky. It struck the wing, which sizzled white and neon blue in the darkness. I screamed, jumping out of my seat.

I closed my eyes and saw the plane falling, falling, and all the people screaming, bags tumbling down on our heads—and then the crash, the explosion and death. I envisioned my father and Anna hearing the news over the phone, their faces draining of color as they attempted to react without embarrassing themselves. How would Alex respond?

The thought of oblivion did not seem unpleasant or threatening, especially since no one would ever blame me for dying. The plane swooped low and then at the last minute rose again and continued circling and shuddering in the storm. A child in the back began to scream. Across the aisle a woman held a rosary in her hands, her lips moving silently. The pilot tried another pass at landing, but he pulled the plane up once again and circled. It took four attempts before he managed to continue his descent and land. When the plane came to its screeching halt there were loud cheers and clapping.

Alex rushed toward me as I came through the gate. My knees gave way just as his big arms encircled me.

He drove the rented VW Golf on the two-lane road through the steaming, squat jungle toward the ruins of Chichén Itzá. Alex calculated the miles and his speed on his new dive watch, determining exactly how long it would take us to get to the hotel, so that we could see the ruins in the afternoon. On our way to Hol Cha the next day, we would need to leave by dawn to see the ruins of Cobá. Hol Cha, Alex had learned from his Mexican business associates, was one of the last great secret diving meccas on the east coast. The lagoon was so small, it did not even warrant a mention in the guidebook, which excited Alex, because it meant fewer divers to threaten the delicate reefs. Alex told me he had learned to dive on the Great Barrier Reef while on a business trip to Australia.

"Great white sharks live there," I muttered apprehensively.

"Didn't see any," he said with a smile. He told me that now he never missed an occasion to dive. His favorite diving experience so far had been a two-hundred-and-fifty-foot chasm off of Andros Island.

"You get narced out at a hundred and fifty feet," he said excitedly. "It's like being bombed under water."

"You're shitting me, right?" I said.

"I shit you not."

This is an improvement, I thought quickly. *He didn't tell me not to swear.*

We drove on, pursued by thunderstorms that clattered above our heads and then galloped off, leaving behind a dazzling blue sky and thirsty sun. The steaming road and jungle glittered in the haze like a fairyland half-shrouded in clouds. By two o'clock the earth was baked dry and we arrived at Chichén Itzá in a swirl of dust. The world seemed empty of people.

We waited for a long time at the front desk in the quiet, airy hotel for someone to show us to a room. There was no ceiling over much of the courtyard and the hallways were like balconies, open to the sky and jungle and in the distance, the great pyramids. Alex wanted to go to the site immediately, but I thought it was too hot. It would be stupid to get sunstroke on our first day. He agreed.

Our large room had clay-colored walls and a smooth tile floor. I stretched out on the double bed and listened to the hot wind blow through the wooden slats in the shutters. Alex opened his big, manly, leather overnight bag and that leather-and-spice smell, now cool, piquant, wafted out at me. He stretched out alongside me and lightly touched my breasts through my T-shirt. My mouth watered with desire, not just for him, but for all the world's exotic, far-off places, like this one, where I had never been. Alex's soft, wet mouth pressed mine. I pulled the shirt over my head and lay back, a stranger to myself.

We followed the dirt path through a tunnel of squat, thorny jungle trees and stepped out onto a flat, sandy expanse as enormous storm clouds tumbled in overhead. The city of pyramids stood before us, the same purple-gray color as the clouds. A gust of wind blew dust everywhere. I had read that the whole city of Chichén Itzá had been excavated from the jungle by Western archeologists, and reconstructed stone by stone to appear exactly as it had over two thousand years ago. A bolt of lightning cracked the sky, and for a moment I was acutely aware of the millisecond of geological time in which I existed. What had happened to the arrogant, powerful people who had built this place? I thought of home, and wondered if a new culture of indomitable giants would be digging the ruins of our skyscrapers out of the wilderness someday.

No rain fell and the storm moved on. In moments the sky was blue again and the land and the pyramids appeared dust-colored and tranquil.

I gripped the enormous corroded chain that ran up the center of the steep, high steps of Kukulcan, the largest pyramid, and facing forward, I began to climb, following Alex upward. I was out of breath long before I reached the platform at the top, on which stood a little square edifice with arched doorways on two opposing walls, a temple or shrine to the ancient gods. I rose to my full height and, looking down, realized I couldn't see the steps I had just climbed. The platform appeared to be suspended in the sky. I broke into a sweat, convinced that I was going to fall hundreds of feet to the thick jungle canopy below. My knees collapsed and I found myself crawling into the little shrine. The whole pyramid seemed to be rocking madly as if it were trying to shake me off.

I'd had a nightmare like this before, of being at the top of something extremely high that was rocking, and holding on with my fingertips, unable to climb down. I crouched in a corner, my back pressed into the wall, and squeezed my eyes shut.

"Just look at this view, Celeste!" Alex called from outside. I could hear the click of his camera.

"Alex," I said, but my voice was hardly a whisper. "Alex!" I cried hoarsely.

He came in and stood over me. "Montezuma's revenge already?"

"No, it's not that. I—I can't see the steps. I can't move."

"You're acrophobic. You have to reason your way out of this, Celeste. The fear is all in your mind. Tourists have been climbing this thing for years."

"It doesn't matter. I can't."

He sat down beside me and crossed his legs. "This happens to people all the time. They never have it, then one day they do. It's nothing to worry about. But you're going to have to get down off this thing, Celeste. So let's just talk about it for a minute. There's that chain down the middle of the steps, remember the chain?" He was talking to me as if I were five years old. "You can just keep listening to me and go backwards. Back yourself right off this thing."

A memory flashed through my mind. It is summer and I am nine. My mother and I have left my grandmother in Bordeaux and we are in Italy, traveling from city to city, spending her meager savings in fancy hotels and restaurants and clothes shops. In Pisa, we walk around the very top of the Leaning Tower. This is before they put up a railing. My mother leads me by the hand. I feel no fear at all because she won't let me fall.

I started to cry.

"I can't." The terror and the panic were familiar.

"Give me your hand," Alex said gently, calmly. I forced myself to give him my hand.

He guided me backwards and I crawled with eyes closed to the edge of the platform and onto the steps. He placed my hands on the chain and said, "Go." I could hear people's voices, questioning, curious, but nothing mattered at that moment but getting back down to the ground. Slowly, my face to the stone, eyes screwed shut, I crawled downward. As I slowly, cautiously moved backward Alex talked, his calm voice complimenting me on how well I was handling the situation.

When we reached the bottom, it was a good five minutes before I was able to speak.

Alex gazed at me with a mixture of concern and curiosity. This was not the Celeste he knew. This was a surprise to him. I felt vulnerable, and that made me angry.

*   *   *

I WAS LYING PEACEFULLY on a towel on the hot, white sand reading *Wide Sargasso Sea,* a better choice, certainly, than Proust. Just behind me was our large, whitewashed cabin with a thatched roof, one of maybe ten, but almost all were empty this time of year. Above my head the palms rustled in the breeze, and tiny waves licked at the shore. Suddenly Alex came running down the beach, back from his first excursion to the Hol Cha dive shop, and I could tell by the look of excitement on his face that I wasn't going to like what he had to say.

"For only two hundred and fifty dollars you can pass the PADI certification course in three days," he said, not even slightly out of breath, "and you can be my dive buddy forever!"

My heart started pounding. "Oh, Alex," I said lightly. "I think I'll just sit here on the beach and read."

His face collapsed in disappointment. "Celeste, just try it. Once. For me, please?"

Feeling put-upon and under scrutiny, I consented. After yesterday's fiasco, I didn't want him to think I was a wimp. "Okay, but if I hate it, I'm not going to go through with it."

"Good girl!" he cried. "If you absolutely hate it, you can quit. At least you'll have tried, right?"

"Right."

Dive number one: The dive master, Dave Francisco, was as big as a baby whale, and so serene he reminded me of a Buddhist monk. We were floating in the perfectly clear, calm bay in six feet of water. I wore the cumbersome scuba vest called a "buoyancy compensator," which was pumped full of air. Strapped to it on my back was a heavy air tank. The weight belt, cinched tight around my waist, dug into my sides. He was telling me in a jovial voice that he was from Santa Cruz,

California, and that Hol Cha had the best diving he'd ever seen in his life. For love of diving, he'd given up civilization and now lived in a trailer on the beach with a pet iguana and a parrot for company. He said that he had better conversations with the parrot than with most humans he knew, and that although the parrot's English was still limited, his Spanish was flawless.

I kept nodding, smiling, while telling myself there was nothing to worry about, all was well. I was sweating so heavily that my mask had already fogged up. *I don't want to fail and look like a coward and a fool!* I thought.

Dave gave me the okay sign, which he had just taught me, index finger and thumb in an O; I returned it, and abruptly he let the air out of my vest. I sank to the bottom.

I knew that I was supposed to breathe through the regulator that I held clamped between my teeth for dear life, but I couldn't seem to. My lungs seemed to explode, and wriggling like a dying fish, I paddled frantically for the surface. My dive master pulled me panting and heaving toward the beach. I washed up at Alex's feet. I looked up and saw his crestfallen face.

"Don't worry about it," my dive master said, "this often happens the first time out."

Yes, of course, I thought, *it must happen all the time because what fool would want to do this?*

"You want to take a break?" Dave asked.

I shook my head. I'd rather have drowned than face Alex, so I pushed off and we paddled back out for try number two.

This time it was only a question of pride winning out over sheer terror. I forced myself to breathe through the regulator. The air felt cool and very dry in my mouth and seemed to rush into my lungs and expand there without any effort on my part. A strange sensation, breathing under water. Listening to my lungs working was even stranger. I sat on the bottom and thought, *Okay, so far so good,* and did not see a thing but sand flying around and my dive master's masked face and wavy black beard. He kept giving me the okay sign, so I figured I was doing fine—quite well, in fact, for a person with advanced agoraphobia, nascent acrophobia, and incipient hydrophobia.

Lunchtime. We sat at the al fresco bar under a thatched roof, and Alex was swearing to me that diving was one of the coolest, greatest experiences he'd ever had in his life.

"I want a margarita," I said, turning to the waiter. "Excuse me, sir? Could I have a margarita please?"

"You can't have a drink before your afternoon dive session," Alex said.

"I'm not going back this afternoon, Alex, so you'd better just shut up and leave me alone if you want me to continue doing this."

He sat there sulking as I sipped my drink, feeling like I'd won a small victory, though certainly not the war.

Fortified, with Alex long gone on his excursion, I decided to go back for my second dive. This time, after the drills, which involved taking off the vest under water, taking off the weight belt and putting it back on, and clearing my mask of water, my dive master led me on an underwater tour of the shallow bay. There were some beautiful little fish, indigo blue, gold, silver, rainbow-colored, and several larger yellowtail snappers who were fearless and came right up to my mask and peered at my face. I also saw a flounder and a small stingray that quickly skittered off, leaving a tiny cloud of sand. It was interesting, but a religious awakening it was not.

We returned to the dive shop and there was Alex with the other certified divers, elatedly discussing the five-foot moray eel they had scared out of its hole, that had sliced a bait fish in two with one snap of its jaws.

"How was it, Celeste?" he asked me hopefully.

"It was fine," I mumbled, rinsing out my equipment in the freshwater trough, like my dive master had shown me.

"Give it a chance," Alex said, and squeezed my shoulder.

* * *

WITH EVERY DIVE, the underwater drills grew more complicated and depth increased; I had to take the regulator out of my mouth and blow bubbles, inflate my BC through my mouth, share a regulator with my dive master, and ascend slowly. I had to take my mask off completely and put it back on, emptying it of water by blowing air out my nose. All these drills, he told me, were so I would know what to do in case anything ever went wrong.

"Like what?" I asked him.

"Oh," he said in that calm voice, "you know, getting caught on some coral at the bottom, or running out of air, things like that."

"Does it happen often?"

"Nah," he said vaguely.

* * *

THE NEXT DAY, I had my first open water dive. After the compass drills, Dave and I cruised around in about forty-five feet of water. We came upon a sea turtle swimming lazily through the deep blue. We tried to follow, but it moved away too fast.

Back on the motorboat, Dave told me that this species of sea turtle was almost extinct, due mostly to overfishing. There was a rescue operation taking place just down the beach. Experts were gathering the turtle eggs and delivering them to hatcheries, where the baby turtles were kept until they were big enough to fend for themselves in the harsh world.

That afternoon, I passed my openwater test, and afterwards saw the most incredible thing—three four-foot spotted eagle rays swimming together like birds in formation, their black-spotted wings flapping in slow motion, disturbing nothing. They were so unlike anything I'd ever seen, they could have been from another planet, another galaxy entirely.

When we returned to the dive shop, Dave handed me the written exam to take home and told me with a grin that I was on my honor not to cheat. Alex did offer to help me with the math problems involving the dive tables. But that was only after I threw the PADI book against the wall and threatened to tear up the exam.

Later that evening, Dave, Alex, and I celebrated at the outdoor bar.

"Tomorrow you'll be a certified diver, and you'll love it, you'll see," Alex said. He was so proud of me he let me order a fourth margarita.

"Mm-hm," I said.

"You know, you really should try a night dive while you're here," Dave said.

"What a good idea!" Alex said.

"You're nuts," I cried. "I won't dive at night! In the dark!"

* * *

ALEX AWAKENED in a good mood and stated that as recompense for my passing the PADI test, we would drive to Matlan and spend the day exploring.

The main street was lined with tall buildings and the tourist shops carried overpriced Mexican clothes and amulets. We bought presents for our families, earrings for me, and a big white cotton shirt for Alex.

Gazing up at the tall hotels along the beach, I imagined them under water. "How tall is that building, Alex?"

"Oh, about a hundred feet."

Tomorrow I would be diving as deep as that building was tall. My heart began to beat hard, my mouth went dry.

At sunset, we found a crowded bar on the beach that had an uncrowded veranda. Why would they huddle inside, I wondered, when this was so much nicer?

Just as the waitress went off with our order, a loudspeaker announced the beginning of the bathing suit contest. Everyone began to cheer and shout. Annoyed, I looked out at the horizon in the fading light. The water and sky were the same silvery-taupe color, one a shimmering reflection of the other.

About twenty feet in front of us, a lone couple lay stretched out on the beach. The fellow had straight brown hair, the ends sun-bleached to pale gold. He was leaning back on his elbows, his large shoulders hunched. There was something familiar about the folds of skin around his neck and the angular shape of his shoulder blades. He turned his face toward the girl and my breath stopped.

"What's the matter?" Alex asked.

"Nothing. I think maybe I know that guy." I gestured with my chin. "Remember Sebastian from the picture? Well, I think that's his brother. I'm not sure."

I was sure, I just wasn't sure I wanted to talk to him. I hadn't seen Nathan for over seven years.

"Go take a look," Alex suggested.

I got up, slipped off my sandals, and walked on the soft sand that was fine and cool. I skirted the couple but watched them in my peripheral vision, and went down to the water. They were kissing now, and he was not paying attention to me at all. The water was so warm, it was warmer than the air. *Should I go up to him?* I wondered.

The sky glowed a strange greenish hue in the west. To the east, the world was darkening quickly to purple. I waited a moment, and then, resolved, turned and started back. They did not look up from their kiss.

I sat down across from Alex and sipped my margarita. I was strangely out of breath, as if I'd run a long way.

"So is it him?"

"I'm not sure."

"Why not call him, yell, 'Nathan,' and see if he turns around?"

Nathan took a long swig off his beer bottle and put it in the sand, next to several empties that stuck out at strange angles, like old gravestones.

I had once heard that it takes seven years to overcome heartbreak. I supposed that must be right. Seeing Nathan brought to mind again that December day during my sophomore midyear finals, when Sebastian called with the news of Sally's suicide, and how I sat in stunned silence until the phone rang again and it was Nathan, and upon hearing his voice, I decided to visit him up at Harvard.

Nine

AFTER THE CALLS from Sebastian and Nathan, I sat for a long time in the dormitory kitchen. Everyone had gone to the libraries or to exams and I was alone. When I stood up finally, my knees were shaky and my head whirling. I went to my room and gathered up my books, and walked across the frozen green to the Science Library, which stayed open all night. There was no need for me to stay in there all day and then pull an all-nighter, I was prepared for my exams. But I had to keep my mind occupied.

I fell asleep in a leather chair sometime near dawn, and dreamed I was standing at one end of Sally's overpass, behind a tall fence. I couldn't see the road below, but I could hear cars rushing by. Across the way, Sally was walking slowly toward me, down a green sloping lawn. She was wearing shorts and a T-shirt, despite the cold. The noise of cars was deafening. She was taking her time crossing the overpass, looking around as if enjoying the scenery. Then she smiled at me and beckoned for me to join her. Still smiling, she lifted one leg over the railing, then the other, then gripping the rail firmly behind her, took an indecisive step. My fists beat against the fence. She turned her face toward me once more, but it was no longer her face, it was my mother's, and her expression was so desolate, so filled with pain, that I tried to cry out, "No! Wait!" but my voice failed me. Then she let go, and I started screaming. I woke up soaked through with sweat. There was no one around; above the long empty stacks the fluorescent lights droned like beehives.

Shaken, I went home and got into bed. I had the same dream again, but this time Sally was running. She did not stop, or seem to notice me standing on the other end of the bridge. Gripping the overpass railing, she swung both legs over at once, without hesitating. At the last moment she turned her head toward me, and again, it was my mother's face, wearing that look of utter hopelessness and devastation.

* * *

WITH ONLY TWO DAYS left before Christmas Eve, I phoned Anna and told her that I had some work to make up at school and I'd arrive home in time for Christmas Eve dinner. I ran back to my dorm after my last exam and packed up my car and drove up to Cambridge.

A wet and heavy snow was falling when I parked at the end of Nathan's street of old brownstones. My stomach was cramping with anticipation. As I locked up it occurred to me that I hadn't thought of Sally all day—only Nathan and what it would be like to be with him.

The door to his apartment was open. I walked in. Nathan sat on a tired old couch in the small living room, framed by his two longhaired roommates. Nathan was taking a hit off a foot-long bong pipe. He looked me over blandly, holding his breath, and exhaled a cloud of smoke that enveloped his head.

"Hey, Celeste," he said, and coughed. He pounded his chest with a fist. "Take off your coat. Have a seat."

I felt ill at ease. The three of them were looking at me in silence. The short walk in the snow had drenched my coat. My boots dripped onto the floor, my hair was plastered to my head in long patches. He introduced me to the two fellows, who shook my hand and left, muttering some excuse.

"Want a hit?" he asked me.

I shook my head. He put the bong away behind the couch. "How about a drink of something? Rum? Vodka?"

"Either."

He got up and went into the kitchen. I heard him opening and closing cabinets, the fridge.

"Nathan, do you think this is a mistake? Because I can leave."

"Absolutely not."

He came out extending a drink to me. It was dark rum and tonic with a wedge of lime floating in it. I took a sip and looked at him.

"What happened to Sally really sucks," he said. "But it wasn't your fault."

I went to the window and looked out at the wet flakes falling heavily against the darkness. Only a few cars were left on the street, there was an end-of-the-semester feeling in the air.

He walked up behind me and began nuzzling the back of my wet head. His arms reached out and held the windowsill on both sides. The old longing came back, hard as a knot, powerful, pulsating in my lower abdomen. *So this is it*, I thought.

He left and returned a moment later with a warm towel, probably left on a radiator. He began to dry my hair with both hands, encircling my head with the towel. He led me back to the couch and we sat down facing each other. He kept rubbing my head until my hair was dry and fluffed out wildly around my head.

"There," he said. He looked at me closely. "When you were fourteen you had a baby face, with little pudgy cheeks."

Abruptly I remembered the discussions he used to have with my brother about girls. "Did you ever screw Olivia?" I asked.

"Who's Olivia?"

"You know, the Catholic one who wore all the makeup and gave blow jobs."

He laughed. "You remember everything! That was just talk. We *heard* she gave blow jobs."

"What about your IQ, was that true?"

"That was true," he said solemnly, as if he were admitting something unpleasant about himself.

"So what was your score?"

"One-eighty." There was a pause. "What's your brother doing these days?"

"Oh, he's going to go to law school in the fall—finally—like my dad always wanted."

"Surprise, surprise," Nathan said. "Sally was sick, Celeste. You couldn't do anything for her."

"I have these dreams—" I started, but couldn't finish. "Oh my God," I put my face down on his lap and was overcome by tears. His hands passed gently through my hair as I cried.

"I've thought about you so much," he said. "Once I even borrowed a friend's car and started down to your school, but I chickened out. I figured, oh shit, I don't know. I figured Bass would never forgive me."

"He will," I said. "He always forgives everybody."

He lifted me easily and carried me into his bedroom. It looked just like his room had at home, with a dark blue spread and bookshelves all along one wall, lined two deep with books. Another wall was covered with photographs: his family standing in front of the Eiffel Tower, in a market in Marrakech, Nathan and Jack and me at one of Sally's running meets. He's shoving an ice-cream cone in my nose, and Jack is laughing. Sebastian must have taken the picture.

Nathan smelled exactly as he had so many years ago—of tobacco, of pot, of some mild soap, of his skin-smell, which was a little like a brand-new clothbound book.

He was tender but not deferential. He lifted my sweater over my head, then unsnapped my bra in one swift click. He lowered it off my shoulders, staring at me without guile. I felt embarrassed and crossed my arms. He moved them away and started licking my nipples slowly, going from one to the other as if they were two different flavors and he couldn't make up his mind.

For me there had been only Sebastian and a boy at school who'd walked me home after we'd both had quite a lot to drink at a party. But there had never been this overwhelming feeling of wanting someone so much. I now felt I understood *Romeo and Juliet* and *Tristan and Isolde*. Their behavior seemed oh so sane. I believed then that there was always a price to pay for great love, that no one ever got anything that extraordinary for free.

I wondered if Nathan felt it too. Or if this was just the way he was with everyone he slept with. I felt crazy jealous, and afraid.

"Nathan, stop—I—"

"Shh," he said. "Don't get up, Celeste."

Off came my jeans and panties in his firm hands. I lay back and watched him as he knelt between my legs.

"Nathan, the door—"

"Oh yes, the door," he said, and got up to close it. In a moment he was back. He pulled me by the hips to the edge of the bed and pushed my knees up to my chest.

"From now on it's just us and whatever happened before doesn't matter," he said, and began to lick me. Soon I was telling him to fuck me, which he did, by pulling me onto his cock as he sat with his legs spread on the floor. It seemed that we shared one mouth, one heart, one sex organ. Like the intersecting circles I used to love to draw with my compass as a child, each overlapping section belonged no more to one than to the other. Our outlines appeared to have merged too and I could no longer tell where I ended and where he began.

* * *

"**CELESTE?**" Alex asked, reaching for my hand across the table. "Is something wrong?"

All at once, I noticed how dark it had become. The couple had not budged. Nathan placed his large tanned leg over the girl's thighs, and she laughed as he whispered in her ear. Inside the bar the patrons were shouting and jeering at the bathing suit contestants.

"No. I'm sorry. I was just wondering if it's him. I haven't seen him in six or seven years. Anyway, he looks busy right now."

I watched them, feeling aroused but not jealous, just curiously detached.

The winner of the competition was announced. She came outside and stood on the veranda among her admirers. Loud voices congratulated her. I turned to look. She was in a string bikini and had blond hair piled high on her head. She was apparently a bodybuilder. Her muscles looked chiseled and hard.

"God, that guy and his girlfriend look like they're about to do the wild thing right here on the beach," Alex said, laughing.

"Come on, let's get another drink," I said.

"I thought you hated this place."

"It's all right."

The breeze raised the hairs on my arms and I shivered.

* * *

IN MY MIND'S eye I could still see Nathan's college room perfectly.

His bed was a wreck, the blankets and sheets on the floor, and I sat hugging my knees and shivering as he returned carrying drinks and jumped up on the bed. He pulled the sheets and blankets off the floor and arranged them carefully around me and then around himself. We sat there, looking at each other in silence. His hair was hanging down in front of his eyes, making him look youthful and innocent.

"I love you, Celeste."

"Not as much as I love you. And anyway, I've loved you longer."

"Bullshit," he said, and laughed. "What do you want for dinner?"

"Do we have to go out?"

"No, Chinese or pizza delivers."

"Chinese!"

We stayed in bed for two days. At some point the roommates must have come and gathered their things and left for Christmas. I never heard or saw them again and didn't care at all if they heard us. We never left the room except to use the kitchen or the bathroom. On the first morning he ran us a bath with strong-smelling sea-kelp bath salts and he carried me in and deposited me into the old, high tub that had feet. Naked, his penis swinging from side to side, he went out and returned carrying a frosty bottle of Veuve Cliquot and two tall champagne glasses. He'd been working part-time at a liquor store and had hoarded quite a reserve.

He got into the tub, handed me the glasses, and popped the cork on the bottle. The champagne flowed into the bath. He filled our glasses and we drank. Then he put the bottle and the glasses on the floor and began to wash me from head to foot with a soft sea sponge.

As I lay back in the warm, steamy water, he told me that he was thinking about quitting school and traveling. He wanted to go to Central and South America and study those cultures by *being* there, not by reading *One Hundred Years of Solitude* and learning Spanish by parroting a gringo.

"Would you come with me?" he asked.

I just stared at him and smiled, dazed.

"I don't know," I finally said.

The mind, he told me, was a great incomprehensible mystery.

"Magic exists, it's just a manifestation of the side of the mind we don't understand. About a year ago I taught myself to read the Tarot. I've read every fucking book on the Tarot I could find." He lifted my foot and began to scrub the bottom. "The Queen of Swords kept coming up in my spread," he continued. "I kept wondering who the hell she was. This unknown Queen of Swords. What were she and the Death card doing in my spread? And the Eight and Nine and Ten of Swords— nightmares, insomnia, worry kept coming up. Love, the Queen loves the King of Swords, that's me. Well, you're the Queen. That's absolutely sure. Air sign, a worrier, one who has suffered losses and is going to suffer more of them in the future. Definitely you."

"Jesus, you sound like Sally, Nathan. Stop already."

"Do you want me to read your cards for you?"

"No!" I cried, unglued by his description of his cards.

After carrying me back to bed, he stood naked at the stove and made corned beef hash and fried eggs. He brought them in on a tray and we ate in silence. I thought I had never tasted anything so good in my life.

I knew that if an angel offered me a chance to be anyplace in the universe, I would not leave.

* * *

ALEX HAD BEEN talking but I hadn't heard a word he'd said. Just as the waitress brought us another margarita, Nathan and the girl stood and playfully swatted the sand off each other's bodies. They put on T-shirts and began to collect their empty bottles.

"Nathan!" I shouted, without thought. He straightened and made a slow circle, looking around, tottering as if he were standing on a rope bridge. The girl looked right at me; taking his arm, she pointed. Nathan pushed his hair away from his eyes with the back of his hand and squinted. I waved. His face lit up, and he laughed. He came toward us, weaving slightly, and said, "Well, I'll be goddamned."

The girl walked up behind him. Her tousled, sun-bleached blond hair hung in front of her unlined, darkly tanned face. She was young, perhaps twenty, and her skin was smooth and taut.

"Giovanna," he said, "this is—a very old friend of mine."

"Old is how I feel," I said.

Giovanna looked from him to me to Alex with a perplexed but friendly expression. Nathan said to her in Italian, "This woman is the only woman I've ever truly loved." Giovanna smiled understandingly.

"Giovanna's from Milan," he said to us. "I'm helping her with her English and she's helping me with my Italian."

"I see," I said with good humor.

She said, "She's very beautiful," in Italian and laughed. Alex stood up and extended his hand over the veranda's railing.

"I'm Celeste's fiancé, Alex Laughton."

"No way!" said Nathan.

"Way," said Alex.

"Well, congratulations!" Nathan said. He looked Alex over carefully, but then his eyes focused on me with a fierce intensity. "Of all the places in the world to run into you. Come have dinner with us! A little place down the road."

Alex called the waitress over and paid the bill with his American Express platinum card, and I felt ashamed.

"Sounds good to me," Alex said. "But we've got a long drive back to Hol Cha, so we shouldn't stay out too late."

We followed Nathan's Suzuki motorcross bike down a winding dirt road through the canopy of trees. Nathan was flying over bumps and holes, raising dust and zigzagging all over the place.

"He's a wild one, isn't he?" Alex said.

* * *

I WAS NINETEEN when I spent those two days in Cambridge with Nathan, and up until then, there had been only one other time in my life when I'd felt completely happy to be alive—the trip my mother and I took around Italy when I was nine. Both times had been colored by a certain recklessness, by heavy drinking (in Italy, by my mother; in Cambridge, by Nathan and me), and by an intangible sense of impending doom. On both, we seemed to be attempting to stop time; but what we feared from the future, I had no idea.

Late the second night in Nathan's bed, I curled into a ball and hid, wrapped tightly in a cocoon of sheets, frozen, unable to express the pain I was feeling. The next day was Christmas Eve, and I would have to leave him. He stretched out alongside me and held me firmly, not saying a word.

"I'm supposed to fly to Houston tomorrow morning," he finally said. "But if you want, I'll just blow it off. We can stay here. Or I'll come home with you. Is that what you want? I'll do whatever you want."

"And then what?" I asked. "And then school starts again and you'll be gone."

"Time and distance are just concepts," he said. "It's all relative. Nothing on this planet short of death could stop me from being with you."

My heart fluttered with joy at his romantic words, but in my mind, I clearly heard the word, *Bullshit. Bullshit. Bullshit.*

* * *

ANNA DID NOT say much when I called to tell her I was bringing Nathan MacKenna home for Christmas. The news of Sally's death had given me a certain leeway. Driving down I-95 with Nathan, I felt that I'd been given a reprieve from the grayness of reality, and I decided to try not to think about the future for at least a few days.

We stopped in town to buy presents for my family. Snow was falling. The sounds of Salvation Army bells filled the frosty air, which bubbled and popped and tickled the nose like champagne. For once, the couples and children did not make me feel lonely and excluded, for

I too felt loved. Nathan held my hand as we gazed, stupefied, into store windows.

"What do you want for Christmas, Nathan?"

"You. Just you. Every night, all night long. I swear I've never felt this good in my life." He kissed my face, my hands, his warm mouth leaving wet trails on my skin that stung in the frosty air.

Later, we got into my car loaded down with silly gifts for my family, and kissed again, our thick coats keeping a distance between us. Slowly Nathan slipped his hands inside my coat, encircling me tightly. Snow was falling heavily, and I felt like we were kids kissing behind a curtain at a party.

Our lips separated, we breathed in the cold air, looking at each other in silence. On the sidewalk just outside the window, Mr. and Mrs. Newlyn—Sally's parents—materialized out of the snow. They were walking slowly, arm in arm.

"Oh, my God," I whispered.

Nathan looked. They were staring straight before them, as if focusing on some point in the distance. Their faces had aged twenty years since I'd last seen them, the lines hardened into masks of perseverance that revealed their grief and shock. They looked like refugees from a war-torn country. Were they out Christmas shopping? They still had another daughter, and a grandchild. People, I realized, didn't stop living when tragedy struck. It stopped my breath. A gust of wind blew snow against their faces, and Mrs. Newlyn winced and gripped her coat collar shut over her throat. Mr. Newlyn put his arm protectively around her back and guided her slowly past our car windows.

I never saw them again. I wrote them a formal, careful letter on Christmas day, and received in response a printed letter that they had apparently sent out to friends and family, signed by Mrs. Newlyn in her girlish, rounded script.

Later that night, Nathan, my brother Jack, then twenty-two and about to enter law school, and I were watching a late-night rerun of *Star Trek* in the den when the phone rang, and I heard Anna answer it. Shortly she opened the swinging door to the kitchen in her bathrobe and slippers.

"It's for you, Celeste. It's Sebastian calling to wish you a merry Christmas."

Nathan and I looked at each other. My brother grinned evilly.

I went into the kitchen, picked up the receiver, took a deep breath, and said hello.

"How are you doing?" he asked. "I was worried about you after I called you the other day. I called later on, but no one seemed to know where you were."

"Bass, listen. Nathan's here."

"With Jack?" Sebastian asked evenly.

"With me."

"Okay," he said slowly. "Okay. I understand."

"Do you want to talk to him?"

"Does he want to talk to me?"

I didn't know if he did or not. "Yes," I said.

I went out to the den. "Nathan," I said. He got up and followed me into the kitchen, where the receiver lay on the counter. He picked it up.

"Hi, Bass," Nathan said evenly.

I left him alone. I don't know what Nathan and Sebastian said to each other; I never asked. I went back to *Star Trek,* the episode where Captain Kirk has been thrown back in time. He's forced to decide between letting the woman he loves die, thus saving humanity; or saving her, which by some cruel twist of fate would cause the Nazis to win the war, changing the course of history.

Nathan came back looking solemn, his eyes dun-colored and impenetrable. His conversation with his brother did not stop him from sneaking into my room later and pulling the mattress off my bed and laying it on the floor. He pulled me down on top of it and pulled off my nightgown with his smooth, unwavering hands.

* * *

THE MEXICAN RESTAURANT was tiny and had a dirt floor. Christmas lights were strung across the tops of the screen windows. As we entered Alex warned me not to drink the water.

We sat down, Alex and I on one side of the rickety table, Nathan and Giovanna on the other. Alex and Nathan glared at each other calmly, like the two skinny wild dogs at Hol Cha who circled each other tirelessly in their eternal search for food.

Nathan was apparently a regular, and chatted in Spanish with the waitress. He ordered four shots of Quervo Gold. Giovanna smiled all the time and seemed to be listening, although how much she understood is anyone's guess. I decided to pretend I didn't understand Italian in case they said anything that I should know.

The shots arrived. Nathan shook some salt onto the back of his hand

and raised his glass. He licked the salt and said, "To you guys." I licked the salt from my hand and we clinked glasses and drank. Alex dispensed entirely with the salt thing, tipped his glass, and downed the shot without the slightest change of expression. I stuck a wedge of lime in my mouth and sucked on it. The tequila finally hit bottom and exploded, sending a wave of warmth through my legs and chest. Nathan ordered four more, and a round of beers.

"I just read a book," Nathan said, "about the Burgess Shale."

We looked at him in silence.

"This guy who wrote it, I studied with him at Harvard for about twenty minutes. It's the best goddamn book I ever read. Well, one of them."

"I think I read a review of it in the *Times*," Alex said. "They found some strange fossils there, right?"

"Right. Well, the proposition is as follows: Homo sapiens evolved due to a total accident of fate. This shale is chock-full of previously unrecorded, presently nonexistent phyla. Like twenty-six varieties or something. There are only four phyla in the entire insect kingdom, by the way. Totally weird stuff—so why did all these phyla die off suddenly and this one little wormlike creature evolve into man?"

"But one book doesn't discount hundreds of years of scientific study and almost two thousand years of theology," Alex said. I wanted another shot.

"It sure as shit does," Nathan said. "People didn't listen to Galileo at first, did they?"

"How's Sebastian?" I asked, changing the subject.

Nathan looked away for a moment, his eyes vague. "Paquita! *Quatro mas, por favor!*

"Bass is fine," he said, turning back to me. "Navy's putting him through law school. He married a girl—get this—named Sebastianna. Sebastian and Sebastianna! Isn't that the greatest!" He slapped the table and laughed. Paquita set down four fresh shots, and Nathan slid one toward me and one toward Giovanna.

Alex drank his down and said, "That's it for me. I've got to drive."

"To Sebastian," Nathan said, his eyes misty and unreadable. We salted our hands and tossed back the shots. The warm glow was beginning to darken the corners of my vision, and to my relief, the pounding of my heart was finally subsiding. I wanted him to order more.

"Paquita!" Nathan yelled. *"Tres mas, por favor."*

"Don't overdo it, Celeste," Alex murmured in my ear.

When Paquita put the drinks down, Giovanna reached for hers hungrily and tossed it back without salt. Her enormous hair, sandy-colored and jungle-like, was falling across her eyes now. She looked at Nathan, then at Alex, and licked her lips.

My vision was closing in. The room became hazy and a feeling of goodwill toward all overcame me.

"I just got my scuba certification!" I cried out.

"No way!" Nathan said.

"Oh, yes, way," Alex said.

"You're pulling my chain, Celeste."

I felt Alex's back and arms tense beside me. I shook my head.

Nathan told us that he led dive tours for one of the local shops once in a while, when he needed cash. Mostly he bartended in one of the big hotels. This was not what I'd imagined for his future.

"The tourists are jerks, specially the Japanese," Nathan said. "They step all over the reefs!"

Paquita brought the menus and more shots. I had to close one eye in order to read the print.

"Yes, well, if I had to do it all over again," Nathan said, as if continuing a previous discussion, "I'd be a marine biologist. We're destroying our environment and it's so apparent in the ocean. Global warming is killing off the plankton and pretty soon we're going to be fucked, my friends, *fucked*! When I dive I never touch anything, not even empty shells," Nathan concluded gloomily.

Alex stared at him for a moment and said, "What a bunch of horseshit. I hunt, I fish. I pick up whatever I want when I'm diving."

I felt terribly confused.

"It's a miracle we're not living in a fucking wasteland. If everybody was like you, we would be," Nathan said.

"I'm going to the ladies' room," I said, and pushed my chair back. I found it difficult to walk.

"Don't put any toilet paper in the john!" Nathan yelled after me.

I heard Alex ask Giovanna, speaking very slowly and loudly, "Howa. Longa. You. Beena. Here?"

"Sree," she said. I glanced back. It looked like she was holding up three fingers.

Above the sink was a dirty mirror cracked down the middle. I turned on the faucet. The water was piss warm and smelled like sulfur. I splashed some on my forehead, and looking up, saw two fractured and disconnected sections of my face staring back at me. I couldn't remember what I was doing here. I leaned against the grimy wall to think.

* * *

THAT SPRING semester of my sophomore year, he was at my college more than his own, staying for long weekends that stretched from Thursday to Monday. Lying on my bed, he would read poems by Frederico García Lorca, Octavio Paz, Neruda, and César Vallejo; and sometimes Theodore Roethke, while I studied at the desk.

He'd read a verse or two aloud in a slow, undulating voice. Often it would be Lorca.

Great stars of white frost
come with the fish of darkness
that opens the road of dawn . . .

Although he never wrote his own papers, he thought I took too long to write mine and decided to help me. He asked me what had interested me most in *Anna Karenina,* and I said, "The death of Levin's brother."

"Okay, so we'll do a comparison between the death of Levin's brother and the death of the Master in *Master and Man.* That's short, you can read it in an hour. And we can throw in Ivan Ilych too." He thought for a few minutes, then dictated my opening and closing paragraphs. The paper began something like this: "In Tolstoy, Death comes wearing different masks. At times his face is that of the Grim Reaper; other times, an angel bringing an epiphany of light . . . "

Now it was a simple matter of filling in four pages of illustrative quotes. What before had taken me an entire weekend of working day and night to accomplish now took only an evening.

After reading my paper, my Russian Studies professor suggested that my senior thesis be an exploration of death throughout Tolstoy's fiction.

* * *

SOMETIMES, in the afternoon, we'd lie on my single bed and talk about concentration camps. My obsession with them had started long before my current class in Twentieth Century Europe. As a child I'd often dreamed of dying in a gas chamber.

"In another life, maybe you did," Nathan said.

He brought me books by Hannah Arendt and Primo Levi and told me about the different philosophies on the nature of survival. Nathan believed the writers who said that hope was the prisoner's worst enemy. Seeing a blade of grass on a spring day could kill a person, he told me gravely, whereas oblivion, nothingness, could keep you alive.

"You would have survived," I told him, "I know it."

"Who'd want to?" He shook his head. "I would never have allowed them to separate us. Fuck them, the sick sons of bitches. I would have refused and been beaten to death or shot," he said matter-of-factly.

Ten years had passed since that year, yet there were still certain songs I could not listen to without remembering those late winter days—the taste and smell of Nathan lying beside me, the faded daylight coming in through the blue Indian tapestries we'd tacked up for curtains over the large windows. There was Sting's clear, lamenting voice singing "The Bed's Too Big Without You," which amused us, given the size of the single bed in my dorm room; and the country and western singer Emmylou Harris, Nathan's favorite, singing,

There he goes gone again

same old story's gotta come to an end . . .

I knew that I was buying time. I knew he was flunking out and Harvard would ask him to leave sooner or later. But it was better to forget about such things. I still hoped he would somehow catch up on his courses. Our favorite songs were about heartbreak and being out in the world alone, but for the moment, I was neither, and the songs made me painfully grateful for my own happiness.

And years later, hearing even one bar of these old melodies on the radio, I still rushed to change the station, refusing to remember.

* * *

ON A CRISP, bright day in April, Nathan stopped by, unlocking the door with the extra key we'd made him. He looked like he'd stopped at a bar downtown after arriving on the Greyhound bus. It was the middle of the afternoon and I was sitting at my desk, reading for the third time Prince Andrew's death in *War and Peace*. Prince Andrew in his final moments dreams that Death is knocking at the door, and he feels he must get up and keep the door from opening, but he can't. When Death arrives, he is liberated from the weight of his earthly existence, and feels sorry for his loved ones who stand around his bed, weeping. He tries to be gentle and communicative with them, but knows he has already left them behind. Tears were streaming from my eyes.

I wiped them away quickly, watching Nathan as he crossed the room and sat heavily on the bed.

"I'm through," he said. "Harvard asked me to leave."

He told me he'd decided to go down to New Orleans for Jazz Fest, and then he was going to travel through Mexico to Central and then South America. Keep on going south till he hit the tip, he said with an uneasy smile. He didn't know when he'd be coming back.

"Come with me," he added after a pause. My pulse quickened.

"Why can't you just pass your fucking classes?" I cried. "You're smarter than everybody else! What the hell's wrong with you?"

"Why does it have to be bad? You can't imagine what a relief this is to me." His tone was calm, his eyes red-rimmed, as if he hadn't slept. His face was set, determined, his eyes inscrutable.

He's leaving me, I thought, panic-stricken. *He says he loves me but he's leaving me. If he loved me he would stay. Therefore he doesn't really love me.* Nothing would allow me to escape the logic of this syllogism and it made me sick to my stomach. My mouth went dry and I clutched the edge of my desk till my knuckles turned white.

"You're just going to leave me, that's it?" I said, my voice shaky.

"I asked you to come with me."

"I can't just walk away from my classes! From my life!"

"Why not?"

"Because this is where I'm *supposed* to be!"

"You want to marry a banker or a lawyer, is that it, Celeste? Because if that's true, it's not me you want."

I'd never thought that far ahead. I'd never really believed that our relationship would be allowed to last. It seemed to me that God was the biggest tyrant of all, lining people up at His giant station, separating wives and husbands, mothers and children, and deciding with the flick of a finger who would live and who would die. I watched Nathan as he sat at the edge of the bed looking at me. *He's weak*, I thought coldly. *He's unreliable.* Yet I was filled with admiration for him. What courage—to walk away from all responsibilities, to shrug off life's burdens, disregarding the consequences!

This is a fork in the road, I thought with awe. My consciousness seemed to lift out of me and float high above the scene. I felt detached, yet I was aware of the enormity of my next words, whatever they might be. Two futures stretched before me and nothing in the distance was clear. I wanted to know the outcome. I weighed the choices coolly. Life on the road with him. I had some money from my mother, much more than he probably had—his parents were paying for Harvard, but they had no intention of subsidizing his peripatetic journeys—I had the semester to finish, classes had already been paid for. But, my God, to be free, with him, unencumbered by responsibility, by the past . . .

"Read my cards," I said abruptly.

"Maybe this isn't a good time." He looked uncertain, boyish, and I didn't recognize him.

"Read them. You believe in them, read them."

Thoughtfully, he reached in his backpack for the leather pouch he kept the cards in and handed them to me.

"Shuffle them," he said, and sat cross-legged on the floor. I sat down across from him and did as he said. "Think about what you want to ask," he said. "Cut the deck in three with your left hand."

I did. He moved so that he was beside me and laid the cards out in a fan, seven across, five down. There was too much to take in. I did not know the cards but I recognized the Death card. I saw another with three swords crossing through a red heart. A charioteer in armor with a crescent moon over his head. An upside-down queen holding a wand. An old king looking into a cup. I saw many, many swords: a knight brandishing a sword, riding a winged horse; a woman sitting up in bed, gripping her hair while swords flew overhead. In the last row was a card of a beautiful woman standing in a vineyard, and all around her hung large clumps of purple grapes. She wore a gauntlet on which a hooded falcon perched.

"What's this one?" I asked, pointing to the card.

"Your benefactress."

My grandmother, I thought. *She lives in a vineyard.* A disconcerting longing for her overcame me.

"Let's start at the beginning," Nathan said, taking a deep breath. "Here's your past—your mother, the Queen of Wands. Fiery, fierce, loyal, beautiful, unreliable. But she's still in your present, still very much on your mind."

"What does that mean, Nathan?"

"I don't know what it means, I'm just telling you what the cards say. You're going to have more sadness. But you're going to survive it and eventually you're going to be happy. You need to look within yourself for the answers to your questions. Who is this older man here? Is there some man in your life I don't know about?" He said this with a slight smile, knowing that we were so obsessed with each other, the thought of someone else never even crossed our minds. "The King of Cups—not your father, surely. The World card just behind him indicates he's come from far away, a foreigner. This is a man with heart and spirituality."

"Maybe Viktor," I said, referring to Viktor Bezsmertno, a Soviet political refugee who was being sponsored by Rudy Brown of the Russian Department. Viktor had survived World War II as a child, only to end up in a Siberian work camp in the early fifties, for writing and publishing harsh facts about life under Stalin. Once, he had escaped and tried to hijack a plane to the West. In all, he'd spent twenty-two years in Siberia and the last four in exile in Gorky, trying to emigrate to the U.S. He was a tall, gap-toothed, gray-bearded man whose eyes were blue and wise.

Rudy Brown had been bringing him to our Second Year Russian class to help us in conversation practice. He was the first Soviet Russian most of us had ever met, and we discovered that he had an affinity for scotch. He hated vodka. A few days after his first visit, my five classmates and I took a bottle of Johnny Walker over to his small, barren apartment. He insisted we stay and drink it with him. The only thing he'd brought from Russia was his dog Bika, a huge sheepdog who wagged her tail hard. Viktor told us, after several big glasses of scotch which he drank warm and straight, that he'd gone to prison so young he'd never had a chance to make love with a woman. Now, he said, it was too late.

"It's never too late!" one of the boys blurted in his rudimentary Russian. We all laughed and Viktor smiled, blushing. The boy was right. There were too many strong-willed divorcées and widows around the college; Viktor's days as a virgin were surely numbered.

He said that while in jail, he'd often considered suicide, but instead he had kept faith that God would reward him, in heaven if not on earth.

"Nu, kto eto, Bog?" But who is God? I asked in my halting Russian.

He looked at me for a long moment. *"Kto eto Bog?"* he said, nodding his head thoughtfully, *"Bog—Bog!"* God is God.

Viktor had survived the unimaginable, and now he was starting life in a new country, in a new language, with absolutely nothing. He poured the last drops of scotch into our glasses and asked us to come back tomorrow. He told us we made him feel useful.

* * *

"Well," Nathan continued, "this Viktor is going to be important to you somehow."

A few months before, Viktor had introduced me to Varlam Shalamov's work. A single mimeographed story from an underground Soviet press. He held the pages and turned them with tenderness and care. When he handed them to me to take home, it was as if he were trusting me with a newborn child. For years I would pursue the elusive Shalamov, until he became one of the subjects of my Ph.D. dissertation.

"This is me, I guess," Nathan continued, tapping a card. "I'm in your obstacle line. The Knight of Swords charging off. But I'm not leaving your life, Celeste, I'm all over your future, too. See, here, I become the King of Swords. And then you've got this benefactress who's going to play a role."

"So?" I said in a controlled, calm voice.

In a tone sapped of all its strength and energy, he said, "I don't see any obvious travel cards in the immediate present, but that doesn't mean anything. We make our own futures, Celeste."

I nodded slowly. I realized then that I had known all along what the cards would say. He came toward me, his face serious and sad. We kissed and stretched out on the rug among the cards. We undressed each other hurriedly. He pulled me astride him and held my hips as I wrapped my arms tightly around his neck and shoulders. He let out a small cry, but I didn't loosen my grasp. I felt like I'd been given my death sentence and I saw no reason to deal with it decorously.

* * *

"DO YOU WANT me to stay a few more days?" he asked as we lay on my bed at sunrise, each having feigned sleep for most of the night. The syllogism would not leave me in peace—*He says he loves me but he's leaving me. If he loved me he would stay. Therefore he doesn't really love me.*

"What for?" As I heard the coldness and anger in my voice, I couldn't imagine why I'd said that, because I wanted him to stay more than anything else in the world.

"I'll always love you, Celeste," he said in a hushed voice.

"Just go," I told him, rolling against the wall and covering my head. Soon I heard the lock click softly behind him. I lay there for hours, thinking there was still time to change my mind, to catch him. I did not leave my room for the rest of the day and night, even when Candace, who lived two rooms down on my hall, knocked at dinnertime and then later in the evening when she was heading out to the pub. I kept wondering where Nathan was now. Was he packing? On a bus? Was he thinking of me?

When the sun rose the next morning and I was still lying there, staring at the ceiling, I realized I had no choice but to get up. That afternoon I went to a doctor in town who, it was said, was good for a prescription of sleeping pills. He was an elderly man whose hands shook. Broken blood vessels made a landscape of red rivers and tributaries of his nose and cheeks. I told him I needed something to help me sleep. He assured me it was the anxiety and pressure of classes. I told him I didn't care what it was, I couldn't sleep. He reluctantly gave me a prescription for Valium and scribbled down the name of a local psychologist.

I went back to my room. There was most of a bottle of Nathan's rum on a shelf and I drank half of it and felt absolutely nothing. So I took a Valium, and another, then a third, washing the little yellow pills down with the rum.

Someone knocked on my door after eleven and said I had a phone call. I stumbled down the hall and dropped the receiver before getting it somewhere near my ear.

"Celeste? It's Sebastian. My parents just called and told me Nathan left Harvard. Is he with you?" For a second his voice had sounded so much like his brother's that I gasped, and let out a small cry.

"I guess not. Are you all right?" he asked.

"Fuck no," I said, and laughed dryly. "Sally had the right idea, you know." I hung up and made it back to my room without another thought for Sebastian.

He borrowed a car and showed up at my door three hours later. He made coffee as I ranted and raved and threw things around the room.

Sleep finally came, and I dreamed of my mother's cool arms embracing me, of Nathan's long solid body lying in my bed. But even in sleep I knew that they were gone, and a cold, bone-aching wind crept into my dreaming room and I awakened screaming.

Later, when the morning sun broke through the spaces between the curtains, I sat up, startled, and found Bass asleep at my desk. Scanning the room with throbbing eyes, I saw a pair of Nathan's shoes sticking out from under the dresser, old Docksides, the outside heels worn down from the way he walked slightly bowlegged, heel to toe. He'd probably kicked them under there long ago, on his way to the bed. My heart seemed to stop and I gasped at the enormity of my loss.

Sebastian opened his eyes with a start.

"Oh, Bass, I'm so sorry to put you through this."

"Don't say that. You'd do the same for me."

I blinked at him, wondering who he thought I was.

* * *

FOR YEARS AFTERWARDS, I obsessed about the day Nathan left and tried to imagine how life would have turned out if I'd gone with him. The notion of packing up a few things and cleaning out my bank account seemed so romantic. I couldn't figure out why on earth I hadn't gone with him.

His long, arduous, passionate letters began to arrive, filled with our secrets. They gave me hope, and hope brought on despair.

Nathan was standing in the hallway when I stepped out of the little bathroom, my face oily with sweat.

"Are you all right, Celeste?" he asked, studying me closely.

"I'm just fine!" I said too loudly, staring back.

"He's okay. At least he doesn't look like you could fuck him in two," he said matter-of-factly.

"You know what? Go to hell, Nathan." I tried to push past him but he blocked the passage with his arm.

"Are you serious, Celeste? Do you love that man? Are you really going to marry him?"

"Yes," I said, but I turned my face away. He was too close, I could smell him, feel the heat of his skin.

"You could stay here with me," he said evenly.

"Yeah, right. You, me, and Giovanna."

"Giovanna's just here on vacation. We like each other but it's not serious between us, Celeste."

"But Alex and I are serious," I said with a shrill laugh, "we're engaged to be married."

Back at the table, our lobsters had arrived. Alex was trying to explain to Giovanna mergers and acquisitions.

"Cerveza. I buy cerveza," he said, grabbing a bottle of beer and one of hot sauce. "Cerveza, y I buy Tabasco, y I make Cerveza-Tabasco *compania mucho grande. Comprende?*"

"Aha," she said, nodding with a small frown. Abruptly, she grabbed his beer out of his hand, drank a large swig, and licked her lips, smiling.

"Bbrrrr," Alex stuck two fingers above his head like antennae. "Tele-visiono," he said. "You know Grupo Telemedia? Me," he pointed to his chest, "me make Grupo Telemedia mucho grande."

She smiled nervously. Nathan ordered another round of shots.

As I picked up my glass, Alex swiftly moved it out of my hand and slid it away. I tried to get it back but he took me firmly by the wrist and held me close. He called Paquita over and crisply handed her his Platinum card, which she accepted and brought back a few moments later. Giovanna and Nathan gazed at us with detached curiosity, in silence. While Alex read over the bill I grabbed the shot and downed it. He looked at me for a long moment without saying anything and then turned to Nathan.

"I'm very sorry to break this up, but we've got to get back to Hol Cha," Alex said pleasantly, pulling me out of my seat. Through a blurry, wet haze of lights I saw Nathan and Giovanna stand up.

Outside, the crickets were loud and the night smelled of flowers and the sea.

Nathan came out and stood in front of the screen door. "If you want to write me, Celeste, write in care of the Grand Hotel. Grand Hotel, Matlan, Mexico, okay?"

"'Kay, Nthn."

Alex got into the car and slammed the door. For a moment, I hesitated. I saw myself stepping off of fate's path; all I had to do was walk ten feet. I could say to Alex, *I'm sorry. You are wonderful but I have to stay here now. This is where I belong.* I had lots to say, to Nathan, to Alex, but I found I couldn't at that moment talk at all.

I fumbled for the door handle, tripped and fell, and Nathan came running toward the car. He lifted me to my feet, opened the door, and helped me inside. "Oops, there you go," he said gently.

"Thnmn."

Alex stared straight ahead and I could feel his anger crushing me and squeezing the air out of the car, the way the sea presses in on you as you drop deeper, deeper . . . I leaned up against the door to get away from it.

The drive home was utterly silent, the little car a submarine floating through inky blackness.

"Will you be able to dive tomorrow?" he finally asked in a controlled, even voice, as we drove through the luminous whitewashed gates of Hol Cha.

"'Course!" I said, and slid into blackness, aware only that I wanted to cry.

* * *

I CAME TO OUT of the blackout facedown in the bed. I was crying, sputtering, mumbling, "How could you do this to me? How could you do this to me? Has no time passed at all? Why am I here?" Suddenly someone was on top of me.

"Nathan?" I mumbled. An arm locked hard across my throat. I could barely breathe. I struggled to free myself but the arm squeezed more tightly and I began to gasp for air. He pushed into me, his cock like sandpaper against my dry walls.

I tried to cry out, to tell him to stop, I shook my head to get free of his bulging arm. He grabbed a fistful of my hair and held my head still. I gave up, went limp. Still with one arm around my throat, all of his weight pressing down on me, he let go of my hair and began to slap my ass and thighs, hard. I started to cry. When he was done, he shoved me away, and I slipped right off the bed. He turned his back and went to sleep. I lay curled in a ball on the cool, smooth tiles, unable to move.

The next morning I awakened with the shakes, feeling like I'd taken a hit of speed. My body smelled of something turned, of sweat, sex, booze, and underneath all that, his cologne gone bad. I wanted to throw up. My eyes burned like there was sand in them. There was blood on the sheets. Alex was gone. I looked around the room and was relieved to see that his belongings were still there, my fear of being left alone, penniless, in the jungles of Mexico, greater than the prospect of facing him.

I stumbled into the shower and stood under the hot jet for a long time. Then I slipped on some shorts and a T-shirt and went to find him.

He was in the restaurant, sitting by the open shutters, talking on his cell phone. Outside, palm trees rustled in the blinding sunshine. He acknowledged me by pushing a chair out with his foot. He talked for a minute more, but then he must have seen something disturbing in my face and abruptly said, "I'll call you back," and put the phone away.

"Alex, what the hell was that?" I asked. I was shaking so badly I could hardly lift my glass of orange juice. I put it back down, not wanting it anyway. I felt guilty, and ashamed, as if I'd been punished for doing something terribly wrong.

"What are you talking about?"

"Last night."

"I thought you wanted it," he said simply. He surreptitiously buttered a roll and popped half of it in his mouth.

I put my head between my hands. I felt too sick, too weak, too guilty, to argue with him.

"You were pretty toasted. I guess you're too hungover to dive."

My mother had once told me that one of the ways you can tell if you have a drinking problem is if your drinking starts to impede your daily plans. I was not about to let last night's binge affect today's dive.

I looked up at him, my eyes aching. "I'm not hungover, Alex. I only had three shots."

Alex tossed slices of papaya into his mouth with brusque, staccato gestures. "Four shots," he said matter-of-factly, "and two margaritas before that."

"You're angry because of Nathan, is that it?"

"He was your lover, wasn't he?" There was a cynical bite in his tone, an icy look in his eyes.

"He was my love," I said quietly, and pushed my chair back. I rushed out into the brain-splitting sunlight as tears began cascading from my eyes.

* * *

SWEATING, NAUSEATED as I sat on the undulating dive boat with the heavy equipment on my back, I ignored Alex beside me and looked down at the deep blue water. My heart and bowels constricted. I had visions of monsters rising up from the depths and taking away my legs. When the dive master counted three, I held my mask to my face and my regulator tight in my mouth and threw myself backwards off the boat. There was a splash and a moment of deep confusion, then I straightened out and looked around. I let the air out of my BC and sank, watching Alex beside me.

My mind went blank. I became a spaceship swooping down toward an unknown planet, enveloped completely in the silent, deep blue womb of the cosmos. There was no sound except for my lungs breathing and the air bubbles escaping from the regulator.

Just beyond the reef, the bottom dropped away suddenly, straight down for thousands of feet. I floated out above the last coral growths, into the open void. It was like jumping off a cliff and not falling, flying like I did in dreams. Beyond the hundred feet or so of visibility, the blue turned into a dark and threatening void; I swam back to the plateau. At the crest of the drop, schools and large solitary fish passed by, following the current. Hundreds of little neon blue fish rose and fell in cloud formation. Yellowtail snappers came up to my mask by the dozens and looked into my eyes. *Hi there*, I waved to them. In a flash they moved off, a yellow tornado through the blue. A group of barracuda passed by like a moving, glinting silver wall. At the mouth of a cave the dive master left some bait, and a huge green moray eel came out and snapped it up in its sharp-toothed jaws.

Feeling more secure, I swam off by myself to inspect some long neon yellow tubular sponges that were growing perpendicular to the ninety-degree incline. About sixty feet away, slinking toward me through the blue, was a large gray shark. I saw a white patch on the tip of the dorsal fin. I screamed into my regulator but there was no one around to hear. The smaller fish did not seem disturbed, nor did the shark know the terror it caused in me. It passed close, the sleek body pulsing with muscle. *Everything here is as it should be*, I thought, bewildered by its beauty. The shark was simply part of the fine, serene order of this universe; and so was I. I lost all perspective for a moment and felt no fear, no anxiety about the future. Only now—this instant—seemed important.

Alex was not close-by, so I swam after him, and as though in slow motion grabbed his arm and pointed, but by the time he turned and looked, the shark was gone.

I did not become frightened until after I got back on the boat.

"I saw a big shark!" I said to Alex as a chill crept up my spine.

"How big?" he asked, impressed.

"More than six feet." I held a hand high above my head.

"What did it look like?"

"It had a white mark on its dorsal fin."

"A white-tip reef shark," he said with awe. "Did you like the moray eel?" He was smiling proudly, pleased with me. I felt redeemed.

I nodded, smiling foolishly. I sat back and breathed in the warm air. The ocean had washed away the vestiges of the rancid smell. The fierce sun immediately began to dry my diveskin suit. The boat rocked gently beneath me.

Everything is back to normal, my mind whispered to me. *Everything is as it should be. He meant you no harm.*

Ten

WE'D BEEN BACK only a week when the deadly lethargy crept back into my bones. I sat on the M11 bus that runs up Amsterdam Avenue, holding my eighth graders' poems and essays in a folder on my lap, and stared out the window in a daze. I'd had a hard time leaving the warm cocoon of my bed that morning, but forced myself because of the kids. A few months before, I'd gone to a party on a Monday night and called in sick Tuesday. The next week, the kids pouted and were sullen and one girl said, "We thought you quit. We thought you change your mind about us." I never went out on Monday nights again. Last week, they'd been angry at me for going to Mexico and changing our meeting day, and teased me about my tan.

Beyond 125th Street, the sidewalks were strewn with litter and some of the buildings had plywood over the windows. I opened the folder and glanced through the kids' poems from last week, making sure I'd picked out the most interesting ones to read aloud to the class.

I had never, after my first visit to the school, been afraid to go there on the bus. Columbia University stretched to 125th Street, if you counted student and faculty housing, so really I was only going ten blocks beyond what was safe and familiar to me. There was an order to the daily routine that I had become a part of, just in my short walk from the bus stop to the school. People hung out on the graffiti-marred stoops, but most of the time danger was not in the air. Some days, something felt off, I didn't know what, but my senses were so attuned to the movements and faces that even the slightest variation made my ears prick up, and then I walked a little faster. But nothing bad had ever happened to me; no one had said an unfriendly word in my four semesters of teaching. I felt protected, as if by a magic aura.

The teacher I worked with was a woman in her mid-forties named

Ellie Horowitz. I'd met her a year and a half earlier at a pro-choice consciousness-raising seminar that Anna had coerced me into attending, at the house of a fairly well known feminist writer. Anna was not a feminist and did not care about feminist issues, but she was adamantly pro-choice and to my father's great chagrin, she refused to vote Republican because of their stand on abortion. Once, he blocked the door when she was heading out to catch a bus to Washington with the "local dykes," as he so graciously put it; she was wearing a straw hat and white gloves and carrying a Statue of Liberty banner with blue writing that said "Keep your laws off our bodies."

"Anna, if you walk out this door," my father had said, his face wild with rage, "I don't know *what* I'll do."

And she responded, "Well, I know what *I'll* do if you don't get out of my way—I'll divorce you."

Now it was just one of the things they did not talk about.

* * *

THE ISSUE UNDER discussion at the seminar was how to educate the young underprivileged women of America so that abortions could be avoided in the first place. The people who spoke didn't seem to have a clue about the inner-city kids they were discussing. I glanced at Anna and made a disgusted face.

Then a woman in her mid-forties, with long, dark, gray-streaked hair, wearing a lower-calf-length flowery skirt and Timberland work boots, got up and said, "My name is Ellie Horowitz and I teach at MS 47 in Harlem, and what you're saying is just lovely and full of good intentions, but let me tell you about these kids. I mean no disrespect, but I know these kids and what you don't understand is the problems they encounter every day. You are talking about educating the young women of America, but who are you really talking about? Dalton girls? The communication gap is cultural, and very deep-rooted. And I don't see you ladies of authority and privilege building a bridge between you and them. I don't see you lecturing up in Harlem." She pushed her hair back indifferently, her olive-toned skin reddening perceptibly under the women's scrutinizing glare. "But that's not even the point. What we need in this country is to reach out to these girls on *their* terms, in *their* territory and *in a language they can understand.* And that is precisely what is not happening."

Pleased, I turned to Anna and smiled while inside I gloated with a little evil self-satisfaction. Anna ignored me and sat with her back straight in her prim suit.

I went up to the woman after the meeting and introduced myself.

"I really liked what you said," I told her as she looked me over with suspicious, cool gray eyes. "And I agree, except for one thing. I've been calling the Board of Education for six months, trying to volunteer in the public schools, and all I've been getting is the runaround. They don't want anyone who isn't certified to teach in the public system. It's like *Catch-22*—you can't teach unless you've taught before, and you can't have taught before if you don't have a certificate," I said, blood rushing to my face as well. "I'm a published writer, and I want to teach children how to write creatively. Why do I need a certificate for that?"

She looked at me as if she could tell everything about me in one long glance. "Have you ever taught before?"

"I've been teaching at Columbia for two years."

Abruptly she pulled a notebook out of a large canvas bag and wrote down her name and phone number. "These kids aren't college students, let me tell you," she said. "But what the hell. Come up to the school next week. This year I've got a disruptive class of eighth graders. They're not Special Ed, you understand. Just difficult. Smart as hell, actually. They just get passed along from grade to grade, nobody gives a shit. It's a sin. So now I've got 'em, and they're not ready for eighth grade. Don't expect too much. We'll give it a shot." She shook my hand, holding it firmly.

* * *

MY TRYOUT DAY came in December, just a few weeks before the Christmas holiday. Feeling like a hypocrite, I took a cab. The driver was an elderly black man whose name, I saw from the registration, was Robert Johnson. When we passed 125th Street, he said, "I don't mean to be curious or nothing, but what are you doing up here?"

I told him I was going to try to teach creative writing to kids in junior high school.

"No kidding. What for?"

"You know, to maybe get them to like writing. Write about things that matter to them," I said. I looked at the back of his bald head, but couldn't tell what he was thinking. I asked him, "How dangerous is it up here?"

"Not too bad," he said evenly. "Come payday, Friday, ain't too good. Crackheads mug people for their paychecks. Otherwise ain't too bad."

When I paid him, he turned to me and said, "God bless you, lady, and have a good day."

I walked into the overheated classroom feeling like I wasn't wearing any clothes. There were five rows of desks, seven deep. A rumble of voices slammed into me. Black, gold, and hazel eyes looked me over with amused curiosity. A Hispanic girl was looking at herself in a pocket mirror, combing her hair and slapping at her neighbor, a large-shouldered black boy with a handsome, devilish face. Ellie Horowitz screamed at the class in a loud, shrill voice like a police siren, and they settled back to watch me in silence.

I took a small papier-mâché container out of my bag, along with *The Paris Review* and two other quarterlies that had published my stories over the past few years. They made a small, neat stack on a corner of the desk.

"This may look like nothing," I told them, "but getting short stories published in these magazines is one of the hardest things in the world for an unknown writer to do." I held up *The Paris Review* and opened it to the second page. "These are the stories I've published. Here's my name, Celeste Miller, in the table of contents."

"How we know that's you?" asked the boy who had been teasing the girl next to him. He smiled. His front teeth were broken and jagged.

"Here, there's a picture of me in this one." I handed him *Glimmer Train* and passed the others around, and they glanced at them without much interest. Only the one with my picture captivated them.

I opened the little papier-mâché box filled with colorful metal Soviet pins that I had bought in Moscow in 1984. Printed on them in Russian were slogans like "GLORY TO THE FATHERLAND OF THE USSR" and "THE WORKS OF MARXISM/LENINISM LIVE ON!" and "GLORY TO THE COMMU-NIST PARTY OF THE USSR!"

"I brought these pins back from Russia years ago, to give to people as souvenirs. The Russians were very nice to me," I said. "Families invited me to their homes and fed me, often when they didn't have much food them-selves. I've never been this far uptown in my life, but I'd like to come back and teach you creative writing. I'd like each of you to take one of these pins as a gift from me to you for allowing me to visit your classroom today."

"How come you starting at the front of the room?" someone called from the back. "That ain't fair!"

I moved to the back, allowing their hands to reach into the box and pick a pin.

"Miss! Hey miss, what's this one?" a girl asked.

"Call me Celeste," I said. The pin was a red star with a photograph of baby Lenin at the center. "That's Lenin as a baby. He was the founder of Russian communism."

"What this one say?" A girl with mahogany-colored skin held up a representation of the world, a blue sphere, with an atom bomb broken in half.

"It says, 'No to atomic bombs!'"

The girl was looking at me with great wary eyes. "I thought they *wanted* to bomb our ass," she mumbled in a tired voice.

"That's like saying that everyone in America agrees with the president."

"Shee-it," she mumbled, and attached the pin to the lapel of her blue-jean jacket.

Ellie Horowitz had brought her little boom box, as we'd planned, and I put in a cassette of a wistful, romantic piano improvisation by Keith Jarrett.

"Okay, everybody, I just want you to close your eyes and daydream."

They started giggling and looking at me as if I were crazy.

"Man, I'm gonna fall asleep."

"Come on, you do it anyway in class and get yelled at for it. Just close your eyes and breathe easily. Breathe in, one, two, three, four . . . "

The eerie, dreamy music wafted through the room. Many glanced at their neighbors to see if they were being made fun of, but slowly they began to close their eyes.

"If any of you really don't feel like doing this, I invite you to step out into the hall or go to the library," I said equably.

Behind me, Ellie Horowitz yelled, "Yeah, and I invite you to go to Mr. Sender's office!" No one moved.

"In a minute I'm going to play the music again, and I just want you to write down what you were daydreaming about. There's no right or wrong about it. Pretend that your hand is getting an electric signal straight from your brain. I don't care about your spelling or your grammar. I want you to break your sentences up wherever you feel like it. If you don't want me to read yours out loud to the class, then write 'Don't Read' at the top. This is between you and me."

When the music ended, there was utter silence. Quickly, I pressed rewind, knowing I could lose them in the blink of an eye. The music began again, wistful, slow, sad. Quietly, they began to write, bent over their desks, covering their words from their neighbors' glances.

"If you have any questions, just raise your hand and I'll come over to your desk," I said.

Hands went up. I walked among the desks, bumping into book bags and legs. Most wanted to ask me about spelling.

"How you spell *heaven*?"

"Spell it any way you want," I said. "I'm the worst speller in the world, so don't ask me."

Shyly, they began to turn their papers toward me as I went slowly through the rows, looking over their shoulders.

Sofyah, the girl who had taken the peace pin, wrote:

I HAD A DREAM

I had a dream of peace.
Peace everlasting peace.
In this dream all through
out the land was peace.
No killing no drugs
no guns no war.
Just peace.

"It's beautiful," I told her, and placed my hand on her shoulder for a second. She looked at it, looked at me, and smiled faintly with closed lips. I moved on, filled with joy. The handsome boy in the front who'd been teasing the Latino girl wrote a poem called "Alone." His name was Ramel.

ALONE

I dreamed that I was homeless on Christmas day
I was walking through an alley
I was all alone
There was no place to go
I was sad and lonely
I was thinking about that night
and how I would feel after Christmas day.

"Sunset" was by a boy who sat by himself, by a window in the very back:

SUNSET

As we head off
into the sunset
Who knows what

Lies out there
as we are
on a journey
to a far away place.

After my first semester, Ellie suggested I apply to The Writer's Way for funding. The grant came through, and I started getting paid to teach my class. But the greatest reward was that, this term, I'd found a writer. He was an eighth grader named Derrence Skinner who couldn't spell and never talked in class. He sat staring at the ceiling with a dreamy expression while mayhem raged around him.

Today, after class, I was taking him to apply for a highly coveted spot in a summer program for gifted children. I had broken my own solemn rule to stay out of their lives, and the prospect of spending a few hours with a fourteen-year-old boy who'd never said more than twenty sentences to me was daunting. I didn't know how to talk to him. He made me feel the way I had when I visited my grandmother in France. I could speak the language, but I was never sure that I wasn't using the wrong idiom and inadvertently insulting someone.

Derrence was quiet, shy, well liked. He wasn't a troublemaker but neither was he a good student. Ellie said his grades were mediocre in all his subjects and next year he was going to one of the biggest, roughest high schools in the city. I showed her his work. She agreed that he had an uncanny ability with words, but she couldn't find a way to reach him. He tested badly and hated reading the assignments. Yet when I first read his work aloud to the class, they clapped and cheered. This eighth grade group thought of itself as unflinchingly cool and had never clapped before.

"Does the writer want to identify him or herself?" I had asked hopefully. At the time, I still didn't know all of their names. A hand in the last row went up slowly. A thin, brown-skinned boy with braces put up his hand, staring down at his desk.

"I swear, Derrence, this poem brings tears to my eyes," I said. The kids laughed and jeered.

"You one crazy woman!" a Latino girl in the front said with a smile.

One day, I wrote just one word on the board in capital letters, INJUSTICE, and put a nostalgic Chopin "Impromptu" on the boom box. This was Derrence's response:

We never ran, we never played,
we never got along.
We never looked, we never watched,
but someone always did.
We always smile, with cigars in our mouths.
We never dream, we never sleep,
we never go in peace.

* * *

THEY LIKED TO tease me about the clothes I wore and the expressions I used, like "fabulous," "excellent," and "wonderful," and how choked up I got when I read them something really good. But I knew that they loved the attention and the compliments I paid them. They often wrote about fear, and drive-by shootings in the streets, and ricocheting bullets that killed passers-by, family members, close friends. Some wrote with devotion about their parents, others about how little their parents understood or knew them.

I began to take a group of five or six kids to the library after class to work on extra projects; students who showed particular talent or just enthusiasm, or ones I thought were most neglected. Everyone wanted to go. I felt sick at heart knowing that I had to concentrate on those who would benefit the most.

The first day, the librarian made them all spit out their wads of gum and warned them that if they didn't behave, she'd throw us all out.

In this much more intimate setting, they began to tell me about their lives. Shatisha, a small, skinny, dark-skinned girl with a tuft of wild and wiry hair, told me that she'd been homeless for two years and was now in foster care. Her stories were always about other homeless people, how she felt sorry for them when she saw them in the street. I asked her if she could write about her own experience. She said no. She said she didn't want her classmates to find out.

Rosalia, an A student with waist-length black hair and almond eyes, told me that she was in love with a boy called Alfredo who was in another eighth grade class. "Oh my God," she looked up at the ceiling and pounded her chest dramatically with her fist.

"Oh boy," I said to her, "I remember that feeling."

This made the table of girls giggle and snort.

"You married, Celeste?"

"No. But I'm getting married in July."

"No shit! Who you marrying? Is he cute?"

"Bring him here for show-and-tell," said another girl.

I started to laugh, picturing Alex standing at the front of the room as I described his accomplishments.

Derrence was off in a corner by himself, writing furiously.

On our way out, the librarian said to me, "I don't know what you're doing but I've never seen them like this before. As far as I'm concerned, you can bring them back anytime."

I walked down the hall surrounded by them, feeling like the Pied Piper, light-headed with happiness.

* * *

FOR THE NEXT MONTH Rosalia wrote sexy, passionate, rhyming love poems to Alfredo, but suddenly her poems became filled with tearful recriminations and jealousy. Rosalia liked me, but she pouted and then ignored me when I spent too much time with Derrence. Two weeks before, she'd asked me why I liked his work better than hers. I told her that her poems were excellent but she didn't push herself, that she'd gotten rhyming down, and now she needed to stop the rhymes and concentrate on herself and not Alfredo. Last week she'd handed me a rhyming love poem about José, her latest love interest.

"What about yourself? What about not rhyming?" I asked her.

"Oh, man, it's too hard what you asking for."

I shrugged and went over to check on Derrence. "Where is your family from?" I asked him.

"Costa Rica," Derrence mumbled in a barely audible baritone as I leaned over his desk.

"Your father too?"

"No." He shook his head. A moment later he murmured that his mother was remarried and that he did not get along with his stepfather. For the first time I realized he had a Hispanic cadence to his speech.

"My mother want to send me to summer school to get me out the house. I hate that summer school, man. So boring. Teach you what you already know!"

Without giving it any thought, I asked, "Do you want me to see about getting you into a special writing program? I think there are places like that. Workshops for young people. Something like that?"

"That be good," he said in a neutral voice. I couldn't tell if he really wanted me to go ahead or if he was just saying yes to be polite.

*   *   *

I MADE PHONE CALLS to different nonprofit organizations for kids and made arrangements with Derrence's mother and the school to take him for a few hours the coming Tuesday. Freedom to Think, a nonprofit Harlem group run by a man named Winston Jones, had seemed the most promising, although Mr. Jones had said that their funding was limited to children who lived in the neighborhood. Freedom to Think was near the school but Derrence lived in the South Bronx.

I'd nevertheless convinced Mr. Jones to at least talk to Derrence and take a look at his work.

Now I got off the bus and crossed the street toward the school. A clammy suffocating haze hung over the city. Entering the building was like crossing into a strange world of noise in which time and space had completely different values. Time was parsed out in fifty-minute segments, and space was what you took for your own. In the dark blue halls I usually had to duck and weave to avoid crashes; the noise level made thinking impossible.

I had a few minutes until the bell so I walked along the hall looking at the artwork that had recently been taped to the walls. There were perspective drawings of buildings and roads; New York cityscapes; mosaics of faces made of little cut-up pieces of magazine paper; paintings of seas crowded with large, frightening fish. I paused at a drawing of skyscrapers. At the forefront, the sharply angled rooftops loomed gigantic, covered with antennae. Way down below at their skinny base was a slim avenue heading straight toward the top of the page, the horizon. I felt a small presence beside me and turned. A boy of about twelve was looking up at me with serious eyes.

"You like it? It's mine's."

My gaze shifted back to the work. "It's magnificent! You have talent." I turned to him, but he had wandered off.

*   *   *

FREEDOM TO THINK was only a few blocks from the school. Derrence and I stepped out of the noisy, dark-halled school and into the bright midday sunlight. Derrence must have felt at least as strange and uncomfortable as I did, although his face did not divulge anything at all. I saw that he had dressed up for his interview with Winston Jones. He wore new purple jeans cinched with a belt below his hips, the crotch hanging down at his knees, the legs draping in folds over new high-tops with two enormous straps like aerodynamic wings on the sides, and a purple jean vest that matched the pants. Underneath the vest he wore a yellow and purple striped hooded shirt.

"Listen, Derrence," I said, "I'm just trying to offer you some other possibilities here besides summer school. You don't have to say yes to this."

"I know," he said quickly.

"Mr. Jones, the guy who runs the place, he told me they have a photography and poetry workshop that meets twice a week in the afternoon."

"I like that," Derrence said. His voice was so quiet and low, it was hard to hear.

"Do you read books?" I asked him.

"Nah. I watch TV. But I like true books. I don't like ones that's not true."

"They're all true," I said. "Novels just change things a little."

I only had two sessions left with my students, and I knew I might never see him again after that. There was so much I wanted to tell him.

"You know, Derrence, I think you're *very* talented. I think you're a writer. Do you know that or do you just think I'm crazy?"

He laughed without a sound. "No."

No what? I didn't ask. I didn't push.

"Don't be nervous with Mr. Jones," I said, swallowing hard.

The walls of Winston Jones's office were covered with drawings, poems, and photographs by students. There were also love notes to him. "Winston I LOVE YOU!" "Come home and live with us!" Books and folders were stacked waist high on the floor. Before us stood a tall, square-shouldered black man with shoulder-length, light brown dreadlocks. He wore faded jeans, a blue oxford shirt, and a striped blue and red tie. Derrence seemed to be trying to hide behind me. I wished I could have prepared him better.

"I'm Celeste Miller, Mr. Jones," I said, stepping forward and putting out my hand. "This is Derrence Skinner, the student I told you about."

Mr. Jones had piercing, intelligent eyes that looked hard to fool.

"Hey, man, those are some fly shoes," Mr. Jones said to Derrence, who didn't respond. "Do you like to write?" Derrence gazed lazily upward and around at the pictures on the walls and said, "Kinda."

"I brought you some copies of his poems," I said quickly, reaching into my bag. Mr. Jones took the folder and glanced at the copies I'd made, and said, "Mm-hm. You're a good writer."

Silence from Derrence.

"You interested in photography, Derrence?" Mr. Jones asked.

"Yeah," he said vaguely, looking down at the floor now. I wanted to interrupt, explain that Derrence was shy, but I knew it was best if I sat in the proffered chair and stayed quiet. Every once in a while Mr. Jones appeared to glance in my direction, an inscrutable expression in his eyes.

"Where do you live, Derrence?" he asked.

"Bronx," Derrence said.

"That's out of our usual jurisdiction. We take kids just from around here."

My heart sank. "But he goes to MS 47 just down the street. I've been teaching for a while, Mr. Jones, and I really think Derrence has an unusual talent."

Mr. Jones sat back in his swivel chair and smiled. "This workshop teaches you to take photographs and then develop them. You write poems to go with the pictures you take. At the end we have a little show of everyone's work. What do you think of that?"

"I think it's good. But I don't know about taking pictures. I don't have a camera or nothing."

"We give you the camera. *Lend* you the camera. If you lose it, you're in deep shit." He laughed, and Derrence's face remained impenetrable. Mr. Jones leaned back in his swivel chair, crossed his arms, and chewed on the inside of his cheek for a while.

"Well, we got space for you if you want it," he said finally. "But you got to be responsible about it," he warned. "If I give this space to you, that means some kid in this neighborhood who has a right to be here won't get his spot. You interested?"

"Yeah," Derrence said in his flat voice. "I like to try it."

We stood up after Mr. Jones did.

"Ms. Miller," he said, "you're with The Writer's Way?"

"Yes, but I volunteered for a semester at MS 47 first."

"Give me a call sometime. I'd like to hear about your teaching methods."

"I will. And if it's okay, I'd like to come back to see the exhibition after the workshop."

"Of course," he said. We shook hands.

* * *

OUT IN THE STREET, the sun beat down fiercely. I asked Derrence if he was thirsty. He said yes as I led him toward a bodega. At the door he stopped for a moment to see if I would open it first. When I did, he stayed back and then followed me in.

We stood in front of the glass refrigerator, staring at the soft drink cans. I could see the reflection of the two Hispanic men behind the counter, gazing at us with curious looks. Me in my little black skirt with white polka dots and cotton blouse, Derrence decked out in his new outfit.

"What do you want? A Pepsi? Something else?"

"Coke be good," he said. I pulled out two cans, a Coke and a Diet Coke, and took them up to the counter. One of the men handed me two straws as Derrence stood back and gazed vaguely at the ceiling.

We left and walked in the direction of Broadway.

"You know, Derrence, it's only like twenty blocks to Columbia University, there's a really good bookstore there. I'd like to get you a couple of books. Do you need to get back to school?"

"Nah. Nothing going on there. My mom she don't get home to after five anyway."

"You get along well with your mom?"

"She's okay. Busy. She always wanting me to go to church with her. I hate that church, man. I hate what they say—you don't believe like us, you don't come here every Sunday, you gonna go to hell. You believe that?" he asked, glancing at me out of the corner of his eye.

My head was pounding from the heat and from the realization that he wanted an answer. I thought of Primo Levi and suddenly wanted to cry.

"No, I don't believe that. I don't think God belongs to any one religion or any one group of people. The Christians say he's one way, the

Arabs say another, then they fight over it. Kill each other. I don't believe anybody has a right to tell anybody else what God is. God belongs to everyone. It's people who say God punishes. People fight over God."

"But like, so you believe in God?"

For me God existed in Primo Levi's writing, in the moments of reprieve he described when one human granted another respect in that godless wasteland of cruelty. The skeletons of buildings stared at Derrence and me with their empty eyes. I had to make a choice to face things and try to help him, or live with my own eyes closed. I felt something lift out of me and float above us, watching us walking down the street.

"Yes, I think there is a God," I said carefully. "I don't know who He is, though. Maybe God is kindness. Treating everybody the way you'd like to be treated. You know what I mean?"

"When I go in the store, they always look at me like I'm stealing something. I never steal nothing!" he said, looking at the ground. "They look at me like I be some garbage or something."

I wanted to tell him he was perfect, beautiful, I wanted to hug him. He would have been horrified.

"That's why you have to read!" I said instead. "You have to educate yourself so that no one can hurt you. I'm not talking about what they teach you in school; I wasn't a good student when I was your age. But if you read, you'll be able to protect yourself because you'll be smarter than the people who would just as soon hurt you as let you be."

"I know that!" he said with a burst of emotion.

Enthusiastic, I went on. "I don't know what it's like to be fourteen and black, but I know what it was like to be fourteen and white and a girl without a mother and to feel totally lost and confused."

He said nothing, walked with his face down, sipping his Coke.

"And being scared and angry doesn't help anything. I'm still so damn angry and scared I never have time to feel good!" I said.

"I know what that is," he said. He nodded solemnly and we walked on.

At the bookstore, I let him wander around. I followed him and pointed out a few writers I thought he might like. James Baldwin's *Go Tell It on the Mountain*. Richard Price's first novel about the South Bronx, *The Wanderers*. There was an anthology of minority poetry; a new novel by a Puerto Rican–American about Spanish Harlem and the crack blight. I pointed out Toni Morrison's early novels, the slimmer ones that would not appear so intimidating to him. He took them all off the shelf one by one and looked at the covers, front and back. He looked up at the poetry section and, piling all the books into the crook of his arm, pulled out a thin pink volume entitled, *Love Poems Throughout the Ages*.

"Rosalia like this one."

"Okay. You can give it to her tomorrow." I took it from him and he went back to his pile and tried to make up his mind.

"Take one from each author," I said, thinking what the hell.

By the time we got to the cash register, Derrence was carrying quite a pile of books. He solemnly placed them on the counter in a neat stack and stood back and gazed around with that blank expression. The clerk ran up the bill. I didn't even glance at the price as I handed him my credit card.

"You don't have to read all these now, but they'll be there for you when you want them." I reached into my bag and pulled out *The Paris Review* with my story in it. "Here, you can have this too. I signed it for you last night. You don't have to read this either. I just wanted you to have it."

I walked him to the subway stop at 116th and Broadway. He had a long ride home. At least it wouldn't be dark for a couple of hours.

"Don't be scared of Freedom to Think," I said quickly. "It'll be a lot of fun, I think. Listen, if you want you can call me and we can talk about it. You want to call me?"

"Yeah." He took out his notebook and a pen and started writing my name out carefully. I gave him the number. I hoped he'd call me, but I didn't think he would.

"Be careful on the way home," I said stupidly, and patted his arm. "You know how to get there from here?"

"Yeah," he laughed, and turned to take the stairs. Halfway down he looked over his shoulder and waved.

"Oh please, God," I mumbled under my breath, "please help this child."

Eleven

THE WEATHER FINALLY broke and the following Saturday afternoon was bright and cool. The ladies kept exclaiming as they arrived, loaded down with gift-wrapped packages in fancy shopping bags, "What a perfect day for a bridal shower!"

The windows of my friend Daphne's duplex were open onto the narrow Greenwich Village street. She had the ground and second floors, and from her living room upstairs we could hear birds and leaves rustling in the trees, and conversations and laughter on the street below.

A few latecomers rushed into the room, and as Daphne said, "Everyone's here, let's get started," I found myself looking toward the door. Someone was still missing, but who? It struck me like a blow to the chest. Candace. My bridal shower should have been her responsibility. Somehow I felt I was betraying her, although I knew this was absurd.

With Candace gone, Daphne had volunteered. Although we didn't see each other much anymore, she was still my second-oldest college friend. Daphne had done everything right: gone to Harvard Law School, become a corporate lawyer, bought a Village apartment that had tripled in value. The only thing she had trouble with, it seemed, was finding a husband. Her mother reminded her of this whenever possible, and Daphne would say, "I don't need a husband, I need a wife."

Daphne seated us in a circle, and I was reminded of games of spin-the-bottle. Since my friend had an obsessive passion for organization, she had planned an "hour shower"; giving each guest a specific hour for which to buy me a gift. It didn't make a difference to the ladies—they bought me pastel-colored slips, teddies, and nighties from Victoria's Secret for the morning and afternoon as well—why not? The most amusing gift was Lucia's.

"For 11 P.M.—" her card read, "Something smooth, black and silky."

In the box, wrapped in pink tissue paper, was a Ray Charles compact disk.

Anna's gift was for midnight, a frilly pink negligee and nightgown from Saks, with a card that said I was free to exchange them if they weren't in my taste. None of this stuff was my taste. I slept in old, extra-large T-shirts with the neckline cut out.

When we were finished, there was subdued conversation and finger sandwiches and more champagne.

I wanted to raise my glass to Candace, but I knew they would stare at me, their soft features darkened momentarily by worry. People didn't want to talk about unpleasant things. I chased away these thoughts with a wide, silly smile that made my face ache. As Alex often told me, I was just blowing storm clouds over a perfectly clear blue sky. I drank another glass of champagne, hoping to dilute my gloom.

* * *

IT GREW DARK around seven-thirty and as though on cue, everyone left except for Lucia and me. Daphne popped the cork on another champagne bottle and they began to talk about hitting a nightclub for old time's sake. The wine had not lifted my spirits; it had given me a headache that sat like a loose pack of marbles in the base of my cranium. Feeling dizzy and confused, I told them I was going to lie down for a little while. I slipped away, down the circular staircase to Daphne's bedroom. I could hear them above me, laughing about the old days when the four of us would go to the Ritz on weeknights and stay out till it closed; the manager was a friend and we drank for free. They never mentioned Candace, but I knew they were probably thinking of her, too.

I stretched out on Daphne's queen-size bed on which large pillows were piled, and closed my eyes. I couldn't stop my mind from dwelling on that other time.

Candace and I had been roommates our freshman year of college, thrown together by an exceptionally wise or foolish computer, because we couldn't have been more different.

I arrived first, alone, driving my secondhand Volkswagen. I had refused my father and Anna's help; my family had never been good at transitions, saying hello, saying good-bye. Propelled by some false sense of humility and a desire to avoid making any kind of self-aggrandizing statement, I'd brought one suitcase that held my four pairs of jeans; my large collection of T-shirts, ones for dressy occasions, hanging around, and sleep; a few cotton turtlenecks; four winter sweaters; and an assortment of unattractive bras and underpants. I also had a box containing all the novels I had read in high school, and a portable electric typewriter that Anna had given me the Christmas before.

Candace and her parents, Jacob and Samantha Black, burst through the door fussing and shouting, with four sweating freshman counselors bearing three enormous trunks. Her parents were tall but stoop-shoullered. Samantha wore a velour fuchsia pants suit and expensive gold jewelry. Jacob looked like an undertaker.

"I'm going to see if the bathroom is clean," Samantha announced, turning on her heel and leaving the room. Jacob tried to tip the freshman counselors, who vigorously shook their heads. "Are you coming, Jacob?" Samantha yelled from down the hall. He followed Samantha out without a word.

"I'm an only child," Candace said apologetically, once we were alone. "They're older. They worry."

I gave her an embarrassed smile. While Candace walked around inspecting the room, I noticed that her right hip was noticeably higher, and protruded more than her left, which gave her walk a slightly off-balance, stomping lilt.

"Not much room," she said, and began to unpack. She had planned for every natural disaster—blizzards, earthquakes, hurricanes. She'd brought all the basic things I hadn't thought of—an electric kettle, instant coffee, creamer, five kinds of herbal tea, extra blankets, medicines, a clothesline, and a little color TV. She had at least thirty color-coordinated outfits and ten pairs of shoes.

"I'm so sorry, I'm sort of pushing into your closet space here," she said from behind the closet door.

"Go right ahead," I said. Looking around, my side of the room suddenly seemed desperately empty.

Samantha and Jacob returned from the bathroom and announced that before every shower Lysol should be sprayed, and flip-flops worn at all times. Samantha proceeded to warn Candace about various illnesses that might afflict her over the course of the semester, advised her to have emergency phone numbers at her fingertips, and warned her to stay away from wild boys who would present themselves as respectable.

Finally Jacob said, "Time to leave the honey bee in peace." They sprayed her with kisses and tears. It all made me uneasy, and I sat at my desk, pretending to read.

"Phew!" Candace said as soon as the door was closed. "So where's the liquor store? Let's buy a big bottle of something and celebrate."

With that first shared magnum of white Folonari wine, I felt a great warmth toward her. I had never met anyone so energetic, so filled with goodwill. In a moment of uncharacteristic abandon, I confessed my distrust of people, especially of groups, and that I had never felt I belonged anywhere.

"But you're so beautiful!" she cried. "Let me handle things and you won't feel that way anymore. Pretty soon everyone will want to belong to *your* group."

I had never thought of myself as beautiful. When I looked into mirrors, I only saw my flaws.

* * *

I REMEMBERED with longing the spring days when Candace and I would buy a magnum of white wine, put it in a wastepaper basket filled with ice, and sit with our books on the hilly campus green from noon until the sun went down.

Candace would read her fat economics textbooks and gossip about school affairs with anyone who happened by, while I tried to concentrate on my Russian language or literature notes, terrified of failing even though I had an A average. By midafternoon, I was too loose to be afraid and I would lie back happily and stare at the sky. But Candace would keep on working and talking.

She was involved in every social affair, from organizing the holiday semiformals to running the student union's dances. She went to every party, terrified of being left out. In our senior year she ran unchallenged for class secretary, which insured that she would remain the recipient of juicy gossip and important social events well into old age. I teased her mercilessly over her compulsion to socialize. I didn't understand until she finally took me home. It was during Thanksgiving break of our senior year.

In her little girl's room, still pink and white, a small white vanity stood in one corner and teddy bears and porcelain dolls smiled down from every shelf. She suddenly said, "I want to show you something," and went digging through cardboard boxes stuffed with old clothes until she found what she was looking for—a barbaric contraption, four long metal rods that formed a jacket with a collar at the top. It looked like a medieval instrument of torture. She was shy about undressing in front of people, but that night, stripping quickly down to her bra, she put it on.

"I keep it to remind myself," she said, and laughed good-naturedly at her reflection in the mirror, while I gaped at her in disbelief. "It's a terrific antidepressant. I needed to catch up! For the whole four years of high school I had to wear this fucking thing and I couldn't wear normal clothes. Granny *shmattes* and maternity dresses, that's all. Forget about dating."

* * *

WE DECIDED to live together in New York City after graduation. Candace found our apartment through an ad in the *Village Voice*. I let her take care of everything, installing the phone, calling Con Ed, dealing with the landlord, whom she needled into lowering the rent by a hundred dollars.

Her parents, of course, were horrified by our living conditions. Our one-bedroom railroad flat was just off Amsterdam Avenue in the Eighties. There were drug dealers on the corner. Graffiti marred the dirty, skin-colored bricks of the front stoop leading to the heavily barred front door. The walls all leaned to the right. But we could easily afford the six hundred dollars a month rent. I was starting my Ph.D. program in Comparative Lit at Columbia, and she a training program in one of the big corporate banks. The first thing she did was become friendly with the drug dealers on the corner, figuring it was good form. As we were strolling home from a bar late one night, I heard her say, "Hi there, Ace! How's it going? This is my roommate, Celeste. Celeste, meet Ace."

"Yo, baby," said an enormous black man standing in the shadows. "Need any weed? Whites?"

"Maybe another time," she said gaily, pulling me along.

* * *

CANDACE COULD DRINK all night, change her clothes, and go to work with no sleep at all. I would lie there moaning while she traipsed around the room in matching pink towels, one around her torso, one wrapped turban-style around her head, singing, "Oy, oy, oy, oy, a shikker is a goy, oy oy." The old song had become a joke between us; her parents thought I was the bad influence, because they believed Jews as a rule didn't drink. *They* didn't drink at all. But Candace could drink me and ninety-nine percent of the fellows we knew right under the table.

Spring break of senior year, in a Fort Lauderdale bar, she'd won a beer chugging contest against a football player from the University of Alabama. He was a good loser, though. "What the hell school are y'all from?" he said in a deep, sweet voice as he smiled down at us from his formidable height. He had a little upturned Irish nose, a face boiled pink from the sun, and was as wide as a door.

"A fancy-shmancy Little Ivy League school where they teach you how to drink," Candace responded, holding her trophy aloft, an enormous brandy snifter with a chesty purple mermaid plastered on the glass. She had an absurd tan—brown in front and white on the back, like a piece of toast put on broil by mistake.

He invited her to take a stroll down the beach.

She came back to our bungalow hours later without her trophy. As she undressed, sand spilled from her bra but she didn't seem to notice.

* * *

CANDACE NEVER DOUBTED that she'd made the right decisions concerning her life, while I was constantly doubting myself. I had no idea what I was doing in New York, pursuing a Ph.D. when I didn't want to be a college professor. I wanted to write. I wrote every day; short stories about loneliness, about my father and Anna, about Nathan MacKenna, who'd chosen to travel through Central America instead of finishing college. His most recent letters were from Chile. What he was doing there, I had no clue. In the back of my mind I was always waiting for him to show up at our door like he always had, in his torn-up jeans, unshaven, with his backpack and nothing else to his name but his passport. I imagined Candace would smile at him and say, "Why, Nathan, how nice to see you," as though he'd been by just a few days ago. She'd fix him something to eat and take his dirty clothes down to the washing machine, while I'd sit quietly, inhaling his presence, anxious to take him to bed.

* * *

CANDACE WAS the only person I let read my stories. She was a harsh critic, and would not let up until I got something right, but, when we felt a story was finished, she would mail it out to small presses and quarterlies, writing a brilliant, self-confident letter for me to sign. Rejections were finally followed by an acceptance from *The Paris Review* for my best story, about the first time Nathan left me, in the spring of my sophomore year.

I was thrilled that *The Paris Review* had purchased my story; for at least a week, I believed in myself. I felt I had a future as a writer.

Meanwhile, it was inconceivable to Candace that my future would be anything but brilliant. "Oh, come on Celeste," she'd say, pulling me up from my bed. "Come to this party with me. Flirt with the magazine editors! You've got to go for it, Celeste!"

* * *

THAT FIRST YEAR in New York, when the weather changed, Jacob and Samantha drove a small U-haul down from Boston filled with all of Candace's spring and summer clothes. This operation was necessary because we didn't have enough closet space in our small apartment to accommodate her complete wardrobe. For a whole afternoon Samantha and Candace sorted through her winter things, wrapping suits in plastic to take back to Boston, and making a donation pile for the Salvation Army. Jacob sat in the kitchen reading the paper.

"I'll just leave the sweaters in the street, Mom," Candace said. "The homeless will pick them up in a minute."

"No, no, no. I'll take them back to Boston and give them to the Salvation Army, the proper way," Samantha insisted, as if this were a huge burden but one she wouldn't think of refusing. "You don't wear this lovely shirt anymore? What a pity . . . "

That Samantha knew every shirt and blouse and sweater of Candace's, I found astounding. I was certain that my father and Anna couldn't have described a single article of my clothing if a gun were held to their heads.

That night Jacob and Samantha took us out to dinner and at Candace's suggestion we went to Wolf's Deli, a brightly lit tourist trap on West Fifty-seventh Street where the waiters wore tuxedoes. Once we were seated, her parents sat with stiff backs, glaring suspiciously at the waiter and barking out questions about the food, as if certain that caution was all that lay between themselves and food poisoning. Candace ordered a second glass of wine before the food arrived and I noticed her mother wince. I was dying to order another one too, but didn't. Jacob and Samantha kept kosher, but when they weren't around, Candace ate everything. The past Thanksgiving had been my second with them in Boston, and Candace and I had stayed out very late dancing in a club in Faneuil Hall that Saturday night. Early the next morning we were awakened by Samantha's vigorous vacuuming. We stumbled into the kitchen, where a plate of bagels and a crock of butter sat on the counter. "Eat," Candace said to me as she searched the fridge for the Maxwell House can and some juice.

"Knife?" I said, and she indicated the flatware drawer as she went about making coffee; I reached into the drawer and pulled out a steak knife. By the time she turned around it was too late, the butter was smeared all over the jagged edges of the knife. She gasped. Then giggling, she plucked the knife out of my hand and ran with it to the sink. I started to apologize. "Shh," she said, rinsing quickly. "They'll never know." She said a prayer under her breath and put the knife away just as Samantha came into the kitchen, looking grief-stricken and exhausted with black half-moons under her eyes.

"What time did you get in?" she said, her voice quivering.

"Oh, I don't know, Mom, it wasn't that late."

"I stayed up all night worrying!" she said, then burst into tears. I stood against the cabinets, appalled and guilt-stricken. Candace threw her arms around her mother's shoulders and led her away. They sat head-to-head on the living room couch for a long time, Candace cooing and whispering as Samantha continued to weep.

* * *

CANDACE WAS ON so many political fund-raising and charity committees that there was always a black tie event on Saturday nights. Sometimes loneliness compelled me to accompany her. Afterwards, we'd end up in some crowded bar. I'd attempt to drag her out of the embrace of a sweet-talking drunk man in a rumpled tux, his clip-on tie askew.

They all said the same thing: "I've fallen in love with you. I've never met anyone I could talk to like this." The looks I threw them were so filled with contempt that Candace would turn to me, a hand on their chest, and laugh and say, "I'm just having fun, Celeste."

Finally, I'd leave her in that dark and deafening maelstrom of spilled booze and cigarette smoke, and go outside to find a pay phone. I'd call my best male friend, Branko, another recent graduate, and if he was not otherwise occupied, I'd go to his place and we'd have a few drinks. He had a massive collection of videos, and we liked to make an all-nighter of it, watching both *Godfather*s or both Terrence Malick movies back-to-back.

At daylight, he'd take me downstairs and put me in a cab. If Branko wasn't home, I'd call Joe Coutinho, a man five years older than I who was a producer at ABC News, whom I'd met at one of our college fund-raising cocktail parties. He wore tweed jackets and khaki pants. He had all kinds of good advice concerning my "postpartum" depression. If he wasn't busy, I'd ask him if I could come spend the night.

I don't know where Candace went with the men she met in bars, but she never brought them to our place and never stayed out all night.

The next evening, Candace and I would stay home, silently regrouping, and I'd cook a French meal for us. She loved when I cooked. About eight P.M. the phone would ring, and Candace would jump to get it. But it wasn't for her; it would often be Joe Coutinho, hoping that I'd decided to give up on Nathan once and for all. I'd put him off with vague, friendly talk. Or it would be Branko, checking up on me, making sure I was all right.

* * *

THAT SAME SPRING, I heard about a yoga guru who could fix crippled backs. People said he was a genius, so I convinced Candace to see him, just because she had nothing to lose. Exercise was not her passion, to say the least. But she finally agreed to go, dragging me along. He assured her that yoga would help and she diligently took classes twice a week. She really liked the people she met there and came home full of new information about New Age books, marriages, movies, divorces, and diets. I wondered when she ever had time to exercise.

The guru warned her that recovery would come slowly, and only after a certain amount of pain—he said she had to work through the pain of her childhood—and Candace told him she'd never felt pain in her life.

After a month, she quit.

"Are you out of your mind?" I shouted when she told me. "Are you quitting without a fight? You'll never be able to carry a child unless you develop the proper muscles in your back!"

"I'm never going to have children anyway," she said, brushing it all off with a shrug. She took a swallow of white wine out of a tall, thick, indigo blue stemmed glass. There was always a magnum of white wine in the refrigerator. She said it helped her sleep.

"What do you mean you're never going to have children?" I cried.

"That's ridiculous." I still believed then that all girls found husbands and had babies. It was just that we weren't in any rush to settle down.

"No it's not," she said simply. "I know. Don't tell me how to live my life, Celeste, Madame Babar, Queen of the Elephants. I don't tell you how to live yours."

"Yes you do!"

"No, I don't. I know you're still waiting for Nathan to come back and that you don't love Joe Coutinho, who is as lovely and successful a man as you'll ever find. But I don't judge you. There's a big difference."

"You're lucky, I guess," she said with a sigh, "to love someone like you love Nathan. I've never loved anyone like that."

"What about Brian?" I said, remembering the two-hundred-and-twenty-pound football player Candace had dated our sophomore year.

"Brian!" she threw her head back and laughed. "Brian raped me," she said.

The silence in the kitchen breathed.

"What?" I whispered.

"I never told anyone. You in particular. I didn't want a fuss." She was quiet for a moment. "It was awful," she said. "He hurt me."

Then she told me the story: a classic date rape case—he walked her home and pushed his way into her room. He knew she was afraid, not only of him but of what people would say if she cried out for help.

I wanted to find Brian, wherever he was, and kill him.

Being on the Student Judiciary Committee herself, she'd seen too many cases of girls taking boys up to the student court on accusations of date rape. No one ever believed the charges and the girls became objects of public derision and contempt. So Candace simply ended her relationship with Brian.

"Maybe I led him on," she concluded, shrugging heavily.

For a moment I was unable to speak. "You should've taken the son of a bitch up on charges!" I yelled, making emphatic waving motions with my arms. I knew I never would have told either, and I felt ashamed. "You should've raked him over the coals!" I pounded the kitchen table.

She laughed mirthlessly.

"That's what I love about you," she said. "You never give a shit what people think. I didn't want anyone to know." She gazed at me sadly.

I told her then, in a determined but gentle voice, that she would find the man who was meant for her someday.

Twelve

THE HEADACHE that had started upstairs in Daphne's living room as a pack of loose marbles had grown big and taut as a bowling ball. The bed was rocking like a rowboat in a storm. Feeling that I might throw up, I went into the bathroom, closed the door, and ran the tap in the sink till the water was ice-cold. I cupped my palms and splashed my face. I looked at my blurry reflection in the cabinet mirror and saw puffy half circles below my eyes and lines curving downward from the corners of my mouth. Mine was not the happy, expectant face of a bride-to-be.

I switched off the overhead light, put the lid down on the toilet, and sat with my elbows on my knees. The rectangular window cast a blue shadow into the small bathroom.

Suddenly those deeply buried emotions exploded within my rib cage and I started to cry. My lungs strained as they expanded; I doubled over, as if to stave off blows. I knew these were the tears I had never cried for Candace, and I wept for a long time.

I remembered a cold, bright winter day, our second Christmas season in New York. We were walking down Fifth Avenue, bundled up in hats and scarves, window-shopping. Candace loved holidays, Christmas in particular. "So what if I'm Jewish?" she told me. "I love the decorations and the spirit." She liked to buy presents for all her friends.

Trump Tower was under construction, and up high on its scaffolding, five men with wind instruments were setting up to play.

"Oh, goody!" Candace said.

"Silent Night" burst forth like a gift from the angels. Stopping dead in my tracks as though I'd encountered a wall, I began to cry. Candace had never seen me cry before. She called my name softly and hugged me to her chest.

"Celeste. I'm here. You're not alone."

"I miss my mother," I wailed. "I miss the way it used to be when I was little. She loved 'Silent Night.'"

"Your mother is with you," she said. A chestnut vendor was staring at us, his weather-beaten face half-covered by a thick blue scarf. She wiped my face with her gloved hand.

"Chestnuts!" she said. "Let's buy chestnuts like we did last year. You love them." She handed the vendor a few dollars and said, "Give my friend your best chestnuts. She's sad today." He handed her a little brown bag and gave her back her money.

"Merry Christmas," he said.

"And Merry Christmas to you, too," she said.

Remembering, I was startled by even more violent tears. I wrapped my arms around my shins, unable to look up. Candace was the closest friend I'd ever had. Everything that was hers was mine, and mine, hers.

Except Ed.

* * *

CANDACE AND I had been living together in the city for almost three years when she met him through some friends in banking, a brother and sister of Nordic descent named Nils and Birgitt, who were, of course, tall, thin, and blond. They, in turn, had a girlfriend and a boyfriend who were also tall, thin, and blond. Ed was curly-headed and dark, like Candace, but they were both tall and thin, too. When I was with the six of them, I felt like a person standing among trees.

Ed was their one struggling artist friend and they always paid for his dinners and drinks. Candace was enthralled by the idea that he was writing a novel. She began to read his early chapters and give him criticism. He'd been working on the same eighty pages for two years, but Candace believed in him without reserve, the way she did in me.

Ed took to spending nights at our place rather than taking the subway home to Brooklyn. She asked me if I would mind sleeping on the futon in the living room. I told her of course not, and Ed began to sleep in my single bed across from hers. When I'd get up to pee in the middle of the night, I'd hear them talking heatedly in low whispers.

I asked her one day why she preferred sharing the bedroom with him rather than the large futon in the living room.

"Would you sleep in the same bed as Branko?" she said, snorting at the absurdity of this thought.

"Of course not."

"Exactly. Ed and I are *friends,* Celeste."

I eyed Ed with suspicion, because I felt uncomfortable around Candace's banking associates, who were too athletic and enthusiastic and had never read a novel in their lives. I couldn't imagine what Ed saw in them.

By then the late-night bars we frequented had begun to depress me. They were packed with people who yelled over the jukebox at the top of their lungs and spilled drinks. Everyone seemed to want to have sex as fast as possible regardless of whether they were incapacitated by liquor.

* * *

ONE NIGHT, we went around the corner to Simpson's for a hamburger and the place was unusually crowded. Candace grabbed the maitre d' by the arm and said conspiratorially, "Ted! Can you do something for me? I don't want to wait." Smiling brightly, she added, "You know I'm a good customer." I was embarrassed. Ted's expression remained aloof, but he seated us at the next available deuce.

The waiter was harried and mixed up Candace's drink order, bringing her gin instead of vodka.

"*What is this shit?*" she yelled at him, making a disgusted face. When we got the check, she wouldn't tip him.

"Candace, he's tired." I took several dollars out of my wallet and laid them on the table.

"*I'm* tired!" she cried. "I've been working all day, at a *real* job."

"Jesus, Candace," I muttered, shaking my head.

"I'm paying for my meal!" she said. "I expect service!"

"That could be me, you know," I said icily. She stared at me as if I'd just spoken to her in Arabic.

"*I* could be waiting on you." *No, no, that's not true,* my inner voice said, *because at heart you're not courageous. If you didn't have money, you would've gone to law school, like your father wanted.* A chill skittered up my back. The muscles in my face ached with shame.

* * *

FOR YEARS, I'd studied Russian and I'd longed to go to Russia to improve my skills, and to learn discreetly about Varlam Shalamov, the elusive concentration camp survivor who had written *The Kolyma Tales* and whom no one seemed to know anything about. I applied for a six-week language program in Moscow and was accepted. Then I became afraid of leaving home. I vacillated. The group was leaving on June sixteenth. Candace encouraged me, knowing that for years I had talked about visiting Russia.

"What do you think," she said, "that I won't be here when you get back?"

Memorial Day weekend was approaching. She asked me to go out to Montauk with her, to stay with Birgitt and Nils. Candace and I had spent every Memorial Day together for the past eight years, and she felt it was "bad luck to break old habits." She promised it would be quiet and relaxing. We'd go to the beach, avoid the touristy bars. I agreed, because I didn't want to stay alone in the city and didn't want to visit my father and Anna in Connecticut.

* * *

ON SATURDAY EVENING we all went to Gosman's dock at the Montauk port and ate lobsters out on the quiet, moonlit deck. Seagulls squawked at us from above, and swans glided by on the still water.

I seemed to be the only one who did not have a clear vision of the future; Ed, even, had his novel. I was intimidated by their clear-sightedness, their calm, self-confident faces. Ed, who had ended up next to me, asked me if I intended to use my Ph.D. in Comparative Lit to teach. I said I wasn't looking that far ahead—I was still doing research for my dissertation, when Candace said gaily, "Celeste had a short story published in *The Paris Review!*"

"I didn't know you wrote," Ed said.

"Well, it's not what you'd call a profession," I said, laughing nervously. The rest of them were staring at me as if Candace had just said that I dove off cliffs in my spare time.

"I know what you mean!" Ed said, and at once we were coconspirators against the rest of them. He asked me who my favorite writers were. I told him that at the moment I was concentrating on Primo Levi and Varlam Shalamov, the subjects of my dissertation. He'd never read Levi and hadn't heard of Shalamov, but wanted me to tell him more. I got enthusiastic, explaining that Shalamov was fairly unknown, even in his own country. I was going to Moscow for six weeks that summer to try to learn more about him. Ed nodded at me encouragingly and began talking about *The Seagull,* saying it was the best play he'd ever read.

"Hey, miss! Miss!" Candace shouted at the waitress who was passing by in the distance with a large tray of drinks. Candace held up her empty daiquiri glass, making an angry, impatient face. When the waitress returned, Candace said, "Damn, a person could die of thirst waiting for you!" and ordered another round for the table. Furious at Candace, I asked for a shot of tequila. Ed said that sounded great and ordered one as well.

The drinks arrived. Time passed and I became relaxed. Ed, who had changed the subject to Martin Scorsese, had begun to seem very attractive.

Just as we were figuring out the check, he kissed me, a long, sweet probing kiss, right in front of his friends, and it never occurred to me to stop him.

*   *   *

CANDACE AND I followed the others back to the cottage in our rented car. Her silence made me feel defensive. *I hate your yuppie friends,* I wanted to say, *and sometimes I even hate you, because you're changing. You and I are moving farther and farther apart.* I was getting ready to say this, getting ready to fight.

As I took in a breath, she said matter-of-factly, "I *love* him, Celeste. I've never told him. I've loved him since the beginning, but he only loves me as a friend. He confides in me, depends on me. I'm sorry, I should've told you." She sighed. "They *always* want to be my best friend."

How could I not have seen this? "I'm not interested in him," I said quickly.

She said with uncharacteristic harshness, "Don't give me that shit, Celeste."

That night she and I shared a room with cardboard-thin walls. I lay on my back inches away from her, staring at the moonlit ceiling and listening to everybody's breathing, wondering which exhalation was Ed's, where Ed was in the house, and whether he was thinking of me.

*   *   *

AFTER THAT WEEKEND, Ed stopped staying over at our place and began to call me during the day, when Candace was at work.

* * *

THINKING BACK on Ed, which I often did during my worst sleepless nights, when my life's every mistake and regret crouched in the dark corners of my room, I tried to comprehend why I pursued this dalliance with Ed. I liked to think that I had for a moment believed he might be the one I had been waiting for, the one who would make me forget Nathan. Sometimes I thought that together, Candace and I had been building up momentum, like snowballs rolling downhill that would inevitably hit some jagged rocks. Or was it simply that I'd had too much to drink on the two occasions I met with him? This was the excuse I used to shrug off all my misadventures.

* * *

I MET HIM ONLY once after Montauk, for drinks down in the Village, in a dark bar. Knees touching under the table, we talked in low voices like a stealthy, adulterous couple. We drank vodka martinis, discussed our writing and how hard it was to write in a place like New York. Laughing, we made a ghoulish list of all the writers we could think of who had come to a bad end. The two names Ed came up with were the obvious ones (Hemingway and Fitzgerald). I had wanted more originality from him. After our fourth or fifth drink he invited me up to his friend's loft around the corner, to do some lines of coke. He told me he was watching the guy's cats while he was out of town.

I thought about it for a moment. Who in her right mind would turn down a few lines of coke?

The loft was apparently under construction, tall scaffolds stood against the open brick walls. The long, echoing space smelled of an over-flowing litter box. There was a film of white plaster dust over everything. Ed sat on the couch and a puff of dust rose around him. He spread lines on a large mirror that had "Budweiser" written in red across the center of it. It was hard to tell the coke from the plaster dust. He passed me the mirror and a rolled-up dollar bill. I sniffed up the lines and handed the mirror back to him.

His face to the mirror like Narcissus at the pool, Ed told me twice that there had never been anything between him and Candace. As he glanced up, a stealthy, guilty look shadowed his dark eyes. A knot of anger formed in my throat. Didn't he care about her at all? It was becoming increasingly clear that he was not the one. I longed for Nathan again, with a pain that tore at my stomach like hunger, or fear.

We kissed for a while on the dust-covered couch and he got a hand up under my shirt and caressed my breast through my bra. Guilt left an evil aftertaste on my tongue and in the back of my throat. Ed stopped to spread more lines. I got up to leave, looking around for my jacket.

"What's up?" Ed asked, pinching his nose and sniffing.

"I've got to go," I said vaguely.

"Stick around, I've got plenty more of this." He held up the dollar bill.

Luckily I was one of those people who could walk away from coke. I could go home to bed while others gnashed their teeth and begged their dealers over the phone to bring more. I picked up my jacket and slipped it on. I began to slap the dust off my arms.

"Well, I guess I'll see you later," I said.

"Let's get together in a couple of days," he said uncertainly. "Like, Thursday?"

"Sure," I said.

He was sitting there dumbfounded, the bill still in his hand, as I turned toward the door.

* * *

OF COURSE, I told Candace I'd been out with Joe Coutinho, the editor from ABC News.

"Oh," she said sweetly, "I thought you were with Ed."

"No," I said. She looked at me for a long moment, searching my face, and I was forced to turn away.

* * *

I HAD AGREED to meet him again, but when the day came I called and left a message on his machine that I was sick. After that, I stopped picking up the phone and let the answering machine take his calls and erased the messages before Candace got home. I don't know if she still saw him with Nils and Birgitt, but he never again spent the night.

Candace and I didn't discuss Ed or anything else that was troubling us. I saw discomfort and pain when I looked into her eyes; I wonder if she saw the same in mine.

A few days passed with no further calls from Ed; then a final message. It was on the machine when I got home from Columbia.

"We had so much fun the other night," his voice whined lewdly, barely recognizable, "I thought you and I really had something going. You were *hot*." He made it sound as if we'd slept together. Furious, I returned his call with my own message. "Listen, you son of a bitch," I said, "if you call me one more time, I'm going to talk to the cops."

I hoped and prayed that would be the end of it.

* * *

I STARTED HANGING OUT with my classmates in the quiet of the West Sider bar up by Columbia. I would put off coming home until I thought she'd be in bed.

One night I had a bad dream. I was alone in the apartment and all of Candace's things were gone. An icy wind was blowing through the empty rooms. I called out to her as I walked, but I couldn't find her. I awakened on the futon, in a sweat, still drunk from the shots of tequila I'd had at the West Sider, but already shaking and hungover. I stumbled blindly into the narrow hallway that led to the bedroom, and bumped into a muscular, naked stranger. He was only a silhouette, all I could see were the whites of his eyes glinting dangerously.

"Who are you?" I said, trying not to let him know how scared I was. "What are you doing here?"

"I have no fucking idea," he muttered angrily. I pushed past him and into the bathroom, locking the door. I sat on the toilet for a while, trying to decide what to do. When I came out, the light was on in the kitchen and the front door was wide open. The silence breathed and ticked. I closed and locked the door and ran to the bedroom. Candace was on her back, spread-eagle.

"Candace!" I shook her. "Candace! Damn it!"

Finally she stirred and opened one blind eye, like a person emerging from a coma. "Candace! Who was that guy? There was a naked guy in the hallway."

"Wha' guy?" She lifted her head as if it were an impossible weight, and looked around. Her clothes were strewn everywhere, her bra hung over the top of the lampshade as though it had caught there in midflight. "No guy here. You mush be dreaming," she said, and her eyes rolled back in her head.

I brought this up again the next day, but she vehemently insisted that there had been no man.

"You brought a total stranger into our house! He could have

killed you! And me! You had a blackout, Candace." I was furious; I wanted her to admit the truth.

"I've never had a blackout in my life," she said, outraged. "I'm not talking about this anymore."

* * *

I **DON'T KNOW** how long I stayed doubled over like that, weeping in Daphne's bathroom. Finally, exhausted, I felt a certain calm return.

The tiled room was darker, still tinted that disconcerting blue. The faucet dripped. High-heeled shoes were clicking impatiently down the circular stairs.

Daphne found me sitting on the closed toilet with my head cradled in my arms. She flicked on the light, which buzzed to life over our heads. I looked up at her, wincing.

"You're as white as a sheet," she said. "Are you all right?"

"Did you invite Candace?" I asked. Daphne's hazel eyes went round and stared at me.

"No, of course not," she said quickly, and wrapped her arm around my shoulders. She pulled me up and walked me away from the bathroom, as if it were to blame. "I'm sorry, honey," she said.

"I have a headache," I murmured.

Daphne led me back to the bed and gently helped me stretch out on the soft pillows. "I'll get you some Advil." She rushed off, returning in a moment with a cold compress, a glass of water, and two pills. "Here. Just rest a while," she said softly.

I closed my eyes.

* * *

I **MISSED CANDACE** terribly while I was in Moscow. Varlam Shalamov proved more elusive than I'd expected. Few people would admit they'd heard of him, even fewer that they'd read his work. Once, at a dissident's house, I was shown a mimeographed copy of one of Shalamov's stories. I had seen one once before, while in college. It had been smuggled to the West by Viktor Bezsmertno, another dissident. "Shalamov came home after more than a quarter century in the Kolyma camps," the dissident in Moscow told me. "He was living here peacefully, writing. Then some fucking American professor smuggled *The Kolyma Tales* out of Russia, translated and published them in the United States. As punishment, the government put Shalamov in a mental institution, the worst one we have, right here in Moscow. He died there, without visitors, without friends. Alóne."

How many people would remember him? I wondered with a sinking heart. How many would know that he left the single greatest literary testament to the atrocities of Stalinism? It became even more imperative for me to get home and finish my Ph.D. dissertation.

* * *

FROM MOSCOW, I sent Candace the most outrageously Communist postcards I could find. Lenin in red addressing the lumpen proletariat; the Soviet flag with hammer and sickle blowing in the wind; Young Pioneers with red scarves tied about their necks, helping the elderly. I wrote her six postcards in six weeks. They'd started out jocular and grew more and more apologetic, until they became hysterical. Finally I begged her to explain her silence.

She never wrote back. I decided that for once I would confront my problems head-on, face to face, as soon as I got home. I'd tell her the truth about Ed. I'd tell her he wasn't worth the saliva I was using up, explaining to her that nothing had happened and he meant nothing to me. I was certain that she would listen to me. It wasn't too late.

* * *

I HELD OUR apartment door open with my shoulder and threw my heavy bags in. An envelope skidded across the kitchen floor. In it were Candace's apartment keys and a note.

Dear Celeste,

You must think I'm a total moron. I heard Ed's messages, including the lewd one that said what a good time he had with you that night. You erased them before I got home but I always called in from work to check messages. Why did you lie to me? I could've handled it if you'd told me the truth. I don't want to stay in New York anymore. This is a sick place. I'm going home to Boston where I belong. I had the PO hold your mail. You can go pick it up. Please don't call my parents looking for me because I don't want to talk to you. Who are you? You are not the person I used to know.

Candace

On the kitchen table were the first two of the six postcards I'd sent her from Moscow. The card she'd given me the night before I left stood on the bookcase in the living room. I picked it up. It was a cartoon of a mouse flying on a goose's back, in the midst of a flock. I opened it. The caption read, "Have A Nice Trip!" Below that was Candace's girlish, large round print. "Stick to your dreams and you will find your way."

* * *

I WROTE HER several letters, sending them to her parents' address. They came back to me unopened. I was afraid to call them. I checked periodically, but Candace still did not have a listed phone number in the Boston area.

When I finally gave up the apartment we'd shared to move in with Alex, I found the card again, covered with dust, between the refrigerator and the wall. Jittery-kneed, I sat down on the bare floor. I'd completely forgotten about that card. How had it ended up behind the fridge?

"Have A Nice Trip!"

* * *

TWICE A YEAR, the alumni magazine arrived with Candace's class notes inside, and every time, my heart constricted in my chest. I could barely stand to open the magazine, but did nevertheless. All class mail was directed to her parents' home. She wrote high-spirited, enthusiastic notes, gossiping about who had gotten married and who'd had a baby. She never failed to mention alumni she had run into in Boston, and that she was not married and didn't have any prospects. She was doing well, working in a commercial bank, living alone in the city, and still "partying hardy with my old college buddies."

The day after my bridal shower, I forced myself to call Samantha and Jacob. Samantha picked up, and a moment later, I heard a second receiver click. "Is that you, Jacob?" she asked. "It's me," he said, and that was all.

I told them I was engaged.

"How lovely," Samantha said coolly. "I'll be sure to tell Candace. Well, good-bye then," she said, and hung up.

I held the receiver with a trembling hand. Finally, when the dial tone beeped busy, I set it down.

I went to the window and looked down at Seventy-ninth Street that seemed so tiny, far below. The long, straight canyon stretched all the way to Fifth Avenue and Central Park. If you could see through the tall green trees of the park, you would find a curving path to the West Side and Amsterdam Avenue and our old apartment—cramped, crooked-floored, but filled with our dreams. Where had they all gone? Was I indeed a person whom Candace no longer knew? Did I deserve the punishment she had meted out?

My forehead pressed against the cool glass, I prayed for the first time in a very long while, for God to let the answers come to me.

Thirteen

AFTER MY BRIDAL SHOWER, I started napping too much during the day and having insomnia at night. I worried about everything, especially the kids in Harlem. I had one visit left with them the next week, and after that, I'd never see them again. I didn't know if I'd helped them. I had tried to help them. Also, my short story collection was not progressing. Whenever I sat down to write, I found myself weighing what had happened in Mexico with Alex. No matter how often that inner voice chastised me—*it was your fault, you were drunk and you acted like a jerk*—some other part of me would not let it go. Something terribly wrong had happened.

As I lay in bed at night, the anger I felt made my heart beat too fast. I'd put on the headphones and watch the Discovery Channel to calm my jangled nerves, while Alex slept unperturbed beside me.

* * *

ALEX'S MOTHER called on Friday afternoon while I was napping. Aurelia was in town for a couple of days and suggested dinner on Sunday evening at Nero's, the restaurant where the rehearsal dinner would take place, to go over details with Alex, the owner, and me.

Later I awakened to Alex's handsome, tired face peering over me. The setting sun cast pink ribbons of light through the blinds, onto the wall across from the bed.

"Hey, lazybones," he said. "I figured I'd surprise you and bring home dinner."

"Your mother called before," I murmured, stretching. "She wants to meet us at Nero's for dinner Sunday night."

"Good," he said.

I got up and perched on the kitchen counter with a glass of white wine while Alex took fresh-grilled tuna steaks and a large assortment of seasonal greens and vegetables out of a white paper bag. He got out a salad bowl and poured in the greens and the container of herb vinaigrette.

"Wow, Alex. This is really nice."

When the salad was ready, he carried our new large wooden bowl to the dining table and set it down. He lit candles in our new candlesticks, set the table with our new silverware, new dishes. The table looked pretty, expectant. We sat and ate in silence for a while.

"Alex, I think maybe I should go talk to somebody."

"What do you mean?"

"You know, talk to a shrink or something. I'm just not feeling well. I can't sleep at night and I can't wake up during the day."

"Maybe you've still got that bug," he said. "Why do you think you need to talk to a shrink?"

I treaded gingerly. "Well, for a while now I've been—I've been haunted by all sorts of thoughts . . . "

"Haunted?" He looked away. He took off his glasses and fogged them with his breath, then wiped them with his napkin. "Celeste, listen. Wait till the wedding's over, then do whatever you want, okay? I just don't think it's a good idea to start digging up stuff now. Not right before the wedding." He put his glasses back on, lowered his eyes to his plate, his flushed ears betraying his discomfort.

After a while he said, "It'll be nice to see my mother, it's been since, what, March? I hope she's put together her guest list like she said she would. She's not really reliable when it comes to this kind of thing."

After I cleared the dishes, he took the wedding file out of his briefcase and spread the papers across the table and looked them over. He had computerized the master list, which held the alphabetized names and addresses of people who had been invited, and he had added a little square in the margin where he could "X" in their RSVPs; there was a "Shower" list with all the gifts listed next to the names of guests; there was a "Wedding Gifts" list, which included date of gift received and a check box for when the thank-you note had been sent; and the "Rehearsal Dinner" list, incomplete because his mother had not supplied him with the names of her guests.

Alex's father would not chip in for the rehearsal dinner, so Alex was splitting the tab with his mother. Aurelia, who was ministering to HIV-positive babies in Zaire, had suggested Nero's because she had gone to college with the owner, Maria Nero, who would surely give Alex an excellent price. Alex was not thrilled that the food was Italian, but he asked around and was told that Nero's was an excellent, well-established restaurant, so we went to dinner there several times to taste different dishes and plan the menu.

Alex was a little concerned about the seating arrangement, as both sides of the family were coming and his parents had divorced when he was a small child. They did not see each other and had nothing in common except for Alex.

"I'm glad she's deigned to visit before my trip to L.A.," he said. "This thing has to be finished before I go."

I had forgotten that he was going away for most of next week. I was ashamed at the relief I felt.

Aurelia arrived thirty minutes late, as was her wont. She marched in, Amazonian in height and assurance. "Hello, hello, sweeties!" she cried.

"Hello, Mother," Alex said. She gave him a hug and then me, pulling away just as I attempted to plant a kiss on her cheek. They didn't kiss in his family either. *That's right,* I thought, *it's the French side who kisses.*

"So tell us about Zaire," Alex said when everyone had finally settled down. He crossed his arms on the table and leaned forward expectantly, smiling with his fine white teeth.

"Zaire was terrific, but Uganda! Oh my Lord. In one village, we attempted to demonstrate the use of condoms by sliding one over a broom handle. On our follow-up visit the next day, they proudly showed us their broomsticks with the condoms we had given them stretched over the handles!"

Alex and she chuckled at the same moment. Sitting between them, I had the odd impression of looking at two representations of the same face—one older and more feminine, but otherwise they were nearly identical. They both had short, thick, dark blond hair and unfathomable, deep-blue eyes. On the few occasions I'd spent with her, I'd listened in bewildered silence while she told of meeting Mobutu ("I called him a big ninny, he loved it"); of almost sitting on a crocodile in the Amazon jungle ("Well, I just thought he was a log, you see"); of flying across America in a hot air balloon with a millionaire she'd been dating ("Hank just loved to show off"). She had seen so much that nothing could get a rise out of her anymore except the sight of starving children and oppressed women. I liked what she did. I even liked her politics. But I didn't like the way I couldn't see behind her eyes.

They each ordered a rum and tonic. I ordered a bottle of Pellegrino water, hoping to make a good impression.

"So why were you late *this* time?" Alex asked, and reached across the table and punched her lightly in the arm.

"It was Frederico, of course. He didn't have his keys so I had to wait—"

Alex interrupted her. "Let's talk about the rehearsal dinner."

After they'd finished their drinks, Maria Nero sent over a bottle of Chianti. Alex rushed to fill our glasses. He was clearly in some kind of excited state.

"This is pretty good wine," said Aurelia. "Maybe we could order this for the rehearsal dinner."

She picked up the bottle and topped off my glass, which I hadn't yet touched. It seemed too much trouble to refuse, to say, *I'm trying to cut back,* so I decided to sip it carefully instead, make it last.

Alex had taken several large gulps and was now topping off his own glass.

Our pasta dishes arrived, and Alex began to ask his mother about her guest list. He was planning the order of the toasts and wanted to know if any of his mother's friends were going to speak.

"Alex, I have no idea!" she cried. "That would take the element of chance totally out of it."

"Exactly," Alex said. "I don't want people going on forever about all the stupid things I did in college."

She chuckled amusedly. "Oh, you mean like when you beat the crap out of that football player for insulting your black friend and had to take a leave of absen—"

I looked at him, my mouth agape.

"Mother, I don't mean that *at all,*" he said between his teeth.

"Well, I haven't made a list yet, Alex. And I think I'll just leave it up to you."

Alex fell silent, brooding.

Another bottle of wine arrived, and later, a bottle of champagne with our dessert, three slices of almond espresso cake, the house specialty.

"Maria is spoiling us tonight!" Aurelia exclaimed.

Alex brusquely filled his champagne flute to the top. Bubbles slipped over the rim and down the stem. He filled his mother's glass, then mine.

"Well," Aurelia said, raising her glass, "I'm glad the whole thing is settled, then. To you, Alex, for doing such a good job. You'll organize this much better than I ever could. I just hope you won't invite too many of your father's stodgy friends."

"Of course not," Alex said, smiling gruesomely. He produced a folded sheet of yellow paper from his shirt pocket and slapped it down on the table; the glasses jumped. "This is the list so far. Now, I want you to sit there for a minute and *think* about who you want to invite to this rehearsal dinner."

Aurelia waved it away. "Oh, I'm sure you can do this without me, Alex."

"Mother," Alex said in a pointed tone, "I want you to have a say in this."

"But I just had my say. I have to go to Mississippi tomorrow, and I'll be gone for a week at least, this is very important to me, Alex, I—"

"And this isn't," he muttered, looking down at the table, a flush spreading over his cheeks. In one swallow he finished off his champagne and refilled his glass.

"All right," Aurelia said with resignation, "Let me see who you've got there. You don't like my friends anyway."

The tips of his ears had turned bright red. Something was beginning to surface from the depths of his calm, still eyes. Watching him, I had a sudden, frightful vision of him overturning the table.

Aurelia glanced at the list and slid it away. "Well, we'll have to ask Frederico, of course," she said vaguely. "And the doctors, let's see— Isabel Green . . . "

He drank his champagne down and stared at his mother with watery eyes.

"Oh, Alex," she sighed . . . "stop being such a tight-ass, will you?"

That was clearly the wrong thing to say. A series of sentences shot out of his mouth like bullets, although he never raised his voice.

"When I was a little kid you left me alone with a moronic maid so you could traipse around the world and take care of other people's kids. It's my fucking *rehearsal dinner* and you couldn't even give me an idea of who you wanted me to invite. You can't ever fucking pretend to care. You're the most selfish, self-involved person I've ever met. How unfortunate for me that you happen to be my mother." Then, quite calmly, he added, "Why am I surprised?" and began to tap at the corner of his dessert plate with his small fork.

Aurelia stared at him, startled, her pink lips slightly parted, exposing her small, even white teeth. "My God, Alex. I did the best I could—I was a single mother."

"You weren't single for thirty seconds. Peter, Hank, John, and now,

I'm sorry, what's his name? Oh yes, *Frederico*. You had time for them. You had time for med school when I was a kid and you certainly had time to graduate at the top of your class."

"I played tennis with you, I paid for your tennis camps. I paid for Choate all by myself, for God's sake!"

Alex didn't say anything, but stared down at the crumbs on his plate and began to smash them with his fork.

"And every vacation we went somewhere where you could practice with the best pros. I did the best I could. I had to live my life, too, after all."

Alex filled his glass again and lifted his flute.

"Alex, put down that champagne glass," I said in a murmur.

His head snapped toward me and he eyed me with icy contempt. "The pot calling the kettle black, don't you think?"

"Not tonight," I said, flushing, glancing quickly from his mother to my half-filled glass.

"Whatever," he said, sighing deeply. "It doesn't matter. I'll take care of it. I've been taking care of myself since I was five years old."

His face looked unfamiliar; he'd become a frightened little boy. In the trembling corners of his mouth I saw glimmers of the grown-up struggling to regain his composure. I was disquieted, and afraid of him, and the floor below me seemed to drop away. I reached for my flute and drank the champagne down in one swallow. With a trembling hand, I lifted the bottle and attempted to nonchalantly pour more into my glass.

"I did the best I could," Aurelia said in a quiet voice, staring at me with a pleading look. "His father wouldn't even give him the money to rent a tux for his senior prom. I had to do everything. I don't understand why . . ." her voice trailed off.

"I'm sure you were a terrific mother," I said. "You did a great job." I put my hand over hers and smiled weakly. Her long, thin fingers felt chilled beneath mine.

"Well, if that's all," Alex said, standing up and squaring his shoulders.

And he left the restaurant very much as his mother had entered it.

"Give me a call tomorrow?" I said to Aurelia, and ran after her son.

I found Alex two blocks up, demolishing a bus-stop shelter. He had lifted a metal trash can and was flinging it repeatedly against the shelter's shatterproof glass wall, which was beginning to crack. Empty paper cups, plastic bottles, cans, and food-stained wrappers flew from the can and skittered about him.

"Alex!" I screamed. "Stop!

People across the street were stopping to watch, while on our side, they hurried past as fast as they could. I came up behind him and tried to hold his arm. He pushed me aside as if I were no heavier than a jacket. I slammed into a parked car, my ribs crashing against the hood.

Frantic, as if possessed, he kicked and punched the thick, crumbling glass out of its casing. The chunks of glass tumbled to the pavement like ice cubes from a huge bag. We heard a cop car siren approaching, and Alex suddenly straightened and gazed around him. He grabbed my arm and dragged me running down a side street toward the next avenue. On the next corner he hailed a cab and shoved me in before getting in himself and slamming the door. His liquor-heavy breath came in gasps. The cab driver's eyes glinted in the rearview mirror like fish passing in a dark tank. I gave him the address.

Alex shouted, "Shit!" then buried his face in his bloodied hands. I couldn't tell if he was sobbing or just breathing heavily. I sat pressed against the door, afraid he might explode again.

"They've never given a shit about me, either one of them. I was a mistake," he said between great heaving sighs. "That fuck my father wouldn't even loan me money for MBA school. I didn't ask him to *give* it to me, for Christ's sake. And that cunt Babs! She fucking hates me!"

I sat frozen, stunned. "It's all right," I reassured him. "It's all right."

But he didn't seem to hear me.

* * *

ALEX LURCHED into the bedroom, dropping his clothes on the floor as he went. He shut the door and the line of light beneath the door went dark.

Later, after two large cognacs, I joined him. As Alex slept soundly beside me, I put on the earphones and watched a show on the birth and death of stars. The narrator said in a deep, measured voice that our own sun would nova in approximately 4.5 billion years. I was struck by an image of the bed being sucked into a tiny black hole and the whole room being pulled in behind it, then the building, the city, the continent, and finally the Earth, until all of it was nothing but a speck of dust floating in space.

* * *

I AWAKENED to the sounds of his packing. He was in a hurry. I sat up in bed and watched him glide quickly about the room, speaking to himself, checking things off a mental list. He was in his blue suit, clean shaven, his fair hair slicked back and his little round glasses glinting brightly.

"Alex, are you all right?"

"Socks . . . gym socks . . . I'm fine," he said, looking toward me with a small frown.

"Alex, you were very upset last night."

He stopped what he was doing and stood immobile for a moment, looking down at me. "I'm sorry, I was a little drunk. My mother just . . . sometimes she makes me angry. It's been a long time since . . . listen, I don't want to discuss this now. I'm fine. I don't even remember what I said." He glanced at his watch. His knuckles were bruised and scabbed. "I'm running late." He opened and closed his hand a few times, looking at it as if he didn't recognize it.

"How are you going to explain that?"

"I never have to explain myself. Besides, it'll scare the shit out of the guy across the table."

He stood in the doorway for a moment, seeming so poised, so strong and in control, so grown-up, I felt as though I had witnessed some kind of rip in time, and this reality had nothing to do with the other, dark reality of last night. My ribs ached where they had smashed into the car hood.

He said, "I'll call you from L.A. Okay?"

"Alex, it's not okay!" I said, suddenly hysterical. "You tore down a fucking bus shelter last night! It's not okay at all!"

"Celeste, you don't need to use that kind of language," he said in a calm, fatherly voice. "I don't have time to discuss this right now."

"You never have time, Alex. You *never* have time!"

"You're overreacting, like you always do. Why don't you *do* something today, instead of just sitting here worrying about nothing? Go to a museum or something."

"Don't you fucking dismiss this, Alex. Don't you dismiss me!" I shouted. "You can't leave with this hanging in the air!"

"Why are you shouting, Celeste? You're way out of control."

I wanted to throw the bedside lamp at him. "*I'm* out of control? *I'm* out of control?"

"I can't talk to you when you're like this," he said. He walked out, letting the front door slam behind him.

Fourteen

I HAD TO KEEP BUSY, not think about Alex, so I spent the morning typing the best of the children's poems and stories and gluing their drawings onto the pages, so that I could take the anthology down to The Writer's Way before lunch so they could make copies. I'd pick them up later in the day and take them up to the children tomorrow. I had the whole week to get this done, but now I was on a mission. To *not* think about Alex.

On my way back I stopped at the mailbox. A letter from my grandmother was among the junk mail and bills and wedding RSVPs. I recognized her thin, vertical script on the thick, eggshell-colored envelope.

For the past nine years, my grandmother had sent me a card on my birthday and at Christmas and Easter, and I'd responded from time to time with a saccharine Hallmark card, bearing only my name. Yet I'd sent her an invitation to the wedding with a little note that read: "I do hope you will come—Celeste." I never expected that she would, and now my heart skipped and jumped. I couldn't wait to get back upstairs and open the envelope. The letter was in French. My grandmother had told me that she could read several of the Romance tongues, but she'd refused categorically to learn to write or speak anything but French, which was, in her opinion, the only perfect language in the world.

Chateau Laroq
Cadaujac
7 June

My very dear Céleste,

Please forgive my delay in responding to your invitation; however, I have been waiting to see how my husband Albert is faring after his most recent cardiac arrest. It appears recovery is slow and therefore I will not be able to attend. This causes me sadness and I do hope you will consider a voyage to France to visit me before I die. Your husband of course is welcome as well. One would not make the same mistake twice! (ha ha, a little joke).

So many issues were left unresolved between your mother and me and also between you and me at the close of your last visit. Could it have been nine years ago already? Please do write to me. You may not believe me but every day I expect a letter from you and am always pained when one never arrives. How is it that I have managed to make such a horrendous mess of things?

Regardless, I do remain your loving and devoted grandmother,

Sophie de Fleurance de Saint-Martin

* * *

I READ IT again upstairs, pacing back and forth in the apartment. I didn't know what to do with myself.

So she isn't coming, I thought, and my skin prickled and itched from the inside as impotent rage tried to surface. With that unwanted emotion came dread, and the thought that warned, This is all wrong. You don't belong here.

I had never really expected my grandmother to come, so why was I having this reaction now?

I lifted the venetian blinds on the living room window and pressed my face to the glass. The leaves of the ficus tree tickled my neck and shoulder. I'd brought it in from the hall one day; most of its leaves had fallen off and the earth in the pot was cracked and gray. Some heartless person had just left it there upon moving out. Now it was green and well and grateful.

"What do you want?" I said to it as if it had interrupted me. "You want some water?"

I went and got the plastic water pitcher. As I poured, I looked out at the street, stricken senseless by the sun. Inside, cool air hummed quietly through the vents. Way down below, a taxi suddenly swung around the corner and smashed into a red station wagon that was waiting at the light. Both tiny drivers got out swinging their fists and kicking up their legs. It was like watching a battle scene in a silent film. I began to feel dizzy and moved away from the window.

* * *

THIS ALBERT was a new husband I had not met. Her last one, the one who had been suffering from gout at the time of my mother's funeral, had died in 1982. My grandmother had written me a short, crisp note informing me of the death of *le Professeur*. Apparently he had died peacefully in his sleep. I didn't know why she called him *le Professeur*, for he had been a pharmacist whose family had fallen on hard times. I had first met him when I was nine and my mother and I visited for two weeks in the summer of 1969, and I retained a vivid picture of him as an old man who looked like a plucked rooster. He had a few tufts of downy white hair on his head and a beak nose and loose, clammy skin. He walked around grumbling as if the world made a full-time job of affronting his sensibilities. All his fingers were webbed except for the thumbs, a congenital defect that he would be happy to tell you went back seven generations. He had fairly good dexterity, however, and liked to grab hold of me and pinch my cheeks between his webbed fingers and his thumb. I was fascinated and disgusted by his hands and stole glances at them whenever I could. His fingers were clearly formed and pressed together under a thick layer of skin that wrapped around his hand like a bandage.

Every Christmas for as many years as I could remember, my mother had sent him a pair of gloves. She searched for the right pair for days, combing the fancy men's departments with me in tow, finally settling on fabulously expensive lambskin designer gloves. She mailed them off in a chic box with a little exuberant Christmas note, and waited impatiently for his response. Invariably, a note arrived in January, thanking her for her lovely and thoughtful gift, but inquiring as to whether the designer might have available in the same size and of similar quality, a pair of mittens. He never returned the gloves.

* * *

AT DINNER in my grandmother's large, candlelit, echoing dining room, we sat at the long, dark oak table that had been in the chateau for generations and generations.

"Come here, *mon petit*," my grandmother said in a tender voice, "I want to show you something interesting."

I jumped down off my *annuaires* and skipped over to her side, fluttering daintily in my brand-new lemon yellow tulle dress that had a lace petticoat, sleeves, and collar, and a large bow in back. It had come in a gift-wrapped box all the way from Bélina, one of the most expensive children's stores in Paris—a present from my grandmother, along with an ancient porcelain doll whose blue eyes closed when you laid her down and who had a brand-new yellow dress as well. My grandmother had told me that the doll had belonged to my mother when she was a girl.

My grandmother took my small hand in her strong plump fingers and placed my fingertips over some dark grooves in the wood of the tabletop at the place to her left where no one sat.

"Do you feel the grooves?" she asked me quietly. "There are four of them, just like fingers. Feel how dainty. They were surely made by the fingertips of a lady. A lady from a long time ago who sat next to her husband at this very table and fretted. What about—we don't know. Imagine how long she must have sat here and worried to make such marks! She was one of your ancestors, perhaps Madeleine de Figeac de Fleurance, who died in 1742—"

"Pff," said my mother, blowing air through her pursed lips. "Don't fill her head with such nonsense, Mother!"

"What?" said my grandmother, as if shocked. "It's the truth! You're the one who is unreliable in this family, Nathalie, not I."

Le Professeur clucked heartily, nodding from his seat at the opposite end of the table. I looked at him and felt my heart turn to ice—a big floating iceberg in a dark, cold sea.

"She doesn't lie!" I cried out. "You're the one who lies!" I pointed at him. He laughed, his whole body racked with mirth.

"You're right to defend your mother," said my grandmother. "That's a good loyal girl. But you mustn't point. I wish my daughter defended *me* that way . . ." Her voice trailed off unhappily. "By the way, Nathalie," my grandmother said to her daughter, smiling at me as she rearranged a curl in my hair, "I compliment you on *Céleste*'s proficiency in our language. With a little work, one wouldn't be able to tell that she is not French."

* * *

ALTHOUGH THE Chateau Laroq rouge had been rated among the Crus Exceptionnels in the Graves 1953 and 1959 official classifications, my grandmother complained that the rating should have come much sooner and she believed certain of her best years were superior to Chateau Haut Brion's first growths and that her white was always given short shrift for some incomprehensible reason. She was extremely proud of the fact that Chateau Laroq had stayed in the Fleurance family for over four hundred years, never succumbing to the pressures of foreign multinationals, as so many others had in the Bordeaux region. This was what we discussed as my grandmother took me on long late-afternoon walks "for the constitution," through the rows and rows of ripening grapes. The soil, speckled with gravel stones the size of fists, sloped gently toward the banks of the Garonne. The chateau itself stood in the middle of the vineyard, and tame-looking woods and pine forests stretched far into the distance. There was an enclosed pasture behind the chateau where a few old Thoroughbreds wandered aimlessly through the warm, mild days.

"Your real grandfather de Saint-Martin was poor but exceptionally bright and very handsome. He never did a thing but read and study. He read every single book in the library. He was nice to the children and left me alone, bless him." My grandmother leaned over a clump of little green grapes and inspected them closely through her bifocals, ignoring me completely for a long time. "Good," she said, and moved on. "Let me give you a little advice, *Céleste*," she now said, taking my hand in her plump, dry one. "Although you may be too young for it—marry a weak man. Have your affairs with strong ones, to be sure. But the smart Fleurance women have always married weak men, which is why we have succeeded in keeping the vineyard.

"You are half-French," my grandmother said sternly, "and you must never forget that this place, this land and our wine, is yours, too. Sometimes I wish that your uncle François was less of a cretin and more of a man. I also wish I'd had more children to carry on the tradition. I fear that François will sell after I die—why not? He's greedy and stupid. Your mother is so much brighter than he. A rebel and a wild one, she is, yes, but so much brighter . . . Wouldn't you like to come back and live in France with your old *Bonne-maman* who adores you?"

"Oh yes!" I said. Obviously, the relationship between my mother and *Bonne-maman* had somewhat improved for her to even suggest such a thing. "But what about *le Professeur*?" I asked with a certain concern.

"*Ah, lui!*" she said, shrugging. "He means no harm. He's just an old fool."

* * *

MY MEMORY is filled with mild, sunny days and the smell of rich wine at every meal, poured in great drops into my water glass; the exquisite lengthy meals that ended with *hachis Parmentier* on Sundays, the cook having ground up all the leftover meats from the whole week, covered them with a layer of milky mashed potatoes, and baked the deep dish in the oven. And there were lavish gifts from my grandmother, the best one an enormous brown bear from Le Nain Bleu in Paris, who arrived in a large cardboard box.

"Stop it, Mother, you're spoiling her," my mother said to my grandmother the day the bear came.

"Pff!" said my grandmother. "It won't hurt her a bit. You've picked up that Calvinist ethic, I see," she added pointedly through pursed lips, which made my mother storm out of the room.

"She's not so bad," I said to my mother gingerly that night as she was tucking me into bed. "Why do you always get mad at her?" I had been wondering why my mother had prepared me to meet a monstrous old witch when my grandmother was really a very appealing, kind and generous lady.

"Pff!" said my mother. "You don't know her. She's trying to buy you, can't you see that? She's very charming when she wants, but what a viper!"

* * *

A FEW DAYS LATER, they had a terrible fight. Doors slammed and voices crashed against the stone walls downstairs, echoing up to me in the warm, still night. My mother burst in like a black tornado and packed me up in a rush. She was flushed and distraught and seemed deflated, as if her clothes were suddenly loose on her frame, as if my grandmother had sucked out all her strength.

"What? What?" I cried, sitting up in the large bed.

"We're leaving, that's what," my mother said.

"Can I take the clothes? Can I take the doll and the bear?" I asked apprehensively.

"Not that damn bear, he's as big as you are."

"I'll carry him, I swear!"

"Oh, all right. But if you ask me to carry him just once I'll throw him out. I will," she warned.

Early the next morning Georges the chauffeur drove us to the Bordeaux train station. We got on a train heading for Italy without saying good-bye to my *Bonne-maman*. The bear, whose name was Monsieur Laroq, took up a whole seat himself.

"Aren't we going to say good-bye and thank you?" I asked my mother, because after all, that was what she'd always told me to do.

"No, we are not going to say good-bye and thank you," she said, imitating my whiny singsong and making a face. I wanted to kick her in the shins and run back to my grandmother's house.

Repenting, the lines in her face softening, she said with a coy smile, "But I tell you what we're going to do, we're going to spend all the money I have in my special bank account and we're going to live like queens! Then and only then we'll go home."

* * *

MY SOPHOMORE year came to a close in a rush of exams and papers. My grades were unbelievable. I'd gotten four A's and an A plus. Only I knew that I had been concentrating so hard on getting through my classes and homework each day so that I could go out drinking with Candace. As a result I hadn't thought about the summer at all. The prospect of three long hot months waitressing again in Connecticut seemed unbearable. I didn't want to sit there waiting to hear from Nathan, whose most recent impassioned letter had come from Oaxaca, Mexico. A feeling of uneasiness and dread came over me whenever I thought of him. I felt we'd left things completely unresolved, and every time he came to mind I broke into a cold sweat of rage that utterly paralyzed me and made me want to jump out a window. It was easier to deal with the loneliness and the sadness of longing for him than to admit to myself the rage I felt toward him.

I seized upon the idea of writing my grandmother a letter asking if I could come visit over the summer holiday. It seemed the perfect escape, and in my enthusiasm I began to remember fondly the large, cool stone chateau with its high slate roof, the pond with carp, the crickets singing all night, the rich, succulent vineyard, the woods, the Garonne River flowing by in the valley below, and my grandmother's old racehorses that roamed long-legged across the field.

She wrote me back a sprawling, enthusiastic letter and enclosed a check for five thousand francs to purchase my airline ticket. She told me she would combine a visit to Paris with my arrival, so that Georges her chauffeur could drive us back and we could avoid the long and uncomfortable train ride to Bordeaux. To my grandmother, taking a plane from Paris to Bordeaux was a sacrilege. Planes polluted the air and made noise. Trains were the only civilized way to travel across land. I wasn't about to argue with her.

* * *

SHE MET ME at Charles de Gaulle Airport, a space age monster that had not been there when I was nine and that frightened me now as I stepped off the plane, hungover from the drinks I'd had to calm my fear of flying. She was standing in front of everybody at the gate, much shorter than I remembered, solid and round as a boulder in her well-pressed dark blue linen suit.

"*Bonjour, Bonne-maman,*" I said in a shaky voice.

"*Mon Dieu,*" said my grandmother with a gasp. "*Mais tu as vraiment mauvaise mine!*" My God, but you look awful! She reached up and placed her small hand on my cheek. "What's the matter, my darling?" she asked.

"Heartbreak," I said indifferently, with a certain bravado. "*J'ai le coeur brisé.*" And I laughed, although tears were threatening. In the touch of her hand, the smell of her wrist, I recognized the essence of my mother and realized with a shudder that my grandmother was much more familiar to me than my father or Anna. She was, I saw now, the last link to my mother, whom I had loved with a fierce and terrible devotion that bordered on obsession because I had always feared, from the youngest age, that I might lose her at any moment.

"*Mais si, mais si,* everything can be fixed, even *le chagrin d'amour,*" my grandmother said with confidence. "Come along, let's get your bags. You have two whole months to tell me about it."

Le Professeur was waiting in the Citroen, she told me, because he could hardly walk, due to his advanced gout.

* * *

THE CHATEAU LAROQ had not changed from my child's memory. Only, the dramatic circular towers with their round, pointed slate roofs that stood at each corner of the main structure did not seem so tall now. The stone terraces that descended in layers to the vineyard did not seem so vast. The wide marble staircase leading from the center of the front hall to the upstairs bedrooms was no longer the formidable obstacle it had once been.

The second-floor bedrooms sprawled out along a wide corridor that split off in two wings from the main structure. The walls and stairwell of the main hall were decorated with ancient paintings. The furniture was a mixture of different *siècles,* mostly Louis XI and Louis XIII. My grandmother pointed to objects, naming their period, and said that the Fleurances had always liked those two Louis. At the foot of the staircase were two incongruous gigantic *Empire* vases that depicted Napoleonic battles in heroic panoramas. I looked back at them as we climbed the stairs and my grandmother said with a shrug, "Oh, those were there before. That was my great-grandfather Alphonse Fleurance's addition—he loved Napoléon, what can one say?"

She put me in my mother's old bedroom, which had a four-poster bed and a view of the horses in the field and the pine forest beyond.

Before dinner we drank an exquisite *apéritif*—some kind of clear liqueur made from plums. *Le Professeur* shuffled around in silence, grumbling and clucking to himself. He stepped between us, in the middle of a conversation, switched on the TV news and sat down, turning the volume up full blast.

"Let's go out to the sunroom," said my grandmother. "The poor old man is as deaf as a pot." She laughed heartily, and for a moment I almost felt sorry for him.

* * *

A WIND RUSTLED outside the glass walls of the sunroom. The sun was a burning orange ember perfectly outlined above the distant woods. It dropped quickly behind the trees until just a tiny sliver was left, then nothing. Above, the sky displayed a vast spectrum of pinks and reds. We had been traveling all day and I was tired and dazed. In a cage above our heads green finches chirped loudly among the jungle of blooming plants. My heart tightened as I remembered the plants at my mother's kitchen window and how she had loved and tended them. My grandmother cooed to her birds.

"We could have a fancy wine-tasting party, how would you like that?" she asked. "Would that lift your spirits?"

"Whatever you like. I'm so happy to see you again, looking so well."

"Pff," she said, blowing air upwards out of her pursed lips, as my mother used to do. My eyes filled with tears.

"I don't know what's wrong with me!" I cried. "I'm sick!"

"Love can make you as sick as *la grippe,*" she said. "Tell me what happened."

So I told her the whole story, starting with Sally's suicide, as I rocked in an ancient wicker rocking chair and watched the stars making their appearance in the darkening sky. I told her about the dreams I'd had of Sally and how suddenly her face became my mother's. I saw something change at once in my grandmother's face. Her skin turned ashen as her eyes hardened to pebbles, her entire body stiffened and became fortresslike. I quickly changed the subject and told her about Nathan; his passion, his wild streak, his brilliance, his sadness.

"He sounds completely mad," she said, her eyes becoming bright once again. "Like a wild horse. Aren't they sexy when they're like that!" She used the English word "sexy," which made me laugh. She never, for example, said "weekend," an expression that was vastly accepted now in French. She would say *fin-de-semaine.* She could not suffer the bastardization of her beloved language.

"He speaks French perfectly, and also Spanish and some Italian. He went to school in England, you see—"

"Good, good." My grandmother nodded approvingly. "Those English schools teach one manners. Where is he now?" she asked, leaning toward me with curious eyes.

"He's in Oaxaca, Mexico. In some hotel. Can you believe, *Bonne-maman,* he already got himself a job working on the excavation site of some ancient ruins."

"Do you want him very badly?"

I stared at her in silence, exposed by my weakness.

"If you really want him badly, I'll get him for you—no, no, don't look so shocked. I'll send him a round-trip ticket and he can fly back to Central America or South America or wherever he wants to go afterwards. He surely wouldn't turn down a free ticket to France, now, would he? Do you know the name of the hotel? Thank God the telephones in this country have improved in the last ten years. We'll call Mexico and talk to him. Surely Mexican hotels have telephones!"

I must have looked stricken, because she hurried toward me, pulling me to her large breasts, imprisoned in their rock-solid brassiere.

"Now now, don't *worry* so. I'll get him for you, I will." After a moment she added, "I think I know someone in Oaxaca. Someone quite important in the government, I believe . . . Don't worry, *Céleste.*"

For a day and a night I didn't sleep as my grandmother made international phone calls and attempted to locate Nathan. Finally the Mexican diplomat brought Nathan by chauffeur to his large estate, and when she finally got Nathan on the phone it was past midnight in Bordeaux.

Her side of their conversation was simple and straightforward. Meanwhile, I stood in a corner of the living room, tearing at a handkerchief and biting my nails.

"Young man," she said to him in French, "I am Sophie de Fleurance de Saint-Martin, the grandmother of *Céleste*. It is imperative that you join her here in France . . . Yes, at Chateau Laroq, but really you don't need to know anything except that I'll have my secretary send you an open-return ticket to Paris. From Paris you'll take the train to Bordeaux . . . It doesn't matter to me what city or country you return to—you can go to Devil's Island for all I care . . . No, she's not well at all and I'm terribly concerned. In this case, young man, money is of no concern."

With her money my grandmother could move mountains, or refuse to, which seemed more often the case when she was dealing with the rest of her family who sniveled, begged, and nipped at her heels.

It was precisely the kind of adventure Nathan would not turn down, and I felt ashamed for bribing him this way. But it didn't matter—to see him! I imagined heroin addiction must be like this. The sweats, the fear, the sickness of the spirit; and then, with one shot, your blood commingling with the liquid drug, you become whole again and life turns sweet and beautiful and pain is just a vague memory, obliterated for the moment.

* * *

WE WERE LATE in arriving at the Bordeaux train station because *le Professeur* had insisted on driving us and at the last minute he could not locate his keys. As I searched the living room and hall in a panic, I was certain that he had mislaid them on purpose and once again felt that old, bitter, icy hatred for him.

My grandmother and I rushed through the crowded station toward the gate in search of Nathan. There he stood, alone and unperturbed among the shorter heads rushing and bobbing past him, ruddy, suntanned, in jeans and a large blue Mexican shirt, his hair long and wild. I felt my knees collapse just as my grandmother's hand grasped me firmly by the elbow. He came toward us, loping, and took us both in his arms. With my face against his shirt, I could hear my grandmother's muffled, embarrassed laughter.

"But this isn't at all *comme il faut!*" she cried.

For an instant I felt at home, at peace, and so close, so very close, to heaven.

* * *

SHE GAVE HIM a room in a distant wing.

"Do whatever you like, just be discreet," she said to me. "The domestics gossip." That evening she went off to bed early and never asked any questions. When we touched, I knew his smell, his curves, his heartbeat, as if we'd been together the day before. He wanted me to make noise, and tried all his best moves to get me to cry out, but I wouldn't. Not in my grandmother's house.

At breakfast the next morning, she offered Nathan a shot of her one-hundred-year-old cognac from a chateau *"pas trop loin d'içi."* She never offered anyone her special cognac, and I was surprised to see two small tumblers on the tray instead of one. My grandmother poured the cognac, a morning ritual, from a crystal decanter into a small, thin crystal tumbler, which she then twirled around and held up to the light. *"Quelles jambes!* Would you just look at those legs!" she exclaimed as the thick, rich liquor dripped in perfectly even, tiny lines down the inside rim of the glass, burning a deep amber color in the early morning sun.

"I find it adds a little something to the day," she said to Nathan, pouring. "But one is enough!" she warned, holding up her plump index finger. "You need your strength, after all," she tittered. Nathan looked up at her with his mischievous eyes and smiled coyly, his nose in the tumbler. I felt uneasy and turned my bright red face away.

"I'm pleased that you are appreciative of such a fine thing," she said, patting his shoulder. "I never trust a man who doesn't like fine wines and good cognac."

* * *

MY GRANDMOTHER, who was extremely well read, spent hours in her sunroom discussing literature with Nathan. For some reason, she reserved these discussions for him, as if she thought I was incapable of discussing literature with her myself, or perhaps she simply thought it wasn't *comme il faut* for a young woman to show off her intellectual capabilities in this manner. I didn't let this bother me and just sat and listened as they argued heatedly about, for example, translations. Nathan insisted that Aylmer Maude's translations of Tolstoy were definitive. My grandmother countered that his point was moot since Tolstoy couldn't possibly translate well into a language as messy as English. Tolstoy, she insisted, had to be read in French. They argued also about the different movements in poetry. My grandmother didn't like *les espagnols,* which for her encompassed all Spanish-speaking poets, because she found all that magical realism too carefully orchestrated. Nathan said he disagreed categorically with that assessment. She told him with a snort that he was a romantic dreamer; he told her with a mercurial smile that she, too, was a romantic dreamer but unwilling to admit it.

"No, no, my dear young man, I'd *like* to be a romantic dreamer but I simply can't afford *not* to be a pragmatic and narrow-minded old lady."

* * *

WE DRANK large quantities of wine, which we chose ourselves from the ancient, dust-covered *caves* with their rows of bottles that my grandmother said had been the favorites of great leaders and kings. She said she only opened them on special occasions and this visit from her beloved granddaughter classified as just that. Nathan became fascinated with the process of wine making and she took us on a long tour of the *chais,* the sheds where the wine was aged in oak casks.

Once, she even let Nathan read her cards. He told her that she would get married again in the not-too-distant future and that her new husband would be energetic and passionate. She liked this very much and opened a very fine bottle of champagne that she had bartered for a bottle of 1968 Chateau Laroq. As we toasted the wisdom of the cards, again and again, I did not tell her that I couldn't tell the difference between this particular champagne and a good Veuve Cliquot.

* * *

SHE THREW a wine-tasting extravaganza, a seven-course dinner, accompanied by wines from all over France. She invited all the friends and relatives and wine connoisseurs from the neighborhood, explaining to us that this was not a real wine tasting, just a faux one. She introduced me to everyone as her long-lost American granddaughter. They told her that I looked very much like her, which pleased her and made her blush. No one ever mentioned my mother. This was not surprising, as the French never discussed family matters such as health, death, or divorce in public.

* * *

NATHAN STAYED for three weeks. He planned to return to Oaxaca for a few more months and then travel south to Guatemala.

The night before he left, as we lay curled together in his large bed, he told me that no matter where I was, he would always love me and that he admired me for going my own way.

His face was buried in the pillow when he said carefully, "I hope you've started going out with other people."

I threw the sheets back and began to dress in a blind rage.

"Shh," he said, "you'll wake everybody up. Come back here." He got up and pulled me back onto the bed. I struggled and kicked but he held me down. He began to tickle me, and I to punch him, until we both were laughing.

"Just promise me one thing," he said quietly, caressing my neck. "If you meet someone else, you'll let me know."

It seemed to me at that moment that I might wait for him forever.

"I promise," I said.

The next day he took the train back to Paris.

* * *

I WAS IN a torpor for the first few days. Hoping to distract me, my grandmother suggested a shopping trip to Paris, but I didn't want to leave the grounds of the chateau.

I began to dream of my mother again. One night, I opened my eyes to find her sitting at the foot of the large, canopied bed, smiling at me sadly. She wore a loose white nightgown and her thick hair hung limply around her pale face. Her lips were slightly open, as if she were about to speak to me.

"What? What?" I cried out, startled, blinking into the darkness. The white curtains rustled in the breeze.

* * *

WHILE MY GRANDMOTHER and I were walking through the pine forest one afternoon, she asked if I wouldn't like to stay in France and finish my studies at the Sorbonne. I could have her apartment off Avenue Victor Hugo. I remembered the dream of my mother sitting on the edge of my bed.

"*Bonne-maman*, do you ever dream of my mother?"

"Your mother?" She glanced at me suspiciously and there was a hard edge to her voice. "Why do you ask such a question?"

"Lately I've started dreaming about her again. I feel like she wants to talk, but she never does."

"Pff. You mustn't think about the past, *Céleste*," my grandmother warned, and we walked on.

* * *

A FEW DAYS before I was to leave, she again brought up the subject of my finishing college in Paris. She said she would introduce me to interesting people, and in the spring take me to her private box at Longchamps and Auteuil. Feeling fraudulent and unequipped for such a life, I told her with a certain coolness in my voice that I would have gone with Nathan to Mexico if I hadn't intended to return to my school in the States. She became despondent, sitting for hours in her rocking chair with a shawl draped over her shoulders, sipping a large snifter of brandy.

"You're so much like your mother," she muttered sadly.

"What did you and my mother fight about that night, *Bonne-maman*?" I asked.

She sighed deeply. She seemed to be considering the wisdom of telling me.

"It was about you," she finally said. "Nathalie wanted to come back to France with you. She was afraid your father wouldn't give her any money. I offered to give her all the money in the world if she would come back and live here with me. But she wanted to be in Paris, to put you in the bilingual school there, so you could be with other American children . . ." She paused and rocked, taking a small purse-lipped sip of her cognac. "I said I wouldn't have it. I said you would be sent to board at the French girls' *lycée* where all the Fleurance women went. Your mother wouldn't hear of it. So we fought, and then she took you and left."

I remembered my mother's bright, open face as we sat in an outdoor café in a Florence square. The sun was blinding as it ricocheted off the white paved stones and the fountain's lapping water. She sipped Sambuca and I an extra-sweet cappuccino. She asked me in French if I thought the Italian man at the next table was a baron or a count. I glanced at the handsome, curly-haired man with piercing blue eyes.

"He's a prince!" I said in a whisper.

"Well, then!" she said, and stealthily hiked her skirt up over her delicate knees. She glanced at me out of the corner of her eyes, giggling like a little girl.

"Stop it, *maman*!" I said, turning away in embarrassment.

She was so beautiful, he naturally turned his chair toward us and began a conversation. They talked about the museums.

"Do you know what my daughter said today about the Renaissance paintings of Jesus? She said, 'Why don't they let that poor man down?'"

He paid our bill and asked us to join him for dinner. This happened quite often, and my mother was always graceful and aloof, icy but charming with her bright coy laugh.

Only once did she leave me alone, sneaking out of our hotel room after I was asleep. I awakened to find her gone and ran out into the plush, quiet hallway with my bear in my arms. *"Maman!* Where are you!" I cried. Locked out of the room, I stood in the hallway, weeping and howling in terror and banging on the door. Someone must have called the night clerk, for he came and took me down to the kitchen and sat me and Monsieur Laroq up on a chopping block while the cooks and the waiters, off duty now and getting ready to go home, stayed to play with me and offered an array of desserts from the refrigerator. I ate two *bombas*, vanilla ice cream in a puff pastry with melted chocolate on top, and a slice of mocha cake. One young waiter named Antonio, who had a black mustache, made a rabbit out of a napkin and made it jump around.

The night concierge yelled at my mother when she came in, and threatened to call the police.

"Maybe you are French, madam," he cried, "but here in Italy we don't treat our children like that!"

She was humiliated and ashamed and told him to mind his own affairs as she jerked me away from my new friend Antonio and dragged me upstairs.

"We should've stayed with *Bonne-maman*," I grumbled. "She never left me alone. If she knew you did, she'd be very angry at you."

My mother looked at me wide-eyed, as if I'd kicked her in the stomach.

At the end of August we ran out of money and went home. Our absence had not caused my father to return all worried and remorseful as she had hoped. In fact, he had taken to staying all week in his studio in the city. She did not cry anymore but paced our big, empty Connecticut house in her pale blue bathrobe, smoking and drinking scotch.

* * *

REMEMBERING ALL THIS in a flash, I watched my stiff-backed grandmother rocking, a self-righteous look on her face, and I thought, *My God, she could have helped her, but she didn't!* Our lives could have been completely different. I was overwhelmed by a fury so sharp it pierced my chest and I could barely breathe. Having totally let go of my senses, I stood up and, before running from the room in tears, yelled at my grandmother, "If only you had helped! You killed her! It was your fault she died!"

* * *

I CLOSED the blinds, put the water pitcher back in the kitchen cupboard, and went to my desk. The letter I wrote was in French, and took me a long time to compose.

> *June 12*
> *New York*
>
> *Dear Bonne-maman,*
>
> *The past few months have been very difficult ones for me as I've been forced through circumstance to look at the past. Getting married I suspect makes one review things that one doesn't particularly want to review. I was sorry to get your letter because I was hoping beyond hope that you would be able to make it to my wedding. I have no one but you from my mother's side and I feel the lack of contact with you deeply.*
>
> *I need very much to apologize to you for what I said that day at the chateau. It has been so many years since her death and yet I can't seem to stop missing her. I also can't seem to remember what exactly happened. I would like to get better, to move beyond the past and live a happy and full life. I miss you terribly and often and if you still want me, I will come visit you. We will be in France in the middle of July for part of our honeymoon.*
>
> *Please forgive me. Your devoted granddaughter,*
> *Céleste*

I licked two twenty-five-cent stamps and put them on the envelope. Abruptly, without considering, I took a wedding invitation from the pile of leftovers and stuck it in an envelope. I wrote Nathan's name, in care of the Grand Hotel, Matlan, Mexico, and put two stamps on the envelope. I ran out into the hall and dropped both letters into the mail chute before I could change my mind.

Fifteen

AFTER I DISTRIBUTED the anthologies I asked the kids to sign my copy.

Dear Celeste please come to my high school next year. From Sir.

Thanks for being here. Love Shatisha.

Peace from Jhamal.

I learned so much thanx, Rosalia PS Thanx for the book of love poems. I read it all the way two times already.

Derrence wrote nothing but signed his poems with a grand, impressive signature. I'd printed four of his poems, one more than any other student.

Ellie Horowitz stood in the front, reading the anthology with great interest. "You kids wrote this?" she shouted. "I don't believe it! *You* kids? Jhamal, *you* wrote this beautiful love poem? Hell, I'd go out on a date with you if you wrote me poems like that."

"You wish," said Jhamal.

"Every word is theirs," I said.

"Do I get to sign your copy, too?" she asked.

"Of course." I handed it to her.

Dear Celeste, she wrote, *This isn't good-bye, I'll see you next fall. You're a pleasure to have around. Best wishes on your wedding day—Ellie Horowitz.*

After every student who wanted to had signed my copy, and I'd signed theirs, I stood at the front of the room trying to think of something to say. I knew that the chances of more than a handful of them making it to college were slim to none.

"You're all wonderful bright kids. You deserve prosperity and happiness. I hope you'll go on to college because you have a right to go. And if any one of you ever needs a letter of recommendation, Mrs. Horowitz will know where to find me."

They gazed at me with their inscrutable eyes.

"Okay, well, good-bye, then," I said.

"Good-bye, Celeste!" they shouted.

"Thanks for teaching us!"

"Yeah, thanks!"

"Have a good life and shit!"

I walked out into the hall, still empty and quiet. My heart felt heavy. I peered through the rectangle of glass in the door and saw Ellie Horowitz's mouth wide open in a shout as she resumed her lesson, pointing to something on the board. The kids were at their desks, talking to each other and half listening, looking bored. It seemed as if I'd never been there at all.

I gazed at the drawings on the blue walls of the hallway, listened to the hum of voices behind the closed door, and sighed. It was time to go.

I walked a few paces and a hand tapped my shoulder. I turned. It was Derrence, his gangly arms fidgeting at his sides.

"I read your story," he said in his absurdly low voice. "I liked it. It was good."

"You liked it, really?" I felt my face break into a smile.

"Yeah. It was easy to read," he said. "Now I'm reading James Baldwin. I like it," he said as if surprised. "It's good. Very interesting. I can understand almost everything." With that, he smiled and his metal braces flashed in the fluorescent light.

"Are you going to go to Freedom to Think?" I asked him.

"Yeah," he said vaguely. "And my mom said thank you for the books."

"Thanks, Derrence." I put out my hand and he shook it limply. Our eyes stayed locked for a long moment as we stood there, not knowing what else to say.

"And my mom says you must be one nice lady."

"You can still call me," I said. "Just to talk. About school or whatever."

He nodded gravely. "Thanks," he said. He stepped back and after a moment, waved.

I watched him until he disappeared into the classroom, then I walked out into the sultry day. The sky had turned the color of bruises. The streets and buildings glowed that strange green hue. Just as I got to the bus shelter, the sky opened up with a crack of lightning and rain began to fall with a loud clatter. I hadn't brought an umbrella. Of course. If Alex had been home, he would have reminded me. He listened to the weather report every morning. As I stood in a corner of the bus shelter looking out at the curtain of rain, I wondered why I couldn't remember to do the simplest things by myself.

The Eighty-sixth Street crosstown bus was crowded with sweaty, wet people in a bad mood. I was squeezed in near the back and watched the street to keep my mind off my discomfort. People were running with newspapers over their heads. Some stood under awnings, gaping at the rain. It was dark as nightfall outside.

At Central Park West, a very tall man stepped onto the bus and stood at the front, amidst the crowd of heads. His curly chestnut-colored hair, the designer sunglasses, his tailored European suit caught my eye and made me blink and stare.

Branko—my heart leapt, though I knew it was impossible.

I tried to get a better look at the figure but the crowd up front was too thick. I could not move forward, the aisle was still packed tight with people. As the bus swung around a double-parked car, the heads at the front all swayed at once in a wave and I caught another glimpse of his face. Although his eyes were hidden behind dark glasses, in that moment I saw his hair, the aquiline nose, his thin-lipped mouth again—and he so resembled Branko that my breath caught in my throat.

I kept my eyes on the spot where he stood to see if he would get off right after the park, but he stayed on. When the bus reached Madison, he was one of a torrent of people who poured out onto the sidewalk. Quickly I pushed my way to the back door.

As I stepped into a cold stream of water in the gutter and was hit in the face by a blast of rain, I questioned my sanity. I stood on the sidewalk, circling, looking for him in every direction. At last, I caught sight of his large frame looming above the others, moving swiftly down the avenue. He had opened an enormous black umbrella that swayed along a full two feet higher than the rest. The rain swept horizontally between the buildings, as if sprites were shaking out invisible sheets.

I picked up my pace, but still he remained half a block ahead of me. I followed him for several blocks, dodging umbrellas and passersby who stared at my rain-drenched clothes and face. He turned into a building on the corner and disappeared.

The building was a brick church whose sooty basement windows opened onto the street. The rain suddenly stopped, and I heard clapping from inside. I looked down into the room through a clean space in one of the windows and saw a crowd of people sitting in rows, facing a small podium. It was a peculiar sight, the dank, hot room completely packed with sweaty faces smiling and laughing as if the heat and rain were no bother to them at all. On a side door hung a sign, a white triangle in a circle on a blue background. There were cheers, followed by more clapping.

A man in his forties with a slender build and salt-and-pepper hair stood outside smoking a cigarette, watching me. He was wearing a T-shirt, jeans, and black lizard cowboy boots.

"What's going on in there?" I asked him, out of breath.

He looked me over with a peculiar smile. "A meeting. AA," he said.

"Why are they clapping?"

"They're celebrating people counting days." His dark eyes took me in. My hair was hanging in a wet clump over my face. I pushed it back and wiped water from my forehead with the back of my hand.

"Counting days?" I asked.

"You know, how many days they've been sober," he said. Smiling as he held up the smoking butt, he added, "My last vice." He chucked it toward the gutter. "Time to go in," he said. "Want to come?"

"No thanks," I said, ill at ease, wondering why he'd felt compelled to ask me in. "Did you see a very tall man in a suit go in about a minute ago?" I asked him.

"No," he said with a twinkle in his eye. "This is an anonymous program, you know what I mean?"

"Thanks," I said, a prickly hot flush rising to the surface of my skin. I abruptly turned east down the street.

* * *

A **STARTLINGLY CLEAR** image of Branko came to mind as I walked briskly toward home. It was of the first time I saw him, the first week of junior year, in my Advanced French Lit class, a fellow so tall he barely fit into the space between the desk and chair and kept shifting noisily, stretching his long legs and grumbling. The professor stopped speaking and stared with annoyance at this newcomer, who kept readjusting his body behind the tiny desk. His hands were gigantic, the white Bic pen he held looked like a cigarette in his fingers. His hair was curly and chestnut-colored, like my mother's. He had a large square chin, a long, narrow mouth, and a small, straight nose, slightly rounded at the end. His features were so perfect, he looked like Michelangelo's David. And like the David, he was enormous. Much too big for someone my size to date.

"That's not a Parisian accent you have," his deep voice boomed high above me as I was gathering my books to leave.

"Bordeaux," I said. "My grandmother owns a vineyard there."

"Really? How interesting."

He told me he'd lived in Paris, on Avenue Foche, from the age of six to sixteen. He'd gone to the Ecole Bilingue, he said as we walked down the hall together.

"I almost went there," I said, surprising myself. I never offered such information to strangers; I didn't like to talk to people I didn't know, so I rarely met anyone new unless I was with Candace, who did the talking for both of us.

Out on the street, he stood calmly, stretching to get out the cricks, in no hurry to go. "This is a gut for me," he said, patting his flat stomach. "I need to get my grades up. I took a year and a half off. Went to Vail. Taught a little skiing. Hiked in the summer."

"I guess that's why I've never seen you before," I said.

"I saw you, though. I saw you the first day of your freshman year when you were registering. My name's Branko Yeretich. B-R-A-N-K-O. Want to smoke a joint?"

"I don't like pot."

"Well, how about a drink, then?"

It was not like me to follow strangers home, certainly not sober. Except that he did not feel like a stranger to me even then; it seemed as if I'd known him for a very long time but hadn't seen him in a while.

He shared an off-campus house with some upperclassmen, a red house that stood on stilts on a steep hill. A rickety outdoor staircase led up to the first floor from the sharply sloping lawn.

He'd turned the downstairs dining room and living room into his "quarters," as he called them. African masks, Indian statuettes, ancient spears and swords hung on the walls. Above the desk was a series of large black-and-white framed photographs of a swarthy man whose features were much like Branko's. In each picture the man was smoking a nonfilter cigarette, holding it in different ways, as if it were a prop. In some he seemed pensive, in others he wore a cryptic smile.

"Your father?" I asked. Branko nodded without looking up. He was busy rolling himself a joint.

"Where did you get all this stuff?" I asked.

"Oh, traveling," he said lightly. Thoughts of Nathan loomed fresh and sharp in my mind.

"So where's the fancy stereo?" I said, and laughed a little. He lit the joint.

"Haven't had time to buy one yet," he said, holding his breath.

Nathan would like this guy, I thought.

"How about a rum and Coke?" he said.

"Sure."

We sat around for the rest of the afternoon, talking about France, and feeling like strangers in both countries, never quite fitting in either place. Finally he glanced at his watch, rubbed his stomach, and shouted, "Dinnertime!"

We wobbled back down toward the main campus, discussing the college's different eating clubs and cafeterias. I told him I hadn't joined an eating club yet.

"Come have dinner with me at Delta Phi. I wouldn't join a fraternity for all the tea in China—but their food is excellent! Be my guest tonight, then tomorrow you can join if you like. Then we can have dinner together every night!"

* * *

A CRACK OF THUNDER jolted me out of my reverie. I found myself standing in front of a fancy bathing suit shop, staring at the headless white mannequins in bright flowery bikinis, my reflection superimposed over them in the window. The rain fell in huge drops around me, my T-shirt and jumper were completely drenched, my hair hung in my face, dripping. *No wonder that man asked you into the meeting,* I thought.

When I got to our apartment, the air-conditioning sunk right into my bones and I began shivering. I stripped off my clothes and got a towel from the bathroom to dry my face and hair. In the mirror, my stunned reflection stared back at me. I looked at myself closely and could not fill in the space between the person I was looking at and me. It seemed someone else was standing behind me, watching.

I put on a bathrobe and went back to the living room, where I noticed the new crystal decanter from Tiffany standing on the bartop, filled with brandy. I took a step toward it. Out of the corner of my eye I saw the red light on the message machine blinking. I went over and rewound the tape. There were six hang-ups, no messages. Alex.

Then I heard Lucia's lumbering, saturnine voice asking why I hadn't called her in a week.

The last one was from Anna, who said she was in town at her sister Theresa's, and asked me to call her back.

I looked up Theresa's number in my phone book.

"Yello-o-o?" Anna's voice sang out after the first ring, startling me.

"Anna, it's me."

"*Yes,* Celeste! Eighteen days and counting," her voice sang. "How do you feel?"

I didn't know what to say. "Alex is in L.A.," I murmured incongruously.

"Celeste? Is something the matter?"

"Yes, in fact, everything is the matter and I don't know *what* is wrong."

"Pre-wedding jitters?" she said sympathetically. "Want to have dinner with me tonight?"

"Must be the week for family dinners," I said gloomily. "Aurelia was in town."

"And how *is* the prodigal mother? Still taking on the Dark Continent single-handedly?" she asked airily. In the next breath she told me to meet her at her sister's at seven.

I had a couple of hours to kill so I stretched out on the bed, where I tossed and turned and fought to rid my mind of images of Branko.

After a while I gave up and lay there as the storm's darkness filled the room.

* * *

THE FIRST WEEKEND of junior year, there was a big dance at one of the fraternities. Branko and I stood together by the keg, getting mildly drunk. A premed junior who had been my TA in Psychology came over and started talking to us. Branko ignored him, his gaze wandering aimlessly as the fellow talked.

After a while, Branko said to me, "I think I'm going to go downtown to He's Not Here. Want to come?"

I looked up at him, puzzled. I was having a good time, enjoying the attention. I shook my head. He leaned down and said in French, "If you stay here you're going to get into trouble."

"*Ça va,*" I told him, smiling vaguely.

So he left and I began to dance with the premed student.

"Parlay voo Fransay? Wee, wee, madame. Vous es trez beautifool," said the premed student in my ear. I laughed. As we danced close I thought of how nice it would be to wake up next to someone again, to be held and rocked to sleep. I wanted to make love again.

But when I awakened in his bed near dawn, sick and disoriented, I felt homesick for Nathan. At first light, I left the premed student's ground-floor apartment through the window. He never stirred.

* * *

TUESDAY, after French class, Branko caught me in the hall.

"Want to come over?"

"Why not?" I shrugged, trying to be calm, cool.

"You were bad this weekend," he said with a teasing smile, shaking his index finger at me.

"Yeah, well I don't want to talk about it if you don't mind," I said stiffly.

He had bought an enormous sleek black stereo with speakers that came up to my waist.

"Check it out," he said, and put on a record by The Cars. *"I don't mind you coming here/And wasting all my time."* The walls held as the little glass panes in the French doors rattled.

"Jesus Christ!" I yelled over the bass. "I was only kidding about getting a stereo."

He poured rum and pineapple juice in diamond-cut crystal glasses that reflected a rainbow of light.

After a second drink, he said, "We're alike in some ways. It's funny how we found each other."

"I think it's more like you found me," I answered, still peeved that he had mentioned my weekend indiscretion.

"Whatever. We both have French backgrounds. My father died when I was fifteen. We've both lost a parent." He began to roll a joint.

"How do you know about my mother?" I was getting more defensive by the moment.

"Someone told me," he said.

Who knew about my mother? No one knew except Candace. There were several people at the college from my high school. Maybe it had

come from them. It annoyed me that people would label me as someone who'd lost a parent, as if that somehow determined my character.

"My mother died when I was ten," I said coolly. "I don't remember
her very well."

"Why do you say that?" he asked without malice, bemused by my statement. "Losing my father was the worst thing that ever happened to me in
my life. I try to keep his face fresh in my mind. Sometimes he fades, and it
scares the shit out of me. That's why I hung the pictures up."

*   *   *

IN OCTOBER, the trees on campus turned to burnt sienna.
Leaves tumbled and waltzed in the wind across the main green. After
French class, Branko said, "I have a surprise for you," and led me outside.
Parked at the curb was a silver convertible Porsche.

"It's a '65. What do you think?"

"I don't know anything about cars," I said. "It's cute."

"Cute!" he cried. "Come on." He jumped over the door like I'd seen
men do in the movies and opened the passenger side for me. I shut the
door, took a few steps back, and took a flying leap in myself. Students were
stopping to look. I felt like we were in a James Bond movie, escaping.

He drove up to the apple orchard that stood on a hill just beyond the
town. It was still warm enough to keep the top down.

"It's good to get away," he said. "See what's going on in the world. That
campus is too fucking small." There was a long silent time as the world
blurred and roared. "Do you want to go out with me?"

"No," I said. "I'm in love with someone else. It's been six years."

"Ooh," he said, sucking in air. "That's bad."

"It's just love," I said with a trace of cynicism.

"I really like you," he turned for a moment to look at me. "I feel like I
can be honest with you."

"I like you too. Going out would just mess things up."

"See what I mean," he said. "We're too much alike." With that, he
drove off the dirt road and into the orchard, slaloming between the trees, in
and out, going fast. The engine howled.

I felt free for the first time in months. Laughing, I reached up and tried
to pull a gold-red apple off a tree. My effort reminded me of the carousel
rides of my childhood, how sometimes you got a wooden stick with which

you tried to pull down the golden ring. When you got it, you felt special, as if angels were watching over you. As we swung under the branches an apple tumbled into my lap.

"Where did you get the money to buy the car?" I asked him, biting into the gift apple that was sour and sweet and a little hard.

"I have some money," he said evenly.

He told me that his mother's family from Kentucky was wealthy. "They started in the coal business, but now they own racehorses and real estate." He told me his father had been a Serbian prince whose family was thrown out of Belgrade after Tito seized power. His father had then lived in Paris and New York, attended high society functions, and lived the expatriate royal's life. He met Branko's mother at a society ball. The father had named his son after a great-uncle, an enormous bear of a man who had apparently been involved in the conspiracy to assassinate Archduke Ferdinand.

Branko told me his parents had separated after his father came down with lung cancer. "She killed him," he told me, his voice flat. "My mother broke his heart. He was the best man I've ever known. We were like this," he crossed his long fingers, holding them up for me to see. "I miss him so badly that some days I can barely stand it."

* * *

I MET BRANKO'S mother and older brother Roderic in November, during parents' weekend. I had just waved good-bye to my father and Anna and was walking home across the main campus. Mrs. Yeretich and her two sons were strolling up the cement path. The wind was blowing and leaves twirled frantically around their feet. I turned away, uncomfortable in my knowledge, when he cried out to me in his booming voice.

"Miz Miller!"

I stopped as they came toward me. Mrs. Yeretich was tall and thin, blond, with a pale square face and high cheekbones. She wore a dark mink coat and exquisite two-toned Chanel pumps. Roderic looked like Branko, but shorter and darker; he had a tight, closed-lip smile. I felt sorry for anyone who had to spend his life being compared to Branko.

Roderic took my hand and planted a soundless little kiss on my knuckles. Mrs. Yeretich smiled, a wide, luxurious smile that didn't seem connected with anything that was going on. Branko seemed cranky and out of sorts. In the past I'd only seen him like that when he was hungry. I'd learned to get him to food quickly when his mood changed suddenly that way.

The four of us talked for a few moments about absolutely nothing, Branko edgy and fidgety all the while. Before they left, Roderic handed me an engraved card with his name and phone number on it. He asked me to call him if I was ever in the city. "We'll go out to dinner, go dancing or something." There was a suggestive gleam in his eyes. I stood there, stunned, holding his card.

* * *

BRANKO HAD a friend in the Navy who sent him postcards of naked girls from exotic ports of call. An auto mechanic named Henry showed up at Branko's off-campus house now and then, smelling of diesel oil. He had also befriended a call girl he'd met at a party in the city a few years before; occasionally she called him collect in the middle of the night to discuss her love life. But certain people simply didn't interest him.

Candace and I lived in a small two-bedroom apartment that year, in a university-owned high-rise. The first time he came to visit, the three of us sat around the kitchen table drinking beers, when she began to talk in her usual loud, enthusiastic voice about the goings-on around campus. Branko pretended interest, stared off, drummed his fingers on the tabletop, stifled yawns.

When he left, Candace told me she didn't like him. "Who does he think he is, just quitting school and going off *skiing* for a year and a half?" He had broken one of her cardinal rules: you don't drop out of school, no matter what is wrong. "He's a spoiled rich kid with an attitude problem," she said dismissively.

Yet she forgave Nathan the same transgression. But then, Nathan had a deep fondness for Candace and thought she had an excellent sense of humor.

* * *

BRANKO WAS fascinated by the waiflike girls with shaved heads or green hair or pierced noses, who seemed on the brink of emotional collapse and wore white lipstick and black nail polish and smoked nonfilter cigarettes. Spotting one of them sitting alone in a dark corner of the pub, Branko would get up, stroll over, and engage her in conversation. Having listened in on too many of these discussions, I knew the topics varied from the girls' devotion to punk rock, their militant feminist ideals, their drug-war stories, their infinite boredom with life, to how their daddies were threatening to cut them off. I found that they were always willing to talk at great length as long as it was about themselves. I told Branko that he was wasting his time.

"I don't know, I think she could use Doctor Branko's hot beef injection," he'd say with a smile.

Mercifully, these relationships never lasted more than a few days.

Sixteen

BRANKO TOOK ME to stay at his mother's Fifth Avenue apartment for a weekend just before the Christmas holidays. The apartment had high, eggshell-colored walls with hand-carved moldings and large windows. The living and dining rooms had been carefully decorated in cream and rose. Delicate egg-shaped objets d'art decorated the dark wood side tables, shelves, and mantelpiece.

She threw a dinner party in Branko's honor. Cocktail hour went on forever. Finally, around ten o'clock, Branko and I were directed to sit together at one end of the long oval dining table opposite his mother and Roderic—the host couples at opposing ends of the table. Branko, whose face was flushed from the drinks he'd had before dinner, proceeded to pour us glass after glass of expensive white wine. By the end of the main course he was mumbling and laughing to himself. Suddenly he tipped his chair onto two legs, raised his arms, snapped his fingers, and began to sing a Serbian folk song in his booming voice. Mrs. Yeretich's guests stopped talking and stared at him for an awkward moment, then went back to their conversations as though nothing were amiss.

Once the guests left, I began to wash dishes, hoping to make up for whatever gaffe I had helped Branko commit. Mrs. Yeretich told me in her pleasant, neutral voice to leave it, the maid would clean in the morning. But I insisted, and accidentally smashed to bits her glass espresso decanter from Italy.

"What a pity," she said in that smooth tone, "it can't be replaced."

Later, Branko tucked me into the guest-room bed, which had a big satin spread that matched the velvet drapes. "Good night, little devil," he said, kissing my forehead. "Don't worry about the espresso pot, she'll get over it."

The next day we went shopping on Fifth Avenue. He bought himself a navy blue cashmere coat at Saks that was as big as a blanket, and he bought me a pair of black leather boots that were so soft they felt like socks. At my insistence, we went to six different stores looking for Mrs. Yeretich's glass espresso pot—but she'd been right, of course; it could only be purchased in Italy.

"Can't fly to Milan this weekend!" Branko said, clapping his hands together and rubbing them briskly.

"Branko, it's not funny," I said in a pinched tone.

*   *   *

AFTER THE Christmas holidays, he decided to have a serious relationship. He said he was lonely, and needed to "ground himself a little."

He found Estelle, a tall, green-eyed freshman. She was considered one of the great beauties of the incoming class. I liked her fine, although it seemed fairly apparent that they had trouble conversing.

About three weeks later he stopped by and sat at my kitchen table, all fidgety and unfocused.

"What's the matter, Branko? You're fidgeting like you're in French class."

"I don't want to go out with Estelle anymore but I don't know how to tell her."

"Just tell her it isn't working out."

"Can't you tell her for me? Make something up. Tell her you and I are in love. Hell, she'd never know the difference."

"Come on, Branko. Do your own dirty work."

Then came Titsia, a Dutch girl with impenetrable blue eyes, a great beauty of the sophomore class. She didn't like it when he stopped in the street to talk to me. At parties, she'd stand a little to the side, scowling, as he engaged Candace and me in conversation.

Branko liked to dance with me because my mother had taught me "le rock," the French jitterbug, Branko's favorite. But after he started dating Titsia he never asked me to dance, and this pissed me off.

One day after French class he told me she was crazy.

"I could've told you that," I said with a snort.

"Bat shit," he said. "Completely. Plus, she's a switch-hitter. I don't like that. Too much competition as it is."

In the spring he had a romance with a senior named Margaret. She was his date to the Delta Phi spring semiformal. They stumbled in, laughing as they held each other up. She wore a strapless dress of green sequins. He left her propped against a column and took me out to the balcony that overlooked a garden. He handed me a white pill.

"What's this?"

"A Quaalude," he mumbled. "Great for sex. Margaret's got a dealer in the city. I just advanced her five hundred dollars to buy a pile as high as Mont Blanc. She's going to sell them here and pay me back, and meanwhile I'll get a supply for free." After a moment, he said, "God, I can't figure her out."

"And that makes her interesting, right?" I made a sour face and swallowed the pill with a swig of gin and tonic.

I woke up the next morning beside one of Branko's housemates, a guy named Ned whose father had recently died in a plane crash. At first I had no idea where I was. Then I saw Ned lying on his belly, his pale, high-waisted behind exposed to the world, one arm thrown over the side of the bed. The last thing I remembered was walking out of the party into the crisp spring night and telling him to read Emily Dickinson's death poems because they would help him deal with his grief.

I stumbled out into the hall in my rumpled evening dress and ran smack into Branko, who apparently was just returning from Margaret's, his bow tie askew and his eyes bloodshot.

"Celeste," he said, shaking his head, a deeply pained expression on his face. "Jesus Christ."

"Branko," I said, my voice trembling, "I'm no slut—I've only slept with five guys my entire life!" I ran for the door and didn't look back.

A month later Margaret came back from a long weekend engaged to her ex-boyfriend, Lance, who'd graduated the previous spring and now lived in San Francisco.

* * *

IN APRIL, Nathan showed up at Candace's and my apartment unannounced. He was gaunt and unshaven and his skin ashen.

"My God, where have you been?" I said, my stomach knotting as I stepped away from the door. "You look like shit, Nathan."

"We haven't heard from you in months!" Candace added, wringing her hands.

He sat down at the kitchen table. Candace turned to the stove and put the kettle on for tea. She took some whole wheat bread out of the fridge and stuck the slices in her toaster.

"I was in Nicaragua, hanging in the mountains with some Sandinistas. I got dysentery and for, like, a couple of weeks, I thought I was going to die.

"That's why you haven't heard from me," he explained, looking at me with haunted, exhausted eyes.

Branko showed up with a paper he needed to have typed and I introduced them, feeling jittery and confused.

"Yeretich. Yeretich," said Nathan thoughtfully, emerging momentarily from his daze. "You wouldn't happen to be related to the Yeretich who was involved in the conspiracy to assassinate Archduke Ferdinand?"

"In my arms!" Branko cried, coming forward with his long arms outstretched. Nathan glanced at me with mock concern, an eyebrow raised. "That was Great-great-uncle Branko!" Branko reached into the breast pocket of his rugby shirt, "Look here, I have a joint of gold Colombian . . ."

Nathan smiled. "It's good to be back," he said.

"So, the point here," said Candace thoughtfully, "is that in order to get Prince Branko to part with his pot, one needs to be an expert on World War I?"

Branko laughed, and passed Candace the joint first.

A little while later the four of us drove downtown in the Porsche and sat in He's Not Here and drank pitchers of beer and shots. Branko and Nathan played pinball for shots. Nathan lost, but nothing of consequence seemed to be discussed.

On the way home, Branko said, "Now, this is the kind of guy I see you with."

Nathan squeezed me to his bony chest as I sat between them, straddling the gear shift.

"I want to be the godfather of your firstborn child," Branko said.

"You've got a deal," said Nathan. "You can be our sugar daddy."

"Wait a second!" Candace said from the back. "Celeste said I could be the godmother of her first child. Is that going to work out, Prince Branko, or are we going to fight over the poor kid?"

"No fighting allowed," I said.

At that instant, the future seemed perfectly clear and bright. I saw Branko as an important, famous businessman, a philanthropist who would find revolutionary ways to help the poor and suffering; in ten years Candace would be the highest-ranking female banker in the U.S.; and Nathan and I would be expatriates living in some far-off land, raising brilliant bilingual children, and writing novels read by the entire world.

I felt empowered, unstoppable, courageous.

I thought we would accomplish great things. I never imagined that success would come at the price of facing terrible, difficult choices, and taking responsibility for their results.

Nathan stayed a week and then went on to Houston to visit his parents, whom he hadn't seen in a year.

He called from there to tell me he'd decided to stay. His father had gotten him a low-level job at Exxon, and Nathan had enrolled at the University of Houston for the summer semester, to try to make up some credits. When he called me with the news, his voice was flat and toneless.

* * *

THAT SUMMER Branko took me to Block Island, Martha's Vineyard, and to the Hamptons. One Friday he drove me out to Amagansett to stay with a group of friends who'd rented a house on the beach. We left New York at two in the morning. I was terrified of the crazy way he was driving, but I sat back and watched the road fly past, because I knew I would never get hurt as long as I was with him. When I wasn't with him, bad things happened to me. Branko was my guardian angel, even if he made the two-and-a-half-hour drive to Amagansett in one hour and twenty-five minutes.

I remember the white-hot beach, the wind blowing sand into my eyes, the waves big and threatening, and a blue flag flapping above the lifeguard stand.

"Come into the water, Celeste," Branko urged. I shook my head. "Don't be scared, I won't let you drown. It's really thrilling."

In the water, he held my hand. "Okay, we're going to have to go under this one," he said as an enormous wave rushed toward us, foam curling over its crest. We ducked and the wave crashed over, pulling the sand out from under my feet and knocking me over. Branko never lost his balance and never let go of my hand, and I knew as long as I didn't let go, I'd be safe.

* * *

I ALLOWED NATHAN to string me along for one more year, with his love letters and phone calls, and one visit at Christmas. But just before my graduation, he took off for Nicaragua again and I realized that he was never going to settle down. I couldn't support the rage—the sadness was nothing by comparison—the rage was like lye poured into my mouth, and me fighting to spit it out, to not swallow, as it seeped into my esophagus and stomach.

I began to stick very close to Branko, who always made sure I got home at night. Sometimes I slept on his couch when the trip home seemed too much to handle.

One night he found me in his bathroom after a party, my hands wrapped around the toilet bowl; I was retching. He bent down to wash my forehead with a cold, damp cloth.

"You're going to have to let him go, Celeste," he said gently.

I burst into tears and began howling as I crumpled into a ball. Branko stretched his legs out around me and took me in his arms. For a long time he rocked me without a word. Hours later I awakened curled up in his arms. He was asleep, sitting up with his back against the door.

* * *

THAT SPRING I went to visit Columbia University after I'd been accepted into the graduate program in Comparative Lit. Branko suggested I call his brother Roderic, who was still taking courses there as a Continuing Ed student. I was afraid to go up to 116th Street alone anyway, so I did. He offered to give me a tour of the campus.

He didn't like Columbia—the classes were too large, the administration a bureaucratic bourgeois hellhole, the neighborhood rife with drug addicts and bums. He took me to a health food restaurant overgrown with tropical plants and told me he'd given up meat, alcohol, cigarettes, pills, and marijuana. He was studying yoga intensively and sociology casually.

"Is Branko still in denial about our father?" he asked after we'd been served large tumblers of carrot juice.

"What do you mean?" I regretted immediately that I'd asked that question, because I didn't want to hear what Roderic had to say.

"Our father was a playboy and a drunk. He loved Branko—handsome, athletic like him—but he used to force me to ski even though I hated it and had a bad leg. He called me a coward. My mother would take my side against them, that's why Branko is angry at her."

I sat there, mouth agape. Roderic smiled evenly as if he were enjoying himself, but I could see that he wasn't calm, his blood was pumping furiously through the artery in his neck. There was something alight in his eyes.

"My father completely manipulated Branko." After a while he added in a clipped murmur, "God, you really are pretty but you are clueless, Celeste."

* * *

ON THE LAST DAY of exams week, the final deadline for late paper submissions, Branko walked up to me in the post office.

"Celeste!" he said, rubbing his hands together and cocking his head, "I've been looking for you everywhere. How about typing up a history paper for me? I'll pay you."

"I don't want your money, you jerk. Bring it over right now."

"Problem is, I haven't finished it. It's a ten-er. I have four pages done."

I looked at the clock on the wall. It was eleven in the morning. "That's it, Branko baby, you're going to be here another semester for sure."

"Can you come over? I'll write. You type. You can catch a tan on the lawn."

As he finished each page he would run down the rickety steps of his house and bring it to where I sat on a pillow in the grass with the typewriter in front of me on a crate. I was wearing the bathing suit he'd bought me the summer before in Amagansett.

Branko's last college paper was on the social conditions of the peasantry in the prewar Austro-Hungarian Empire. His thesis was that they were to blame for their lack of education, the landed gentry having offered them every opportunity for advancement. He'd found only a few quotes to substantiate his argument, citations taken out of context and originally used in the textbook to prove the converse.

"Branko, your professor isn't going to like this, I'm afraid."

"What do I give a shit if he likes it? My father told me this and it's the truth."

He cracked open our first beers at three o'clock. An hour later, I wasn't even proofreading for typos. At four-fifty, he grabbed the last sheet from my hand.

"Yes!" he cried. "Adios, college!"

* * *

IN NEW YORK, he worked for an investment bank for a while before starting his own venture capital company called Baobab, after the tree in his favorite book, *The Little Prince*.

Branko gave seed money to companies who built miracle-seeking medical inventions: a leg and back brace for paraplegics that would make them walk again; a "breakthrough" hearing aid that was implanted in the inner ears of the stone deaf. Nothing came of them, but he kept trying, looking. He joined Greenpeace and the Rainforest Alliance; he funded Save the Whales so that the organization could patrol international waters in search of Japanese whaling vessels.

* * *

ONE DAY he met a six-foot red-headed model on the subway. He told me their eyes locked above the heads of the other passengers. She got off at the same stop and handed him her phone number. Her name was Josie.

She had a pale face with a perfect, thin nose and large hazel eyes. She was friendly and open and I liked to look at her. She loved to dance, and at parties she and I rolled back the rugs and contorted ourselves into strange invented dances from mythical countries, holding postures as Branko watched from the sidelines, amused.

I told him I thought she was the one. But he shook his head. He told me she was on the rebound. A few months before they'd met, she'd come home and found her husband shot to death. There was blood everywhere, splattered on the walls and floor. Apparently he'd been shot over drugs. Branko was vague. He told me she woke up screaming every night. She wanted no commitments. After a short while, they parted amicably.

* * *

IT WAS MY twenty-second birthday and Candace and I were sitting in the kitchen discussing our plans for the evening when there was a knock on the door. We stared at each other for a long moment; the buzzer in the lobby hadn't sounded. She looked through the peephole and opened the door, sighing heavily. Nathan stood there, wearing a leather jacket and biker boots. He was carrying a large black motorcycle helmet.

"You know, Nathan, this is growing old," Candace said quietly.

Without a word he took three bottles of Veuve Cliquot champagne out of his knapsack and placed them on the kitchen table.

"Happy birthday, Celeste," he said evenly.

"Happy birthday, Nathan," I said.

He told us he'd recently taken a job working as the manager of a liquor store in Cambridge. He hadn't liked Texas or Texans, they were loud and obsessed with the size of things. The job at Exxon hadn't worked out either. He was considering reapplying to Harvard. Candace was right, it was getting old.

Much later, we went to bed on the futon in the living room. I was too drunk to be able to appreciate his hands caressing me. He tried everything, but I only lay there as if I were part of the mattress. I thought that his hold over me might be waning.

In the morning, feeling like an old building with no doors or windows to protect it from the wind, I said, "Nathan, I don't want to see you again."

He nodded slowly, and watched me as he dressed, taking his time as if this were the most normal morning in the world. Finally, he took his helmet, and left without a sound.

I lay there in the gray morning light, feeling an emptiness unlike anything I'd known. It seemed I'd finally reached that place called The Future that I had so often contemplated while in college. But The Future didn't look anything like I'd thought it would. I didn't understand what had gone wrong.

* * *

WHEN I CAME HOME from my six-week language program in Russia to an empty apartment, to Candace gone, Branko was the only person I called. Two days passed before I was able to face talking to him.

"Branko, I don't know what to do," I said into the receiver. "Candace left for good."

"It's over a guy, right?"

I didn't say anything.

"Just hang on," he said, "I'll be right over."

He arrived with a frosty bottle of Stolichnaya, a welcome-home present. Sitting in the kitchen that was still filled with Candace's presence, I waited for emotion to overtake me. I waited and waited, just sipping at the shot glass of thick, cold Stoli Branko had placed before me.

"Why?" I finally asked him quite calmly.

"Why what?" He waited for my response. I felt exhausted, drained of strength.

"Why anything, Celeste? Why my father? Why your mother?" After a pause he added, "It was always an imbalanced relationship."

Whatever he meant by that, I didn't want to know.

* * *

WE RESUMED our old habit of having dinner together at least once a week, and going to a party or a film from time to time. Several years passed.

Then one lonely night, much like any other night, I didn't want to go home alone. Something about the darkness, the empty streets, the late hour, terrified me. Branko was matching me shot for shot. If only we could stay in the cozy neighborhood Irish bar, McNamara's or whatever, until the sun came up, but they finally turned the lights on and told us to go home. I told him I was afraid and he came back to my apartment.

We undressed in total silence and darkness and stretched out on the futon, where I'd been sleeping since my return from Moscow. I hoped I was doing the right thing. His body was both too familiar to me and too unknown.

Afterwards he lay on his back in the dark for a few minutes, then said, "I have to go."

"Why?"

"My eyes—my contact lenses are going to dry up and blind me."

"Take them out, you can put them in a glass of water or something."

"No. I gotta go. I'll call you tomorrow."

* * *

HE DIDN'T CALL for three weeks. We hadn't gone that long without speaking since we'd met. Furious, scared, I finally made the first move.

"Branko," I said, "what the hell is wrong with you? We've been friends for years. Why are you treating me like a one-night stand?"

There was a long silence.

"We could've at least discussed it," I continued. "You're avoiding me." He didn't say anything for a while.

"I'm sorry, Celeste. I feel like . . . I feel I've done something very, very wrong."

"We were drunk, what's the problem? All these years I thought you wanted to sleep with me."

"My life's completely out of control, Celeste. Listen, give me some time, all right? I need to think about things."

*   *   *

HE DISAPPEARED for two more months.

When he finally called on New Year's Day, he sounded as normal as if we'd spoken only days before. I was angry, but also relieved. We agreed to meet at a Mexican restaurant on Columbus Avenue the following evening.

He ordered immediately, two burritos, a taco, an enchilada, and a chili releno. "And make them really spicy," he told the waitress. The whites of his eyes sparkled like new china and for once, there were no purple circles beneath them.

"Anything to drink?"

"A club soda with a lime for me," Branko said, sitting back.

"A club soda?" I said. "Why go to a Mexican restaurant if you're not going to drink margaritas? Come on, Branko, have a margarita with me."

He shook his head solemnly. "I quit," he said. "Just for today."

"What do you mean, just for today? You drank yesterday but you won't drink today?"

"I mean I'm choosing not to drink today."

"Well, do you mind if *I* have one?" I asked irritably.

"Not at all."

I ordered a margarita and a couple of tacos. But he had taken the fun out of it; we would not be partying tonight.

Sitting back in his chair, he sighed, and said, "That night that we . . . you know . . . I felt so horrible about it. It was a real low for me. I care about you, Celeste. You're my friend. I'm so sorry."

"Listen, we've been friends a long time. We had a lot to drink. It doesn't matter."

"But it *does* matter. It matters."

There was a long silence. The waitress brought our drinks.

"You know what else?" he said, drinking half of his club soda in one gulp. "I feel like I haven't accomplished a goddamn thing in my life."

"You're twenty-nine, Branko, don't panic."

"It's not that. If you died tomorrow, you'd leave something tangible. Your stories. That's important. I haven't done anything."

"You've saved a couple of whales," I said, and laughed. He didn't crack a smile.

"I'm serious, Celeste."

Our dinners arrived, covered with brown sauce. We ate for a while without talking.

"Maybe my biggest accomplishment will be to quit drinking," he said.

"I thought you already quit."

"It's been two months, but every day I say it's just for today." After a moment he added, taking a deep breath, "I'm in so much fucking pain . . ." His voice trailed off. After a while he said, "One day you look around and say, wait a minute, where's my life? But I'll tell you something, compared to most, my bottom was pretty high."

"Your bottom was pretty high? What the hell are you talking about?"

He said calmly, "I didn't end up in the gutter like some people. Some people have to lose everything before they quit. Some people never quit. You hit one bottom and then just go right on through, down to the next one. You lose your job, your family. You might end up in the fucking street, and still not stop. It's a total miracle that I quit when I did. And it was all because of you—because of that night!"

"Jesus Christ, Branko, I didn't think I was that lousy in bed."

He smiled, and I noticed in the pale candlelight that he was blushing. I felt like I was ten years old and this grown-up was trying to explain sex to me for the first time. I had only the vaguest idea of what he was getting at.

"What would it take—what would it take, Celeste, for *you* to quit?"

"You are really bumming me out," I said, and tried to laugh.

"You know, we've had some really good times together. I'm going to Vail tomorrow for a while, that place always has a way of rejuvenating me. Will you do something with me when I get back?"

"Sure, what?"

"I'd like to take you somewhere, a surprise, will you just come?"

"Sure," I said glumly. "If it'll make you happy."

* * *

HE WALKED ME a few blocks north.

"When you first quit drinking, they tell you to stay away from people, places, and things that make you want to drink."

"Who's they?"

"Other drunks who stopped drinking. For me, you're one of those people I had to stay away from. That's why I haven't called you."

"Jesus Christ, Branko," I said, my voice knocked out of me. "Fuck you."

At Columbus and Seventy-seventh, he stopped. The wind whipped through the deserted school yard on the corner, sending bits of paper and old cigarette butts scurrying through the fence. He threw his arms around me and squeezed me tightly. With my face pressed up against his chest I felt even more like a child. I looked up at him under the street lamp and smiled weakly.

"I love you, Branko," I said, my eyes filling with tears.

"So. I'll call you in a few weeks, when I get back."

"Definitely," I said.

"I love you, too." He stepped back, looked me over with serious eyes. "Be good, Celeste. Try to take care of yourself." With that, he zipped his down coat to his neck. I stood at the corner, watching him stoop against the icy wind as he walked away. At Seventy-sixth he turned and waved.

A strange and frightening thought passed through my mind in that instant: *You'll never see him again.*

I wanted to shout at him to stop, to turn around, come back with me to my place, or come sit downstairs in the corner bar. But I let him go.

I turned and headed home, feeling the icy wind in my bones.

* * *

A WEEK LATER, in Vail, Branko was skiing fifty miles an hour down a narrow catwalk in over a foot of powder snow when the tips of skis sank and stuck, catapulting him out of his bindings and sending headfirst into a tree. His ski partner found him moments later. On val at the hospital, Branko was brain-dead, but his heart went on ting resolutely for three days.

She swallowed hard. "Your mother? I never knew her, you know. Let's go ahead and order."

"I went to Japan once," she told me, picking up a California roll with her chopsticks.

"Really?" I didn't know this, but it didn't seem odd. I knew nothing about her past, or how she'd met my father, or their courtship. I'd always liked it better that way.

"Yes, I went to Japan with my first husband, Jordan. He was a jazz musician and one summer they played in Japan. It was fun. Altogether life was great fun back then—but he was a junkie. I was so young, I didn't know what was wrong with him for the longest time. Why are you looking at me like that? You think your generation invented drugs?"

Her mood went from ebullient to teary. I laid down my chopsticks and took a long, slow sip of my drink.

"Sometimes I feel I haven't been a good stepmother to you. I just never did enough to make us close."

"You did a fine job, Anna, you really did."

She reached into her little handbag for a tissue and dabbed at her eyes. "You never really liked me. I know you loved me—love me—but we were never friends."

A large dish of sukiyaki arrived and was set at the center of the table. She stirred the vegetables and meat with her chopsticks.

"The best one was Branko," she said without looking up. "I always had a secret crush on him. He was rich, handsome, and nice. I never could figure out why you two didn't—"

My heart was pounding against my rib cage, as if fighting to get out.

"How can you say that, Anna? I don't need this shit," I said in a low, cold voice, and pulled my legs out from under the table. "I'm getting married in less than three weeks. What's the matter with you?"

"Oh my goodness! Don't go! I'm sorry!"

I sat back down, angry.

"I just can't bear to think of you making the same mistakes I made. Do you know why I never had kids? I had an illegal abortion years ago and that damn drunken quack botched up my insides. Jordan couldn't have handled kids, he couldn't handle himself.

"Life is all about settling happily for less than one expected," she went on, looking down. "Your father *thinks* he's content. But now he gets these headaches and can barely move from the pain. He's become an avid bird-watcher, did you know that? He says it helps him relax." She raised her eyes and they seemed hopeful and vulnerable. I felt intolerably sad.

"No, I didn't know that," I said in a quiet voice.

"Oh, yes. He's very serious about it. Has these brand-new binoculars, and keeps a little book. He found a baby bird that had fallen out of a tree. He brought it home and tried to feed it, but it died. He cried like a little boy."

I tried to picture my father crying over the tiny corpse of a bird. It was impossible to imagine. When I'd last been home to try on my wedding dress, we'd come across each other in the kitchen. He was getting ice cubes from the freezer.

"How are you, Celeste?" He looked at me expectantly with eyes the color of old jeans.

Hope rose in me. "Well, actually, I'm having an incredible time teaching in Harlem. You wouldn't believe this boy Derrence, Dad, he's so bright! He's been writing poems about . . . "

Watching him closely, I saw boredom already settling over his eyes like a thick fog. I had always assumed that I bored him, but today, lurking behind the fog I saw discomfort. He felt trapped around me. Did he see my mother when he looked at me? Perhaps I reminded him that he had walked away from her in her illness, and ignored his children.

I kept talking but the enthusiasm had drained from my voice; he wasn't hearing me. My voice trailed off. He smiled, nodded, and walked away, through the swinging door.

* * *

I REALIZED as I listened to Anna that I'd treated her much as he treated me, a difficult thing for me to accept.

I sat there, stunned. "Anna," I said slowly, barely audibly, nausea rising in waves from somewhere down in my legs, "Anna, how did my mother die?"

"How did your mother—" she repeated, looking at me and then glancing away.

"I can't remember what happened. My father told me she had a heart attack, I think, but I have this blank in my memory."

"Oh for God's sake, Celeste, all these years I thought you knew and just didn't want to talk—"

"What?" I put down my chopsticks. One rolled off the table and onto my lap. My throat closed as if a fist were squeezing it shut. I picked up my glass of sake and drank it down. Anna immediately refilled it.

"Celeste," she said in a whisper. "You don't know? Oh for God's sake." She lowered her face into her hands. "I thought you knew. Everyone else knows."

And then I said it as if it made the most perfect sense in the world, as if I'd always known it, and the beast of fear who'd hidden for so long behind every unfamiliar corner had known it too and wanted to shout it in my ear.

"She killed herself," I said numbly.

Anna nodded, without looking up.

"How?" I asked.

"She took all her pills and drank a bottle of booze," Anna said quickly. "Apparently it was a miracle that the maid—what was her name?"

"Mathilde."

"—that Mathilde found her before you did. Your father made me swear never to discuss—"

"I was ten years old!" I cried, squeezing my eyes shut. "Everyone was out, they left me *alone*." I saw myself wandering around downstairs, turning on all the lights, calling out, *"Maman! Maman!"* She always waited anxiously by the kitchen door for me to come home, as if the ride on the school bus were a treacherous journey. She never left the house and I knew something was terribly wrong.

"I *waited* for Mathilde to get home before going upstairs. It wasn't a fucking miracle." I took several deep breaths, gathering my wits. "Why did *he* lie to me?"

"To protect you. To protect your feelings. You were just a child."

"No, it's because my father's a coward," I said.

"Your mother was an alcoholic," Anna said, suddenly defensive.

I shouted back, as if she'd just insulted me, "What about you? You drink more than she did!"

"I don't have a problem with alcohol, and certainly not with pills," she said with authority. "I never even take an aspirin! *You'll* have to watch it, you know, Celeste. These things are hereditary." With that, she refilled our empty glasses and we both lifted them to our lips.

Where did one draw the line, then? Was it in the way one behaved when intoxicated? Toward the end, only one drink would make my mother wild and blue, and she'd repeat the same thing again and again, as if she'd completely forgotten. Anna, on the other hand, could drink and drink and she only became more ebullient and laughed more loudly. Was that it?

Was that the difference? Branko hadn't lost anything, so why had he decided to stop? Because he had fucked his best friend in a drunken stupor? This seemed patently absurd to me.

"Thank heavens that Alex isn't much of a drinker," she added thoughtfully.

"Oh, he drinks," I said. "He's just a control freak. I'm going to go talk to a shrink," I said with renewed conviction.

"If you must, wait until after the wedding. Now," she said, quite satisfied, "want to go to the Carlyle?"

I didn't want to go home to an empty, dark apartment. Even if it was a beautiful space that reigned high up in the New York sky.

* * *

THE BAR IN THE CARLYLE was no less dark and more brooding. Anna sent a drink over to the piano player, who looked up and waved toward our table after "My Funny Valentine."

"I used to know him in my other life," Anna whispered to me.

I was on my second brandy when the piano player said, "My old friend Anna Carruthers is here, maybe she'd like to come up and sing a song?" Anna smiled, her blush showing even in the dim candlelight, but she shook her head.

"I'd need several more drinks before I'd be willing to do that," she mumbled, clasping the cameo at her throat as if it were a reminder of who she was today. "Ha, ha, your father would have a heart attack!" She slapped the tabletop with her palm and took a sip of her gin and tonic.

After the set, the piano player came and sat with us. He looked much older up close, with a handsome face ravaged by deep wrinkles. He had a quiet, smooth voice.

"Anna, long time no see."

"Pete."

"How do you do?" he said to me.

"My daughter, Celeste," Anna said. "Pete Brown."

"Passing through?" Pete asked.

"Just passing through," Anna said with a smile.

"Well, good to see you, Anna Carruthers. Come up and sing a song."

"It's Miller now. Anna Miller. Those days are long gone, Pete. I don't even sing in the shower anymore."

He tapped the table, and got up. Moments later, the waitress in a tiny black dress arrived with another round of drinks from Pete.

"My darling Celeste," Anna said in a mumble, close to my ear, "you're going to have to learn to forgive. It's so terribly important as you get older to *forgive*."

"*Forgive!*" I cried. "How about learning how to tell the truth first?"

"I know," she said somberly, "being young is so very hard."

Anna and I were weaving by the time we left the Carlyle. Hooking her arm through mine, she led me toward Fifth Avenue through the stifling night.

In the Hotel Pierre, we walked down a labyrinth of corridors until we finally came upon the bar. There were a few couples sitting in dark corners and one lonely fellow at the bar. The bartender approached and Anna said very succinctly, "A Martell and a gin and tonic, please."

She turned to me, cupped my chin in her hand, and leaned very close. "I'm sorry. I'm so sorry that you've had to go through this now. I had no idea you didn't know. I do love you so." A pearl-sized tear fell from her eye.

"Don't cry, Anna," I said, moved by her emotion. "I love you too. Everything's going to be fine now. We can be friends, we really can."

She pressed her cheek to mine and I felt a tear slide onto my hot, damp skin.

"Ladies," said the bartender, looming above us on the other side of the bartop, "we'll have none of that in here."

"Oh, what are you talking about, silly man!" cried Anna. "This is my daughter." She turned my chin toward him. "Look how beautiful she is."

Anna stood in front of her sister's building and waved as my taxi sped away. The streetlights cast a luminescent glow in the thick haze that hung over the deserted avenue. There was no breeze at all.

The taxi stopped at a red light. I was too dazed to think. Just then I caught sight of a very tall figure through the windshield, his outline fuzzy in the haze. Once again my heart recognized him before my mind did. Branko had been dead over a year, I reminded myself. This time the man was wearing jogging shorts and a torn-up T-shirt. My hand instinctively reached for the door handle. Just then he glanced in my direction. Our eyes locked, and I was unable to breathe. He smiled and ran past the cab, tossing his thick curly hair away from his face.

The light changed and the driver turned a corner and sped off.

* * *

AT HOME, I collapsed onto the couch and stared at the dark TV screen. There were eight hang-ups on the answering machine before Alex left a message asking me to call him at his hotel in L.A. It seemed like he'd been away a year. Reflected in the screen I saw the couch and the coffee table and myself, sitting there demurely, all perfect and in order like a commercial for some household appliance. Except my vision kept going in and out of focus. No way was I calling him now.

I picked up the remote control and with a wavering hand flicked to the Discovery Channel.

A mountain of snow was collapsing on the screen. "Avalanches are common in the Himalayas," said the narrator in a confident voice, "and we were unprepared for the losses we suffered. Two Sherpas in the first avalanche, and Krauss, the Pulitzer Prize–winning German photographer, in the second."

A long, bright, orange and red centipede of Sherpas with heavy square bundles on thin brown legs was weaving up a steep, stony incline. The camera cut to two stills of smiling men whose faces were so wrinkled, it was impossible to determine their age. The Sherpas who had perished in the avalanche.

Next came a wide-angle shot of an enormous expanse of snow. Suddenly the white ground opened up, exposing a bottomless ice pit.

"Even more dangerous are the ice crevasses because you never know where one will surface. We lost our best Sherpa to an ice crevasse. A man who'd been climbing Everest for twenty-five years."

I thought the narrator's voice was much too self-confident for someone who'd witnessed so many deaths. I was seeing double, so I covered one eye with my palm, a late-night driving technique during college. I focused on the screen.

Climbers were camped in small Day-Glo orange tents as a blizzard raged around them. They were smiling, their cracked, sunburned faces aglow with excitement.

"Even though I was the principal financer of this Mount Everest expedition, I was not one of the fortunate ones who made it to the peak. You see, being the richest, or the best climber, or the most physically fit doesn't matter here—it's who is in the best position to make that last major effort on the final day. Evans, who planted our flag, was relatively inexperienced, compared to the rest of us. But he was well rested because he hadn't exerted himself as we had on previous days. I was just too damn exhausted by the time we reached the Hillary Step, the last big obstacle. But in the larger sense, it really doesn't matter who planted the flag. It's the team effort that makes such an expedition worthwhile."

I flicked off the television and sat in the dim light, breathing deeply.

A long time must have passed before I stumbled into the old guest room, now my office, where a carpenter had built me wall-to-wall bookshelves. On the bottom shelf was an old photo album I hadn't looked at in years. I opened it at random and came upon a picture of Branko standing proudly, legs and arms crossed, in front of his Porsche. The pages were yellowed and the plastic protective bindings had come loose. As I fumbled to right the pages, pictures tumbled out all over the floor. I threw the album aside, and bending to retrieve the pictures, stumbled to my knees.

I picked up a photo lying facedown on the rug. It was one of Branko and me at the Delta Kappa Half-Assed Semi-Formal. I am sitting on his lap with my leg extended straight out, wearing a black silk décolleté blouse and silk boxer shorts with black lace stockings and a garter belt. Branko is wearing the top half of one of his European suits, complete with vest and tie and button-down cotton oxford shirt and gold cuff links. He's also in boxer shorts, with cowboy boots and an enormous black cowboy hat he'd bought in Colorado. We'd had a good time dancing that night, until I got alcohol poisoning from drinking Purple Jesus, a grain alcohol punch Branko had warned me to stay away from. In the middle of the party, I stretched out on a couch and closed my eyes. Moments later, Branko tried to wake me but I was out cold. I was barely breathing and he couldn't find my pulse. He slapped me, got me to my feet, and poured black coffee down my throat until I vomited. Afterwards, he walked me around the block for several hours.

I picked up another photo. It was of Branko, Candace, and me in our red graduation robes, the silly square tasseled hats cocked on our heads. A large group of us had been up most of the night, drinking champagne, sniffing cocaine, dancing like escaped lunatics on the campus green. Our three youthful, uncomplicated, sweaty faces smiled moonily at the camera. What did we know?

Anyway, I had never believed myself to be one of the strong or the brave.

Eighteen

AT SEVEN on Friday morning, Alex called me from his office.

"Hi there," he said in a shaky voice. "Where have you been?"

I didn't answer. He went on. "I took the red-eye. I wanted to get back. Want to have lunch with me? We could meet in the park."

I thought for a moment, trying to clear my head. "Okay," I said.

I slept for a few more hours, then drew a bath. I washed my hair, taking my time, luxuriating in the feeling that the storm had finally passed and now I was ready to face the blackouts and frayed power lines. I intended to tell Alex about my conversation with Anna, and to discuss with him the issue of my drinking and of my need to see a shrink.

By the time I entered Central Park at Fifty-ninth Street, my courage had waned. I spotted Alex standing down the path by the pony run. He was observing the little children who sat demurely in the pony cart, knees together and tiny hands clasped in their laps. On his face was an amused smile. It was close to noon and the park was crowded with mothers shouting and chasing children, and homeless people resting on the shady benches that lined the walk. Alex was one of the few men in a suit. I saw the young mothers smile at him approvingly. In a moment he turned his head in my direction. Without thinking, I slipped in behind a tall man walking in front of me.

When I reached Alex, he was facing the pony run again, still smiling at the little kids.

"Hi, Alex," I said. I had been completely alone for more than thirty hours, not speaking to a soul.

He took me into his arms and held me close. "This used to be my favorite place when I was little," he said into my ear. His voice had lost the lacquer of testiness that had bothered me so much before his departure, and his spicy cologne smelled reassuringly familiar.

"Want to go to the zoo?" he asked. "I haven't been here since they've redone it."

Glass had replaced all the bars I remembered from my childhood. We sat down on the shallow steps surrounding the tank of seals and watched their feline faces glide by in slow circles. Their movements were as liquid as the water. I thought of scuba diving again and grew excited.

They coasted past, first in one direction, then the other.

"Wouldn't it be fun to dive with seals?" Alex asked, taking my hand and holding it between his soft, dry palms. "There's a kelp forest in northern California that's teeming with seals."

"I saw it on the Discovery Channel," I said. "Great whites frequent that kelp forest, too."

"You and the Discovery Channel," Alex said, smiling. "I've been trying to call you for two days. I was worried."

"I'm sorry. Look! They're watching us!" The seals had come around again and were turning to look at us as they passed by. With the flick of their tails, they sent a shower of water onto our shoes. Alex took out his white handkerchief, wiped off his black wingtips, and dabbed at my tan slingbacks.

"Celeste, I've been thinking," he said. My heart began to pound again. The sunlight seemed awfully bright and I squinted at him. "Everything is not perfect between us," he said.

"That's for sure," I said.

"I don't remember exactly what happened the other night with my mother, but I'm sorry if I upset you."

I could feel rage simmering below the surface of my skin. I kept my voice calm and smooth. "Alex, you scared the living shit out of me. How am I supposed to live like this? Never knowing when you're going to flip out!"

"You're right," he said, surprising me. "I guess I haven't really dealt with that stuff."

"Why do you push me away, why don't you talk to me about things?"

He watched the seals for a while, thinking. I focused on the curve of his ear and jaw, the way his hair ended in a smooth line at his strong neck. He was beautiful to look at.

"I feel insecure around you," he finally said. "Like that time you were reading Proust. How the hell am I supposed to compete with that?"

"It's not a competition, Alex."

"I think you're smarter than I am. You're an intellectual, a teacher."

"I'm not an intellectual."

A crease forming between his brows. The sun glinted off his glasses. "I wanted everything perfect with the wedding. All I wanted was to take care of you, make your life easy. Make you happy. And I think everything I do is just never enough."

"Maybe you wish I were someone else," I said. "Someone without a history. Listen to me, Alex. I had dinner with Anna on Tuesday and she told me that my mother killed herself."

"Oh, Jesus," he said quickly, and pressed me to his chest. "Jesus, Jesus, what a terrible thing."

"They lied to me, Alex," I said, pulling away from him to look into his face. "I just didn't know; they should have told me. I'm going to see a shrink," I added resolutely. The sunlight was so blinding, I had to shield my eyes with my hand. I swallowed and said, "I think we should go see someone together."

"Okay," he conceded. "I think that's a good idea."

We sat in silence. Finally he said, "But not now. Not till after our honeymoon."

"It seems like maybe not such a good idea to start now, you're right. Since we're getting married in just over a week."

"How could your mother do that to you?" he said quietly. "Kill herself like that and leave you, a little girl? What a selfish thing to do."

I swallowed calmly. "It took courage, I think. *I* couldn't do it. When I was younger and in a lot of pain, I thought about it, believe me. But I never could do it."

I wanted to bring up the other thing, the drinking, but couldn't seem to broach the subject.

"No wonder you're depressed." After a moment he added hopefully, "Maybe you need pills."

His words were reassuring for some reason. Pills might fix me, I thought, put everything back in order. Maybe that was the problem. Maybe I'd inherited my mother's depressive condition. In the quiet buzz of noon, I pressed my face to Alex's chest and heard the steady beating of his heart, the small, excited voices of children surrounding us, and water slapping against glass. The children's voices reminded me of the feeling of loneliness and exclusion that had always haunted me, even while my mother was still alive.

"Alex . . ." I started, without looking at him, knowing that what I was about to say could have disastrous consequences. *Alex,* I was going to say, *Alex, my dearest Alex, I have a drinking problem* . . . But this seemed far too cataclysmic, far too definitive. *Now, now, don't overdo it,* my mind warned. *If you tell him that, you'll never be able to take it back.*

So I asked him in a calm, even tone, "Alex, do you think I drink too much?"

"You drink a lot," he said after a moment of thought. "But you're not— definitely not—an *alcoholic* or anything like that. It's not like you drink every day. You're just a heavy social drinker. And you've been going through a stressful time lately. But look how much you've cut back since we've been together. We're going to keep it that way, right?"

He looked at me very seriously. A huge sigh of relief wanted to escape from my lungs, but I wouldn't let it for fear that he would take notice. *Everything is back to normal. Everything is as it should be.*

I decided, just as a precaution, not to drink until the wedding.

Slowly he kissed my cheeks, my neck, behind my ears, my lips. His mouth tasted cool and sweet, like fresh water after a long ocean swim. I felt desire stirring in me, a tiny flame of hope reigniting.

"I'm going to take the afternoon off," Alex said. "Let's go home and go to bed."

"Let's," I said, breathing against his neck. He took his cell phone out of his breast pocket and called his secretary.

"Lorraine."

Apparently she had something very important to tell him because his whole face went rigid in concentration.

"What the hell is he talking about? We went through this yesterday. He's not to talk to their lawyers. I told him not to! Well, just get him on the phone right now . . . I'll hold."

"George again?" I said, aiming for humor. My lips trembled as I smiled. But he had already forgotten I was there.

I waited a half hour while he talked on the phone, trying to fix whatever had gone wrong. I knew that if he took the afternoon off, he would be anxious and ill-at-ease, resentful of me for taking him away from his work.

I put my hand on his arm. I could feel his hard biceps through his light, summer wool suit. "Alex," I murmured, "it doesn't matter. Go back to work."

He looked relieved. "I'll be there in a minute," he said into his cell phone, and folded it back into his pocket.

* * *

PRESIDING OVER our rehearsal dinner in Nero's restaurant, I couldn't take my eyes off the mirror that ran the length of the opposite wall. I looked at us, the bride and groom at the center of a long rectangular table, backs to the fresco of Venice, appearing to be seated in a gondola about to pass under a bridge. Beyond the bridge were gondoliers in striped shirts, floating in their gondolas in a sapphire blue Grand Canal. How happy and beautiful the couple looked, he in a new charcoal gray suit and she in a new shimmering blue dress with tiny white polka dots, her new sapphire earrings flashing prisms of light.

On each table, small white candles burned in crystal sconces, their golden flames reflecting in the wine glasses and sparkling off the ladies' jewelry. Laughter and merry voices echoed through the room.

But Alex's voice in my ear brought me suddenly, with a pang of regret, back into the party.

"Why aren't you drinking the wine, Celeste? I ordered Chateau Laroq just for you."

The ruby wine shimmered in the ballon glass just before me, untouched. I looked at it, thought about it from every angle once again. Even my taste buds were screaming in outrage. My stomach churned, my hands and feet itched. I wanted to drink the Chateau Laroq so badly, I could already feel its tangy, velvety sweetness coating the back of my throat, and the burst of heat in my chest on its way down. I hadn't had a drink since my dinner with Anna eighteen days ago.

If you haven't had a drink in eighteen days then you don't have a problem, my mind told me.

But then I thought of what the man outside the church had said: "They're celebrating people counting days." Every day I'd counted off to myself, and every day I'd felt proud, as if I'd accomplished something. Normal people didn't feel that way if they went a couple of days without a drink. They surely didn't *count*.

As each day had passed without a drink, my anxiety increased, along with the rage and self-disgust, and the fear that accompanied them, that pricked at my skin from the inside.

Alex, for some reason, had seemed deeply threatened by my resolve.

* * *

LAST MONDAY, he called from work at ten P.M. and said he wanted me to meet him at a nightclub his coworkers were taking him to. I told him to go without me. I was already in bed and did not want to get all dressed up and go to a club, where there would be lots and lots of alcohol and I would want to drink.

"What the hell is wrong, Celeste?" he said impatiently.

"Nothing is wrong, I just don't want to go out, that's all," I said. He hung up on me, and came crashing in at four-thirty in the morning like some kind of bulldozer. He crawled into bed and I pretended to be asleep. He grabbed hold of the collar of my nightgown and ripped it right off my back. He held me down with the weight of his body. I struggled to free myself.

"Alex," I hissed, "get the fuck off me."

"Don't you swear at me," he said through clenched teeth. His big hands encircled my throat and began to squeeze. I couldn't breathe, felt my face beginning to explode. I reached over and grabbed the bedside lamp and brought it down on his head. It hardly fazed him, but he was surprised enough to let go of my neck.

I sprang out of bed and ran to the bathroom, and locked myself in. He banged his fists against the door. "Don't make me break this door down!" he shouted.

"Go away!" I shouted back, looking for some kind of weapon in the cabinet under the sink. Not much there besides toilet paper. I picked up the plunger. "Go to sleep, you're drunk!"

"I'm going to wait right here till you come out," he said.

I pulled sheets and towels and blankets out of the closet and laid them out on the floor. "That's okay with me," I said. "I'm going to sleep in here."

As I lay on the bathroom floor with the bath mat and a blanket between me and the tiles, the absurdity of the situation was not lost on me: how many times had I passed out cold on a bathroom floor? And here I was, not a drop of booze in me, sleeping again on a bathroom floor.

At six A.M. he woke me up, knocking politely, and cleared his throat. In his most reassuring and sheepish voice, he said that he needed to get his shaving things. I was so angry, I couldn't speak. We passed each other like strangers getting on and off an elevator, eyes never meeting.

* * *

H E C A M E H O M E from work earlier than usual that evening, carrying a small, pale blue Tiffany shopping bag, which he handed to me. Inside was a little blue box with a yellow Post-It attached: "Mr. Laughton: I hope this is what you had in mind! —Lorraine." Apparently he had forgotten to remove the note.

Inside the box was a pair of sapphire earrings in the shape of large tears. "They're beautiful," I said glumly. "Lorraine has good taste."

He shot me an angry glance and chose not to say anything.

Knowing that he would not be happy about it, I told him I'd decided I wanted us to take a week of our honeymoon to go see my grandmother in Bordeaux. "I need my family," I said.

"I thought you hated your grandmother," Alex said as he began to take off his suit.

"Of course I don't hate my grandmother," I said. "In fact, I'd like to see her very much."

"I'd like to stick to our original plan if you don't mind, a week in Venice and a week in Capri," he said evenly. "After all, it is our honeymoon."

I told him I wanted to go to Bordeaux.

"I don't want to go to France and sit there like a jerk while you talk to everybody in French."

"So it's the thing of me knowing something you don't," I said dryly. "Anyway, I speak Italian, too."

"I should never have told you that," he muttered. "Let's go out to dinner, I'm going-stir crazy. How about Le Bistro?"

Le Bistro had *great* martinis. I did not want to be tempted. "I'd rather stay home," I said. "I made a *salade Niçoise*."

He looked at me with an annoyed frown. I'd seen him look at the doormen this way, when he was expecting an important package from the office and it had apparently been misplaced. For a moment, I was crippled with the realization that I had absolutely no idea who this man was, and that last night he had almost strangled me.

And for the first time since my dinner with Anna, I suddenly really wanted a drink. There was a bottle of Stoli in the freezer and it was calling to me. My knuckles turned white as I gripped the couch pillow beneath me in an effort to stay seated.

Enraged and disgusted, I refused to back down. "Alex, I want to go to Bordeaux to see my grandmother."

I realized, of course, the argument had nothing whatsoever to do with Bordeaux.

* * *

ALL DAY Wednesday he called me from work, circling me like a shark, coming in for a nudge, attempting different approaches in the hope that, exhausted, I'd finally give up. I decided that I'd fight him to the end.

He said in a honey-coated voice, as soon as he came in from work, "I had Lorraine call the travel agent; she found out it would cost us nine hundred and eighty-six dollars each to change our tickets to fly to Bordeaux."

"Since when do you care how much things cost?" I said in an equally honey-coated voice.

He said, "What if I plan a vacation for us next Christmas to go just to Bordeaux and stay with her for two whole weeks?"

I knew this was a bribe so I said, "Bordeaux isn't at all beautiful in December." I had no idea if this was true, but it sounded fairly plausible to me. He was silenced for the time being.

* * *

"I'M NOT GOING to Bordeaux," he said to me on Thursday morning. This was the night of his bachelor party. His New York friends had waited until the very end so that Alex's best man, James, could arrive from Oregon.

I tried to envision him sitting with my grandmother in her sunroom and a horrible feeling of embarrassment overcame me. He wouldn't be able to discuss literature with her. He'd proudly tell her about mergers and acquisitions and my grandmother would peer at him with her coldest expression, her inscrutable eyes filled with a contempt that Alex would not even recognize.

I knew he would not back down and that I'd lost the battle.

"Okay, Alex," I said, my voice quivering with rage, "*fuck* Bordeaux! Next fall, I'll go by myself."

"You don't have to swear about it," he said.

* * *

ALEX CAME HOME early from work to help me greet his best man. James had driven his Nissan Pathfinder all the way from Portland. He was a large fellow with fine hair so pale it seemed white, a small upturned nose, and round cheeks. He wore a lumberjack shirt, jeans, and Timberland boots. When he entered the apartment, Alex stood back and frowned, looking him over.

"Jesus Christ, Jimbo, you're taking this nature stuff way too seriously," he said with a chuckle.

"You're darn tootin', Attila," James said, also laughing. "And it's *Doctor* James to you now."

"A man with a doctorate in environmental science is about as useful as a whore with a Ph.D. in public health. Please tell me you brought a suit."

"Don't know if it still fits," James said. They slapped each other on the back, having a good laugh.

They had a few rum and tonics while I sat on the couch with a Diet Coke. Alex got his second electric guitar out of the storage closet and dusted it off. They plugged both guitars into the huge black amplifier Alex still kept in the living room, although he never played anymore, and they began to twang and rift. The bottle of Stoli in the freezer came to mind.

The walls thumped and thudded as a feedback scream threatened to shatter the glassware. The Stoli began calling to me like a homing beacon. I went to the freezer and opened it. There was my beloved friend, Stolichnaya vodka, a dusting of frost covering the bottle. I saw a pint of Rocky Road ice cream and took that, along with a spoon, into the bedroom and put the headphones on and turned on the TV. I could still hear their guitars and them howling, "You neeeed coolin' baby I'm not foolin' . . . "

I watched a documentary on the mating rituals of birds of paradise, taking slow, deep breaths, and prayed for these bad feelings to go away. *You're just nervous,* I kept telling myself.

Shortly, Alex came in to tell me they were off to the bachelor party. I smiled and waved, not removing the earphones.

* * *

THEY CAME IN at around two and started with the guitars again. "I'm a cowboy with a six-string on my baaaack!"

Later, when Alex stumbled into the bedroom, I attempted to confront him. Perhaps this was not the best moment, but time was pressing. Tomorrow was our rehearsal dinner; the next day, our wedding.

"Alex, why do you hurt me when you're drunk?"

He stood with an arm against the dresser, tottering slightly as if on board a ship. I thought that maybe he might hurt me again tonight, and that James would have to come in and rescue me, and this might not be a bad thing.

"Hurt you? What the fuck are you talking about?" he said with a rapacious smile, his red eyes ablaze. "You know something? You're a total drag when you don't drink."

With that, he pounced onto the bed, rolled over, and passed out.

* * *

ALEX HAD LEFT by the time I awakened the next morning.

I made coffee for James and waited for him to get up. He finally emerged from the guest room/office, his hair standing on end and his big face bloated and pasty.

"Why do you call him Attila?" I asked lightly, fixing him a cup of coffee. The booze he'd consumed the night before emanated from his pores in a toxic mist.

"Oh, you know. He was pretty wild in prep school and college. He had guts, though." James's eyes lit up at some memory, full of admiration. "Took on half the Yale football team one night. I was there, I saw it. They thought he was nuts, started calling him Attila.

"He's calmed down quite a lot. You're a good influence."

I asked, gambling that James knew about this, too, "He told me about his wife. The order of protection and all that." I let my voice drop conspiratorially.

"Oh yeah, that," he said, looking down and shaking his head. "It was an accident. It's really easy to dislocate a shoulder. He never meant to hurt her." After an uncomfortable silence, he said, "Say, is there a gym in this building?"

* * *

AND EARLIER TONIGHT, at our own rehearsal dinner, we stood together, the beautiful, happy couple, greeting our guests at the door. I had promised myself, as a reward for not drinking for ten whole days, that tonight I would have a cocktail.

Hurry up please, it's time, I heard in my head as Alex and I hugged Aurelia and shook hands with her new boyfriend, Frederico, a thin, stoop-shouldered man with a black mustache who was only a few years older than Alex.

"Champagne, madam?" a waiter asked me, proffering a tray.

Take it! Take the glass! But I knew I was in such a state that if I started now, by the end of the night I would be dancing naked on the table, if not in bed with one of the waiters.

"Could I please have a glass of Pellegrino water?" I asked him sweetly, shocking myself. *What? But you said cocktail time!*

* * *

AND NOW IT was dinnertime, and we were having our appetizers, shrimp cocktail, which I hadn't touched, for my mouth was so dry I could barely swallow.

I thought that if I reached out and drank down the glass of Chateau Laroq that Alex had just reminded me he'd ordered as a special surprise, my discomfort, my rage, my fear, would instantly abate.

So what the hell is holding you back?

People, places, and things, Branko had said. Here I was, smack in the middle of the maelstrom. No wonder I wanted a drink.

"Celeste?" Alex said again. "I spent a lot of money on this wine."

"Yes, it must have been difficult for Lorraine to get such a big order on such short notice."

I saw rage in his eyes. If we'd been alone, he might have tried to strangle me again.

"My grandmother would've sent you as many cases as you wanted for free," I said, my voice quiet from the knot in my throat. I turned away, glanced quickly in the mirror across the room and saw there a happy, perfect couple smiling at each other. I felt wrenched in two.

Why can't you believe what you're seeing in the mirror? Why can't you just be happy, accept it? Drink the wine and everything will be all right.

I turned back to Alex. "I don't want any," I whispered, smiling so hard, two points of pressure pulsed dully at the base of my skull.

"What the hell is wrong with you?" he said between his teeth, also smiling, eyes on fire.

"I have a drinking problem, Alex," I said smoothly, in an equable tone.

"I already told you, you don't have a drinking problem, Celeste. Why do you always have to ruin everything?"

My heart raced, my ears rang with a rhythmic pounding. I wanted to lift the glass of Chateau Laroq and dump it on his head. My hand reached out and encircled the glass.

Fuck it. Fuck it all! Drink it!

A zephyr tickled my neck and the tiny hairs there bristled, as I remembered what Branko had said: *Some people have to lose everything before they quit. Some people never quit. You hit one bottom and then just go right on through, down to the next one. What would it take—what would it take, Celeste, for you to quit?*

"God, help me," I whispered.

"What?" said Alex, frowning. Just then someone down the table asked him a question about his latest big merger, and he turned away from me. In the mirror, at this distance, his face appeared aglow with happiness instead of rage.

The wine glass still shimmered before me, full and ruby-colored in the light. At once everything became clear, as if the lights had been turned up full blast in the room. I looked around, blinking as if I were seeing them all for the first time. There was Aurelia, one table away, her eyes opaque with boredom as she listened to Aunt Theresa's husband, the plastic surgeon—Alex had put them next to each other because they were both doctors. Theresa's husband placed his hand over Aurelia's and leaned toward her, practically drooling onto her chest. Two tables away, Theresa watched, ignoring the conversation at her own table, stiff and anemic and malcontent. Catching his wife's eye, the doctor pulled back his hand and reached for his wine glass.

At another table, Anna's pale, oval face was smiling frantically at Chester, Alex's father, whose elastic mouth grinned back, oblivious. Nodding at Chester, she lifted her highball glass to a passing waiter and jiggled the ice in a quick, impatient gesture.

I filled my glass with Pellegrino water and took a sip. It had the nonexistent aftertaste of disappointment. I had to think of something better to drink, but what? I couldn't think of a thing. What had I drunk before? As a child? I'd been drinking alcohol for so long, I couldn't remember.

My brother, Jack, sitting at the end of our table, looked old tonight, his skin flaccid and gray. He was drinking double scotches on the rocks, talking heatedly about corporate law to Lucia, whose stolid face displayed quiet surprise that this man was my brother. In a matter of a few years he'd gone from a longhaired, pot-smoking rebel to an overweight, middle-aged man in a suit.

I looked at my father, tall, stately, expressionless in his own dark suit. He hadn't glanced my way once all night. His face seemed bleached, as though he'd been put through the wash with Clorox. He topped off Babs's glass with Chateau Laroq, then refilled his own. He drank it down. I was reminded of those dinners after my mother's death, when he'd drunk away her wine cellar as fast as he could. Maybe he wanted to get rid of the Chateau Laroq tonight as well, another harbinger of bad memories.

Babs smiled at him encouragingly, as if she had made it her mission to bring him out of his shell, as though his shyness were an adorable character trait rather than some kind of malignant deficiency. In the next moment I hated him so much I wanted to point a gun at his head and shout, "Tell me the truth! What do you feel?" But I knew that even with his life threatened, he'd only stare back, confused, and say, "What on earth do you mean? Are you not well, Celeste? Should I call a doctor?"

Of course I'm not well, you son of a bitch! How could I possibly be well?

What a fucking mess, I thought.

No, it's not a mess at all! If they're all fine, then you're fine too. Why won't you believe it? Drink the wine and forget this nonsense. You deserve it, you haven't had a drink in ten days.

Fuck you too, I thought. I'm not drinking the goddamn wine.

You're not going to make it. You can't live without drinking for the rest of your life! You're a loser, anyway. Your mother abandoned you and your father doesn't even like you.

But I remembered something else Branko had said that last night: just for today.

Hear that? I thought. It's just for today. Alex turned to me once again.

"You're having champagne when it's time for the toasts," he said in a whisper, close to my ear. "You're embarrassing me, Celeste."

"Go fuck yourself, Alex," I said, smiling at him from ear to ear. His head snapped back as if I'd slapped him. The muscles in his jaw pulsated. My heart began to pound. I felt afraid of him.

"Just shut the hell up, do you think you could do that?" I said, and pushed the wine glass away toward the middle of the table. "And if you tell me not to swear one more time, I swear to God I'll get up and walk right the fuck out of this restaurant."

Nineteen

"**WELL, THAT WAS** a nice party," Anna said from the passenger seat. In keeping with tradition, I was going home with my father and Anna to Connecticut to spend the night. I wouldn't be seeing Alex till four P.M. tomorrow, when he'd greet me in front of the judge in the rose garden at the end of the garden path. From the backseat I watched my father's broad shoulders, his short, pale, graying hair that didn't touch his white shirt collar, as he stared straight ahead at the road. Every once in a while he patted his forehead with a handkerchief. Anna was in excellent spirits and I wanted desperately to shout at her to shut up.

"That Aurelia is really something!" Anna snorted. "Flirting like that with Theresa's husband!"

"I think it was the other way around," I said from the back in a harsh murmur, dangerously close to losing control.

"Pardon?" said Anna.

"Nothing."

I stared at the back of my father's head and imagined taking an ax to it. The thought was somehow comforting. If I opened my mouth and said anything to him, it would surely be terrible. Unforgivable.

Oh my God, this rage, I thought. How am I going to live with this rage?

I sat glaring out at the highway and the black night, watching the yellow lines slip away under the car as Anna chattered on.

* * *

UPON ENTERING the vestibule, my father dropped the car keys into the silver dish Anna kept there, stretched his back with his arms extended, patted me quickly on the shoulder, and said, "You looked lovely tonight. It was a lovely party. Everything was lovely. Well,

I think I'll pack it in. I have a terrible headache. I want to nip it in the bud, so to speak. Tomorrow's going to be a big day for all of us!" He lifted his hand, backed away rubbing his palms together briskly, and turned to climb the stairs. As I watched his tight, square back recede, I imagined firing on him with an Uzi and watching his body roll down the stairs.

"Yoo-hoo, Celeste!" Anna called from the kitchen. "Come join me for a little drink."

I went in through the swinging door. She was pouring gin from the bottle she kept in the freezer into a short glass.

I sat down at the table and dropped my head into my crossed arms.

"Why, Celeste," she said, "what's the matter? Everything was simply lovely tonight."

"Oh, for God's sake, Anna, open your eyes," I said numbly.

I didn't look up to see her expression. I was thinking hard about tomorrow, about the feelings I'd thought I had, was supposed to have, but simply didn't have, for Alex. How could ten days have changed things so much? Why had this happened? Which was insane, to marry him feeling this way, or to not marry him and have everybody think I was crazy?

I looked up. "Listen, Anna," I said. "I'm having serious doubts about getting married tomorrow."

She stood frozen at the counter, her face muscles quivering. She kicked off her high heels, shuffled toward the table, and collapsed into a chair.

"For God's sake, Celeste," she murmured. "My God. It's almost one A.M. I think you need a little nightcap. How about a brandy?"

"Thanks, but I don't want a drink." I kicked off my heels, too. Suddenly the thought of hot chocolate appealed to me. My mother and Anna used to make me cocoa when I didn't feel well as a little girl.

"I want some cocoa."

"Hot chocolate this time of year?" She got up out of the chair and went to the cabinets to look. "Cocoa," she said, shaking her head.

She poured herself another shot of gin while she placed a cup of milk in the microwave. "You know, Celeste," she said airily, "people often get the jitters the night before their weddings. I, for example, took to my bed and cried for three days before I ran off with Jordan." She took a sip of her drink. "But then, of course," she mused, "we were eloping."

She brought the steaming cup back and placed it before me. I took a little sip. It coated my taste buds, my throat, soothingly burned my heart and stomach. It seemed at that moment the best thing I'd ever tasted in my life.

"I can't stand him," I said flatly, my strength returning. I drank the chocolate fast. "I need some more," I said, holding up the empty cup.

"But—excuse me for saying so—couldn't you have realized this before tonight?"

Could I tell her? I waited for my hot chocolate, my face a stolid mask.

"Listen, Celeste, it's late," she said very logically, composedly as the microwave buzzed. She brought me back the cup. "You've been under a great deal of stress—what we talked about that night at dinner, about your mother—well, you know what I'm referring to . . . Think. There's still time. You may wake up with a whole new attitude."

I decided to tell her the truth.

No! No! Don't!

"Anna, I think I'm an alcoholic."

She stared at me for a split second, then threw her head back and laughed. "That's ridiculous, Celeste, whatever gave you such an absurd idea?" She glanced at me suspiciously. "You haven't been going to those religious meetings, have you?"

You see? She's right. Now, put some brandy in that hot chocolate and we'll just pretend all this never happened.

No, I thought. She's afraid.

Oh, right, everyone in the world is wrong and you're right, as usual. Why not have a drink? After all, why not? Why do you insist on suffering?

I considered this for a while.

A loud whining motorcycle engine roared in the distance. It seemed to be coming up the hill. The noise grew louder, until it was in our driveway, and then right outside the house. A strange lightness filled my head.

The engine growled and sputtered one last time and went quiet. I ran to the window and peered out. In a golden rectangle of light, straddling a large dirt bike, was a man in a black helmet, a dusty bomber jacket, black faded jeans, and biker boots. Walking bowlegged toward the kitchen door, he shook out one leg and then the other. He took off the helmet and shook out thick hair that was damp with sweat. It was Nathan. I knocked on the window, laughing crazily as he looked up and smiled.

Anna was just behind me, looking over my shoulder.

"Well, I'll be damned," she muttered, "here comes the cavalry."

"Hey, Mrs. Miller, what's happening?" he asked with a grin, standing in the doorway holding his helmet.

"Hah! What's happening? What isn't happening? Won't you come in, Nathan? Would you like a drink?"

"Sure. Whatever you're having is fine. As long as it's not tequila."

He looked as if he'd had a few drinks already. Perhaps he'd stopped in a bar in town. He looked me over carefully, taking a step into the room. He seemed to be trying to decide if he'd made the right choice, coming by at one in the morning.

"I got your invitation at the Matlan Grand Hotel. I just figured, hell, why not just ride up? I left the day after I got it. I'd been down there too long, anyway. It was time for a change."

Anna handed him a gin and tonic. He took a sip, shifting his weight from leg to leg.

"Am I interrupting anything? I saw the lights on and figured I'd just see who was around." He took a pack of Marlboros out of his pocket and tamped out a cigarette. He lit it with a Bic lighter, inhaled deeply, and blew a stream of smoke out his nostrils. Anna shooed the smoke away.

My small burst of energy had faded. Depleted, I sat down at the table again. My cup was empty.

"Would you like some more *cocoa,* Celeste?" asked Anna pointedly. I held up the cup.

Nathan sat down across the table from me, looking around for an ashtray. His eyes were impenetrable, his face tranquil, unconcerned. Anna put a large glass ashtray down in front of him.

We were silent. The microwave hummed loudly in the room.

"Celeste has just informed me," said Anna in her ebullient voice, "that she is having doubts about going through with her wedding *mañana.* This wouldn't have anything to do with you, Nathan, now would it, hmm?"

He pushed his chair back and leaned comfortably against it with his legs spread wide. "*I* wouldn't want to marry Alex," Nathan said, looking up at the ceiling.

"That's hardly the issue," Anna said acerbically from the counter. She came back with my cup and sat down between us.

Silence.

"I suppose I should be terribly upset and angry with you," she said to me. "But for some reason I'm not. I can't imagine why. Twenty thousand dollars, your father poured into this wedding. The man is going to shit pears if you back out. Pardon my French."

Nathan laughed.

"It's always about fucking money with him," I said, blood rushing to my face.

"What am I supposed to do? Call people in the morning and tell them not to come?" she asked no one in particular. "I mean, some people are coming all the way from California."

"I'll call people," Nathan offered.

"That would hardly be appropriate," Anna snorted. "Oh, the hell with it. I'm too tired and I've had quite a bit to drink. I think I'll go to bed and—as Scarlett O'Hara so aptly put it—I'll think about it tomorrow." With that, she went back to the fridge and refilled her glass. "Ta-ta!" she said, and disappeared through the swinging door.

* * *

ALONE, Nathan and I looked at each other.

"What does Alex say about all this?" he asked finally, tamping out another cigarette and lighting it.

I shook my head. "He doesn't know."

"Hmm," he said. He jiggled the ice cubes in his glass, then he got up and went to the freezer.

"Nathan, do you think you could stop drinking? Like, just stop?"

"Hell no," he said evenly. "The thought alone is terrifying."

"Yeah," I said. "For me, too. If I get through tonight, it'll be eighteen days. I don't think I've gone eighteen days without drinking since I was fifteen."

He came back, sat down. "I know I haven't!" He laughed. He reached across the table and took my limp, cold hand in his.

"I thought you were making a mistake marrying him, you know, when I saw you down in Matlan. I guess I came to see it through. I owe you that much. . . . I'm sorry, Celeste," he said finally.

"For what?" I said flatly, but I knew exactly. I believed our souls had merged once, long ago, and when I'd severed from him, a large chunk had been carved out of me. The gaping hole had never properly healed. But the person here was only vaguely connected to the person he had once been to me.

"You expected too much from me," he said quietly.

"All that doesn't matter now, just help me get through this."

"That guy's not good enough for you. Neither am I."

"Don't make me mad, Nathan. Nathan . . ."

Don't ask him that! The voice in my head cried out.

"Nathan, do you think I'm an alcoholic?"

"Did he call you that?"

I shook my head.

"Well, *I'm* an alcoholic," he said neutrally, without remorse, guilt, or even much interest. I'd never heard anyone use the word so easily.

With that, he went to the freezer, took the gin bottle out, and carried it under his arm through the swinging door into the dark house. I followed him to the empty living room. The moon shone pale and creamy on the beige carpet. He sat in a corner of the long couch and I at the opposite end, stretching my legs out between us. He picked up my bare foot and began to rub it, pressing deeply into the tender arch.

"How's Giovanna?" I asked.

"Giovanna?" He seemed lost for a moment. "Oh, right. She went back to Italy."

He slid toward me, began to rub my shoulders. I relaxed under the pressure of his hands. The smell of gin was strong on his breath, but I was not tempted or repulsed by it.

"You've got a lot more guts than I do to stop like that," he murmured.

"My mother killed herself," I told him.

"Yeah," he said.

"You *know?*"

"Everyone knew. At least, everyone hinted that they knew."

"Why didn't you ever tell me that?"

"Oh yeah, right, just like, in regular conversation. 'So, Celeste, I hear your mother killed herself.'"

"I didn't know," I said, perplexed.

"You didn't want to know."

"So what am I going to do now?" I asked him, bewildered, filled with anxiety at the prospect of tomorrow. He didn't say anything.

"I'm so tired, Nathan."

"Go to sleep. I'm here. Everything's okay."

* * *

THE ROOM WAS still dark, except for the creamy moonlight wafting in through the large French windows. Nathan's back pressed up against me on the couch. We'd slept like this so often, it did not feel uncomfortable or strange. I felt someone nearby, watching. I tried to sit up but was pinned down by Nathan's weight. Lifting my head, I saw a woman sitting at the end of the couch, on the armrest. She was wearing a pale blue bathrobe with safety pins all along the frayed lapels. Her long chestnut hair fell in a mass of curls around her shoulders.

"*Maman?* What are you doing here?" I mumbled.

She smiled, seemed about to speak, and I remembered that in all the dreams I'd had of her, she never spoke to me. I became afraid of sending her away with the wrong words.

"Why do you have all those safety pins on your lapels?" I asked her in French.

"Everything is coming apart," she said in English.

"Why did you tell me a knight in shining armor would come and carry me away? It wasn't true."

"I was afraid you'd never be strong enough to take care of yourself. *I* never was strong enough."

"How could you abandon me like that?"

"Pff! What a waste. There is always another way . . . *Retourne à l'église. Ils te diront quoi faire,*" she said. Then, in English, "Don't be afraid. I will always be with you." She smiled, got up, and walked out soundlessly through the swinging door to the kitchen.

"Wait! Wait!" I cried.

* * *

NATHAN SHOOK ME gently by the shoulder. "Still having those nightmares?" he mumbled, half-asleep.

"It's okay," I said, breathing deeply. "She talked to me."

The next time I opened my eyes, I was facedown, my nose buried in Nathan's armpit. He was out cold, his shoulder, arm, and one leg flung over me. The sun was streaming in through the windows, the air thick and hot in our old, un-air-conditioned house. I pushed his arm away, looked around at the living room, the empty gin bottle on the coffee table, and gasped. But I remembered suddenly, with a feeling of elation, that I hadn't had any booze at all in eighteen full days.

"Celeste, dear!" I heard Anna's high, enthusiastic voice coming from the kitchen. She came wafting through the door in her flowery bathrobe and slippers. She swiftly picked up the empty gin bottle and Nathan's smelly, heaping ashtray. "Yoo-hoo, Celeste! It's ten-thirty, time to wake up!"

I grumbled, tried to pry myself loose from under the weight of Nathan's body.

"It seems to me," Anna said, "that given the circumstances, as a family, we're exhibiting a distinct lack of decorum."

Twenty

I RAN UPSTAIRS to my room and threw off the wrinkled, funky smelling rehearsal dinner dress, replacing it with an old yellow sundress that was in the closet. My wedding gown, wrapped in plastic, hung there expectantly.

I went into the bathroom to wash my face and looked at myself closely in the mirror. *Nothing drastic has happened yet*, my reflection said to me with pleading eyes. *You can still go through with it and have all those things you want so much.*

"What things?" I said aloud.

Safety. Respect. Nice jewelry, good clothes. A big, clean apartment. A place to belong in the world.

The temperature seemed suddenly to rise. Cicadas in the garden below burst into frantic song. I ran the cold water tap and put my head under the stream. A flutter passed over my bare back, like angels' wings.

"Who's there?" I whispered, afraid to look up. I heard nothing but the gentle sound of water running, reminding me of the last time I saw Sally, the day before I left for college. Rain was running off the eaves and it was safe and warm inside my room. She sat on my bed, her yearbook in her lap, and gazed at me with pleading eyes. "Don't settle, Celeste. Go get what you want. For me, okay?"

"Okay," I said aloud. In a corner of the mirror I saw Anna standing in the doorway, still in her robe.

I straightened, watching her in silence as I dried my face. I saw that there was something hopeful in her red-rimmed eyes, as if she were trying to determine if I'd changed my mind. She padded in and perched herself on the rim of the bathtub. She was sweating, a watery film covered her face. Soon, my father would be making Bloody Marys in the kitchen. I knew this as surely as I knew that the sun would set today. Apparently she wasn't finding what she'd hoped for on my face. She shook her head sadly.

"Poor Celeste," she said.

"Why poor Celeste?" I said evenly.

Anna placed her elbows on her knees and her face in her hands. "My God, what am I going to tell your father?"

"I'll tell him. It's my problem anyway, not yours."

"All right," Anna said, getting up with a sigh. "Let's not panic. Let's feed him first, that always has a calming effect."

* * *

THE KITCHEN DOOR was open to catch any hint of a breeze, for the midday sun was beating down fiercely on the house. My father had come down shaved and dressed, in khakis and a crisp white oxford shirt. He was not one to ever step out of his bedroom unprepared to face strangers. Nathan was sitting with him at the kitchen table, still in his dusty black jeans and T-shirt. His beard had grown in, dark and grubby.

Nathan was telling my father about the danger of bandits on the Mexican roads. Anna hovered behind them, pouring coffee.

"A breeze will hopefully kick up off the Sound . . ." Seeing me in the doorway, she fell silent. She returned to the stove, where eggs were frying in bacon grease—my father's favorite. Batter specked with nutmeg for French toast lay in a bowl beside the stove.

My father picked up the folded *Times* at his elbow and opened it in front of his face. Nathan sat impassively, watching a fly crawl across the tabletop.

A yellow taxi pulled up in front of the open door and honked.

"Now, who on earth could this be?" my father grumbled, peering over the edge of his paper.

Anna opened the screen door.

The back door of the taxi flew open and two short, stout legs appeared, struggling to get out. My grandmother emerged, straightening her linen ashes-of-roses suit. Her small, delicate ankles and feet clad in pink pumps did not appear capable of sustaining her substantial weight. On her head was a small white straw hat, cocked to the side so that it almost covered one eye. Attached to the ribbon was a silk bouquet of pink roses the size of a grapefruit.

"I am Sophie de Fleurance de Saint-Martin," she announced.

"Goodness!" exclaimed Anna, running out to help her. Taking hold of an ancient Vuitton overnight case, Anna escorted my grandmother into the kitchen, "We weren't expecting you, Madame—uh—Madame de Fleurance."

"Bonjour," my grandmother said stiffly to no one in particular. "Well, me too, I was not expecting me. And now ze taxi refuse my traveler *cheques."*

I couldn't believe my grandmother was speaking English. A laugh burst from my chest. She looked toward me, smiled, then noticed Nathan sitting at the table, and frowned. She said to him, *"Encore vous?"*

Nathan stood up and went to her with his hand extended. *"Bonjour, madame. Ça fait vraiment plaisir de vous revoir."*

"Pff!" said my grandmother as he kissed her hand. And looking around, she said quickly and softly to Nathan in French, "What are you doing here, young man? This is truly not *comme il faut!"*

The cab honked its horn again.

My father abruptly put his paper down with a loud crackle and glared at my grandmother. A bright flush had spread up his cheeks.

"Well, for Christ sakes," he mumbled, and got out of his chair. On his way out the door, he nodded perfunctorily at my grandmother, who nodded perfunctorily back.

She opened her arms to me. *"Embrasse-moi, mon petit,"* she said loudly. I went and threw my arms around her solid little body. We kissed twice on each cheek.

"Qu'est-ce qu'il fait là, celui-la?" she asked, indicating Nathan with a small nod.

"He came last night. I invited him," I told her in French.

"Hmm," she said.

My father entered, carrying a cumbersome white box with a perfect pink ribbon and bow. His face was now bright red.

"That—that cost over one hundred dollars!" he sputtered. "She came all the way from Kennedy in a cab!"

"I pay you wiz the travel *cheques,"* my grandmother said, shrugging indifferently as she slipped off her little white gloves.

"Would you like some coffee, madame?" asked Anna, pulling out a chair. Nathan had remained standing.

"Of course," said my grandmother, sitting down. Nathan pushed her chair in.

"I wasn't going to come," she told me abruptly in French, taking my hand in her small, plump fingers. Her wedding ring, which she wore on her right hand, squeezed her finger like a rubber band. "But then I received your letter and changed my mind at the last moment. I remembered suddenly what your grandfather de Saint-Martin used to say—he was well educated, all he did was read—he used to say, '*Carpe diem*—'"

"'*Carpe diem*,'" Nathan said, "'*quam minimum credula postero.*'"

"Bravo!" cried my grandmother. "That is Horace, of course," she told my father.

My father was once again hiding behind his paper.

"Seize the day, trust little to tomorrow," Nathan said, hunched over and gazing into his cup as if he were reading tea leaves.

My grandmother abruptly gripped the top of my father's paper, pulled it out of his hands, folded it up daintily, and hid it on her lap.

"Brunch is ready!" cried Anna hysterically from the stove, coming forward with the frying pan. "French toast and bacon and eggs!"

"*Mon Dieu*," said my grandmother. "*French* toast! Hahahah!"

"I'd like a Bloody Mary," Anna said. "Charles, why don't you make us up a batch of your famous Bloodys—would you?"

My father swiftly got up and went to the cabinets and fridge, his face muscles frozen in a determined look, as if every ounce of his being were fighting to remain indifferent.

"I like the Bloody Mary," my grandmother said approvingly. In French, she added, "Your accent has become terrible, Celeste. You sound like a Canadian. You must come back to France."

"*Ecoutez-moi, Bonne-maman*—" I coughed, mumbling quickly. "*J'ai décidé que je ne peux pas me marier aujourd'hui. Aidez-moi*—"

She answered in French, "Is it because Nathan the Explorer has once again returned to claim you?" She made her hard, pinched little face.

"Not at all, *Bonne-maman*," I said quickly. I saw that Nathan was following this exchange as if it were a Ping-Pong match, his eyes shifting from me to her. "Please listen to me," I continued, "it has nothing to do with him, I swear it to you. I am totally to blame. I made a terrible mistake. I thought Alex would give my life a certain order. But he is very . . . controlling."

"So he isn't weak?" she asked.

"*No!* Or perhaps he is. I don't know. He's strong in all the wrong ways. But, *Bonne-maman*, that isn't the point. I don't know who he is!"

"I see. But excellent marriages are never based on love." When she saw that I was not to be swayed by this argument, she asked, "So what do you want from me, *mon ange*?"

"Just help me with him." I nodded imperceptibly toward my father.

"With pleasure," she said, squaring her shoulders, her mouth a tight little knot.

I looked toward my father and saw that he was hunched over the Bloody Mary pitcher, pouring in the ingredients with harsh, quick movements. In a moment he would pour himself a drink and go lock himself in his study.

I coughed, cleared my throat. "Since you're all here, there's something I have to tell you—" I began in a steely, calm voice.

Everyone gazed at me with alert expressions, except my father, who was now taking the cap off the Tabasco. Nathan nodded encouragingly.

"I've decided that I can't marry Alex."

My father stopped shaking the Tabasco, his hand freezing in the air. There wasn't a sound in the room. The cicadas' loud chirrup crescendoed outside. I went on, glancing from face to face.

"Right off the bat, if you're looking for reasons, let me assure you immediately that Nathan has nothing to do with this. I've been lying to myself for a long time about Alex. I was scared to end up alone and broke. I was drinking too much and I thought he could keep me under control. I'm truly sorry about the money you spent on the wedding. I don't know if you can get it back or not. You can have the presents back. I don't know anything else to say." I paused, feeling choked up; tears filled my eyes. My grandmother patted my hand. "My life's been a goddamn mess for years. I'm sick of living this way," I said, my voice cracking. "I'm tired of lies. Of running away from things."

I looked right at my father and he looked away, his face in a grimace. Anna stood gripping the back of a chair, her face pale and alert. Nathan was staring into his empty cup, tilting it toward him.

"Don't cry, *mon petit*," said my grandmother in French. "It's not that serious. You might have married him and awakened feeling like this tomorrow. That happened to me once. And it was too late to do anything, being that I am a good Catholic. Thank God he died not long after!"

My father punched the counter with all his might, sending the Bloody Mary glasses and the celery stalks flying. "I won't have this!" he shouted. "I won't listen to this—this—bullshit in my own house! Twenty thousand dollars, this wedding cost, are you out of your minds? You can't back out at the last minute! I won't allow it! Anna, talk to her, will you?" He turned his back to the room and crossed his arms.

"*Mon Dieu,* Charles!" cried my grandmother. "How you could talk about money at this time? Are you entirely a low-class *petit bourgeois*?

We must talk *raisonablement,* we 'ave avoided this conversation for thirty-three years, but unfortunately the time 'as come."

Nathan stood up. "I think I'll go for a ride into town. Anybody need anything?"

No one spoke or moved. He slipped out, quietly shutting the screen door behind him. A moment later we heard his motorcycle roar to life and fly down the driveway.

"Il faut dire que ce jeune homme est très sensé," my grandmother said to me.

"You stay the hell out of this, Sophie!" my father shouted, spinning around. "This is none of your business. I don't know where you find the gall to barge in here after thirty years and tell me what to do. Where the hell were you when Nathalie needed you?"

My grandmother stood up, fingertips on the table, and stared at him with her coldest, most contemptuous look. "Yes. Yes, Charles, I am guilty and ashamed every day. But let us talk about you for a moment. If you want to start parceling out the blame in front of the child, I will meet your challenge. But I will say some sings I am *certaine* you do not want Céleste to hear," she said evenly. "Now, do we speak reasonably, or do we duel? Because if you want a duel, I am ready for you."

"Oh, no, please, Charles," Anna whispered, her body rigid like a column, "please, do let's speak reasonably."

"I have to go call Alex," I murmured, and rose from my chair.

On my way to the door I could feel all their eyes burning against my back. The door swished shut loudly behind me. There wasn't a sound coming from the kitchen. I climbed the steps two at a time.

"More coffee, anyone?" I heard Anna ask finally, as I reached the landing.

* * *

I WENT INTO their bedroom, which had the only upstairs phone, and shut the door. The bed was unmade, the sheets tangled and thrown back. I hadn't been in this room in a long time. Anna had redecorated after she'd moved in. Now it was pale and modern, black furniture, beige rug, curtains, bedspread. I had never much liked to come in here after my mother was gone. My mother had slept in a wooden four-poster canopy bed with lace curtains and a creamy chenille spread. A bed, in fact, not unlike Alex's.

I hated the fact that their bed was unmade, it was like catching my father and Anna in their underwear. I averted my eyes.

I stood by the bedside table, my back to the bed, and lifted the receiver. I dialed our phone number. I listened, my pulse pounding in my throat, as the phone rang once. Then Alex picked up. I wanted to hang up.

"Hello," said his self-possessed voice. Last night's monster was long gone, and I felt confused again.

"It's me, Alex," I said, swallowing. My mouth was completely dry, my tongue felt thick and useless.

"Well, hello there," he said in his honey-coated voice.

"Alex," I said quickly, "I've been thinking about this all night, and I've come to the realization that I can't marry you."

"I won't discuss this over the telephone," he said immediately, without emotion, as if he'd considered this contingency and had prepared for it. His voice had changed suddenly to his crisp, formal business tone, and I wasn't sure anymore whom I was speaking to. "Don't you do anything until I get there," he added.

"Alex, there's no need—"

"Do you hear me? I'm leaving in ten minutes." With that, he hung up. I tried to call back but the phone kept ringing; apparently he'd turned off the answering machine.

* * *

I COULD HEAR my father shouting in the kitchen from the top of the stairs. I descended slowly and stayed quietly on the other side of the door.

"In all my years!" he shouted. "In all my goddamn years! You're telling me to just chuck this twenty thousand dollars away? Is that what you're telling me?" His voice rose hysterically. "Because if that's what you're telling me, you're out of your fucking minds!"

"*Mais c'est pas possible!*" cried my grandmother. "Shut yourself up, Charles! I always suspected you were narrow-minded and foolish, but I did not imagine you 'ad such bad taste."

"Oh, for God's sake. If it's about money," said Anna in a cold but controlled voice, "I'll transfer ten thousand from my account to yours, Charles. But I have a strong suspicion that it isn't about the money at all. It's about your neighbors and your business associates and your relatives. You are terrified of what they're going to say. 'Look at that family,' they're going to say, 'they're *still* a mess!' I've had enough of this dissembling, Charles. I've had enough. Now, act like a man, for God's sake, and stand by your child."

"*Bravo, madame,*" said my grandmother quietly.

My father said, "You talk some sense into her, Anna. You're a woman."

"The best thing to do," Anna added evenly, "in my opinion, is to offer everyone a drink here, and then sort of announce—anyway, it's too late to call people now. It's past one o'clock. People are coming from all over the country."

"*I* came from France," my grandmother said.

I opened the door and saw that the three hadn't moved since I'd gone upstairs. My father's face was pale and solemn. He glared at me and then looked away.

"Alex is coming," I said helplessly.

"He's coming?" Anna said, eyes going wide.

"He hung up on me. He said he didn't want to discuss it on the phone."

"So you mean there's still hope?" Anna said, her face lighting up. At once my courage evaporated.

You should have a Bloody Mary, I heard in my head. *It would really help you right now.*

I began shivering, a chill rising from deep within my bones. "I need some hot chocolate," I told Anna.

My grandmother glanced at me with concern.

"Hot chocolate! For God's sake, it's ninety-five degrees outside!" Anna said, turning toward the cabinets.

* * *

I STOOD BY my bedroom window, facing Alex. He had arrived in his best pin-striped suit, the one he'd intended to wear for the wedding. He had on his "power" tie instead of the floral Cardin print he'd planned on. It struck me—and I was horrified—that he still intended to get married today. He stood by the door, hands clasped firmly behind him, shoulders squared, wearing a contemplative and serious expression, as if this were an extremely important business transaction.

This side of Alex had always daunted and intimidated me. We'd been staring at each other for only thirty seconds but it felt like an hour had passed. The heat seemed to be stealing all the air in the room.

"So? Talk to me, Celeste," he said smoothly. "This is about Nathan, isn't it? I saw him downstairs. I'm not *totally* stupid," he added, "even if I am not as well read as you."

I turned my face away and stared into the garden below. Not a leaf stirred. At the round cast-iron table under the pink mimosa tree, my grandmother and Nathan sat, sipping Bloody Marys with tall celery stalks in the glasses. I heard her say to him in French, her voice carrying in the hot air, "Your Bloody Mary is much better than *his*."

"He puts in too much horseradish," Nathan said.

"Exactly!"

"I hope I don't have to go up there and beat Alex up," Nathan said contemplatively.

"He's much bigger and—if you don't mind my saying—in much better shape than you," my grandmother responded.

Anna came out from the kitchen. She'd changed into a short, pale blue dress, something noncommittal. The three began to whisper, and Nathan glanced up once at my window.

"Celeste?" said Alex impatiently.

I turned to him. "I didn't want you to come here, Alex. I won't be talked into changing my mind. This has absolutely nothing to do with Nathan. What I can't understand is why you would want to talk me into marrying you, knowing how I feel."

"How should I know how you feel when by your own admission you have no idea how you feel ninety percent of the time?" he said.

"Well, you're right, I've been feeling very confused. Getting engaged brought up things from the past I'd tried to forget, and remembering, I realized that I'm really not okay."

"You're just terrified of commitment!" he said.

"That too, definitely."

He threw his arms up and took a few steps toward the door, but quickly turned back to me. "My father warned me we were too different. I should've listened to him."

"Why *would* you pick someone like me, Alex? Someone as totally fucked up as I am? I'm an alcoholic—"

"Hah!" he cried. "Now, that's a good one! You'll just try any excuse, won't you, Celeste? Why don't you just admit you're still in love with Nathan?"

You can throw words like that around all you like but that doesn't make them true. No one believes you, especially not me!

I sighed and collapsed into the armchair. "God, Alex, I can't talk to you at all."

"I don't understand," he said. "I work long hours but I always make sure to spend quality time with you. I always take care of all your needs—"

"How could you know what my needs are when *I* don't know what they are?" I cried.

"Well, perhaps that's the point," he said, his voice waning, now soft and lulling. "Maybe I know better than you do what's good for you."

He's right. Absolutely right. You don't have the sense of a billy goat.

I looked out at the garden again. People had begun to arrive. I could hear ice tinkling in glasses, hushed voices conversing. A woman passed by in a bright yellow outfit and a large, pale yellow hat.

Alex began pacing. Sensing that he was making progress with the lulling, gentle tone, he waxed romantic about our early days, the moments of tenderness we'd shared; he talked about our apartment and how beautiful my office was now, and the wedding gifts we'd received and had been using and couldn't return. He paused, waited for my response, which didn't come.

I felt my heart, strength, courage, waning. "Alex, let's not talk anymore. Let's just not talk, okay?"

Abruptly he changed course again and became condescending and fatherly. "You have nowhere to go. You have nothing without me . . . "

In the distance, I spied James walking briskly down the driveway in a suit too tight across the chest, dressed for the wedding. My grandmother's quiet voice carried through the open window.

"I was desperately embarrassed when Nathalie married Charles. I begged her not to do it. *Un Américain, mon Dieu!* I thought I'd raised her better. I took it as a personal affront and cared terribly what everyone thought. I turned my back on my only daughter. I have come to the conclusion, in my old age, that the opinion of others is for the dogs."

My brother approached the table. Nathan stood and they shook hands. Nathan turned to my grandmother, his hand on Jack's shoulder, and said in English, "Madame, this is your grandson, Jack."

"Jacques!" my grandmother cried, jumping up. "My grandson . . ." With that, she burst into tears and collapsed in her chair, covering her face with her hands. Jack seemed at a loss, dismayed, but in a moment he took his clean, crisp white handkerchief from his breast pocket and held it out to her.

"Thank you, Jacques," she said, sniffling. "This is too much in one day for the nerves of *une vieille méchante*."

My eyes filled with tears.

"What the hell is so interesting out there?" Alex asked impatiently. "Here we are, our future hanging in the balance, and you're staring out the window!"

Wiping at my eyes, I said in a faraway voice, "Alex, you almost strangled me the other night. In Hol Cha, you raped me."

"Celeste, I think rape is too strong a word."

"A week ago you tore down a bus shelter and the cops came. You're lucky you didn't get arrested. You broke your ex-wife's arm—"

"She dislocated her shoulder in a scuffle."

"Whatever, that's semantics, Alex. Don't you see that you need help, too? I used to think I deserved to be treated like that. But now I see that I don't. No one does."

He breathed heavily, impatiently, and began to pace the room like a caged beast. I became afraid and wanted to call down to my brother and Nathan to come rescue me.

"Listen, Celeste," he reasoned, getting control of himself, "let's get married today. When we get back from Europe, I'll go talk to somebody. We can even go to a marriage counselor. You have my word I'll go. I'll try it out."

What a good idea! You can give it another try . . .

Perhaps he would. Perhaps he'd even change. I turned back to the window. The lawn was shimmering in the heat like a lake. At the end of the driveway, parked cars undulated in clear, oily waves.

"We'll cut back on our drinking . . ." he said hopefully.

My heart sank. It was so clear to me, in that moment, that he didn't understand. I could never cut back. Just one sip and I'd be right back in the bottom of the pit.

"I'm so sorry. I can't do it, Alex."

He began to pace again. "What am I going to tell the office? And what about the plane tickets? We can't cancel them now."

"We'll figure that out. Get a doctor's note or something."

"What are you going to do?" he continued. "Where are you going to go? You don't even have a real job."

I remembered Branko's words: *Maybe my biggest accomplishment will be to quit drinking.* If I did only that today—not drink—it would already be something. Tomorrow, I would go back to the Madison Avenue church basement and ask them for help.

"I'm going to have to learn how to do things for myself," I said, and smiled weakly.

He seemed to be thinking, then said dryly, "Well, I have to ask you to give me back your engagement ring and credit cards." He held out his hand. Nodding, I went to my bag that was lying on the chair and took out my wallet. I pulled out my Bloomingdale's, Visa, and American Express Gold cards. Alex took them and put them in his wallet. I slid the diamond solitaire off my finger and dropped it into his palm. My hand felt much lighter without it.

Alex's fingers closed over the ring. There was a knock on the door.

"Who is it?" I called.

"Uh, Celeste, can I talk to you guys for a second?" Lucia murmured through the closed door. Alex turned on his heels and briskly opened the door. She wore a tight black lace dress and a little black hat with a sprig of white flowers, and was holding a flute of champagne.

"Anna wants to know what to do," she said, standing in the doorway. "Everyone's arriving, the judge is here. They're all drinking champagne. No one knows anything yet. Anna hasn't even called the yacht club."

Alex sat down heavily on the edge of the bed and covered his face with his hands, his shoulders sagging. I went to him and gingerly put my hand on his shoulder. The sounds of laughter and drinks being stirred echoed through the air.

After a few long moments, Alex stood, back squared, face determined, gazed at Lucia calmly, and then turned to me and said, "Celeste and I have come to a mutual agreement that we're not ready to get married. We still care a lot about each other and plan to remain good friends." He paused, searching my face. I saw a hopeful, conspiratorial look in his eyes and understood. I nodded to him.

"Since all our friends and relatives are coming from everywhere to be here today, we think it would be best to have the party. We can't send them home on an empty stomach. We'll celebrate this decision, and our deep affection for each other and our families. Somehow we'll figure out a way to pay Mr. Miller back."

Lucia stared at him, her crimson lips parted, then turned to me with a startled look. I was relieved. Alex had found a solution that was acceptable to him. In time, he would probably believe it to be the truth. What did it matter? Our sense of what was true and what was important had never coincided. But it was fine, I owed him this much.

"Yes," I said, "Alex and I think it would be best." I watched him. He smiled, the corners of his mouth quivering.

"I'll inform them," Alex said, his face composed, almost relaxed now. He nodded once, and left. Lucia stepped into the room. I stared longingly at her champagne glass; she offered it to me, but I shook my head.

"Do you need a place to stay for a while?" Lucia asked.

"I don't know. Probably." My voice didn't seem to be coming from me.

"You're not alone," she said, placing a hand on my shoulder.

"Thank you," I said.

When Lucia and I entered the lobby of the yacht club, my grandmother, my brother Jack, Nathan, and Anna were waiting for us outside the closed French doors that led into the banquet hall. Nathan had finally shaved and changed. He was wearing a morning coat and a white silk shirt embossed with white palm trees, a black bow tie, and black lizard-skin cowboy boots. They all held champagne flutes and their faces seemed less tense. They smiled at me. My brother, in his dark suit, reached out and hugged me stiffly. I was so taken aback by his gesture that my eyes filled with tears.

"No, no, don't cry," my grandmother said, taking Jack's arm. "Why, this is a celebration! It is a great day for the Fleurances when the grandmother meets her grandson for the first time. It is a familial reunion!"

Jack blushed, breaking into a smile. Strains of soft, cocktail lounge jazz and muted chatter drifted out through the closed doors.

"You all right, Celeste?" Nathan asked. I nodded.

I caught sight of myself in the large, gilded mirror, wearing the green silk dress I'd worn last year on the Fourth of July, when I'd met Alex. It had been packed in my "trousseau" for Europe. "Bookends," Lucia had said as she helped me slide it over my head.

"Jacques," I heard my grandmother say, "you must come see your chateau."

"Absolut-ment," Jack said, and lifted his glass.

*   *   *

Now I saw Alex through the glass in the French doors, slapping the back of a young man who was laughing, and then moving on with a strained smile to the next group of guests. I admired his valiance.

I looked around the crowded room for my father but he was nowhere to be seen. As if she were reading my mind, Anna coughed into her fist and murmured, "Your father's coming a little later. He has one of his migraines and had to lie down. . . ." her voice trailed off and she attempted a wan smile.

He would come, or he wouldn't; if I waited expectantly for him, I would be setting myself up for more disappointment, as my mother had done long ago, and surely nothing good would come of it. Suddenly I felt sad and alone. Anna had told me that I must learn to forgive; I imagined she was right, but the road to forgiveness would be a long and difficult one.

My grandmother took me by the arm. "All these people are supposed to be your friends. In a moment you will learn who is worth his weight and who is good for the trash bin. *Alors*. Good," she said. *"On y va,"* and flung open the doors with a dramatic push.

I walked right to Alex and hugged him, planting a soundless kiss on his big, smooth chin. As he held me for a moment in his strong arms, his familiar leather-and-spice smell wafted over me and I felt a pang of regret, but evaporated quickly and my heart felt light as air.

* * *

My grandmother and I stepped out of the banquet room onto the deck that overlooked the Sound. The sailboards had been stacked for the night on the small crescent of beach, and beyond them in the shallow blue water, dozens of small sailboats rocked gently in the swells, their halyards chiming. Beyond the deck a long, crooked wharf jutted out into the waves.

Inside, everyone was dancing to a big band swing tune. Alex was jitterbugging with his mother, spinning her in and out of his arms. She laughed delightedly, tottering on her pointed heels. The sun was beginning to sink behind the sloping roof.

"It is very pretty here," my grandmother said in French. "But you know, Celeste, you may come back to Bordeaux with me."

"I have things to do here first. But I will come visit, I promise. Thank you, *Bonne-maman*."

"Do you need money?"

"No. Thank you. You've helped me so much.". I still had enough money for a few months. I'd find a second job.

Her eyes searched mine for a moment. "Something good has come of this—something wonderful. We've found each other again."

I squeezed her hand as our eyes filled with tears. I turned to the water.

"I'm going out on the jetty," I said. "Would you like to come?"

"I'd break my leg!" She laughed, and turned to go back inside, taking a handkerchief out of her purse and dabbing the corners of her eyes.

I took off my shoes and walked out to the end of the wharf. Glancing back at the yacht club, I saw that a sliver of sun, bright red now, still remained above the roofline. When I closed my eyes, the sliver shattered in a kaleidoscopic pattern. It remained for a while behind my eyelids. When I opened them, the sky behind the yacht club had burst into a rhapsody of fiery oranges and reds, and amidst the white spots that still danced before me, a dark silhouette approached.

Someone tapped my shoulder and I spun around. It was Nathan.

He leaned his hip against the railing and said, "Want to take a trip with me? See the Southwest? I've never been there."

Go! Run with him! There is nothing for you here!

Oh, shut up, I thought.

I looked at Nathan closely. "I can't leave now. Anyway, if I went with you and you didn't stop drinking, I'd drink for sure."

He thought about this for a while, leaning back on the railing with his pointed boots crossed. A breeze rose over the water; a lock of hair fluttered on Nathan's brow.

Finally, he said, "Drinking has never caused me any problems. The day it does, I guess I'll think about quitting."

I nodded, aware of the futility of arguing. His eyes seemed sad, or perhaps just tired. He turned and walked back toward the beach. My brother was standing on the sand by the stack of windsurf boards, a beer bottle in his hand.

"Want to go windsurfing?" Nathan called to Jack, his voice carrying through the air.

"Sure, why not?" Jack replied.

They took two boards from the pile and attempted to attach sails to them. Laughing, Jack fell backwards on the sand. He took off his shoes and rolled up his suit pants. Nathan steadied himself on Jack's shoulder and tugged at his boots. With their dress pants rolled above their calves, they launched the boards into the surf. There was not much wind, and they fell several times in the shallow water. After a while the wind grew stronger and they managed to pick up speed and sail away from shore. Soon they passed the end of the wharf. Jack's tie whipped his face and Nathan's coattails flapped behind him.

Darkness was spreading over the horizon, a purple stain. In the distance the opalescent water and matte sky had become one. High above, gulls swooped and cried in the expanse of blue. Waves lapped at the pylons and the empty hulls of sailboats. I breathed deeply. The sharp, musty smell of algae and fish filled my nose and throat as I ran my fingertips lightly over the weathered railing, feeling the grooves in the ancient wood. Beneath my feet the planks creaked and moaned with the tide's pull; crabs crawled on the mossy pylons, and schools of silvery minnows rocked undisturbed in the swells.

Soon the sails were two small white fins in the distance, slashing the vast, darkening Sound. The wind had picked up, and the sultry haze was lifting.